M-theo

M-theory

a novel

Tiffany Cates

BAOBAB PRESS

ISBN: 978-1-936097-34-0 (print)
ISBN: 978-1-936097-35-7 (ebook)

Library of Congress Control Number: 2020941557

Baobab Press
121 California Avenue
Reno, NV 89509
www.baobabpress.com

Typeset and Design by Baobab Press

*No words are entirely untranslatable; none are en-
tirely transparent:* This passage appears on page
169 and is quoted from "Word Magic" by Adam
Gopnik. *The New Yorker*, May 19, 2014. Print.

For the Brown Line,
its many passengers, and the Chicago Transit Authority in general.

This story would not exist without you.

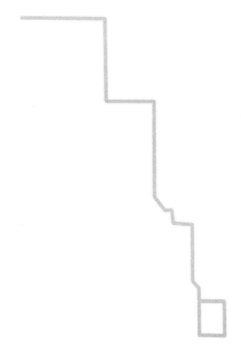

M-theory

There was a knock at the door to remind him that he'd been wearing the same clothes since Saturday. It also reminded him he hadn't washed his hands or brushed his teeth since conversations in a midnight wood whispered sounds of ripping fabric, and the knocking of her skull—a sound much different from the knocking on the door that came again, and again, and again, this time a man shouting his name, too authoritative to be anyone he knew, too callous to be anyone helpful. The knocking came and reminded him that she would have rung the bell—she always rang the bell, she liked its sound, said it donged without the ding and had a long tail. He'd never heard it until she said it, and then it couldn't be unheard or undone—like Lily, calling his name, or Sara sighing yeses into the dark of his room—there was a knock on the door to remind him. And then the door burst open.

The Lady in the Blue Coat

Running late rarely happened, but there were sure signs when it did: the woman who wore heels in ice and snow; the father who allowed his daughter to hit him when he told her "no," and the deaf man who continuously signed only to himself. These passengers all spoke to Donovan James. They all worked to tell him exactly how late he was and what kind of day it was going to be. If he would have been on time, he would have waited on the platform and pulled out his magazine. He would have stood under a heat lamp and the man with perfectly manicured hair would have appeared wearing a jacket too stylish for the windchills. The kids from the Marine Math and Science Academy would have boarded the train with him, walking slowly, taking up too much space once they'd found a place to sit by stretching out their legs and throwing their bags on the seats next to them. The day would have slid on rails. Unfolded expectedly. Ended with a run. But Donovan was not on time, and he knew this because the people who came and went on the train or platform had utility as time pieces.

It was this "timepiece" nature of their existence that allowed Donovan to consider them. He categorized them without scrutiny of his own thought. Placed them on mental lists according to their behaviors and never asked *why* those behaviors existed or why *he* should be the one to judge. The woman in heels, the man with no coat, and the space-sprawlers all fell into the category of people for whom image, whatever that image might be, was most important. Well-defined calves, check. The classic metrosexual, present. Hostile identity-seeking youth, done.

Others were a little more complex and had nothing to do with their physical presentation. Their timing was always poor, in that seeing them meant Donovan was on the later side of being late. There was the man with the hitting child who clearly lacked self-respect—obviously had an emasculating wife and more than likely plotted his own death on a daily basis while doing something mundane like taking out the trash. There was the deaf man who wasn't interested in dying because he cared too much about getting where he was going. He cut to the front of every line, frantically signing and grunting until some form of transit appeared. He would rest his eyes after finding a seat and eventually a snore would develop. Donovan could see the man had grit and purpose, but where he was going, what he was doing, and how he knew when to get off, were all mysteries Donovan didn't have time to consider when catching the 7:15 train. Things were even worse when he'd missed the 7:18.

The morning the lady in the blue coat drifted from one who came and went to one who was considered and categorized, Donovan James wasn't just running little-girl-hitting-daddy late, or even gutsy-deaf-man late, but the kind of late where absolutely nothing around him looked familiar and therefore everything looked new and mildly alarming. It was his first day back after Christmas. He'd overslept, skipped his shower, spilled coffee on his pants on his way out the door, and by the time he was ascending to the platform, he could hear the thunder of the 7:31 train pulling in and then the ding-donging of the doors as they opened.

To one unfamiliar with taking public transit, the art of it may be lost, but there is in fact an art. For Donovan, this involved the utility of door placement and the convenience of exiting. When exiting at Armitage, Monday through Friday, this meant riding the third-to-last train car and entering from the front door. On this morning, however, Donovan breeched the top of the stairs just as the doors were closing and had to jump in before they could shut him out. Third-to-last train car. Back door. His bag caught in the closing process—inspiring the spastic opening and closing of the doors, their accompanying ding-donging, and the prerecorded voice that kept shouting, "Doors Closing," though it was clear they were not. He was by no means the first person to cause such a scene, but frequency didn't dampen the humiliation of being caught in a stuttering situation.

After two very long seconds and several convulsive attempts, he snatched his bag through the momentary opening and tried to ignore the train operator's din, "Do not attempt to board or alight this train while doors are closing," a phrase he had heard many times, just never directed so personally at him.

3

Looking up, he tried to avoid noticing anyone who had noticed him, but the appearance of a contained flame drew his attention. The red and purple of the rising sun shining in through the window behind her had created the illusion of something dangerous until his mind interpreted a speckled white face glowing at its center. It was surrounded by a flame of hair, a mustard-yellow stocking cap, and the robin's-egg blue of her down coat. The lights flickered as the train lurched forward and he couldn't help but determine it was her—zapping the electricity from the train as her pink lips suspended themselves with an upturned tenderness that said, I've been there. A smile that informed him his insertion into the scene had not just been observed but considered.

Standing among the crowd of people bulked by the layers necessary to survive a Chicago winter, he felt momentarily cocooned by their anonymity until other remembrances of the blue coat and yellow hat began to tickle his conscious mind. The blue coat ran; the blue coat waited; the blue coat had watched the world and read weird books, but the blue coat hadn't had a face until that morning. She'd lacked the utility of other riders. She hadn't had a regular routine that allowed any of Donovan's attention to be drawn to her. But her smile, the smile she'd given him, left the lingering sense that she'd been the unobserved observer for more than this singular encounter, and that made him uncomfortable.

It had been years since Donovan had felt the cruelty of being someone's entertainment. Years since he'd discovered running as a form of therapy to keep his mind balanced and his words flowing. But her smile prickled elementary day fears of attentions being drawn to him because he was the sickly kid with the stutter. Like the door, like the door, like the door. His bag caught in a loop of unutterables that had drawn her attention and awareness full-stop in his direction.

Moving as far from her as the space would allow, Donovan took a seat that provided a safe but cluttered view. Her upturned lips may have touched a nerve, but they also animated curiosities that unsettled him, and as he pulled out his most recent copy of *The New Yorker*, a title tickled the part of him that didn't have to view other passengers for their utility. The blue coat knocked on a door in his mind and glancing up, he found her eyes upon him. She too was bulked, but blue and flaming.

He returned his nausea to the page and tried to let the soporific movement and heat of the train distract him. *Chut-chut, chut-chut. Chut-chut, chut-chut.* "*The Eight Serious Relationships of Hercules.*" Even without the author being factitious, the title depicted a complicated love life. Between each ill-fated match, Donovan's eyes felt drawn from the page to rest on something more distant and meditative. The woman looking out the window.

He allowed his eyes to wander over her unfamiliar face and found himself considering which of these lovers she might be. He decided on Ophelia, based on the innocence expressed by the paleness of her skin and the red of her hair.

Ophelia, who had actually been Hamlet's lover, was driven mad by his love or lack thereof . . . *Chut-chut, chut-chut.* Or had Hamlet been driven mad by her? *Chut-chut, chut-chut.*

At Armitage, a flurry of snow and morning commuters separated him from the sight of her, and his attentions were snagged by the familiar calling of his name.

"Mr. James!" Lily, coming toward the end of a four-year relationship with him that involved waiting and transgression and conversations about literature, stood shivering in the wind, ice crystals forming on her lashes. "Welcome back."

The cold had him digging deep into his pockets searching for the warmers kept there because gloves were inconvenient for flipping pages. "You shouldn't wait for me on days like this, Lils. It's too cold."

Lily disregarded him and reached into her bag for a delicately wrapped package of green and red matte paper. "Merry Christmas." She required more than a teacher. She required common sense and the ability to see things for what they really were.

The snow whirled and sprinkled the gift's surface with tiny six-pointed flakes of perfection. Donovan's slightly warmed hands entered the cold with an outward autonomy that only understood his internal hesitation once the package was in hand. "We already exchanged gifts." A hand-made throw in the colors of Man U. A copy of Voltaire's *Alphabet of Wit*.

"Just open it," she said.

Her smile nudged his hands into motion and she waited for the box to be opened before saying anything else.

"I figured you'd need a new one."

The scarf's material was soft against his fingertips, black and gray plaid with a dark red stripe, not the dark green of the one he'd lost but much more sumptuous and inviting.

Tucking the box under his arm, he began to wrap the warm material around Lily, who clearly needed it more than he did, but she stepped away and shook her head. "I bought it for you."

"I know, and I thank you, but your eyelashes are frozen, so let me do this."

Holding her chin up, she stood still and allowed him to wrap the scarf around her neck, and he was suddenly made uncomfortable by the intimacy of the act he'd initiated.

"Did you miss me?" she asked.

His hands found their way back into the safety of his pockets. "I'm glad to be back."

Lily's face showed the disappointment of the unanswered question. She led the way toward the school, leaving him to navigate the slippery slope of keeping her where she was in his life without further complicating their relationship.

"What did you think of *Doctor Faustus*?"

"I think instead of covering 'transgression in literature' every year, you should cover social ineptitude." The pressure behind her words told him they were intended to sting, and they walked the remaining blocks in silence. The mess of children before them slushed down the salted sidewalks leaving footprints that rapidly lost their imprint to the falling snow, reminding Donovan of unwanted words erased from a page.

When they reached the school, he, Mr. James, held the door open for his student and watched her silently unwrap the scarf; the warmth of the indoors already melting its collected snow. "I'll see you during my free period then?" he asked.

Her smile said something he couldn't yet determine while her mouth said, "This is how I know you missed me."

Not needing to say anything in return, he took the scarf and watched as Lily fell into a blur against the other students drifting down the hall. A disappearance that knocked on a door and returned his thoughts to the pale skin, flaming hair, smile of the lady in the blue coat, his previously unobserved observer.

Seven months later, Donovan knew the truth of his relationships and what they had become. His attempts to get what he needed had failed, and now he had to meet the man who could save anything he had left. There were calls made in advance, a waiting for wellness. Routes that needed to be plotted so he could run there, and back, preserving his speech and steadying his thoughts. But the doctor noticed him when he entered the hospital room. A quick glance followed by the double stuttering of eyes trying to pinpoint the exact location of Donovan's familiarity until his presence felt like a surprise to them both.

A tanned hand, still capable of movement, gestured toward a chair, and Donovan did as instructed. Always doing as instructed. He watched the incapacitated body of the detective for the movement it had been capable of when a fifteen-minute conversation set into motion the events leading them all to this room. This moment. This uncomfortable chair made of an easily hosed-down material that lacked the support necessary for a long visit. This keen awareness of his spine and how it moved and bent and made running possible. This conversation that would not negate what had happened but could preserve and make real a memory.

Donovan's eyes caught on a book he'd read, and given, and discussed, and never gotten back. Its presence in the dim-lit room made him uncomfortable, told him there was more happening than what he'd been told, or knew, but that he could contain it if he stuck to the plan. Despite this knowing, he pointed to the bomb on the book's cover and asked, "Where did you get that?"

"Give me a minute," the detective said, "we're almost done here."

The minute stretched with the slow tick . . . tick . . . tick of a clock whose second hand had been stuck between eight and ten for days. Weeks even. A single moment lived in repeat and without escape until the doctor exited the room and Donovan wished to leave with him. Believed he could. Knew his legs were capable.

This proximity to truth made him uncomfortable.

"What can I do for you, Mr. James?"

He looked at the detective and couldn't feel sympathy for him, even while knowing he was supposed to. "I want to know who talked to Sara." What others were willing to forgive felt disproportionate to the information they wanted.

"Sara who?"

"Sara Barrett." Donovan pointed to the stack of newspapers surrounding the book he had questions about.

"I don't know who she is—"

"Her name's in the byline." He thought of rising, approaching the bed, leaning down over the detective in a show of strength and vigor. "I want to know who talked to her."

The detective's fingers pushed the book aside like it was blocking their view of one another before saying, "You could have saved yourself the time and trouble by calling ahead. I don't know who talked to her."

Donovan moved toward the window, away from the man lying in a bed and closer to the reality of how the man had existed three weeks prior. "What the papers are saying about her . . ." To say any of it was true meant everything was false. "It isn't true." Donovan reconsidered his position and kept his eyes on the morning sky. "I want to know who did it and why."

"I'm sorry, Mr. James, I really am, but I'm not the person who can answer those questions for you." There was taunting in his voice. Donovan could hear it; he didn't need to see the man's smile.

"Then why do you have that?" He turned from the window and pointed back at the book.

That book is here to remind you of one thing only.

"This?" The detective picked it up, opened its cover. "A friend brought it for me—"

"It's mine. It's my copy of the book—I can tell by looking at it. Why do you have it?"

Relax. You can be free from cause and effect.

The book shut and the bomb was examined. "It's yours?" The cover wasn't a popular one, there was the accidental mark left by a pen with a loose cap, and the name of the author, signed in red pen along the outer pages—only legible when the book was closed, and yet the detective still asked, "How do you know?"

"Because I know."

He looked at Donovan. "Do you want it back? I don't need it. You can have it back."

"I don't want it back." Not from him. Not like this. Not now. "I want to know why you have it."

"To read. I didn't know it was yours." Donovan watched him. "I'll get a different copy." How his tanned fingers tapped the cover. "Leave this here in case you change your mind—"

"I won't be changing my mind." As long as she didn't give it back, it wasn't done. Donovan moved to stand over the detective, show him that bit of power the man would never recover. "Was it you?" His eyes moved from the detective, to the broken spine of the book, and he determined that all he had to fear was himself. "Sara mentioned your name when I talked to her, so maybe it was you."

Do not attempt to board or alight this train while doors are closing.

"I don't know why she would have mentioned my name. We never met."

Needing to leave, wanting to run, Donovan moved back to the safety of his chair and tried to steady his breath.

There are no little moments.

A memory. Disjointed. The details not quite clear enough for him to grab and hold and make fiction out of what evidence had shown them all to be true.

You have to do what they say, son . . .
She's dead.

Interference

"Look, ma'am, we've done everything we can, and we haven't *seen* a problem—"

Standing in the police station, the mother ripped off her gloves and wrestled a phone from her coat's pocket, "See *this* problem then."

The pictures had been taken under the resistance of the subject and showed bruising on the boy's arms, back, chest, and legs.

"It is *your* job to protect and serve—I want that gang out of my neighborhood. Protect him. Do your goddamn job—"

"Ma'am, that's enough." Masterson stepped away. "We're doing our best here."

"Why aren't you listening to me? My son's being targeted!"

It was nothing they hadn't heard before, but every mother entering the station basically said the same thing. It wasn't their kids—someone else was the problem. Their kids weren't like that, their kids were good, kind, into sports or music or theater. Their kids were always "standing on the corner minding their own business."

Lesley Powell knew that no one standing on a street corner was minding their own business; the mortality rates were too high for that to be true.

"I left the Southside to keep him safe—as soon as I found out I was pregnant—"

"Ma'am." Masterson tried to interrupt but she kept going.

"Now *this* neighborhood isn't safe, and the Latin Kings keep marking up the alleys—all the way to the market. Have you *seen* how frequently they're tagging the market?"

"Ma'am—"

"When they put that shit all over our garage, Jamal and I painted over it. Next day, there it was again, and then they beat him up on the way to school—"

"Ma'am—"

"Don't *ma'am* me! He's ten years old! In the fourth grade! He's just a boy!"

The woman continued to rant and rave, but boys were just who gangs were after. Young boys, vulnerable boys, boys who didn't fit in, boys who wanted to belong, be a part of something, feel like they had control and community. In the fourth grade you could still squeeze through windows, hide behind garbage cans, wander unnoticed with forbidden substances into dangerous places and then buy an ice cream off a vendor without anyone being the wiser. Boys were exactly what they wanted. Everyone knew it, but a lack of officers left the monitoring of potential elementary-aged children involved in gang activity on rotation throughout each district, and this lady didn't have a clue:

"We'll come talk to him." Lesley decided to put an end to the conversation. He and Masterson had been off rotation for three weeks, and he knew the woman just needed to see something different being done.

"When?" She snapped.

"Today, after school."

She didn't say thank you, she didn't say okay, she just gave a short snap of a nod and shoved her hands back into her gloves as she marched out of the station. Masterson's eyes rolled in his head before he too walked away.

Four hours later, as they drove to the boy's house, Masterson was still mad. "Why are we doing this? Blakely and Ranken have been on rotation for weeks—they should be dealing with her."

"We're the faces she knows; it'll only take a minute."

"My ass, it'll only take a minute—you think just because ice-cream sales are down we've got all the time in the world—but it's gonna get warmer, Powell, and you're gonna regret giving this lady so much attention."

"It'll be alright." The correlation between ice-cream sales and homicide rates was a fact Lesley wished he'd never shared. "No more than twenty minutes."

It was just after the New Year, and all the schools were back in session. The cold had left things relatively quiet in the Albany Park district, but Lesley never sat easily in the quiet. Quiet made people comfortable, softened their intuition, allowed things to pass unnoticed.

"You're gonna deal with the kid when we get there. I don't have the patience for kids."

Lesley glanced over at Masterson, "Maybe we should check in with some neighbors while we're there."

"Christ, Powell."

"It will only take a minute. I'll handle the kid, you can run a quick door-to-door."

"It's fucking freezing outside—you realize that, right?"

Lesley allowed him a moment to pout and watched the kids on Ainsley huddle in groups of three and four as they traversed the icy sidewalks toward warmer places. "Just check in with the mom and hit the neighbors on either side, find out if they've seen anything. Make sure you ask across the street as well."

"I hate you."

"Yeah, well . . ."

They arrived at the Dupont home and found it tucked behind a fence-deep pile of untouched virgin-white snow. The single-family homes that surrounded it all bore evidence of play, snowmen, makeshift forts, boot tracks, and dog runs, but this one lacked a sense of life beyond the carefully shoveled drive and walkway, both of which held a fresh layer of salt that crunched under their feet as they approached the door.

"Twenty minutes, Powell." Masterson blew into his hands. "I'm not doing this shit for more than twenty." When the door swung open, there was no "hello" or acknowledgment from the mother. Just a quick flick of a light being turned on in the hall before she moved back into the kitchen. Masterson shot a look before entering and only removed his cap.

Lesley followed the sound of a television out into the living room. The house was clean but not tidy. One window, covered in plastic to keep the heat in; a myriad of Happy Meal toys and junk mail littered most available surfaces, and the television ran in the background—cartoons flashing animated violence and high-speed action to the sound of explosions.

Amongst it all, Jamal Dupont sat dressed in his school's uniform of navy slacks, a white polo, and black shoes. A navy-blue hoodie, unzipped and hanging precariously off one shoulder, seemed to remain on his body only because the hood remained up over his head.

Lesley moved a dining room chair to sit on. "Good afternoon, Jamal."

Raising a remote, Jamal turned the television up just a notch.

"I'm Detective Lesley Powell. Your mother asked that we come by and see what's been going on."

The boy didn't look at him, his head turned slightly to the side, eyes occasionally looking up from the floor in the direction of the television.

"It seems you've been having some problems at school?"

In person, the boy looked younger. His face and belly still held the baby fat of a child, but Lesley could see the man trying to emerge. High cheekbones would be exposed as soon as puberty hit, his shoulders would continue to spread, and his well-defined brow and thickly lashed eyes would convince the smartest girls he was just a sweet misunderstood boy who'd grown up the hard way. Lesley couldn't save him from any of that, but he could potentially help him with this.

"So what's been happening, Jamal?"

The child's shoulders raised, and a sigh followed. "Nothing."

Why did it always have to be "nothing"? Why couldn't one person look him in the eye and say, "This is what's happening, this is who's doing it, and here is the proof." That, Lesley could do something with. "Nothing" left him with exactly that.

He checked his watch when he heard the front door close behind Masterson. "Your mom seems to think you're having some troubles—"

"I don't have any troubles." The speed with which the boy adjusted himself caused the hood to slip from his head, and his eyes caught Lesley's before quickly pulling it back into place.

"How'd you get the black eye?"

"I fell coming down the stairs—"

"You hit your eye falling down the stairs?" People came up with the wildest tales in order to avoid the truth.

"Yeah." Jamal dared him to argue with a firm look before holding out his legs. At least four inches separated the length of his right from his left. "I fall a lot."

13

"And the pictures your mom showed us?"

Without looking, the boy once again raised his legs and gave them a wiggle.

"There's been some gang activity in the neighborhood, a lot of new tags popping up, and your mom reported—"

Jamal rose from the couch, tossed the remote on the cushion, and limped past Lesley. "I need to get out of my school clothes." At ten years of age, the boy was already over five feet tall.

"We can only help if you talk to us, Jamal."

The slamming of his bedroom door was response enough.

"So that's it? That's all you can do?" His mother stood, cross-armed in the room's entryway.

"We'll double our patrol around the school for a bit." It wouldn't hurt to see what was happening while the neighborhood lay frozen. "I'll make a point to be there in the mornings to keep an eye on him." Lesley lifted the notebook in his hand, "I'm assuming he walks Ainslie to Avers?"

"I don't need you to watch my son, Detective Powell." Her words weren't unexpected. "I need you to keep an eye on what's happening in this neighborhood and let those little bastards know they need to be making different choices."

He knew what she needed. The whole city needed it. But there was only so much he could do, and he was doing it.

Tucking the chair back under the dining room table, Lesley slipped back into his coat and gave himself a quick pat-down for phone and keys before considering the notebook in his hand.

"Ainslie to Avers?"

The look she gave him reflected all that separated them from one another. "He walks wherever the sidewalks are clear."

The air was bracing, and Masterson's breath plumed as he spoke with a neighbor across the street. Lesley made his way through salt, street slush, and hidden patches of black ice only to have Masterson turn around and give the wrap signal.

"You talked to all the neighbors?"

"Half of them aren't home." Masterson headed straight for the car and Lesley glanced for clear walkways.

"Why aren't we fining people for not clearing their sidewalks?" He watched Masterson slip on some ice and catch himself with the car's roof.

"It's not our job—you want to add it to the list though?"

Lesley maneuvered his way back to the vehicle, planning each step carefully in order to avoid the dangers of wet feet and hidden ice. "I told the mom we'd double our patrols—"

"Why'd you do that?" Masterson's face scrunched in disgust, "We *can't* say we're gonna do that—what if something else comes up? This isn't even popcorn, Powell—this is a woman with too much time on her hands."

"It will only be a few weeks."

"Fuck you." Entering the car, Masterson waited for Lesley's door to be shut. "I'm going to run background checks on their extended family, see if they have any connections—and when that comes back clean, I don't want to hear another *goddamn* word about this kid."

It wasn't uncommon for close relatives to be targeted by rival gangs. It also wasn't uncommon for an affiliated family member to make gang life look worthwhile to someone who, like Jamal, struggled. Lesley knew better than to poke the injustice of it all, and so he sat in silence while they headed back to the station. He could go patrol the area in the morning, early, see where the snowplows hit, who had time to shovel their walks before kids started making their way to school. He'd find a place to sit and either see something nefarious taking place or find nothing at all. Maybe it *was* the boy's legs that left him bruised. Maybe his mother *did* have too much time on her hands. But Lesley didn't believe that to be true.

Waiting for the car's heaters to warm back up, he thought about how cold it would be in the tin can of his truck and said, "I'll have to borrow Deb's car," out loud instead of keeping it a silent thought. It was a biproduct of being partners for so long. Occasionally the lines between thinking and speaking became blurred.

"What?"

"Deb's car, I'll need it for the morning." Masterson pulled onto Lawrence where the streets had actually been cleared, and Lesley used the moment to move the conversation in a different direction. "She's got split-pea in the crockpot, if you're interested."

"Not tonight." Masterson drove the rest of the way in a silence that remained even after they'd reached their destination. The irregularity of it left Lesley standing in the cold while Masterson exited the car and entered the building without looking back.

"Taking up smoking, Old Man?"

Lesley knew without looking it was Blakely. He'd made the mistake of saying "You must be the new kid" when Blakely first came over from vice and had been "Old Man" ever since.

"Or are you and Tubbo finally having a fight?" Blakely pulled a half-smashed soft pack of Kool Kings from his pocket and thumped it against the palm of his hand until a filter ejected itself enough for him to grab it. "Did you enjoy the Christmas party?" He spoke with the cigarette dangling between his lips while he lit a match. "Did you have a good time?" A puff of blue-gray smoke mixed with the white vapors of his breath.

The production of it all irritated Lesley. "Why don't you have a lighter? As much as you smoke, shouldn't you have a lighter?"

Blakely raised an eyebrow as he took another drag. "It gives me an excuse to talk to people. 'Hey, man, can I bum a light?'" He motioned with his arms like a gangster in a rap video, and Lesley was ashamed for him. "Every smoker sympathizes with needing a light, man. It brings us together."

His point, though lacking any prophecy or eloquence, was noted.

"Your missus have a good time at the party?"

Lesley couldn't help but laugh. "What's with you and the Christmas party? Did it change your life or something? She said she had a good time, yeah, I had a good time. Everyone had a good time."

There was a slight shake of Blakely's head. "Alright. Alright. Calm down." He eyed the parking lot around them, the only movement happening was the falling of the snow. "I was only asking because I had this date and she was like *pow*, if you know what I mean." The fingers, not holding a cigarette, separated in front of him, alluding to an explosion, and Lesley had no interest in listening further.

"I'll see you later, Blakely."

16

Three steps toward the warmth of the precinct, Blakely called out, "Maybe you need a light."

Lesley held up a hand, "I'm good, thanks."

"They think we've got someone on the inside." Blakely's tone had lost its pizzazz and made Lesley stop, turn around, and listen. "I have a friend, who has a friend—"

"Who has a friend who said what?" he asked, walking back toward Blakely. He knew how it went, that vice connections ran long and deep, even well after the fact, but it was cold and there was nothing on his roster that warranted Blakely's solemnity in the moment.

"They said Obuchowski, the one Professional Standards brought in, is here because they think one of us is bent."

"What?" Lesley could feel his face scrunch up in disgust. "Who? Who do they think is bent?" There wasn't a single person he could imagine taking a bribe outside of Blakely himself, and even that required all the sincerity of his imagination.

"You're not gonna like it, Old Man—"

"Who?"

"Masterson."

"That's bullshit."

Blakely flicked his half-smoked cigarette into the bushes. "Just saying what I heard." He exhaled a large screen between them, "But if Masterson was up to something, you'd know it, right?"

"Yes. I'd know." Masterson wasn't the kind of guy who went around making shady deals in back alleys. "And you should probably save those," Lesley motioned toward the plant adorned with half-smoked cigarettes, "save yourself some money."

"It's not about the cigarette. It's about the *opportunity*." Blakely wasn't smiling. "It's *all* about opportunity, Old Man. Are you hearing me?"

"Oh, I'm hearing you alright."

The cold at his feet was too much, and Lesley was done with the conversation. But Blakely's voice called after him again. "We should be friends, Powell."

The problem with spending too much time in vice is that it makes you suspicious of everything. And as Lesley entered the warmth of the building, he wondered how much "opportunity" had led to Blakely leaving the unit.

"Morning," he said to no one in particular as he passed the front desk and received a "morning" back. Two voices attached to two heads he knew didn't look at him either.

Glancing down at the snowflakes on his sleeve, he counted the seconds. Three passed before their tips began to melt ever so slightly. They maintained their resilience to the heat up until he reached his desk and tossed both his coat and gloves onto an empty chair. An act he regretted as soon as the flakes hit the floor and began to melt.

"What was that about?" Masterson stayed tuned to his computer.

"What?" The wet floor irritated him. It meant he couldn't kick his boots off and keep his socks dry.

"Your conversation with Blakely."

Lesley took a seat, thinking about what universe and set of circumstances it would take for Professional Standards to be interested in Masterson. Then he thought about the set of circumstances it would take for Masterson to have seen him talking to Blakely. He didn't like where either pointed. "He wanted to make sure we all enjoyed the Christmas party."

"And did you?" Masterson asked without looking at him.

"Yes, I did." There was a pulling tension, a lingering of something left unknown. "Did you?"

"It was alright. Not much different than any other year outside of the meat." Masterson grabbed the giant white mug from his desk and sipped his coffee. "The meat was better this time."

Lesley finished peeling away whatever layers of clothing he could manage while pulling up a log of recent reports. He narrowed the results to Jamal Dupont's neighborhood.

Lawrence to Foster, Pulaski to Kimball. There had been a minor uptick in home break-ins around the holidays, but that was to be expected, and even looked favorably upon, in neighborhoods where you wanted to monitor gang activity. Members didn't tend to burgle homes where they lived, and thieves, for the most part, wanted to avoid pissing off the wrong people.

Narrowing the reports to tagging, a buckshot pattern began to expose itself. When gangs are spreading, the reports don't just scatter, they also moved away from a central location and, as far as Lesley could tell, the spattering still remained too close to locate a nexus.

"Hey, have you found anything on the extended family?"

Masterson stretched his arms above his head and rocked back and forth like he hadn't moved for hours. "Nope, not yet."

With no affiliations turning up, Lesley double-checked the snow routes and times to know where to place himself the next morning as the kid walked to school. Masterson gave up and made his way to the breakroom where Blakely could be seen having a laugh with the woman who'd come to investigate. The spirit of the room deflated with Masterson's entrance.

Lesley kept his eye on the situation while he gathered his things, trying to recall Blakely's date for the Christmas Party, but he'd not paid enough attention to him or her. His brain kept putting the new woman in her place. Once his things had been collected, Lesley poked his head into the room. "I'm headed home for dinner. You know how to reach me."

"Alright." Masterson stirred his coffee and Blakely rose to leave, but the woman remained at the table with a stack of files spread out in front of her.

"Check you later, Old Man." Blakely moved passed him without making contact. "Make sure to tell the missus I say hello."

Complex Adaptation

"Do you remember the night that Peter died?"

It wasn't a thing he was likely to forget, and Eric Sullivan watched his daughter continue to look through the racks of discounted winter coats while she spoke.

"I think about it sometimes. How it was a perfectly normal day up until that point, and then everything changed."

He couldn't figure out why she'd brought it up there in the middle of Nordstrom two days after Christmas, but the unexpectedness of it made him listen.

"There was music playing, I don't remember the song—"

"Duran Duran, 'Reflex.'"

M stopped and looked up at her father. "'The Reflex.'"

He watched her try to fit it into the schema of her memories.

"How do you remember that?"

The question evoked the imagery like it was happening in real-time. Coming in through the back gate after an argument with his wife; the silhouette of people against the lights strung across the back fence and shining outward from the house. Someone screamed, and people began to scatter. The orange glow of the lights on the cement as it cleared. M, by the diving board, staring into the pool. He came in through the back gate, and his son was dead.

Eric's heart fluttered, just as it had that night. Peter's Hawaiian shirt puffed up over his back. The splash of water as someone jumped in to grab him. The song, suddenly loud and clear.

"'I'm on a ride, and I want to get off.'" He replied. "That's how I remember."

Had it been a perfectly normal day? He'd been over it almost every day for twenty-seven years and couldn't remember anything extraordinary about it until he found his wife being groped by another man in the driveway and a fight broke out.

He believed she'd been accosted and threw the first punch in her honor. He believed it to be the most incongruous thing he'd ever done—hitting another human. But he did it, and his wife started yelling, jumped in front of him to protect the other man, and suddenly nothing made sense. What he came to struggle with five minutes later was that he'd been hitting someone or trying to make sense of his wife's actions while his son, Peter, slipped off the diving board and hit his head. M and Peter were two months into kindergarten when it happened.

A perfectly normal day? Somehow, nothing about that day wound up feeling normal except the heat of the San Joaquin Valley.

There was a pause in her movement, hands rested on down-filled coats. "We rode behind the ambulance with the windows rolled down. I remember thinking I'd feel him wake up. That I'd hear him through the sounds of sirens and wind, and everything would be fine; we'd go back to the party and avoid the pool, and everything would be fine."

The ambulance hadn't actually used any sirens. There was no urgency in transporting the dead.

Eric reached across the rack, not to touch her, but to feel closer to her. "You were young."

"I had no idea what death was."

With the rack between them, father and daughter let the other post-holiday shoppers circle around them for a time that felt other than now and happening.

"We ate cereal for breakfast and watched cartoons in our underwear. That's the only other thing I remember."

Eric tried to recall the sound of Peter's laugh, full-bellied and contagious. He wanted to consider the living details as M commenced sifting through the coats, but his mind fell into the loop of what happened next.

There had been two weeks of holding and crying and arrangements being made. Family, co-workers, and friends brought food and flowers. Flowers he had to watch die. Flowers that didn't make sense as comfort items when he had to pick their petals up off the counter and throw them away. He wanted to put them back, make everything right again, but the flowers just kept dying and the leaves outside began to do the same.

His wife moved out. He went back to work, M back to school. A little over a month later, it was Christmas and the two of them, Eric and his daughter, slept under the tree, she falling asleep to him reading about color symbolism in art—a book well over her head but full of illustrations she spent countless hours looking at.

She drew green people, painted purple suns, and collaged saffron-colored raindrops falling from brown skies. His ex-wife saw it as a psychological issue and put M into counseling. Eric knew she was trying to say something. He just wasn't strong enough to say anything back.

"I'm sorry we didn't talk about it more. About *Peter* more."

M pulled a light blue coat from the rack and brought it up to her nose; breathing it in like it could provide some kind of olfactory knowledge. He knew what the color meant to her. When he found he couldn't talk about Peter's death or her mother's absence, he returned to the book to try and hear what her colors said. That fair blue being a color she snuck into everything represented a reality larger than her own.

"What kind of person do you think he'd be? Peter."

Eric walked around the rack to be closer to her and idly checked the coat's temperature rating so as not to appear grief-stricken by the question. "I don't know, M." There was a burning in his eyes that he tried not to acknowledge. "Beautiful. Talented. Happy." He took the hanger and held the coat so she could slip it on.

"You and Mom would still be together."

Knowing this wasn't true didn't help. He had to remove his glasses and wipe his eyes.

Everything about Peter had been darker than M. He turned bronze in the sun like their mother and had been born with a mess of brown hair and puppy-dog eyes that saved him plenty of trouble during his brief five years.

"You should test the zipper; you want to make sure it isn't broken and doesn't snag on the lining."

Peter smelled different too. He smelled of earth, and grass, and water.

"What do you think?" She gave a little turn and Eric wondered where they'd all be had things been different.

Untucking her hair from the coat's collar, he kissed her forehead. "It suits you. And it will keep you warm."

"I think I love it," she said, running her hands down its front.

Eric noticed bits of dried paint on her hands and under her nails. "It will be hard to keep clean."

Detecting what he saw, she laughed and unzipped the coat, allowing him to help take it off.

M smelled like a crayon box when she was five. A crayon box and pencil shavings.

"I think he'd be doing field work somewhere. Counting bugs or monitoring plant growth. He'd specialize in something bizarre like the mating habits of frogs in the Pacific Isles." Her smile was far away. "He'd still be dirty. That much I'm sure of."

Eric didn't want to talk about it anymore. "Maybe we should invite Alex to join us tonight."

His daughter stared back at him with eyes that said things her mouth was incapable of stating. "To the gong bath?"

"Yes, he might really enjoy it—"

"Have you met Alex?" Taking the coat, she moved them toward the serpentine line of shoppers waiting to check out.

"It never hurts to ask."

"Sometimes it does, actually."

The woman in front of them, laden with thermal underwear and stocking caps, tried to juggle her attentions between the items in her hands and her two restless children. Eric watched as they began swooping back and forth under the lines of rope dangling between poles not sturdy enough to survive their motion.

"Here, let me help you." He took some of the woman's packages and she smiled in his direction. But one child swung, slipped, and jerked a pole down next to his head. There was a screaming of terror rather than pain.

Music. Screaming. Too many people in too small a space. Eric began to feel his heart flutter again.

The mother lost her cool, espoused a few expletives, and jerked the fallen child up by his arm, dropping her remaining packages in the process.

"I've got it." M stooped to pick up the items but Eric felt dizzy and unstable in his movements when he leaned over to help.

A clerk shouted, "I can get whoever's next!" And the herd separated.

Those in front of the woman crept slowly forward through their stanchion channel while those behind them remained still and grew impatient.

Heart accelerating. Child screaming. He couldn't stand the music.

"Are you okay?" Her voice came at him through a fog. "Dad? You're all sweaty, are you okay?"

He tried to steady himself enough to rise.

"Dad?"

He knew it would pass, he just needed a minute, and for the commotion to stop.

"Next!"

The crowd once again moved forward and M helped steady him, taking the packages, handing them off, and then taking his hand.

He held it tight. Eyes closed. Focusing on her pulse and his breathing.

"I can take someone on Five!"

Too many voices. Too much congestion.

"I'm sorry I brought up Peter." Holding him, M leaned her head on his shoulder and he turned to inhale the warm comfort of her. Frankincense, oranges, and turpentine. "I just want to be able to remember him."

Eric let his head rest on hers. "Me too." The burning in his eyes came back, but this time he didn't try and stop it.

Social Expectations

"There's a faculty meeting at lunch today." Ann Barret, a fellow English teacher with bottle-blonde hair and mothering eyes, had been working at the school for over a decade by the time Donovan arrived. "I'm sure we'll have to move rooms at the end of the year. We won't be able to handle the overflow if we don't."

Donovan emptied his bag into piles of organized chaos, thankful the lights were still off, and his disorder could remain hidden.

"Harold and I are doing sushi on Friday. You should join us—seven o'clock at Ora. We could pick you up on the way." Ann not only had mothering eyes, she had mothering instincts as well. She wanted him to be married, have children, live a happily-ever-after that he wasn't sure existed for him. Whether he wanted her to or not, Ann was going to love him. Mother-love him to death if she had to.

The clock read 7:49 and the bell was about to ring but she lingered in his doorway and flicked on the overhead fluorescents. "You should do something about the lighting in here, it's jarring. I have some lamps in the garage. I'll have Harold drive them over."

Tossing his bag onto a chair, he leaned against the desk and watched her eyes plot lamp placement throughout his room. "Does seven work?"

"Seven lamps?"

"Seven o'clock, for dinner. Three lamps will do with how you have things." Her finger extended and whirled in the direction of his circular desk alignment. "We'll pick you up."

"The 50 will drop me right there."

Her arms folded across her chest, skeptical and unbelieving. "Don't forget the staff meeting."

His response choked by the ringing bell.

The students entered with the early-morning fog of not enough sleep and too many hormones. First period was generally like this, and the cold didn't help.

"Alright, which one of you brought me a coffee this morning? I'll chuck your test score and give you an A."

"What if we already had an A?"

Peering along the top edge of each overturned page, he smiled. "Don't worry. You don't."

In the circle, nothing was secret, and everyone's shame was apparent.

The workday ended much like all the workdays preceding it: students— including Lily, more conversations, a farewell from Ann, the staff bathroom, a change of clothes, seven miles around the indoor track, locker -room shower, redressing, and the final exit.

The only variation to his routine seemed to be that blue coats and flaming hair had begun to knock and open doors in his mind he hadn't consented to opening. Her presence ignited the possibility of his own utility to someone else. A utility that didn't necessarily live out of entertainment or amusement but held the potential of something else. Something new and intrinsic within him. Thoughts not previously considered.

Whether consciously or unconsciously, Donovan found himself catching the late-late train for a week. Each time he was surprised it had happened, and yet each time he found himself thinking that if he saw her, maybe he could be shown his usefulness in how she looked at him in return. But the lady in the blue coat remained unseen until Friday, when he consciously decided to leave his house at five and stand on the platform until she appeared, his limbs going numb and the snow piling on his shoulders.

Fifty-nine minutes passed before the doors closed behind him and the train lurched forward. It took him a moment to move. He hadn't expected there to be so much free space surrounding her and, being unsure of where to go, Donovan pulled out his magazine with numb fingers and feigned reading before realizing he didn't want to be seen and considered as That Guy Who Blocks the Doors for No Reason and is therefore a douche-bag.

He didn't know if she looked at him; he was too afraid to see. And at the end of the day, he sat in the circle most comfortable to him and talked to the only people who ever really seemed to listen. "My best friend's getting married in May and I hate it." The students laughed, but he meant it. "I've got to write this best-man speech, and it's killing me because I don't even like the girl."

"Ooh, snap!"

Their laughter caused a twinge of guilt. "No, no, it's not that I don't like her—I'm sorry, that was mean, I shouldn't have said that. What I *should* have said is marriage steals your friends."

"Life lessons with Mr. James."

He waved his hand to calm the class. "Come on, you guys get butt-hurt when your friend has a boyfriend or a girlfriend, but someday that other person is going to be with them *forever*. And it sucks. Just saying."

"You don't want to get married?" a voice asked.

"Of course I want to get married." Donovan looked up and around. "I just wanted to get married first." And that was the truth of it. No one wants to be left behind or become the third wheel.

"You could always ask your girlfriend to marry you, Mr. James. Get married over the weekend—"

"Or move her in. No one says you have to go crazy, man."

Everyone laughed but Lily. Her irritation tapped upon her desk with a pencil, and forty minutes later she left his room without saying goodbye.

Before he could finish packing his stacks of weekend grading, Ann was there standing in his doorway. "It's a BYOB, you know . . ."

"I'll be there, don't worry."

"I didn't say I was worried. I know you'll be there. I just wanted to make sure *you* know you'll be there. Why don't you let us pick you up?"

"I'll see you at seven, Ann."

She left without further argument, and he was thankful. He only had so much will left, and he could feel himself beginning to scatter each time the blue coat knocked.

He ran the track feeling the rhythm of a train running express and tried to ignore its warnings.

Pa-tat pa-tat pa-tat pa-tat pa-tat pa-tat pa-tat pa-tat pa-tat pa-tat.

When he arrived at the restaurant, he found the table was asymmetrical. It bothered him because of how they had situated themselves around it. Ann and Harold sat in the outer seats while another co-worker, Beth, and her husband, Lenny, sat at one of the table's slanted corners. This left two very vacant spaces intimately tucked next to one another at the opposite end.

"Here." Ann took the cider from him, a guilty expression betraying her like a mom who'd promised ice cream and failed to mention the trip to the dentist taking place beforehand. Setting the cider at the head of the table, she highlighted the emptiness of the chair next to his by stating what he'd already determined to be true. "Someone else is coming."

Before the sentence had fully left her mouth, a woman with chestnut-colored dreadlocks and black-rimmed glasses swooped over to Lenny and hugged him from behind. "It's so great to see you!" Beth was queued for a hug and stretched across her husband's torso while the whirlwind of hair and smiles made familiar hellos that involved hand squeezes of implied relationship with Ann and Harold. The attention was on Donovan before he had a chance to sit or fully realize her arrival. "You must be—"

"Donovan. Donovan, this is Sara," Ann either wouldn't look at him out of fear that her offering would be rejected or couldn't look at him due to the shame of her planned entrapment. It didn't matter why. Fear and shame acted as quick modifiers, and Donovan hoped she felt both.

"One of the reasons I love her—she has no shame." Sara's hand was outstretched, and she checked her smile in the window's reflection before looking at him.

"Nice to meet you." The fact that she used a word – *shame* – he'd only just supposed discomforted him, but it was what came next that had him dissecting her.

Reflection checked and greeting over, she placed her hand on his back as she moved toward her seat, like she was preventing him from stepping on her when she passed. It didn't take more than that for Donovnan to begin putting her in a very specialized category of people: reflection-checker, mind-reader, a white woman with dreadlocks, under thirty, thinks men will step on her, wears glasses that should, and do, have their own sub-category, attention-demanding whether deliberate or not—but probably at least subconsciously deliberate, and forward, let's not forget forward.

"I can't believe it's been so long!" Her voice was sugary sweet as she wrapped her arms around Harold.

"Well, if you weren't travelling all the time."

Donovan knew that kind of sugared tone grew in the Midwest, but it was clear she wasn't a Chicagoan—suburbs maybe, but not a born-and-bred city girl.

"I have no *major* trips planned until August, so you'll be seeing a lot more of me." Sara, he learned, was Harold's niece. She, like Donovan, disliked sake; she also brewed her own beer, loved soccer, and had been twice published in *The New Yorker*. Her living was primarily made through an online travel and food blog, but she was working on landing a job with the *Tribune*.

It was not a slow unwrapping. All of this was learned over some garlic-salted edamame and a couple of drinks while Ann, Beth, and their husbands repeatedly stole glances at him to gauge his interest.

A few minutes after they'd placed their actual orders, Sara got up to use the bathroom and Donovan knew the interrogation had arrived.

"So? What do you think?" Beth, a person he'd viewed as a respectable acquaintance up until this point, leaned across the table with a wide smile. "She's great, isn't she?"

He looked around the table, eight eyes watching him expectantly, and slowly nodded.

Knock-knock.

Who's there?

Blue.

He picked up his cider and emptied the glass before agreeing.

Blue who?

You know who. Say it.

Their faces were pregnant with hope, and he didn't want to disappoint them.

Come on. Blue. Say it.

"I actually just started seeing someone—"

Beth sat up and whacked the woman across from her, "I *told* you, I *knew* he had to have a girlfriend—I mean, look at him—"

Ann scrunched her face at Donovan, her arms folded in wounded indignation. "Why didn't you tell me?"

"I'm sorry. If I'd've known this is what you were planning . . ."

Door open, he poured himself more cider and let the contents flood.

The blue coat danced through his mind as they walked to George's for dessert and Sara offered her number. "There's no harm in having friends, right? I mean, we have a lot in common and friends are good . . ."

Their feet hit the sidewalk in unison, and he could feel her eyes taking in his profile between her glances into passing echoes of her own image. The possibility of the lady in the blue coat seeing him right then, walking down the street with a woman, made him determine how he would feel to see her. "I don't think I'd want her taking another man's number."

That night, when Donovan got home and hung his blazer on the hook by the door, he found an Ora business card tucked into his pocket with Sara's name and number written on the back. Holding the card felt like a betrayal to his newly imagined girlfriend. Throwing the card in the trash felt unduly inconsiderate of Sara's attempt to befriend him. So he approached his bookshelf, shoved the card into the pages of a random book, and quickly walked away. Careful not to look at the title.

After his first slip from fact to fiction had taken place, Donovan saw no harm in allowing his mind to run toward the lady in the blue coat and her imagined girlfriend-ness. He didn't have to feel ashamed; he was, in fact, just beginning to see someone. It wasn't a lie. She would appear on the morning train and he would position himself open to her view while trying to read his *New Yorker*. Sometimes, if the sunrise wasn't spectacular, she would look up and around until her eyes met his and grant him a smile that said, You're worthy.

Donovan plunged in and out of time and circumstance. The haplessness of actions, once deemed to be choices, didn't feel under his control or aligned with his will.

"I'm not the one who strung this story together." A nurse entered, checking vitals, administering meds, and the detective continued speaking. "The pieces were gathered, and someone else put them together . . ."

"*Sara* put the pieces together because someone *gave* them to her."

"Do you know her? When you say her name, it's like you know her. Is she a friend of yours?"

Donovan didn't want to answer this question. "Her name's on the byline."

The detective's hand gave a tired wave at his side. "Well, Sara Barrett is not responsible for this, Donovan . . . and if she's right, maybe you were used . . ."

Maybe . . .

she used you . . .

"And Ms. Barrett isn't who you should be angry with." There was a daring about him. The way he watched, the way he waited for Donovan to say the wrong thing. "She highlighted the relationships with other men and, as far as I can tell, helped paint the picture of your innocence."

Are you so innocent?

Emergency cords were pulled—the skirt that rose in the wind; the smell of turpentine survived in her hair—there were lineless tans, ribs and spines, full breasts and her bare toes tucked—

STOP.

There was the rocking of the train, *pa-tat, pa-tat, pa-tat, pa-tat,* her red hair flaming as the sun shone through the window behind her. Doors open on the right at Armitage. A blue coat and gray mittens. Nervous hands adjusting hats and checking bus times. All of this, Donovan knew, had already happened.

Looking at the detective to make sure he heard him. "She didn't have other relationships. Not like ours."

Doors closing.

Interference

It was a quarter past six, and dinner would be ready at seven. The bracing air caused Lesley's earlier interaction with Blakely to flit briefly through his mind, but when he stepped onto the well-plowed-and-salted parking lot his thoughts were diverted toward roads, and sidewalks, and whom they were accessible to.

Lesley decided against the main roads for his drive home because he wanted to see what the conditions were like off the main thoroughfares. He swore under his breath each time his front tires fell into a pit, jerking the wheel out of his hands, making him question tax dollars and how they were spent.

Jamal Dupont lived one foot-bridge away from a different tax bracket, better schools, and more community services. There was a good school on the other side of that bridge, a quarter mile from the boy's home, but the zoning of tax dollars had him hobbling the mile between Bernard and Avers instead of doing what made sense. It pissed Lesley off.

Jamal's mother had moved from the Southside in an attempt to make things easier for him, keep him off the streets. But she was still a single mother trying to raise a son in a city full of crime, and as much as Lesley hated to admit it, the odds were stacked against any young male of a darker shade than white. He'd seen it over and over again—felt guilty about his participation in a flawed system and needed to reassure himself again and again, case after case, that he wasn't part of the problem. But each time his tire fell into a pothole he saw the boy, falling, receiving another bruise, and by the time he entered his home, Lesley was hot with irritation. "Have you seen the size of the potholes around here?"

"Hello to you too." Deb set soup bowls on the table while Lesley adjusted his frame of mind. "It's why I take the train."

They met halfway for a peck on the cheek before continuing about their tasks. Lesley rolled up his sleeves, tucked away his badge and gun, turned his phone off vibrate and set it on the bedside table, and then entered the bathroom to wash his hands, face, and forearms as he did every evening before joining his wife at the table.

He'd assumed Deb took the train so she could read during the commute. She was always buying books for her commute. "I tried to get Masterson over for dinner," he hollered up the hall. "Not like him to say no to split-pea." Drying his hands, he checked himself in the mirror before heading back to the dining room. Deb was dishing up the salad, so he began to pour the wine. "He was in a foul mood though, so it's probably for the best."

Deb took the glass of wine and handed him a salad. "I think it's just that time of year. People reflect and get sad."

Oil and vinegar separated into droplets across his salad, and Lesley reflected upon the lack of ranch dressing. "Masterson? Or people in general? Because I think you're giving Masterson too much credit if you think he's reflecting."

The television ran in the background, filling her silence with the ticking of the Wheel of Fortune.

"How was work?" He wanted the question to be returned.

The television ticked, and the audience cheered.

And then Deb shrugged. "I think Bill has a lot of regrets." Her recent tendency to refer to Masterson as "Bill" frequently left Lesley disorganized in conversation. "It can't be easy to wake up one day and realize you've sacrificed love and family for a paycheck."

"I don't think he thinks about it."

"I do." She dipped a bite of buttered bread into her soup before eating it and then gently whirled the wine in her glass until she could swallow. "And I'm glad he's thinking about it. It's something all of you should be thinking about."

The drug commercial filling the space between her words was for a pill that seemed to cure everything from panic disorder to PMS while also running the risk of increasing all the symptoms one was trying to avoid by taking it.

"I suppose. I didn't know you thought about him like that."

She shook her head. "I'm not thinking about him in any particular way, Lesley, I just think it's natural that he'd be sad." Deb looked past him, over his shoulder, in the direction of the television.

"Masterson isn't sad."

Deb's eyes moved back to her soup. "Well, he *told* me he was sad, so . . ."

The audience cheered as the spinner ticked. "What do you mean he *told* you? When, why, and how would he tell you that?"

Eyes once again on the television, glass of wine making its way to her mouth. "At the Christmas party."

Lesley sat staring at his wife. Blakely's mention of the party, asking whether Deb had a good time. "Where was I when he made his confession?" What he really wanted to know was what had prompted the conversation to begin with.

"I snuck outside to smoke while you were talking to someone."

Lesley leaned back in his seat like he'd been mortally wounded, "Deb, Deb, Deb. We've talked about this. What are you doing? You don't want to smoke."

She began clearing the table. "Well, actually, sometimes I do."

Lesley grabbed the napkins and followed her into the kitchen. "Okay, *I* don't want you to smoke. Smoking will kill you."

The fact that Masterson was sad or depressed fell away from their conversation, and Lesley began citing the same statistics he quoted every time he learned Deb was smoking.

Eventually, she ended the discussion by reminding him how many cigarettes he smoked just sitting *next* to Masterson every day.

The next afternoon, he sat next to Masterson and watched him blow smoke out a barely cracked car window.

"He's got a short leg . . ." Masterson said. "When I was a kid, if you had a short leg and a gimpy walk, you got beat up." If this was Masterson being sad–"What can you do?" He inched his butt out the window. "Life sucks sometimes."

No one in the boy's family could be tied to a gang, but Lesley had convinced Masterson they could sit tight from three o'clock to three-fifteen and wait for the kids to make their way from the school. He watched huddled groups of weighed-down children pass by their car and thought of Jamal's shoes. They hadn't been boots, just black runners, and he wondered if the boy's feet were the same size.

"It's called anisomelia," he said to Masterson.

"What is?"

"The condition of having one limb shorter than the other—I looked it up."

"Of course you did." The car's engine had been left on, but the cold poured in through glass and slightly cracked windows. "I just think the woman is acting out of hysterics, that's all. I mean, I'm feeling right now what my mother must have felt every time I ran into the kitchen crying because my brother *looked* at me funny." Masterson rolled up the window and trapped the remaining smoke inside.

The snowflakes landing on the windshield were perfectly designed to look artificial for over sixty seconds. More often than not, it was the swish of the wipers pushing them aside that broke them; not the heat of the glass causing them to lose shape.

Lesley had been counting, calculating the temperature through their softening points, and he'd come to the conclusion that it was still very cold outside.

"This is a fucking waste of time, Powell—tell that woman to get her kid a therapist and let us do our job."

"This is our job."

"Not right now it's not."

A new huddle of kids approached. There were five in total, and the smallest one hung at the center with a mess of curly hair sticking out between a black coat and gold cap. His chin was tucked down and his hands shoved deep into his pockets while those surrounding him wore reasonable beanies, fur-lined hats, gloves, and scarves.

"Is that Damien Quiles's little brother?" Lesley didn't need to point in order for Masterson to understand who he was referring to. Damien Quiles had spent time in a youth correctional facility after stabbing his mother's boyfriend. His return to the neighborhood hadn't made any waves because he'd stayed mostly out of sight.

Masterson redirected his attention. "Jamal's coming down Lawndale. He must have taken Argyle instead."

Lesley kept his eye on the kids. Latin Kings took pride in their adornments, and the child at the center had clearly taken on the role.

"If she's so worried about him," Masterson adjusted his weight in the seat and watched Jamal cross to the opposite sidewalk, "why doesn't she pick him up instead of making him walk in this shit?"

"They don't have a car." Lesley tried to keep track of the gold cap. "When did they start calling baseball caps 'snapbacks'?"

"Who cares." Lesley could tell by the lean of the car that Masterson was watching the side mirror. "If she doesn't have a car, how the fuck does she manage to be at the station every goddamn day?"

"There's this thing called public transit. You should look into it—"

"Fuck you, Powell."

The group of kids had stopped on the corner a few blocks down. "Maybe we should go around the block. I'd like to get an ID on the others."

"You know it's only going to make things worse for your little buddy here if those kids think cops are watching him."

"It's an unmarked car."

"You think they don't know that?"

Lesley disregarded the comment and had Masterson go around the block. On their approach, one kid looked up and nudged another until they all had eyes on the vehicle and its inhabitants.

"What the fuck did I tell you, Powell? We shouldn't be here." Masterson did one more pass through the neighborhood to make sure Jamal made it home. "I'm sick of this kid."

But Lesley wasn't. There was something to the boy's hobble that tugged at him and, rotating between Deb's car and his truck, wishing there were an alleyway with a wider view, he began reading his morning news alone at the corner of Ainsley and Monticello so that Masterson wouldn't have to deal with it.

It turned out that the kid with the gold cap was indeed Damien Quiles's younger brother Joey. A development Lesley needed to keep his eye on in order to know if Joey was for real or if the cap was just there for show.

It was the same thing day after day though, a hobbling kid, the falling of snow. Lesley grew accustomed to the stillness of what he himself was there to witness. He stopped looking for bogies and tried imagining the kids—what their lives were like and how they came to stand there in the first place. Those kids hanging on the corner couldn't be minding their own business *all* of the time.

More complaints came in. More tags popped up. More reports of shoplifting and random acts of vandalism and violence still emerged. Sure, a more constant police presence might have been useful, but something larger than that was missing in their lives. Lesley was willing to share the blame, but he wasn't willing to accept all of it.

A Brief Refrain

Yvette watched the waiters move around the room and admired the complexity of their overtures. They weren't just taking orders and bringing food, they were peddling a fantasy to any woman over the age of thirty who could afford their menu prices. "I can't remember what it's like to sleep with someone who doesn't smell like engine grease."

They were young, good-looking, well-kept, waiting to serve, wanting to help, eager to please, and she couldn't take her eyes off them. "Imagine that kind of attentiveness in the bedroom."

"It wouldn't happen. And they'd just smell like a different kind of grease."

"Nice, thanks for that." Disappointed, she took up the drink menu and wrestled between the immediate release of something strong versus the slow ride of a flight or a bottle of wine.

M grinned and looked momentarily up from her menu. "I'm sorry. If you had to choose, who would it be?"

A once-upon-a-time game now ruined, Yvette missed the days of being young and single, when she and M could pass their time in a world of "if you had to choose" scenarios. "It's too late. You've killed it for me. Now they all look like unfamiliar sex and smell like a restaurant."

M laughed, but Yvette had wanted the fantasy to last beyond their first drink. Every time she looked in the mirror lately, she saw a slowly evolving version of her mother beginning to appear. Just for the night, for this one evening while she was across the country from her home and family, she wanted the fantasy of something else to exist. The reality of her aging self was a constant presence that left its own reminders.

"I found a black hair on my boob the other day." Clearing her throat, Yvette tried not to look at her friend. "I Googled it, and it turns out it's *completely* normal, but no one ever bothered to tell me that. No one ever said, 'Oh, yeah, Yvette, as you get older, you're going to sprout little black hairs in random places—but don't worry, it's *totally* natural.'"

"Just wait until you find a gray one down below."

"Shut up! Did that happen?"

M nodded. "We should do flights and then pick a bottle from there. I want to stretch this evening out as long as possible." Pushing her menu aside, M took a sip of her water and Yvette watched the glass be immediately refilled by someone whose only job was to keep water glasses full.

"Youth is wasted on the young."

"It was certainly wasted on us. That guy there," M pointed to one of the servers, "he goes to Greece once a year to visit family—stays there for six weeks at a time."

"God, that sounds glorious."

"We could have done that."

"Neither of us has family in Greece."

"You know what I mean."

Their waiter arrived with white shirtsleeves rolled to mid-forearm, exposing meaty veins and a tattoo of roots that disappeared up and under his shirt. Yvette wanted to imagine the man and his decorated body in their entirety, visualize what grew there. But the more he moved and spoke, the less alluring the fantasy became. As much as she missed the possibility of lusty sex unadulterated by a messy house, screaming children, and a constant need to be something for someone else, she was also aware that twelve years of marriage had brought her a kind of comfort she wasn't willing to trade.

"If you could do it all over again," M began, after the waiter walked away, "would you change anything?"

It was a question everyone contemplated at one time or another. For Yvette, it most frequently crept up at 2 a.m. when one of her children cried and she was forced out of bed to deal with vomit or shit. "I try to imagine a life where I'm not known as 'Manny's wife,' 'Junior's mom,' or the lady who needs three gallons of whole milk every Saturday when she does her shopping. But," she shook her head, "I'm not sure who that person is anymore. Or what she'd be doing. Or what would make her happy."

M's smile was genuine and warm.

"How about you?"

Folding her arms across the tabletop, M appeared to give the question serious thought. "I don't know. I probably wouldn't get married. I don't think I was *meant* to be married."

That thought had occurred to Yvette on more than one occasion. It had screamed at her in the church as she stood beside Alex and watched M say, "I do."

M shrugged. "I like to be alone."

"Except when you don't."

"Except when I don't."

Their wine arrived, and Yvette watched her friend smell each glass before pushing the subject further. "How *are* things with Alex?"

Her laugh was the one that meant a nerve had been touched, and Yvette knew the answer before it had been said. "Lonely . . ." M smiled and shrugged. "But you knew that already." Glancing around the restaurant, M avoided her eyes. "There's a difference, you know, between being alone and being lonely. I just didn't understand that in the beginning."

Yvette had known Alex much longer than she'd known M. Although she loved them both, she'd always known it was a disastrous mix. "So what are you going to do? What's it going to take to make you happy?"

M waved her off with a flick of her wrist and a smile. "I would be fine if I could find a guy to keep in a closet, pull him out when I need him, and then tuck him away again when I'm done."

"What you're talking about is a man-slave. You really think you're the kind of person who could have a man-slave?"

"Well, when you put it like that . . ."

"And you'd fall in love—"

"No, I wouldn't."

Except they both knew better. M bore the tendencies of an artist's heart and fell in love with risky combinations of sad, mysterious, and beautiful every day.

"I thought about having an affair."

A platter of meats, cheeses, dried fruit, and flatbread arrived. The two women shuffled things about to create more space and avoided eye contact with the waiter, who had wandered into their conversation at the wrong time.

Yvette considered what it meant to "think" about having an affair and hoped M's words implied that she "thought" about having an affair in the same way Yvette had just been thinking about the waiters. Thinking, but not *thinking*.

"I met someone."

"Oh, God," Yvette needed to rest her head, she didn't want to hear or know anything more than that, yet she needed and wanted to hear every little detail. "Just don't tell me anything I'd have to tell Alex. I can't keep that kind of secret—"

"Nothing happened."

Head still resting in her hand, Yvette dared to look and see if M was telling the truth.

"Nothing happened. It *could* have happened. I thought about letting it happen. But it didn't."

They'd known one another for thirteen years. Yvette knew M's tics and inconsistencies and waited for something to reveal itself. "Who was it?"

"A guy I met at work. One of my students' dads."

Catching a passing attendant, Yvette ordered a shot of Aberlour. The wine wouldn't work quickly enough for a conversation about infidelity.

Infidelity had become one of her largest marital fears. She saw what she looked like when she had time to check her appearance. She felt her own exhaustion and lack of desire for anything more than a full night's sleep and a quiet house. Every movie, song, and television show alluded to someone, not unlike M, turning up in her husband's life refreshed, clean, and unburdened. She'd be sweet. Have good intentions. Provide a friendly ear. Then, one night after a few drinks . . .

Yvette took the shot of scotch and felt its slow burn roll down into her belly. "So what happened?"

"Nothing really." The tables around them passed in and out of laughter and light-hearted exchanges about the food and the weather while M repositioned herself in her seat. "We just talk about things, occasionally meet for a drink."

Yvette closed her eyes and tried not to hear M's words as naïve and leading to trouble.

"It's seriously nothing. I'm telling you this because it's hard. Being married to Alex is hard."

"M, you knew who Alex was when you married him—"

"He forgets I exist!" Her words came out louder than either of them had expected. Cheeks flushed and head bowed in embarrassment, she pushed on. "I am not just alone here, Yvette. I am completely lost and unseen."

There had been times over the course of their friendship that Yvette had wondered if M would be the kind of artist to one day kill herself. Not because she wandered through life depressed but because she held it together so well that no one knew anything was wrong until it was too late.

Watching M drink her wine like water, Yvette felt a mixture of sadness and concern. "I think you need to be able to talk to Alex about this."

M's smile returned, soft, quiet, keeping it together, holding it all in, and making everything appear normal again. "We both know that won't work."

But this was something Yvette knew and understood about her friend. Her smile said many things, and more often than not, it acted as a diversion. "Then you're going to have to leave him, M."

Hidden in Transit

Donovan sat in a single seat trying to read his *New Yorker* while a couple in front of him worked steadily to split his concentration and plant seeds in his thoughts. They were holding a conversation he felt directed to hear; one that continuously moved in and out of his understanding and circled around capital-T truth-statements involving possibility, actuality, and necessity.

There had been a flurry of days in which the lady in the blue coat hadn't appeared. Ten days. Twelve days. Fourteen, not counting week-end days, and Donovan's desire to witness his own utility had become amplified. Felt necessary in order for him to understand its truth.

When the question was asked, "So, you believe, the ability to per-ceive something is necessary for its actuality?"

The words were not lost on Donovan, who had needed to observe his own usefulness since he was six and lost his brother in a park. His father shouting, but not shouting, "What's the point of you if you can't look after your own brother?" The words weren't loud, they were thick with disappointment and stuck to him like honey, attracting flies and excrement that continued to gather even now. *What is the point of you?*

The actuality of his pointlessness, having been seen and verified many times by his father, preoccupied Donovan's thoughts throughout the day. They distracted him from his work, complicated his speech, forced him to skip lunch for a midafternoon run at the gym so he could make it through his afternoon classes using complete sentences and *not* metamorphosize into that stuttering kid.

Layers of honey. He was trapped in it.

It was past nine-thirty. Donovan hadn't noticed until the phone rang, but when it did, and he saw the clock, he knew it was Jimmy.

"Are you busy?"

"Yes." Nine-thirty constituted two truths in Donovan's life: it was too late for his mom to call, and the earliest he would hear from Jimmy on a weeknight. "But what's up?" Understanding this phase in life, he tossed the essay off his lap and onto the pile.

He'll talk about weddings, and people, and other people's life plans.

Jimmy got right to the point. "Tilly wants to know how the speech is coming along . . . She's worried you'll embarrass her or something . . ."

He's afraid you'll s-s-s-s-s-s-tut-ter.

Taking a breath, Donovan sat up straight, closed his eyes, and felt the air traveling deep into his stomach before it filled his lungs. "I'm not going to embarrass anyone."

"She wants you to tell a sentimental story or something."

Donovan shook his head, "We don't have any sentimental stories."

"You'll think of something . . ."

He wants you to sell a lie.

The snow kept everything outside quiet except for the passing of the trains. Donovan didn't hear them anymore. He rarely noticed them at all unless he was really trying to be aware. And he was really trying. "Have you made your World Cup pick yet?"

"No . . ."

He doesn't care about the World Cup. He's turned into your mother. Future plans. Families. What are you doing with your life, Donovan?

"We also need to know if you're bringing a date."

Next he'll be asking about kids.

"You were supposed to RSVP a week ago, and Tilly needs a headcount for the caterers."

"I know . . ."

"I'm going to put you down for one. It's not like you're seeing anyone, and the odds of meeting someone you'd want to bring to a wedding in under four months is crazy. Just crazy." Jimmy was thinking out loud, but Donovan wished some thoughts were quieter.

Knock knock.

No.

Come on. Say it.

Who's there?

He felt the door of blue coat possibility creaking open.

Blue.

Closing his eyes, he tried to center himself. "I haven't responded because I wanted to give it more time." Donovan prepared the lie everyone wanted to hear and wondered how her freckles would sit on his couch. "I've been seeing someone."

"When? Who have you been seeing?"

He doesn't think you'll ever have a Tilly.

Massaging the voice out of his head, Donovan moved to the edge of the couch and attempted to stretch out his spine. "Go ahead and put me down for two—if she can't come, it won't be a big deal."

"It will be. Tilly would never shut up about it."

Why would you ever want a Tilly, when you could have . . .

"But who is this person and why haven't you mentioned her before?"

Blue.

"Donno?"

"Yeah, I'm here."

"Who is she?"

"A lady from the train." The space of his apartment felt too small. His eyes needed to rest on something distant, his feet and legs required movement.

"Is it serious? Because Tilly doesn't want to waste money on people who aren't there . . . Are you sure she'll come?"

It's too late to run.

"Donno?"

Just say yes.

"I'm going to put you down for one?"

Loser.

". . . I want to keep things as amicable as possible."

Amicable wasn't a Jimmy word, it was the kind of word that rolled off Tilly's tongue and into Jimmy's mouth for improper regurgitation.

"Look . . ." Papers to grade. A warm beer. "I should probably get going . . . I've got a pile of work to do here."

"So I'll put you down for one?"

No one sees you.

Rising to leave and having nowhere to go, Donovan walked the circle around bed and couch paying close attention to step, and form, and the combination of textures he felt while treading between hardwood and wool carpet. "Yeah . . . sure . . . why not . . ." The paths of wood that traced lines to radiators not turned up high enough to spit. The swimming of fibers between the toes. Scratching. Tickling. Exfoliating and callousing all at once.

"Can you believe how cold it's been?" Jimmy asked.

He could. Standing on platforms, hours before dawn, forty-below windchill. Waiting to see his actuality cast back in a smile that said, I'm so sorry to have witnessed your humiliation over and over and over again.

"I can't believe the schools are still open."

Following the circle round, Donovan let his eyes skip across titles, over shelves, visit old familiar spines until he found the one that hurled its main character in and out of time and place without consequence or volition. "Yeah, neither can I." Who he was, what he was . . . "Hey, Jimmy," he had no control over it—he was passive in every sense. "I've gotta run." Disengaging the line he took the book from the shelf. Fingers flipping pages. Watching things happen *to* him, Billy Pilgrim's agency lacking.

Donovan too felt passive. Saw his whole life as inert—the shit a fly lands on.

Maybe it *had* always happened this way. Maybe their observance of each other at 7:31 in the morning was a point in time neither of them could escape. But that didn't mean he had no control over what would happen next. Billy Pilgrim could have changed his story. All he had to do was act.

Lying awake in bed, Donovan counted down the hours until he could talk to Georgia. Georgia worked at the Armitage Station, another woman with mothering eyes, but she knew where people worked, and played, and how and why they got sick, their kids got sick, their parents . . . She would know the woman, tell him where to find her, how to track her down, help him discover there was more inside him than a sputtering kid who failed at relationships. And he was prepared for this set of events to take place exactly as he'd imagined them until morning came and the blue coat was there, on the train at Montrose, negating his need for Georgia entirely.

"Doors closing."

Nothing stuck, nothing stuttered, and the train pulled forward.

He chose a sideways-facing seat, closer in proximity than he'd ever dared, and withdrew his *New Yorker*: "Bigger Than Phil: When Did Faith Start to Fade?" For Donovan, this question felt larger than God.

"I thought you'd moved." Her voice stopping his thoughts, flickering the lights. "It's one of those strange things about a regular commute." Her mittened hand motioned. "You never know if you'll see someone again." She had freckles that made constellations across her face, and he followed their map, voices quieting, possibility happening.

"I didn't move." It came out like a hiccup instead of a signifier that he'd like the conversation to continue. He wanted to say there were days, countless morning hours spent waiting for her—that she was the one who'd disappeared, but he couldn't say that and not sound sick.

There was a polite smile as she adjusted her hat with her well-mittened hands.

She thinks you're an idiot.

Chut-chut, chut-chut. Chut-chut, chut-chut.

At Southport, the train filled with winter bulk, stomping feet, shaking snow, and people trying to defrost their faces. The space that separated them felt thick and cloying, hot and clinging to everything. Doctors, lawyers, students, babies, stockbrokers, professors.

What purpose do you serve? What's your utility? What category of person are you?

The train only moved toward their departure.

A white twenty-something male who reads The New Yorker *and adjusts his schedule to wait on platforms.*

"Do you think we can change it?" His question asked without context or warning. A head tilt, lips opening to speak but not releasing any words, he saw her waiting for him to say more. "Do you think we have any say in where we're going?" But his words weren't helping. Her face was bemused, and her hands were in motion. Anxiety pulsed a book from his bag and shoved it toward her.

"What's this?" Confused or not, her mittened hand didn't hesitate to accept his gift.

"A book." Its cover bore the black silhouette of a plane and he watched her thumb trace the white words on the bomb below it.

"Well, I can see it's a book." Her eyes bounced around his face. Mouth, nose, eyes, cheeks, and chin. A complete loop.

You're the weirdo on the train.

He could feel her searching for something more. "I'd be interested to hear what you think," he said.

You can't even hold a polite conversation.

"It's a strange introduction though, isn't it? *Slaughterhouse-Five* . . ." And there she was again, on the fringe of his stuttering self with a laugh that might be at his expense but a smile that said, Come closer, tell me more. "People usually start with smaller things, like hello." He reached to take the book, but she pulled it closer, holding it to her breast. "Are you kidding me?" She laughed, again, face still scrunched in confusion. "You can't take it back now, not after all that." Opening her bag, she slipped it inside. "I'm going to read it . . . Tell you what I think."

He couldn't speak when she looked at him.

Chut-chut, chut-chut. Chut-chut, chut-chut.

Lily stood outside the exit perched between the bars and a trashcan. "Why are you so *late*? I swear, I'm going to die waiting out here for you." His eyes squinted against the cold, but he marched forward instead of lingering. "Bad night?" He didn't have to linger or wait, Lily always caught up.

She pressed forward in conversation, despite the snowflakes blowing into her mouth whenever he checked its movement. A movement he kept testing and determined could not compare to the lady, blue coat removed, comfortably tucked up on his couch, reading his book while he graded papers.

"Are you listening to me?"

"No."

He wanted a picture of her, uninvolved from the coat. He wanted a picture of her unbulked silhouette to add to his fiction, but Lily's contours and long legs kept intruding. He wanted them to stop. For the blue coat's removal to flood.

"What do I need to do to get your attention?"

Flaming hair. Eyes like the earth. Wrap yourself in blue and yellow and gray and then expose what's hidden underneath. Have a smile that says you understand and pink lips that could whisper secrets I wanted to hear. Electrify me with your presence. Have constellations of freckles that will lead me places I never want to return from. Be her. Be free. Be my unobserved observer and make me question my utility. Do you find me funny? Funny queer? Funny ha-ha? Funny strange? Funny interesting? Funny how? Why do you laugh? "Why are you laughing?" He asked.

"Because you're not even . . ." Her dark hair caught more snow as she shook it. "You're not even here right now."

Ann left him a bagel on his desk, invited him over for dinner, said he looked like he wasn't feeling well. "I'm well, why wouldn't I be well?"

She pressed her hand to his forehead. "You don't have a fever, so that's good, but you look terrible. Is everything okay with that girl you've been seeing? What's her name again?"

"Ann, everything's fine, I'm just tired and have a lot of papers to finish grading."

She took offense, but she also took the hint. "Make sure you get some sleep tonight."

The shuffling of pages began. He eased himself out of his seat. "Take the last ten minutes and explain why Jonson chose to use these names." The raven, cocky and unafraid. A crow, cautious until safe. "Don't get into the imagery, we'll get to that later." The parasite, a fly, feeding off others. "Leave your papers on my desk on your way out." And the vulture, patient, circling, waiting for death. Lily's eyes rose to meet his, and he feared what she would see.

Awake in his bed, Donovan thought of the blue coat, imagining her, wondering if she was reading, and what page she was on. When she appeared again the next morning, her pink lips greeted him before he'd fully entered the train and she patted the seat next to her, transforming the possibility of her closeness into a necessary reality.

He could feel the electricity of her eyes watching him as he sat and shook the snow from his bag. "It's cold this morning," she said turning her head back toward the window. The sky was clear, apart from the smoke of the chimneys, which sat suspended above them like props added for effect. He was thankful she'd turned away before he'd looked. It's easier to watch someone who's gazing elsewhere, their details can be more easily examined. "I'm tired of this cold. I want a nice warm beach where I can stick my toes in the sand and drink a beer with lime—a Corona with some salt on the rim." Her smile said, Care to join me? And his mind imagined her toes in the sand, the parting of her lips when she spoke, spiraling questions he needed answers to.

What does she see when she looks at you?

"I try not to think about it." It was said in response to himself instead of her.

Liar.

"How do you not think about it?" She shivered in her seat and he tried to be present, in the cold, she was talking about the cold.

Chut-chut, chut-chut.

How do you not think about it?

Chut-chut, chut-chut.

What your utility is . . . What you're useful for . . .

Chut-chut, chut-chut.

She sees you. Say something.

"It looks warm." He reached out to touch her coat, but did not. The train slowed upon entering a corner, and his fingers retreated.

Caution.

"It's hard to keep clean." It was a matter-of-fact statement she made while he watched her eyes follow his hand and determined he could have touched her and been okay.

"I think it's my favorite color, that blue."

You didn't know that blue existed before her.

Five stops took place before he could summon the courage that her *-ness* inspired. Questions teetered at the threshold of open doors that invited her in to have a seat on his couch, a sip of his beer, her bare toes tucked under his leg. He'd give her a Corona and salt the rim.

Know her. First you must know her.

He chose what was close and felt least invasive. "How do you always wind up in the same seat?"

She smiled and gave a wave of her hand, "I get on at Kimball, so that part's easy . . ."

It begins and ends with her. The line begins and ends with her.

"It's finding the motivation to leave when it's this cold outside that's hard." She looked to the mass of people gathered on the Belmont plat-form. "I hope they don't decide to run express to the Mart."

Train times were calculated from Kimball to Montrose, and a wall of kids from the Marine Math and Science Academy entered, preventing people from getting off. The doors closed and then jerked back open. The emergency cord had been pulled and a stream of people quickly exited while the train operator chastised them over the intercom.

The lady in the blue coat used the bus tracker on her phone. Her gray mittens were thick and bulky but had convertible tops that slid back to expose the upper portions of her fingers. He memorized the location of a few secreted freckles. His favorite lay to the right of her pinky nail on her left hand.

"This is the drawback to 6:42, everything has to run like clockwork, or I won't even be able to run and catch the bus."

The train left the station without turning express. Donovan had been hoping that it would, that they'd have to get off, wait for the next one.

With three stops left, he watched as her attentions flitted between the blanketed world outside and the standing passengers struggling to escape the heat of their enclosure.

Turning ever so slightly in her seat, she observed him in return. A challenge, or a dare, he couldn't determine, but he wanted to win.

"I haven't seen you in the afternoon since last spring." Her surveillance of him screamed out in a statement that put a chokehold around his tongue.

Chut-chut, chut-chut. Chut-chut, chut-chut.

"We used to ride the same train in the afternoon."

Chut-chut, chut-chut. Chut-chut, chut-chut.

"You were usually reading your magazine and still catching the third car."

How long has she been watching you? What is your utility to her?

"What do you see when you look at me?" He asked the question outright and watched her face, eyes darting, taking note of her surprise.

Chut-chut, chut-chut. Chut-chut, chut-chut.

"I thought maybe you were an attorney—"

"I'm not an attorney."

Her eyes squinted as if she could see him better that way. "Are you always like this?"

Weirdo on the train.

"Or do you just never talk to people?"

The unobserved observer tingled something inside of him that he couldn't isolate. It was either complete excitement or total discomfort. Words needed to be taken slowly. His tongue felt too big for his mouth and his lips didn't want to move appropriately. "I never saw you . . . in the afternoon."

She waited, studied, and then proceeded. "Well, I took the first car on the way home. Fewer teenagers." Rubbing her forehead, she looked back out the window. "You still caught the third." Closest to his street. Spring weather. Street running. Snow and ice melted. Exposed elbows and knees. "You're a teacher though, right?" He nodded when she looked at him. "It was your clothes that threw me." Her mitten came up and rubbed her nose, "You're quite dapper, you know," and then adjusted her hat, "with the way you dress and whatnot."

You're uncomfortable.

Chut-chut, chut-chut.

And you should be.

"Is that not a word people use anymore? Dapper?" She was nervous. Her hands fidgeted when she was nervous. Her busy hands, he'd determined, were her armor.

"I don't think so, no."

Her tongue gathered her lower lip for her top teeth to scrape. She rubbed her face with both mittens like she was washing herself. Donovan watched. Time slowed. Every detail pulled into focus. Coat zipped all the way up to her chin, unsnapped, with the faintest hint of a burn mark up toward her lips; the point of a down feather peeked out from the otherwise smooth matte surface where her shoulder met her neck; the thick cable knit of her stocking cap, covering ears, blanketing eyebrows, holding little drops of leftover moisture from her walk to the train.

There was a sigh and a shake of her head, "Well, they should. It's a good word, and it suits you. So, if for no other reason . . ." Her smile said, I'm afraid, while her mouth said, "I teach art at St. Josemaría's. What do you teach?"

Catholic school, spire angels, regular prayer.

Do you believe in God?

"Honors English at Lincoln Park."

Her anxious expression turned to surprise. "I would have never guessed that. I'm worse at this than I thought."

She was a mystery outside of her freckled face and occasionally exposed fingertips. "What would you have guessed?"

"I'm not sure . . . psychology? School counselor maybe?" Her lips were the center of that mystery. Each time they parted they revealed an element of her that exposed a part of him in return.

You're not what she expected.

A disappointment.

She was nervous. Her hands were moving. And there was a brief refrain of thought as the little girl and her emasculated father entered the train marking an inaccurate time, forcing Donovan to check his watch. They were early, the child was subdued, and everything felt off. There was heat, and pulling forward, and lips moving, one stop to go. He needed to see the child hit something, break something, make a mess of things.

"My English teacher didn't wear suits. He wore Birkenstocks with socks and Coke-bottle glasses." He needed things to feel normal. "He also taught anatomy which, as you can imagine . . ." But her laugh told him they didn't have to be. "Do you like teaching?"

He wanted to believe it, to see every detail of the blue coat's inhabitant as a gift. "Yes, I love it, actually." A surprise he didn't know he wanted until it was there in front of him, being opened. "I would never want to do anything else."

She smiled a smile that spoke with her voice. "I believe that about you. I really do. I've seen you with a few kids around the station."

Watching. Waiting. You're not the only one.

The train pulled into Armitage and he stood, allowing her to pass first, watching the way she moved in front of him through the crowd.

"I'll see you later then?" she asked at the bottom of the stairs.

What was there, was there, wrapped or just opened, the anticipation or anxiety never followed by disappointment, and he felt more than imagined girlfriend-ness toward her. "You will."

Her smile was a kiss that would happen. "Great. Good luck out there today."

"You too." He watched her pass through the turnstile and thought about her name. Not knowing it felt somehow like the most intimate withholding.

You can wait.

Donovan had always waited.

That afternoon, Lily stood on the platform, shivering under the heat lamp. He approached her, pulling her stocking cap down over her ears, zipping her coat up under her chin like he'd seen plenty of parents do to their children while waiting in the weather for a train to arrive.

Her smile said, This is how I know you care, even as her hands moved to loosen the zipper from her neck. "What are you doing here? Why aren't you running?"

"I thought I'd catch the train, run at the gym later."

He wondered if he was too late or too early to find what he'd come for. He tried to not notice Lily's eyes when she spoke. "Ride with me then?" They said things he didn't want to hear.

He rustled the hat he'd just tidied, making it a game, making it a joke, making her a kid amongst the other kids on the platform.

"Not today, Lils. I need to get some reading done."

She sought to catch his hand and draw him closer, but someone called her name. Startling her. Freeing him from his last instinct to touch her.

"I'll see you tomorrow."

The confused thought of Lily, how she reached for him, how he wanted her to stay just as she was, without complication, came with an electricity that filled his body and set him on edge until he looked up to find the blue coat, red hair, and yellow stocking cap walking toward him. A slow smile spread across her face, a smile that said both, I'm happy to see you and, I'm glad it worked. "How was your day?" she asked.

"It took a while to get me here, but I'm glad it did."

"Me too. Mind if I join you?"

"I was hoping you would."

The habit of skipping his run while she listened to the details of his day had been easy to start, and even easier to maintain. She didn't look at his pock-scarred face, or the bump on the bridge of his nose caused by Dustin Height and a baseball bat in the fifth grade. She didn't seem to notice that his beard was patchy and perhaps even a bit wiry, or that his skin tone was uneven to the point of being blotchy. She looked him in the eye, hers never leaving his, and he felt her delight in being with him, talking with him, asking questions, remembering specifics, sharing her smiles and laughs and workday tales.

Nothing felt hidden.

Until it did.

Donovan first noticed the ring toward the end of March when, after a very long and cold winter, one could leave the house without mittens and expose more than freckled fingertips.

A tiny gold band. It wasn't a betrayal to him. It was a betrayal to someone else.

The hum of medical equipment drowned out the ticking of the clock and begun to relax him. It settled Donovan's mind toward the detective as he existed in the present. Unthreatening.

"I never thought of her as being single."

"Never?"

This part was easy for him to understand, but everyone else seemed to struggle with it. "From the moment I saw her, she was mine, or I was hers . . . I don't know if there's a difference really, I just knew there was something." Donovan found himself slouched over in the chair, resting his face in the palms of his hands. "Something bigger than I could see, bringing us together."

"Maybe this is it. You, setting the record straight—"

"No . . ." The doctor had recognized him from news stories filled with truths that lacked the details of how and why. "She was meant to show me who I was." That much he knew.

"And who are you, Donovan? What did she show you?"

He doesn't know.

They'll never know.

But he needed the man to see it. He needed someone to believe he had loved, she had loved, and that there had been a *them.* "She smiled at me." Upturned lips, recognizing him. "She smiled and I waited. She spoke and I followed."

It already happened.

"I would have done anything she wanted me to do—"

"It must have been hard then, when you learned she was married."

It was like the man had never been in love, never experienced a mutual relationship, didn't understand that smiles and conversations are what start it all.

Donovan shook his head, not because he didn't want to respond, but because the detective was missing the point. "No."

"No?"

"It wasn't a lie to me. It was a lie to someone else."

"So you ignored it?"

A bit of chipped paint on the metal doorframe gave Donovan a place to focus his attention. It was easy to focus on imperfection. It stood out, and in a weird way highlighted the perfection of everything else. "She loved me." That much was perfect. "Other people may have had her . . . but she *loved* me." The winter had been long, the snow lasting well into March. "The snow came back and so did her mittens. I didn't have to see it."

"And in April, May, June?"

"By July she wasn't wearing the ring at all, Detective Powell. By July, her marriage was over."

The detective smiled a smile, and Donovan looked away.

Interference

Two weeks into his morning watch, in snow and negative double-digit wind chills, Lesley had empirically tested and verified that if he took Deb's car, the heat stayed in and his hands didn't go numb flipping newspaper pages or running Google searches on his phone. Where, on days that he took his truck, even the muscle movement of his tongue became frozen. He'd just entered the station to defrost when Masterson stopped him at the door. "Let's get out of here. I need some real coffee this morning."

Lesley had wanted two things upon entering the station, to empty his bladder and gain some feeling back in his toes and fingers before Masterson arrived. But Masterson was there early, ushering him back out into the frigid air where his thoughts were forced to return to kids and the hobbling caused by a miscalculation of nature. He had nearly forgotten his conversation with Blakely and the probability of Masterson's ennui, but the cold was a constant reminder of what it would be like to limp back and forth in the weather without proper footwear.

"Did you know there's a surgery they can do to slow down the growth of bones?"

Masterson's face contorted in complete disgust. "Jesus." The wind blew tiny particles of ice and snow, diamonds that had both men bringing their scarves over their mouths. "Why would *anyone* want that?"

Lesley found himself relieved to be back in the shelter of a car, even if he still needed a bathroom. "The kid—I looked it up. They can somehow slow down his good leg so the other can catch up." Masterson turned on the heaters and they blew hot air at Lesley's nose and toes, begging him to lean in and feel their heat. "A surgery away from normal."

"Well, I don't know about that."

Lesley held his gloved fingers close to the vent and watched Masterson adjust his coat behind the wheel.

"The kid's off, even without the limp." Putting the car in reverse, he drove around the block before turning right onto Lawrence and a clearer street. Cigarette lit, window barely cracked, and wheels set eastward,

Masterson stayed tucked behind the 81 bus, a technique Lesley knew allowed him to smoke more of his cigarette before they arrived at their destination. "How's Deb?"

"Good." Smoke hung in the air, activating a train of thought that went from smoking, to cancer, to Deb, to a shared cigarette between her and Masterson at the Christmas party, and then landed on Blakely. "At least, I haven't heard otherwise." It wasn't the best time to mention shared cigarettes and potential sadness, and Lesley kept this in mind as he watched the people walking down streets they were meant to stay off of when it was so cold. "How's everything with you?"

Masterson's response came with the pause of a flicked ash out the window. "Fine."

He didn't want his conversation with Blakely to adjust his idea of who Masterson was after twelve years, but Lesley felt a needling he couldn't put his finger on. Lost in his own thoughts, he failed to notice when they'd crossed the river and passed all the usual coffee places.

Once the discrepancy was noticed, he didn't need to ask before Masterson answered his question. "I want a bougasta. We're going to Hellas."

"I thought you wanted coffee."

"It isn't a request." Masterson used "needing coffee" as an excuse to buy himself a pastry or a meat pie more times than Lesley could count, but the exchange felt off.

"It's been a bit since we grabbed a beer. We should do that after work today."

The bus in front of them stopped, and Masterson took another drag. "It's 8 a.m., Powell. I'm not thinking about beer." The brake was released, and the car crept forward.

"Yeah, well, maybe it'll sound good later." The car's bottom scraped as they turned up and into the entrance of Hellas's four-car parking lot. The gnawing Lesley felt aligned itself with the fact that he could also feel his fingers and toes. "Did someone use the car last night?"

"Not as far as I know." Masterson stepped out and peeked back into the car. "You coming in or not?"

Not wanting to wait in the cold, Lesley got out, shut the door, and stepped over a curb hidden by the snow. "The car was warm."

Masterson waited, hands tucked deep into pockets and a scarf wrapped around his face.

"Yeah, I wanted to go get coffee, so I warmed up the car before you got there."

It was a simple explanation that required more forethought than Masterson usually put into things, but Lesley followed him into the bakery without question.

The air inside felt tropical, and the woman behind the counter wore the same pale blue uniform popular in 1960s television. She didn't speak a lick of English, but Masterson preferred things this way, or at least that's what Lesley had come to believe over the course of their partnership.

Lesley's phone vibrated against his chest, and he stepped back and out of the way to unglove, unzip, untie, and untangle himself enough to reach inside and pull out the pulse. The name on the screen bothered him.

"We've got ourselves a bit of a situation here, Old Man." Blakely and Ranken were on rotation so the situation he referred to could really mean only one thing. "Your boy's been picked up. School police caught him tagging. Mom's flipping her shit because the school wants to press charges."

"Of course they do." Lesley stepped further away from Masterson's ear, watching his transaction come to a close.

"Mom's meeting us at the station and she wants you there—her lungs are fully loaded though, so it's up to you." Blakely's tone held the dread Lesley could feel in his gut. "I can tell her you're unavailable—"

"No." Lesley took the coffee being handed to him and tried to prepare for the shitstorm that would hit once he told Masterson. "I'm on my way. We won't be long."

"On your way where?" Masterson stood two steps in front of him, his eye on the counter and the impending meat pie.

"Jamal's been picked up." Lesley reburied the phone under layers of winter clothing and waited for Masterson to move, or flinch, or say something vitriolic, but nothing came. "Mom wants me at the station."

Masterson approached the counter to collect his goods and made his way to the door without checking for Lesley. He didn't say anything their entire ride back. He didn't smoke, drink his coffee, honk at any cars, or take a bite of the bougasta that filled the car with its savory smells. He just drove as Lesley stared out the window.

"This is such *bullshit*!" These were the first words they heard as they entered the station. "What the hell am I supposed to do now? Quit my job?" The mother stood well across the room; her winter layers half ripped off in anger. "I can't afford that—I can't afford to quit my job because you-all ain't doing yours." Blakely and Ranken stood in front of her while Jamal sat to the side, hood pulled up in avoidance until she turned on him. "And *you*—you little bastard—"

At this, Blakely put his hands up and stepped between Jamal and his mother. "I don't think name calling is going to be helpful here, Mom." He nodded toward his partner while keeping his eyes on her. "I'm gonna have you go with Sergeant Ranken while Jamal and I have a little chat. You're gonna need to sign some papers, but Ranken can talk to you about a few city services—after-school and weekend programs that could provide the support you're looking for—"

The woman threw her hands up into the air and laughed. "He's already involved in *programs*—I'm *sick* of programs." Ranken used her momentum to move her toward his desk while Blakely removed Jamal from the area with an exacerbated look in Lesley's direction.

"We can give them a ride home when you're done." Lesley looked at Masterson. "It'll be on the way."

"On our way where?" Masterson didn't look sad, or mad, or under investigation. He just looked tired.

"Wherever we're headed next, I suppose."

Masterson moved passed him and took a seat at his desk without bothering to lose any of his layers.

The woman ranted through the stop-and-go traffic while Lesley watched Jamal in his side-mirror. The boy sat next to her with his hood pulled up and his head bowed, cocked slightly toward her and away from the world outside the window. The boy didn't want to be seen, not by anyone, but if he had to choose, he'd choose to be seen by the woman who called him a little bastard.

The television was on when they entered the house, and Masterson led the mother into the kitchen for a cup of coffee Lesley could already smell.

Jamal paused just outside the doorway to hear what his mother would say when she didn't think he was around, and Lesley gave him a small tap to move him forward. "Come on," but the boy stayed firm. "Let's at least go turn the television down."

The words seemed to be enough to set Jamal in motion. A car commercial was muted, and Lesley gave him a moment of listening to his mother before asking any questions.

"Want to tell me what happened?"

"Can you just leave me alone?" Jamal stood in the middle of the room and kept his eyes on the floor in front of him. "They think I'm a snitch because you're always dropping by and waiting on street corners."

Masterson entered the room with urgency. "A 417 just came through on Pulaski."

With an armed gunman only blocks away there wasn't time for Lesley to respond to Jamal. He stepped out of the house and into a day that yo-yoed from potential tragedy to tragedy for the next thirteen hours straight. When his day was done, he drove the dark twenty minutes back to his home honking at anything that slowed him down, realizing whatever dinner Deb had made would be cold by the time he got there, and the boy's words floated back to him.

"Deb?" Lesley tossed his keys in a bowl and headed toward the bedroom where he could begin his after-work routine. "Deb?" The bedroom was empty, bed still made, no signs to indicate she'd been home and left again. No smell of food prepared and left for him to eat.

He took off his watch while listening to her phone ring in his ear. "Hi, you've reached the voicemail of Debra Powell . . ." Lesley hung up and entered the bathroom to wash his hands, and arms, and face before returning to the edge of the bed to order food.

"It's too late for delivery that far out."

"What do you mean 'that far out'?" He stood and wandered out into the kitchen to scout for an emergency supply of food.

"We only deliver that far during peak hours when we have extra drivers."

Opening the fridge, Lesley stared into its belly and waited for something other than cottage cheese, half-n-half, tomatoes, and the previous week's taco meat to appear. "What if I pay double?"

"I'm sorry."

He'd barely disengaged the line before it rang and the sound almost satisfied his hunger with the possibility of it being Deb, ready to talk about food.

"You need to come up to Swedish Covenant," said a subdued Blakely. "The kid's in the ER."

The hunger pains in Lesley's stomach turned sour, and he was very aware of the beating in his chest. "What happened?"

"He got jumped." Blakely's pause told Lesley what he needed to know before his words did. "It's bad, Old Man. I don't think he's going to make it."

Lesley must have grabbed his coat and keys before he found himself in the garage starting up Deb's car, but the efficiency of his decisions didn't register. Her car required less warming, could handle the potholes down Mozart. Its Bluetooth allowed Blakely's words to remain his focus. Jamal had been found on the dead end of Drake right before the river. Given the injuries, they believed a bat or pipe had been used, but nothing had been left at the scene. A man walking his dogs found Jamal unresponsive and called it in. The boy suffered a contusion, bleeding of the brain, and a fractured skull. He was being taken into surgery. "Mom can't say why he was out there."

The wailing of the mother could be heard as the elevator doors opened and exposed Lesley to the moment. Here, with the woman's swinging arms and broken, shuffling approach, Lesley couldn't retrace his own movements but knew he was too late. The reemergence of space and sound and setting became surreal as her fists landed and Blakely came into focus behind her.

"I told you!" she cried as Blakely pulled her back with comforting arms. "I told you they were after my boy!"

Lesley stood transfixed, trying to catch up, trying to process. But the realness of her grief and the boy's image so distinct in his mind prevented any sense-making.

"You said you'd keep him safe, said he would be fine." Her body began to collapse, and Blakely moved to keep her upright. "And now he's dead!" she yelled. "Dead! Do you hear me?" Turning her away, Blakely tried to save Lesley from the visual of her pain, but it was too late.

Ranken appeared with a uniformed officer and a first-responder, all checking their notes, verifying times, double-checking names, locations, and active protocol, but Lesley stood before the woman. He had approached her and begun to speak before he ever knew what was happening. "I'm going to find whoever did this."

She looked up at him and spit in his direction with whatever strength she had left. "Fuck you, Detective Powell. I don't need your help anymore."

"I promise," he said again. "I'm going to find whoever did this."

An hour later, Lesley watched the child's mother climb up onto the table and lay down next to her son. He tried not to see how she cradled and stroked him, how she covered his unrecognizable face with tears and kisses that would never be enough to reconcile the despair she'd been left with. He stayed at the hospital until the mother had been sedated and driven home by a friend. He stayed until she was gone and they were able to move the boy's body to the morgue.

At 4 a.m., it was just the two of them left, and Lesley stood observing the boy's dead body. He could only recognize him by the length of his legs.

Externalities

The last few weeks of school had always been hectic for St. Josemaría families. It started quietly with the school science fair, then relatives would begin to fly in and stay through whatever Confirmation and eighth-grade promotions were happening between siblings and cousins and other God relations. There were a host of graduation parties, split between houses, friends, and families that stretched until the end of May when the school's largest fundraiser of the year happened. Then, babysitters were hired to watch groups of children overnight and movies and pizzas and sleeping bags stretched from one house end to the other while parents dressed up and said goodbye for the next twenty-four hours of their children's lives. A week after that, the student art show happened, and four days later, the holy grail of every child attending St. Josemaría's—the last-day-of-school barbecue and street fair.

The event included bouncy houses and pony rides. Face painting, water balloons, cotton candy, hotdogs, obstacle courses, Slip 'N Slides, and shaved ice. There was music and dancing and blood and tears, but everyone was invited, and no one had to be anywhere the next day. It was the last hurrah before summer took hold and everyone scattered. They would come back different after that. The summers always changed people.

It wasn't very long ago that Thomas had enjoyed the madness of the season, his community of faith and school and family all celebrating together, party after party, gathering after gathering, missed bedtime after missed bedtime. But moving toward his senior year, things were different. The madness no longer felt celebratory, and he wished he could take it back, recapture the innocence and excitement he once felt for the season.

"Well, things are different now." His girlfriend, Kadi, wiped down tables and tossed her head in the direction of some parents, seemingly free from burden or harm. "It feels like the same people standing over there, but it's not. Those were our parents once, you know." She folded a table and set it just inside the door. "It could be us standing over there in just a few years if we're not careful."

The group she watched celebrated in proportion to how much time, effort, and fundraising they'd put in. Their parents had done their time when they were younger and were now free to volunteer their children as nursemaids and cleanup crew. It all ran in a cycle. He hadn't seen it when he was younger. He'd ran wild until his parents said it was time to go and missed what came after. Children wailing out of exhaustion, nannies and *au pairs* turning up to take them home while their parents stayed to stand in circles, drink from solo cups, talk too loudly, laugh too much.

"We should start a garden club," someone suggested. "Help beautify the neighborhood with a splash of color."

Thomas needed the night to end before every memory of his childhood was ruined. "I need to go grab the chalk bucket from the art room to clean all this up . . . do you need anything?"

Kadi looked up and around and shook her head. "Maybe a sweatshirt if you have one." She was the only good thing about staying late, and he told her as much before heading indoors.

The lights in the school had been shut off hours ago, leaving the dim green glow of the exit signs and years of rote memory to guide him to the basement, across the auditorium, and up the ramp to the art room.

He opened the door, turned on the light, and was startled to find his uncle quickly moving up and away from his former art teacher's seated position. The pink of her nose was visible before she turned away and blew into a tissue.

"Thomas."

"Uncle Nate."

"Everything all right?"

It seemed an odd question to answer when the millisecond before had felt filled with unexpected dangers. "We're cleaning up. I'm here for the chalk bucket."

Mrs. Monroe opened a desk drawer and pulled out a small purse, but his uncle's attentions didn't waver. His hands rose to his hips as he glanced around the room in a typical Uncle Nate stance. "Is it really that late already?" And then he moved to pick up the chalk bucket before Thomas had located the object. "We'd better get moving. Isa will want to go home soon."

Uncle Nate didn't say goodbye to Mrs. Monroe, and she didn't say goodbye to him either. Thomas quickly gathered his sweatshirt and left the room with his uncle. He stopped short of leaving the building with him once they'd crossed the auditorium. "Could you tell Kadi I had to use the bathroom and I'll be out in a minute?"

"Sure," he smiled.

"And could you give her this?" He handed him the sweatshirt. "She's cold and I don't want her to wait."

"You're a good kid, Thomas." It made him uncomfortable how his uncle looked him in the eye in that moment. "Thanks for letting me know what time it was."

Thomas walked around the corner and waited to hear the clang of the outer door before heading back to the art room. He rapped lightly on the door, calling her name while he slowly pushed it open. Just in case there was something. Just in case she needed time to adjust herself and save them both more discomfort.

The purse had been tucked away and the drawer had been closed, but she was still seated in her chair.

She sat there, face held in her hands, elbows resting on her desk, and her shoulders shaking in silent tears.

"Mrs. Monroe? Is everything okay?"

The sound of his voice startled her. She looked up and laughed after she'd seen who it was. "Oh, Thomas . . ." She said, grabbing another tissue and blowing her nose. "I thought everyone had gone." She tossed the tissue in the trash like he'd caught her having a good laugh. "What can I help you with?"

"Are you okay?"

Her body flopped back, and the chair let out the slightest of creaks. "I think I'm just tired." Another creak as she rose. "Really fucking tired." She laughed and brushed away a few more tears before giving him a hug. "Thank you for being here. I needed your face right now." She stood quietly in front of him for a moment, her lips pulled back into a tight smile that left her teeth hidden until she once again covered her face with her hands.

"Are you sure you're alright?"

Turning from him, she grabbed her sweater and put it on. "It's been crazy busy, as you know . . . " She took her hair down, ran her fingers through its strands and then put it back up again. Her appearance would have been freshened had it not been for the redness of her eyes and the blotchiness of her skin. "I'm just tired." She waved off whatever was troubling her. "That's all, I'm just tired." Moving to the door, she let him know it was time to move on. "Kadi told me you're going to Brazil?"

"World Youth Day," he said. He held the door open for her and they headed toward the auditorium.

"That sounds like a blast. When are you leaving? Who's all going?"

Her excitement helped him remember he had something to look forward to. "Some volunteers from the Christi Foundation, I don't really know all the details yet. Nicodemus set it up—"

"Generous of him."

Thomas's feet came to a slow stop somewhere in the middle of the auditorium. It was as if his body refused to let the charade continue. "I'm sorry," he said. Mrs. Monroe stopped as well. He could see the blur of her pale skin glowing dimly in the dark. "Did Uncle Nate hurt you?"

"What? No. Of course not." She stepped forward and took his hand, pulled him toward the light of the exit. "I'm tired. I just need time and sleep and some more time for painting." Using her hip, she pushed the metal door open and moved them out into the cooling night air. Thomas knew this put an end to his probing. "I think I'm starting a new collection."

"You think?"

"Well, you know . . ." Her hands slid into her pockets. "Collections are tricky like that." The softness of the streetlights kept evidence of her crying hidden, "Sometimes I don't know until—"

"Hey!" Kadi, freshly wrapped in Thomas's sweatshirt, bounded toward them and directed her words at Mrs. Monroe, "I thought you left." She searched the remaining adults left hovering around. "Did Alex show up? I haven't seen him."

Thomas saw the expression on the art teacher's face fall and then collect itself into a smile. "No, Alex couldn't make it—"

"That sucks. He promised you."

"I know." Mrs. Monroe held her smile and pulled the two of them into a three-way hug. Thomas could feel whatever she was trying to avoid seeping out through her arms and chest before Kadi excused herself to hold a door across the lot.

"I'll be right back," she chimed.

And Thomas knew he shouldn't, but he wanted to pry deep into the roots of Mrs. Monroe's sadness and help her see that it would all be okay. "I'll pray for you." He understood he didn't know what was happening in her life, but he knew he could help. "You and your heart."

"Thank you . . ." There was a smile, and it was real. "I appreciate that." Mrs. Monroe began to leave and then turned back around. "Will you be at the Papachristi barbecue next week?" Everyone would be at that party, so he nodded. "Great. Remind me to talk to you about a kid in my neighborhood. I'd like to set him up with one of the afterschool programs—I think it would be good for him."

"Sounds good." Thomas watched Mrs. Monroe approach the remaining drinkers to shut them down and send them home. He didn't believe she could falter in her faith or stop doing what was right, but he did believe she was tired.

The church bells announced the ten o'clock hour, and Kadi reappeared next to him. "Happy summer vacation, Thomas Aram." Taking his hand, she kissed his cheek. "Can you walk me home when we're done?"

"Of course," he replied.

Across the parking lot, his uncle opened the car door for his aunt and took a quick survey of the remaining people before getting into the car himself. Thomas didn't want to think about what he'd seen or not seen in the art room, but he did wish his uncle were close enough to God to see the danger of his actions.

Dark Matter

It was easier than one might think to disappear into the fantasy. The lady in the blue coat arrived every morning, Monday through Friday, with a smile that carried Donovan through his day and greeted him every afternoon on the platform where they exchanged the highs and lows of their workdays. He could forget that their time was limited to, at the most, one hundred fifty minutes each week. He could forget her tiny golden band because it didn't play a part. It didn't have the power to interrupt their train rides, or his imagining, or the way her smile said, I'm here for you, every time it spread across her face. Every day, Monday through Friday, Donovan was able to rush from train to home with her girlfriend-ness still fresh in his mind. He could still smell her on his clothes. He could imagine her closer. Less wrapped. Mouth full of sighs and yeses.

But when spring break came, everything involving a routine, or a schedule would cease to exist for ten days, and Donovan's life would be turned upside down, not just in the lack of possibility her absence would bring, but also by the fact that his parents would be making one of their three yearly visits to the city.

The pressure of parental expectations had never been something he was good at enduring. He believed that if he could see her, if he could maintain their train rides throughout his parents' visit, then he could withstand them, and their judgments, and the wild amount of running around they both deemed integral to their time with him.

All you have to do is ask.

Donovan had heard a heart could survive up to 240 bpm, but he wasn't exactly sure it was true when his mouth spoke truths directed at her. "I'll miss seeing you." Her smile said something he wouldn't see, and he pushed on, waiting for the explosion in his chest to happen. "I'd like to see more of you, really." There was a part of her that was his. He knew it, because she allowed him to know. "Do you think that would be possible? To see you more?" Her innocent face and parted lips weren't ready to speak but her eyes, little worlds unto themselves, communicated everything. "I just want you to think about it."

Silence.

Chut-chut, chut-chut.

Normally, Donovan's parents came down from Lansing in March after the last chance of snow had passed, but a never-ending winter had pushed their visit back until after Easter and the end of his break. They stayed at the Winston, where he met them for meals and various Chicago experiences that outsiders assumed made up the city. What he wanted them to see was *his* city. But his parents never saw anything as his unless it was also, in some way, intricately tied back to them.

"How about tomorrow I make you breakfast at my place?"

They were out for the big meat-is-our-specialty meal his father always insisted on, and his eyes never left his plate. "You know how to cook?"

"Of course I know how to cook. How would I survive if I didn't cook?"

"A microwave and takeout?"

His mother, who had grown especially good at ignoring their on-going back-and-forth banter, was even better at it when wine was involved. She took a sip from her glass and smiled up at no one in particular.

Donovan knew her time to talk was coming. "Well, I cook," he said. "I've been cooking for myself for over a decade now."

"You could always have a woman cook for you. That's how I got your father." And there it was. Since Donovan had become an educated adult with a career and a retirement plan, his mother's smile most often said, Give me grandbabies, and Donovan missed the simpler smiles from childhood, ones that just said, I love you. She again smiled a smile not meant for either of them and then took another sip of her wine. "Or maybe it was my charming disposition."

The two men looked cautiously across the table at one another before his father continued the most straightforward of the two conversations. "Well, we've never been to your apartment."

"I know."

"Or maybe it was my body," his mother added. "God love you if that was the case."

"Jesus, Laurie." His father's irritation grew more visible each time she spoke. "It was a combination of all the things, okay? All of them, your cooking, your charming disposition, and your . . . everything else."

"Hmm, for me it was just your orneriness." She winked across the table, this smile saying *I know all the right buttons because I helped install them,* and Donovan knew the wine was doing something other than "working."

"My apartment isn't big. You can see the bed from anywhere in the house—unless you're in the bathroom with the door shut."

His father's eyes finally left his plate. "Your bed is in your living room?"

"Well, I prefer to think my bed is in a bedroom without walls."

His father stared blankly across the table at him.

"But it's up for interpretation."

"Can't wait." One raised eyebrow, that's all his father offered before returning his gaze to his meat.

His mother dipped a sliver of lobster into some sauce before taking a bite and moving the conversation toward other plans. "What do you want to see this weekend?"

He saw his father's eyes roll, as they always did when the question was asked, but Donovan answered anyway. "*See What I Want to See*—it's at Steppenwolf. Some kind of 1950s murder noir."

"As long as it's not a musical," his father interrupted. "I hate musicals."

"You hate *plays*, Donald. It doesn't matter if there's music or not." She tossed him a look before turning back to her food. "How many tickets should I buy?"

Fingers brushed across the napkin, the question asked without looking—words thrown out to remind Donovan that his singledom was a perpetual disappointment to her and a concern for his father.

Donovan let his knife slice into his pork chop. He knew how to stop them both, make her happy, and prove he was a man all at once. "If you want to grab four, that'd be great."

"Four?" His parents spoke in unison, as if finally on the same team.

He couldn't take it back. "There's someone I'd like you to meet."

It wasn't a lie.

Both parents looked at him with the same kind of unintended shock, like he had an eleventh finger they'd failed to notice at birth. And there, in that moment, he found it again, that empowered feeling of simply saying he was *involved*.

It added a lightness to the air that helped him to breathe deeper and sit a little straighter.

"Is it a woman?" His father asked.

"Don—"

"Hey, you know, I've got a right to ask," his hands held up in defense.

"Yes, she's a woman." Donovan knew all too well what his father thought of him. Questioning his utility had started early and was brought on by the way he spoke and acted toward him. "I met her on the train, she's a little older than me and teaches at a nearby school."

"What does she teach?" His mother's eyes were bright and her smile said, Let's plan the wedding.

"Art, she's an artist. She has a studio in her house where she paints."

"Is she any good?" His father, still wanting to find fault where he could.

"Of course she's good."

"What's her name? I want to look her up." His mother's phone already out.

"I don't want you to look her up, Ma."

"Come on, why not?"

"You'll meet her tomorrow."

"Should be interesting." His father raised his wine glass. "To finally meeting someone who understands you." Donovan could cheers to that. "And thank God it's a woman."

Donovan watched over his pint glass as his parents joined him for a drink, and he determined that his relationship with them could have been made better years ago simply by lying.

He bought flowers, an extra toothbrush, a pink-handled razor. He bought shampoo and body wash that smelled familiar and tickled memories of spring. He lit new candles. Dirtied an extra coffee cup, a towel, a washcloth. He used the soaps to fill the space with her scent and dumped half their contents down the drain in case his mother checked their weight to verify the strength of their relationship or, worse yet, his father checked the validity of his character. He lay in bed and whispered "I love you" to the pillow that was her head.

It wasn't an ill-conceived plan. His mother's eyes caught on all the appropriate props and his father assumed that his orderliness was his girlfriend's doing. That afternoon on the pier, Donovan received a phone call. She'd fallen sick and wouldn't make the play.

"She was worried about it last night but hoped she'd be feeling better today." There was a sigh that signaled nothing other than the sweet liberation of a lie adding texture. "Working with kids, they're little packets of disease, man. I tell you."

He saw his mother's disappointment and his father's skepticism, but for the first time ever, when their departure time arrived, Donovan was not relieved to see his parents go. Saying goodbye to them meant saying goodbye to the charade he'd grown rather comfortable exuding—a charade that left him in a constant state of arousal and possibility, even though the lady in the blue coat had not appeared in his life for days.

Resting his head against the train window, he closed his eyes and concentrated on the sun's warmth. It felt good after such a long winter, like the slow and comforting heat caused by skin connecting with skin, a thought that caused the lady in blue to skip knocking before the door opened and a familiar twinge developed in the lower half of his body.

He didn't try to fight it. He could embrace her image, let his body do as it pleased. He knew she was the only one who might watch him closely enough to notice his excitement. And he imagined that too. What she could do for him, what he'd do for her in return.

When the train pulled up to Paulina, laughter flitted in through the open doors, and his body, already on high alert, filled with the electricity that meant she was close. He didn't have to look to see her, he could feel her there before she'd boarded. It was the man standing next to her that Donovan didn't wish to see.

They entered the train holding hands and Whole Foods grocery bags. The man looked like a god disguised as a homeless person. He wore maroon corduroys, a disintegrating T-shirt, and a tan jacket from the 1980s fully equipped with a chevron stripe. The jacket was at least three sizes too small for the man's immensity, and this irritated Donovan almost as much as the messy blonde hair he had pulled back into a bun.

Donovan watched his beaming and oblivious smile as he leaned in and kissed the side of her head. *Her* head, atop an unzipped blue coat. Neck exposed. Smiling a smile Donovan had yet to receive.

The weight of the man's gravity forced Donovan's eyes to close and beg back any image of her prior to that moment.

"Doors closing."

He tried to reach the fantasy where his hands felt underneath her blue coat and her breath was warm like the sun on his face. One where she was his and he was hers. But when he couldn't, and when his eyes opened, the lady in blue was watching him, frozen midsentence like someone entering the event horizon.

The train lurched forward, restarting time, and the man, her god, orbited in the opposite direction toward some seats, pulling her out of the black hole and spinning her round to where her Adonis had landed. She cast one last glance over her shoulder, looking back at Donovan as if he were a memory she wished to suppress.

There were three stops before Montrose. Three stops in which they faced one another from across the train and failed to stop seeing one another. When the time came, he exited through the back door and made his descent without checking her gaze.

"Mr. James!" The voice was familiar but the name out of place. "Mr. James!" There was a light touch on his back and for the briefest of moments he'd believed it to be the blue coat running after him. "Mr. James?"

He turned as he opened the gated door at the bottom of the stairs and let his disappointment walk through first. "Hey, Lils."

She smiled at him the way a woman who knows her looks are worth something is wont to do, then tucked a wisp of black hair behind her ear. "Did you have a nice visit with your parents?"

Her smile reminded him that for three stops he sat facing the red hair and pale skin of a smileless face that said nothing. You are nothing to me.

"It was good, yeah. Thanks for asking."

Weekend charades had been replaced by the image of Adonis kissing the side of her head over and over.

Block it out, take it back, make it a fiction.

"Are you okay?" Lily moved, and the world moved with her. "You look not okay."

He was not okay. "I'm good, just tired. It's been a busy weekend."

"I was just going to pop over for a chai," she said, tilting her head in the direction of Starbucks. "You could join me, decompress." The wind kicked her skirt up, exposing the skin of her upper thigh and she made no move to contain its introduction.

"Thanks, but I'm gonna head home."

Her smile said, It would be better if you stayed, but her remaining innocence said, "Next time then."

The phrase, her smile, and the lingering image of her thigh had him turning away from her. "Take care, Lils."

"*Volpone* was an interesting choice, I think." The words caused the hair on the back of his neck to stand on end and stopped his forward motion. "It wasn't just the lies, or deceit, or greed—it was the production of it all." Her ankle boots clacked along the cement as she stepped closer, the sound causing a brief flash of her exposed thigh to reappear in his mind before he could smother it. "I mean, it's one thing to tell a lie and something altogether different to plant the evidence, isn't it?"

In that moment, Lily was a stranger to him. Holding a mirror, tickling his thoughts, flaunting her long legs and sculpted thighs. He needed to escape. "That's a great point, let's talk about it in class tomorrow."

"Why do you use transgression?" The hair tuck and the smile.

He could smell the various products she used to maintain herself: her shampoo, body wash, lotion, skin-care products, all conglomerating into the underlying chemical smell of social expectation, but also of spring.

You bought Lily's shampoo.

"I teach a section on transgressions in literature every year."

"But why?" Her smile faded as her eyes probed his thoughts. "What is it about transgression that you find so appealing?"

Two hundred forty beats; he wasn't there yet.

And her body wash.

"It was the topic of my master's thesis. We've been over this."

"That still doesn't answer my question." Her eyes traveled back to the door he'd held open for her. "I'd like to read it, see what the allure is." A smile. "Maybe after graduation . . . "

"Maybe after graduation what?"

She wants to fuck you. Sleep in your bed. Bring her soap and share a toothbrush.

Stop.

"I could read your thesis and we could grab a coffee like normal people?" Her new smile said, Be gentle, I'm patient, I'm doing this all for you. His utility to her came fully into view, and Donovan had no idea how to respond.

You could take her home.

"I don't think that's going to be a good idea." There was a flash of hurt in the way she looked at him and his hand reached out to touch her, comfort her, but as his fingers met her skin, he determined it was best to let her go. "I'll see you tomorrow."

Loser.

The wind encircled her skirt as she walked away, lifting it up just enough to reveal where her ass and leg met. Tan round curves coupled under maroon cotton.

Look.

The image shattered the precarious guiltlessness with which he held their previous interactions. It felt calculated and seductive.

Sunshine had warmed the inside of his apartment to a degree that made summer feel less like a distant memory. Evidence of his parents' visit was everywhere, from his carelessly thrown shoes to the to-go boxes filling his fridge. Five hundred square feet made the displacement of any item obtrusive to the eye.

He stood for a moment by the island counter that separated his kitchen from his bedroom/living space and gazed longingly at his unmade bed. His desire to crawl into it and match the blue coat's face and red hair with the exposed thigh and ass he'd just been unabashedly shown was overwhelming, until Adonis's glowing skin, toothy smile, and maroon fucking corduroys appeared to take her first.

Maroon. It's not just a color.

He turned around and hung his coat on a hook by the front door before kicking off his shoes and pushing them into the closet.

Maroon: to leave in isolation without hope for escape.

Anger and discomfort filled his being as he tried to correct the location of objects and repeatedly found himself wishing that Lily had been a random stranger on the train who'd come on so boldly. Someone he could have taken home and fucked without guilt or regret. Someone he could have fucked on the train. Fucked in front of *her*. Fucked for the sake of fucking.

Fuck her. Fuck him—and fuck his patched-up corduroys.

You are marooned.

He threw his running shoes as hard as he could toward the front door. They bounced back at him as if to say, You need to run.

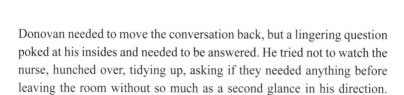

Donovan needed to move the conversation back, but a lingering question poked at his insides and needed to be answered. He tried not to watch the nurse, hunched over, tidying up, asking if they needed anything before leaving the room without so much as a second glance in his direction. "How did you wind up at my apartment?" he asked.

The detective appeared unfazed by the question. "Public records."

"But how?" Donovan saw a life already lived when he looked at the man. "How did you know to look for *me*?" Silver hair and skin made leathery by too much sun.

"You were a question mark that kept cropping up—"

"No." Shaking his head, he watched the old man for a sign that he was getting somewhere, but the detective's limp body left few clues. "There was no reason for my name to be brought up—nothing you were working on that related back to me."

A shift in the room. The detective smiled a smile and his hands began gathering the newspapers his eyes had already examined. "The murders *are* related, Donovan. At the very least, tangentially." Opening papers, flipping pages, he spread the words out and over the table resting above his legs. "I'm sure you've read the articles." Of course he had. "Emily is linked to all parties. A nexus if you will, and the only one no one knew about was you."

"But I had nothing to do with any of that," he said, pointing to the papers.

The detective had already begun to appear sleepy and his speech was beginning to slur. "She knew the boy. She knew about Sticharia." Donovan needed more words before the drugs took their full hold of him. "I needed to see how you related."

It's not about you. It's never been about you.

He waited. Watched the detective fight to keep his eyes open.

You're a pawn in a game.

"It was always about the boy, really." The detective's voice barely above a whisper.

Interference

Six months after the boy died, Lesley woke to the sound of his phone vibrating rhythmically on his bedside table. The clock read 6:15.

"This is Powell."

"Nice of you to answer." Masterson was more awake. "Something's come up and I won't be in today."

Lesley rubbed his eyes in the dark and thought of Deb. "Is everything okay?" Seven months ago, he could still feel the warmth on her side of the bed when he woke. But that hadn't happened in a while. He was up later; she was leaving earlier. They rarely met one another in between.

Masterson was smoking. Lesley could hear him inhaling through the line. "Everything's fine. I've just got stuff to take care of."

He reached to turn on the light, thinking of the tasks he'd need to handle that day and hoping something would happen, some bit of evidence would come through and he could release himself from the weight of the boy's death. He couldn't live with it hanging around his neck anymore. He needed a break in the case, proof that the time he'd invested had been worthwhile. But he also needed a distraction from what his life had fallen into, and Masterson knew both of these things.

"They're sending Obuchowski to meet with the lady on St. Louis. Do me a favor and tag along, would you?"

"Sure, what time?" The lady on St. Louis acted as popcorn filler—a case Masterson had asked for after a spate of summer homicides left them all needing something quieter.

"Nine, and don't make it obvious, Powell." Lesley wasn't sure what he meant by the statement but agreed. "Her file's on my desk."

Masterson disengaged the line without further discussion, and the air-conditioner kicked on. There would be at least one more homicide that day. There was a flicker of hope that when it happened it might bypass their district and not add to their workload. But it was the boy's birthday, and regardless of where the bodies fell, the whole city should be held responsible.

He couldn't move through the sequence of events that led him to this day, at 6:17 a.m. in a dark and empty house, without picturing the boy's body on the table and knowing that his death and the bubble of grief Lesley felt in relationship to it had pushed everything away but his own failures.

The silence surrounding him was a new trend, a variance that began shortly after the boy's death and had since come to mean that no one wanted to be around him for fear they'd have to hear about it. A sourness arrived in his gut, his body feeling the memory just before his mind. The boy had died, Lesley had returned home, and Deb had poured him a cup of coffee. He wasn't yet aware that he didn't want to talk about his feelings or think about how she knew a child had died. He could feel a shift taking place within his world, a falling out and over that separated him from what he thought and what he could hold on to. The death of the boy had propelled him toward the reality of his dying marriage and left him with this single memory of Deb and coffee, the last time he'd felt a "being with" someone.

Standing naked in the bathroom, waiting for the hot water to work its way up the pipes, Lesley observed himself in the mirror. His chest hair had turned gray and his pecs sagged enough for him to know it would only get worse with time. Deb, at least the last time he'd seen her, had her nails done and was wearing a new shade of lipstick.

He tested the water and thought about calling her. It felt like he'd woken up one morning to find his life completely different, but he knew that wasn't the case. Before freshly painted nails, before Jamal's death, before breakfasts together stopped happening and secretly shared cigarettes took place, there had been smaller things. Things they'd done or failed to do and thought nothing of until one day their life no longer held the trajectory of being together. He wondered how long it would last. How long they could continue before this separate life existence became permanent in ways he couldn't take back or make better. The question rode along next to him on his way to work, like a hitchhiker pointing a loaded weapon at all his thoughts and opinions of what happened around him. His wedding band, thick in gold and scratched by thirty-six years of living, looked surprisingly foreign on his finger. Even his gray slacks, matching tie, and white shirt—the same combination of clothes and colors he'd worn since making detective seventeen years ago—felt disembodied.

Sitting in the parking lot of the station, he stared at the dust that had collected across his dashboard and steering column, knowing it had gathered there one fleck at a time. One fleck of shedding skin, clothes fiber, and plant pollen at a time, and he'd done nothing to wipe their tiny corpses away.

There comes a point when things cannot be undone, and as Lesley moved to escape the disfunction of his surroundings, he considered what it would look like to sit there in a new truck. Something unburdened by decay. "I could do that," he said to himself. "Buy a new truck and start again."

The air inside the station was already subarctic. A temperature contrived to invigorate those who needed to maintain their perpetual motion in order to keep up with the chaos happening on the streets outside.

Not everyone needed it. Blakely bounced in the middle of the room, jacked up on caffeine and nicotine—ready to go, ready to "fuck some shit up," and Lesley avoided him as he approached his desk. A chaotic landscape of to-do, done, and almost-done case files that never seemed to go away. He pushed a pile of scraps and notes to one side and stacked the last few days of coffee cups on the other.

"No Tubbo today?" To Lesley, Blakely was Tigger disguised in a hoodie, saggy jeans, and overly white sneakers.

"Not today, no."

Opening the drawer of necessities, Lesley dug past paperclips, pens, pencils, cinnamon-flavored toothpicks, deodorant, an electric razor, and a dozen pairs of black socks before he located his un-encased glasses.

He slipped them on, and Blakely rubbed his nose like a junkie. "It freaks me out when you wear those things, man." The lenses doubled the size of his eyes and bore large scratches. "You look like a basement degenerate."

"Well, we can't all have your looks."

Lesley had initially believed Blakely to be nothing more than a wannabe-hooligan who'd come to rest as an annoyance in his life. Then he realized his behaviors were residue, leftovers from hiding out, getting high, and fitting in with people he'd later help arrest. He wasn't immature, and he wasn't a bad detective. He was just too deep in the filth of things.

"Tubbo say what he was doing?"

Lesley glanced over at Masterson's desk where the only extraneous object of clutter was the lady's case file. "I didn't ask."

"Not cool, Old Man, not cool." Blakely patted the partition as Lesley moved over to Masterson's desk. "You're meant to be *partners*—you gotta be in each other's shit, man."

"Blakely!" As if on cue, his partner entered the room holding coffee and signaling go time.

"You should clean this shit up," Blakely motioned toward Lesley's desk. "There could be something important in there."

Lesley observed their exit before checking his watch. In nine hours, unless something unexpected came up, he'd be standing at the cemetery with a grieving mother who hated him. He'd promised he would take her there. Agreed to hold himself hostage at a birthday party for a dead boy. That was what he could look forward to, and it made him resent the stillness Blakely's absence left in the station.

He eyed the file left on Masterson's clean desk and was reminded of Deb's kitchen, car, and closet space. He wanted the file for distraction, to keep him from thinking of his wife's recently acquired late-night phone habits and freshly painted nails. But a brief glance at the case told him that wouldn't happen.

The woman on St. Louis was an artist, and a man named Nate Aram had contacted the police a few weeks prior regarding items being left in the foyer of her apartment. He had referred to himself as a "concerned friend" but came across more like a jealous lover. The fact is, concerned friends of the opposite sex, especially those attached to a woman whose husband has been out of town for over a month, negated any alarms the situation could have called for. Uniform hadn't even gone out—the report mentioned flowers and bottle caps, items that weren't bells that brought police running.

Masterson had made face-to-face contact with the woman ten days prior when some of her paintings were stolen from her apartment. The neighborhood had been canvassed, the appropriate questions were asked, but the file lacked any photos or descriptions of the paintings, and no actual evidence of a break-in had been found. She had left her backdoor unlocked. Who in their right mind left their door unlocked?

The reason for this day's visit, however, wasn't to follow up on any of the old reports or to provide the woman with any news in regard to them. No, this day's visit had to do with a cat. A dead cat to be exact. It had been strangled to death with blue ribbon and left on her back doorstep.

Lesley squinted up from the file as his lieutenant entered the station and passed quietly into her office. He waited for the door to shut before approaching Obuchowski. "Mind if I go with you this morning?" The artist lived two blocks over and one block down from the Dupont home.

"Sure. Masterson left the file on his desk." She didn't look up from the stacks of papers on her desk. "It should be a fairly open-and-shut case."

It was the first time he'd spoken directly to Obuchowski, despite the fact that she'd been permanently stationed within their precinct for the last nine months. Lesley hesitated to reply as he thumbed back through the file, feeling keenly aware that it lacked the depth of a proper investigation.

"I could use your input." Closing the file in front of her, she tapped it on the desk to straighten its pages and then set it aside before grabbing another one. "You're more familiar with the neighborhood." She looked at Lesley. A fleeting look of familiarity that told him how unfamiliar he was with her.

"Yeah." He rubbed his eyes to clear the details. "That I am."

Her attentions went back to the file. "She's expecting us at nine, so if you have anything to take care of, you should probably do it now."

The station was unusually quiet and everything about her felt weighted. No wonder Masterson had "things to do."

"It will be a pleasure to see you in action, Detective Powell." Her distance existed in her mannerisms but not in her words, as if her mind and her body were following a contradictory set of rules, and she knew more about Lesley as a person than she was letting on.

He returned to his desk, needing to find something not found in the artist's file, and pulled up her website. He didn't know if the stolen paintings were part of a collection or not, but the site had them grouped by showings: *His Dick to My Jane; 4:00 – 4:03 a.m.; Between Drake & St. Louis*; and the most recent, *In Transit*. He decided to work backward through time, find the ones that received the most attention, the ones with the highest price tags, and go from there, but an interior painting of a train caused him to pause and look more carefully. It was full of passengers—all doing their own thing. It made him think of Deb reading her books, and for the briefest of moments he believed he could find her there. See her face. Tell her he loved her. See that she looked happy.

But Deb's face avoided him, and the thought passed. He leaned in closer to read the painting's title.

Hidden in Transit, Not for Sale.

Twenty minutes later, Lesley drove down Drake before turning onto St. Louis. "This is the neighborhood where it happened, right?" Obuchowski was young, and her frankness around topics others now avoided made him not want to talk—especially when everyone knew it was the neighborhood. "This is where that kid was killed."

The driver's seat was unexpectedly uncomfortable, and Lesley attempted to adjust himself while fighting the urge to say the boy died at Swedish Covenant on an operating table.

"It's no surprise the case hasn't been solved." She said it matter-of-factly, as if it were old news and easy to come by. "I imagine the diversity of the neighborhood makes it hard. There's no community amongst neighbors. Too many language barriers."

He tried to roll back his lens, see the neighborhood the way he had back in December and January when furniture marked parking spaces on the street and the earth was a mixture of dirty snow, patchy ice, and shoddily salted sidewalks.

"Do you speak any other languages, detective?"

The neighborhood had been like winter trash, remaining hidden until a cacophony of cicadas called out from trees where people stopped for shade and cars drove by with windows down and music blaring. The more he pressed back on memory, the more obvious his fault became.

"Enough to get by."

"What do you speak?"

She watched him and he knew his reply would be moot. She had read his file. "Hebrew, Arabic, Cantonese—"

"And Masterson?" The heat exposed everything but leads. "He did the majority of the door-to-doors—what languages does he speak?"

"Greek, Russian . . . a little Spanish."

"So you should have had it covered. Between the two of you." Obuchowski sat up as Lesley began to circle the block for parking and spoke before Lesley could answer. "If you could let me off here at the corner, I'd like to check the perimeter, see what's visible from the alley."

He did as she requested and watched her get out.

"Don't push anything too big until I get there."

The car door shut, and Lesley glanced down at the Monroe file. Obuchowski's words, "should have had it covered," replayed in his mind. To say that it *should have* been anything implied that it wasn't, and her words implied that they hadn't done a proper enough door-to-door after the boy's death.

The front door into the artist's building remained unlocked, but there was a buzzer just inside the vestibule that required someone overhead to release the inner door. Lesley stood listening to the footsteps above him, wondering if the lady would come down or ring him up.

When the door buzzed open, he found himself unsurprised that she'd chose that option. She was, after all, the kind of person who left doors unlocked to begin with.

He stepped into the warm heavy air of the stairwell leading up to the second-floor apartment, and his footsteps aligned with those coming from the other side of the door, just before it opened, just before the lady's face appeared, glowing pink, between door and jamb.

"Good morning, I'm Detective Lesley Powell." He noted a hesitation in her eyes and held his badge a little higher. "Masterson couldn't make it this morning."

Upon hearing Masterson's name she stepped back and opened the door wide enough for him to enter. "Sorry." She extended her hand. "I'm M. Thank you for coming."

Her hand was rougher than most of the hands Lesley came into contact with, and the shock of it caused him to look down. Paint clung to a space between the nail and skin of her thumb.

"Can I get you some tea or something? I have iced in the fridge." Freshly showered, she pulled her wet hair back and secured it with a tie, exposing another bit of paint, a streak of gray across the underside of her forearm.

"Tea would be great, thank you." Lesley closed the door behind him as she stepped toward the hall. "I'm sorry to hear about your cat." The smell of her soap clung to the humid air.

"He wasn't really mine," she said as she headed down the hall. There was a damp spot present on the back of her dress where her hair had been resting. "We just sat together sometimes."

Lesley pulled the notebook from his inner pocket and moved into the living room, where a lack of belongings permeated the apartment. "Are you moving?" Perspiration gathering between his neck and collar had him checking the windows. Eleven were visible from where he stood, each as naked as the next.

"No?" A creak in the floorboard alerted him to her return. "I don't know. Maybe?" She handed him the tea. "I forgot to ask if you took lemon or anything."

"This is great, thank you." The glass contained cool beads of condensation that rolled across his fingers. "Where's all your stuff?"

The woman took a seat on the only furniture in the room, a blue denim couch, no larger than a loveseat. "This part of the house rarely gets used for anything." She looked toward the sunroom where a CD player sat unplugged next to some floor pillows. "Alex took his books and papers, but those were in the dining room and all my paintings are in the back, so this is our stuff."

Lesley took note of the scarcity of items and could understand that yes, this *might* be all that someone could need, but any sign of a lived-in mutual life was missing. He wrote the word "transient" to help remember the feeling.

"I'm not really sure what I'm supposed to say or how much you know." The pink lines running through her eyes became observable once she'd stopped moving and Lesley was given a moment to look at her properly.

He didn't have to understand it. He just had to write it down. "The file shows a series of escalating events over the last six weeks." Setting his glass atop the mantle behind him, he saw eight half-burned votive candles. "We're looking for interruptions, anything that doesn't quite fit." His eyes roamed the books lining the built-in shelves on either side of the inoperable fireplace—*The Art of Perspective, Impressionist Landscapes, Textures in Pencil*, and *Slaughterhouse-Five*. Taking a seat on one of the room's radiators, he readied his pen. "Can you think of anything from around then—or just prior?"

She shook her head, "Not really, no. I mean, my husband left around then, but outside of school ending that's been the only difference."

Lesley made note. "And who knew your husband was leaving?"

He watched her mouth twist in thought. "My landlord and my downstairs neighbor? Peter, from the market at the end of the alley." Lesley divided his attention between the notes he made and the paint on her forearm where her fingers idly picked. "Everyone he worked with at the university . . . a few of my colleagues."

"What about your friend, Nate Aram, the man who made the initial call?"

Her fingers stopped moving. "I'm not sure when it came up—but I know he knew Alex was leaving."

Lesley paused to get a good look at her, and she stared right back. "How about your routine?"

She talked with ease about her days and nights. Since summer had begun, her alarm had been set for five o'clock every morning. Once up, she lit the candles on the mantel, turned on some Savasana music, and practiced a few of the eighty-four classic asanas.

Lesley made note to look up both the music, and asanas, because neither meant anything to him.

She set her coffee to brew while she took a shower and then sat on the back porch to drink it and "watch the world wake up." She spent her afternoons painting, walked to the market between seven-thirty and nine to gather dinner supplies, and drank a glass of wine on the back porch most evenings.

"And none of that's changed? No new people hanging around? No old people hanging around more often?"

She shook her head, "As I said, school ended, and Alex left, but my routine's been the same as it is every summer."

"Is your husband gone a lot?"

She took a drink of her tea and looked down the hall. "Not like this. I mean he's not *present* most of the time, but normally he *lives* here." There was a slight smile before her tears began to build. "That's why I liked having Jack to sit with me."

She pointed back toward the hall, and Lesley looked up to clarify. "Jack?" Beads of perspiration escaped his collar and rolled down his back. "Who's Jack?" Flipping back a page he checked to see if he had missed something.

"Jack's the cat. That was his name."

There was relief and not relief all at once. "And how long had you had the cat?"

He could see her mind and fingers working. "I want to say he started showing up after Alex left."

"So about six weeks ago?" She nodded, and Lesley checked his notes, needing to be sure he'd written things down correctly. "Which is around the time everything else started happening?" Again she nodded. "What time did you say you found Jack?"

"Around six yesterday morning."

"And this asana stuff, you said it takes ninety minutes?" It was there, written down, her continued nod affirming. "But you were outside by six yesterday?"

She looked down the hall again and then back at Lesley. "The heat was too much. I got up early because I couldn't sleep."

The temperature in her apartment would have made sleeping impossible for Lesley. Air-conditioning had become a lover that sheltered him from sleepless nights and kept cheese from melting on the counter when Deb wasn't around to make dinner. But he didn't believe the heat was responsible for the discrepancy in her details.

"Do you know what they'll do with his body?" she asked.

A question generally heard under a different context, one where something better than a trashcan would become the body's fate. Lesley didn't feel up to lying, but he also didn't want to tell the truth.

Taking a sip of his tea, he felt the cool liquid slide down into his belly. He tried to stretch the sensation by slowly drinking more until the sound of the buzzer meant he no longer had to answer her question. "That's probably Detective Obuchowski," he said. "Would you mind if I take a look out back while you let her in?"

Melting ice cubes bounced against one another in her glass as she and Lesley parted ways in the hall. Once he'd moved through the smell of her soap, another smell, more familiar but seemingly misplaced, crept in through his nostrils and forced a mixed sense of comfort and uncertainty.

Lesley entered the dining room to find a giant whiteboard covering the wall to his right. At work, whiteboards held all pertinent developments for easy reference and quick updating, but here, on this whiteboard, madness abounded in scrawls Lesley only knew to be equations because of how little he understood them.

He paused before the board in silent awe and wondered what it all meant.

The two women had entered the room, and the artist stood beside him as if she were trying to see what he saw. "Alex is a physicist. I had the board installed as an anniversary gift." She wore a soft smile. "I thought it would keep him home."

The three of them stood silently before the board until Obuchowski asked if anyone knew what it meant.

"I have no idea," Lesley admitted.

"Neither do I," said the artist. "But I *do* know how to tie my shoes."

The sadness of the woman felt bigger than dead cats, but her comment lightened the mood and made Obuchowski laugh. Lesley followed them through the kitchen and out onto the back steps where the cat had been found.

There were four small landings, all connected by steps that led from the backyard to the third floor above them. Lesley wasn't comfortable with the transition of her mood, or the change in the space, or the easy access from the alley below that smelled like a mixture of laundromat, bakery, and sun-roasted trash. "So there's no security from the back."

"No, but I have my neighbors and my neighbors have me."

Obuchowski exchanged glances with Lesley before potholes caught his eye and he wondered if Jamal had ever hobbled past.

"How involved are you with the man who made the initial report? Nate Aram." Obuchowski dove right in without a warmup.

"He's the father of one of my students, and we have a few mutual friends." A large crashing sound below them caused a vein in her neck to pulse, and Lesley moved to look over the landing's ledge. "It's just my neighbor doing laundry," she batted his concern away.

Obuchowski didn't appear fazed by the commotion or the pulsing or the way the woman nervously picked paint from her forearm, but she did seem interested in the next question. "Is Nicodemus Papachristi one of the friends you and Mr. Aram have in common?"

Lesley was unfamiliar with the name, but he caught sight of the woman's movements when it was said. How she pushed wisps of hair away from her face, scratched at the paint, crossed her arms. "I called you about Jack."

"We're just trying to cover our bases." Obuchowski let the words sit between the three of them while she tapped her pen. "The items that were left in your foyer, were they collected by Detective Masterson?"

"No." Her arms unfolded, and her hands slipped into the pockets of her dress where they tapped against her leg and kept the fabric in constant motion. "He told me I could throw them away."

Lesley couldn't believe it. Didn't want to believe it. He avoided Obuchowski's reaction in order to both hide his discomfort and keep his eye on the woman as she moved.

"Did any of the items stand out to you? Hold any significance?"

Lesley wanted her to say no—needed her to say no. But the shuffling of her canvas shoes on the wood beneath her feet told him that wouldn't happen.

"There was a picture of a redhead." The woman was noticeably uncomfortable and didn't look at either of them when she spoke. "It was only significant because she had red hair."

"Can you describe the picture?"

A slow and deep breath. "She was naked. Naked and bound."

Lesley checked Obuchowski's understanding and tried to calculate the likelihood that Masterson wouldn't have asked, wouldn't have found such a thing important. But the news didn't ruffle her in the slightest. "Do you know who the woman was?" The artist shook her head and a wisp of her hair fell free. "Who all knew about the cat?"

Tucking hair, adjusting feet. "My dad? My neighbors maybe?" Cheeks still glowing in the heat. "I didn't really talk about Jack—he just sat with me while I smoked my cigarettes." Her *au-naturel* appearance made her easy to overlook, but her hands used motion when attention was needed. "If you wind up talking to Alex," she said, reaching out to them, "please don't mention the smoking—he's got enough to think about." And her hands were once again tucked away.

Lesley's observance of her physical behaviors stopped. Some lies were lies of omission, others were not. To lie about cigarettes suggested she'd lie about other things. "Your husband doesn't know you smoke?" Bigger things.

"It would bother him. He's got enough to think about."

Secret cigarettes struck a nerve and added imperfections to her character. "What's your relationship with your husband like?" he asked.

Her eyes skimmed his face for the motive behind the question, and the look that finally rested on hers told him she would not be speaking to his brevity but to his potential insinuation, "Alex isn't capable of doing any of these things, Detective Powell." She pointed toward the door leading back into the house. "He can do that in there, all that *Beautiful Mind* bullshit you see on the board, but . . . he couldn't do this." The *this* felt pregnant with meaning she didn't intend, or wish for Lesley to understand, but her words echoed his own thoughts and filled the gaps between intention and interpretation in a way that made them both uncomfortable and began to fill her eyes with tears. "Please excuse me." She headed back into the house and Obuchowski looked up in irritation.

"What was that? Why did you do that?"

Taking a kerchief from his pocket, Lesley wiped his neck. "If she's lying about cigarettes—"

Her shaking head stopped him from saying anything further. "I'm going to go look around the back rooms. You see if she handed over anything to Masterson—anything at all."

Lesley followed her back through the doors feeling like a chastised child, and when he found the woman drying her eyes at the center of the living room, he thought about apologizing but didn't. "Is there any way we could get a list or a look at the paintings that were taken?" Masterson could not have fucked that up.

"I did that when they came to the house." She paused to blow her nose, "The paintings are all from my last showing."

Lesley tucked his notebook back into his pocket wanting to believe it was an oversight on Masterson's behalf, that the list and the evidence existed back at the station.

"Do you know what they'll do with Jack's body?"

He still wasn't prepared to lie. "I could have someone call you if you'd like."

She wiped her face, tucked her hair, and made it clear she wanted to remain composed, but her voice broke and more tears sprang forward. "I just don't want him to be thrown away."

Lesley handed her a tissue and hoped Obuchowski would say something meaningful. But she stood by the door and disregarded the comment altogether. "Give us a call if anything comes to you, some detail you might have missed. Even if it doesn't seem relevant." Instead of giving her a card, Obuchowski nodded toward Lesley. "Keep Detective Powell's information handy, just in case. Someone will give you a call when there's news."

She opened the door and stepped out onto the landing while Lesley handed over his card. "Again, I'm sorry for your loss, Mrs. Monroe. We'll be in touch."

Once the door had closed behind him, Lesley paused to make one last note before joining Obuchowski on the stairs. The sun sat just above the homes across the street, shining through the windows, reflecting light off the dust floating in the air.

"What are you thinking?" They had begun their descent, and she took two stairs at a time.

"I think she's having an affair."

"Do you think it's connected to all the other stuff?"

"No." Before he could say anything, Obuchowski opened the door,

93

and a group of kids walked past the car out front. Five kids in total. All familiar to Lesley. The smallest one still lingering in the middle with his golden snapback.

The kid's eyes moved from the vehicle toward Lesley, and a slow smile spread across his face, tightening Lesley's body. Joey Quiles, he had learned, had been a close friend of Jamal's before black and gold had come into play and standing on street corners had become a habit.

"The one with the hat," she said after they'd passed, "he and his older brother were seen out and around the area the night the boy was killed, right?"

He paused out of fear. "We haven't been able to make anything stick; crime scene was too clean; no murder weapon was found. All the evidence we have is based on a few sightings of those kids—but there's nothing direct. And there haven't been any other leads."

Her eyes followed the group before getting in the car. "Who was first on the scene?"

Lesley hated the question and answered it knowing she already had the answer. "Masterson."

They headed back to the station, where he pulled all the files on the Dupont case and triple-checked Masterson's notes. Searching through the evidence again and again and again. Pictures of shoe prints, teeth, and blood. He checked the statements of first-responders and the man who'd found the boy while walking his dog. He read back through the initial door-to-door interviews and cross-referenced them with the written reports. Circling around and around, until the proximity to the artist, where she lived, and what she painted, came fully into view.

A desperate thought evoked the slimmest of possibilities in her collection titled *Between Drake & St. Louis* and sent Lesley back to her website. He scanned the paintings, the faces, postures, backgrounds, and windows, trying to see if any of the boys showed up, alive or in danger—it didn't matter. It was a Hail Mary pass, but Lesley needed to know if she'd seen something no one else had.

False Horizon

It wasn't a normal practice to leave the store in the middle of the evening to go eat hotdogs and drink beer in a customer's backyard. But it *was* his birthday and he was *meant* to be eating hotdogs and drinking beer—just not in Albany Park with an alley view.

Peter O'Shea had expected a crowd because the woman didn't come across as a hotdog sort of person, but as he approached her back gate, he saw only one other occupant, the limping black kid who stole things from his store. He was "special" because he had a limp; people felt sorry for him and never suspected that his baby face and hobbling disposition would rob them blind first chance he got. He was a ten-year-old thug in the making.

"He's never had a Chicago-style hotdog. Can you believe that?" The glee on M's face told him she was just as naïve as she was a white-girl saint-in-practice. "You're witnessing a civic duty right now. Jamal, this is Peter; Peter, this is Jamal."

Jamal's eyes rose to meet Peter's and they understood one another.

"We've met."

Naïve as to why the situation could be problematic, M turned and pulled a couple of Coronas out of an ice bucket before cracking them open, quickly slicing a lime, rubbing the rims, then salting the bottle tops like she performed the actions for a living. "Today is Peter's birthday," she said, looking at Jamal but handing the beer to Peter. "He was supposed to be at a Sox game, but he got called into work instead." Turning her attentions to Peter. "I'm sorry, and happy birthday." She raised her bottle to his before taking a drink.

"The Sox are getting their asses handed to them anyway, so . . ."

Jamal started cleaning up his space at the table, and M invited him to stay and eat more. "I can't." He cast a look between the two adults in front of him and settled on M's face. "My mom calls at eight to make sure I'm home. If I'm not there," he shook his head as he stood, "you'll hear her yelling all the way downtown."

"Well, we wouldn't want that." She retrieved a plastic bag from the back stairs and handed it to him, "Don't forget this." It was one of Peter's store bags, and he wondered if she'd been buying the kid groceries. He knew he'd confronted the kid after eight o'clock at least once within the last month, stealing Takis while buying a Kinder bar. "And take some cookies."

He and Jamal exchanged a goodbye suitable for the situation, and M closed the small gate behind him before returning to the barbecue.

"He's a great kid," she said, giving the hotdogs a turn. "He has a friend who likes to paint so I give him my extra supplies."

"As long as you're not handing out any spray paint." His store had been tagged three times in the last six weeks.

Closing the lid, she powered through her remaining beer and grabbed another. "I don't think you have to worry about Jamal tagging anything."

Peter didn't feel like arguing and glanced around the space of her backyard, "I was expecting other people to be here. It isn't your usual fare, if you know what I mean."

She laughed as they both looked at the plate of chocolate chip cookies and giant bag of Lay's potato chips sitting on the patio table. "This is for my brother." The sun had dipped down just enough to make its tilted orange umbrella useless for shade, and the chocolate had begun to melt.

"Is he here?" Peter asked.

She shook her head and drank her freshly prepared beer while busying her eyes with looking elsewhere. "He died. Thirty years ago today."

As unusual as it was for him to be drinking beer with a customer he'd only casually spoken with, her response made his being there feel even more out of the ordinary.

"We ate hotdogs, with lots of ketchup. I remember dipping our chips into it and pretending they were McDonald's french fries."

He wasn't sure how to escape the situation and decided to finish his beer.

"Here," she returned to the ice bucket, "let me get you another. This wasn't meant to be awkward."

He recognized the sincerity in her voice and wished he could help lighten the conversation without having to remain.

A van pulled into the drive next door. He could hear its occupants listening to the game on their radio and asked for the score.

"Six-one Tigers." The man turned off the engine and a handful of children jumped out of the vehicle. "I give up." They ran directly to a blowup pool in the corner of the yard and began splashing each other.

Peter imagined his friends at the game, drunk and pissed off. "Happy birthday to me," taking the fresh beer from M, he watched her pour ketchup all over a bunned dog. "You do know you're not supposed to put that on hotdogs, right?" She licked her thumb and nodded. "What was his name? Your brother." The question had more of an effect on her than he'd expected until she said the name, *his* name, and Peter was forced to look away.

"I'm sorry," she said shaking her head. "I know it seems weird. I promise I'm not crazy. It's just a coincidence, really."

"A coincidence that your brother, Peter, died on *this* Peter's birthday?" He pointed at himself and checked for a visual confirmation of her honesty.

"Yes, very much a coincidence." Her head bob was rapid and her eyebrows raised. "Also, the part about your birthday plans not working out and my inviting you here . . . total coincidence. I know it looks bad, insane even." She reached out and touched his arm. "But no one should go without a little birthday celebration."

"Or a memorial." He felt like an asshole as soon as he'd said it, but really, it was bizarre to be there under such morbid circumstances.

"The story continues." She plated up the remaining hotdogs and opened the foil-wrapped buns. "I think it's good to remember that. I'm glad you can help me remember that."

Peter took a long sip of his beer and decided to stay. Joining her at the wrought-iron table, they silently made their plates, both of them trying to pretend the interaction was normal. "How old were you when it happened?"

"Five."

"So you probably don't remember much then."

The sun had dipped just enough to shield her eyes, and she grabbed a handful of chips before answering. "Memory is weird, you know? I don't remember a lot, but I feel like I've spent my entire life trying to cobble Peter back together, befriending people I think contain some aspect of him, trying to paint him, trying to draw him out, help him live, fill the void his death left in my personhood . . . but I can never find him. Not really. The memory of him is like a reality I can't quite make out—"

Peter nodded his head, wiped mustard from his chin, and spoke through a mouth full of food. "Like a pilot trying to find the horizon at night, or between clouds." She waited for him to say more, and he knew he'd fucked it up. "I don't know why I said that. I don't even know what it's called. My friend's a pilot and he said something similar about losing the horizon."

"No, no . . . I love it." She seemed to understand something he did not and took a giant bite of her hotdog. "So their flight is based on an illusion?"

He tried not to notice the ketchup on her cheek and again wiped his own face. "Yeah, something like that. Like I said, I don't really know."

"I imagine there's no way for that not to end disastrously."

"Probably."

She laughed and wiped her face. "So you're saying I'm going to crash my plane."

"*No.*" Her laughter came harder, and he struggled to think of a way to correct himself. "I'm saying . . ." Then he thought of Jamal. "Make sure you're not just flying based on what you think you perceive." That seemed safe. "Be certain that what you're seeing is real."

So It Goes

It was Friday, midafternoon, and Donovan stood on the Armitage plat-form waiting for a train home. His afternoon classes had been cancelled due to an assembly, and he knew he could skip home early without run-ning the risk of seeing the lady in the blue coat. It had been twelve days since he'd seen her on the train with *him*. His chest hurt whenever train doors opened and a woman's laugh could be heard. His chest also hurt while he lay awake in bed at night unable to fall asleep. The image of Adonis's maroon corduroys had killed his ability to masturbate, the only sleep-aid he'd needed in years.

A note had been left on his desk that morning, neatly typed and anon-ymous. He pulled it from his pocket and let his eyes skim the words again while he waited. *For when she spoke, he did not hear the words unspoken, nor see the fire, which plumed smoke from her mouth, ever waiting for his branch to stir and stoke its flames higher. What he saw and heard was trapped in time—the length of a period, the age of her skin, the ticking clock passing one and aging the other. Her fire, waiting, coals hot. Someday, he would remember the skin of her thighs differently, and she hoped they would read like braille under his fingertips. 'Open Me' is all they would say . . .*

Electricity filled the air, and he shoved the paper back into his pocket. He didn't have to turn to know she stood beside him. He could feel her in the skipping of his heart and then the way her arm pressed against his. As close as a train ride.

"So it goes." She said it quietly. "When I saw you on the train, that's what I thought. So it goes."

To the left, down the tracks, a pigeon with a broken wing hobbled close to the third rail, and Donovan knew its life, just like the moment, would end if they weren't careful.

The blue coat moved to catch his eye. "Maybe I should have told you . . . " But he watched the bird and let her stay in his periphery. "I just . . . don't know, it's not like I don't wear a ring—"

"We don't have to talk about it."

His eyes met her abruptly silent expression, and it was her turn to look away. "I think maybe we should, you know?"

So it goes. He could feel the war but didn't know its place. "Look, I don't care about the ring or your husband—"

The lady in the blue coat drew in a breath and turned back to him. "Emily," her name echoed, "but you can call me M, like the letter." Her unmittened hand extended, fingers exposed, drawing his eye back to the details of her and making their impending death feel innocuous.

Was the war in him? Between them? With Adonis and maroon corduroys? He watched her lips when she spoke and slid his fingers across hers, first surprised by the roughness of her skin then embracing it like braille. "Donovan." He would open her. He'd read *her* thighs like braille. *Open me. Open me.*

Without letting go of his hand, she blocked the sun from her eyes with her free one. "It's nice to finally meet you, Donovan." Her smile said, You've already opened me, and he knew he would.

"You too." He released her hand and watched it quickly find its way back into her pocket. Safe. Hidden. Secreted away from him and his thoughts.

The northbound train approached.

The pigeon would die, as would the moment.

"You want to grab some lunch?" she asked.

But not yet.

He followed her in silent anticipation down the stairs, out the turnstile, and fifty feet down the sidewalk to the restaurant next door. This is what he needed. To watch her remove her cap, tuck away her mittens, unzip the coat and slide it off her shoulders. Her girlfriend-ness screaming *Open me* and curing his impotence with simple gestures. He wanted what was his and watched it become real before him. Naked and exposed. Laughing in his bed, on his couch, next to him on the train. Filling him with purpose. Exposing his utility.

This was the inevitable. Her, being his.

She chose a table by the window, platform in view. He watched the way her body moved when she slipped across the stool cushion. The bend of her elbow as she balanced herself on the table. The crease in her skin a detail he wouldn't forget.

Her hair, longer than he'd imagined, fell over her breasts like an extra layer of protection he wished to maintain and brush back all at once. She began to populate his reality as a woman with waist and hips and freckles that flitted up arms, disappearing under a navy dress that left collar bone exposed and the scent of her leaking out.

She could not be the lady in the blue coat now.

Emily, because every girlfriend needed a name.

They stared at one another. He unabashedly cataloged her *-ness* while she allowed it and Steve Miller poured from the speakers louder than necessary. "Jungle Love," the repeated refrain eventually made them laugh.

"Maybe we should have a drink," she said. And there went her hand, reaching for the beer menu, a piece of glitter on her elbow. "Is it too early to drink?"

He would later find that glitter in his bed. "What do you like?"

How many drinks are too many? How many are just enough?

"I'll grab a pitcher."

"You two look cozy. Afternoon date?" A waitress who specialized in small talk and didn't give time for an answer. "What do you think you'll be having?"

The question rubbed against thoughts of what he knew he wanted.

"To long overdue introductions."

He tried to ignore the gold band on her finger when she raised her beer.

"And free afternoons."

But its simplicity sparkled.

Fluids mixed and dribbled to the table as their glasses came together. He watched her free hand move to clean it up while her mouth sucked beer from between her thumb and pointer finger. All her motions swam through him like tiny fish tickling his insides and made it difficult to keep the imagined her distinct from the gold-banded her in front of him.

How many drinks are enough? How many drinks are too much?

When questioned, Donovan said they talked about "everything." When pressed, "everything" included where they grew up; what their parents did for work; her brother, a twin, who died as a child; Donovan's brother, Jay, who still lived at home and smoked pot in his parents' basement; their hobbies; musical tastes; all the things normally associated with "getting to know someone"; and, of course, Kurt Vonnegut's button-pushing Tralfamadorian.

"I don't think it would be a comfort knowing." Her lips moved as people passed by the window behind her and he wanted them to come in. See her. See him.

See us. It's happening.

"I don't want to know that the end has already inevitably happened—that I never had any control—not even in the little moments."

See me. See her. See, it's already happening.

He held silent a moment too long. "Maybe there aren't any little moments."

She was quick to respond. "How is that supposed to make me feel better?" There wasn't a smile, but her face expected an answer.

Having contemplated this idea many times over the last few months, Donovan had come to one conclusion. "My bag got caught in a door, and it happens to people all the time, but *this* time it was different because *this* time I saw you, and that wouldn't have happened if I hadn't stayed up late grading papers, set the wrong alarm, and then woke up at the wrong time and spilled coffee on my pants heading out the door because I was trying to juggle my cup and keys and hadn't got my bag all the way on my shoulder because it got caught on the button that holds that little flap thing—and I wouldn't have been up late grading papers if it weren't for soccer and being a fan and talking to my brother about Man U being beat by Swansea, and don't even get me started on all the 'little' events that took place in order to make that happen, because, believe me, none of them are little. All these things that seem so inconsequential—the button on my coat, needing to post grades, the Wayne Rooney transfer—they all lead to *this* moment—you and me, right here where nothing else matters and everything is beautiful."

She looked at him and laughed.

He tried not to calculate how many trains would pass before they said goodbye, but his thoughts returned to the pigeon as he stood at the bar and felt the rattle of a southbound train pulling into the platform above. A train would pass every six minutes throughout the rush.

So it goes.

The music had been turned down and the crumpled note in his pocket had been handed over. Her chest expanded as she breathed in through her nose and then diverted the air with her mouth.

"Who do you think left it?"

"You." Another train rumbled overhead, vibrating their glasses. He liked the way her cheeks had flushed. "Someone probably found it on the floor and put it on my desk."

Her smile said, You're lying to one or both of us. "I think it's a love note."

From you, to me. You're open. I opened you.

He refilled their glasses.

Three trains later, his hand reached out and took hold of her upper arm when she tried to pass on her way to the bathroom. He watched her eyes try not to look at his hand; they slipped to his chin before floating back up to his eyes like a buoy in a storm. "Do you need something?" she asked.

You. Privacy. My hand under your dress. Lips parted. White teeth exposed. Chest heaving. Freckled skin. What color are your nipples? Strawberry? Penny? Pink?

"Should I order us another?" he asked. They needed another, and though he willed his hand to let go, his fingers had their own ideas and allowed themselves to sneak down the skin of her forearm before fully releasing.

"Pint or pitcher?"

"Both," he said.

Lying in his bed, reading books, window open, cicadas screaming, she would laugh a laugh that burst from her belly.

Touch me. Touch me before you walk away.

"I'll be right back." It was just a whisper.

The space between her reality and his imagination was slippery. She drank a quarter of her beer before taking her seat or setting her glass down. "Maybe we should go after this."

He knew her words weren't an invitation, but he imagined them as such. He also knew she could have left out the word *maybe* and eliminated the uncertainty.

"We should have one more first."

It was an intoxicated suggestion full of possibilities that made her blush.

Sixty trains had passed since he'd ordered their first pitcher. Thirty trains in either direction could have separated them, but she'd stayed, and now the guilt of being seen had kicked in. He watched it play out in her eyes and waited for her to say it had been a mistake.

"I'm not going to be able to do this again, Donovan."

But you will.

"I knew you would say that."

"So you understand?"

The blush of her skin highlighted her freckles, and he shook his head to deny her an easy out. "No."

"Yes, you do."

"Then why'd you ask?" Ready to say a million and one drunken things that all ended with him making a fool of himself, he leaned across the table and let her fingers find his.

"I just want to say . . ." But her mouth stopped there.

What am I to you?

"I'm going to see you again, Emily." Her name was his. "I'm choosing to push that button."

She layered back up. Each addition adding protection, a way to distance herself from him. Her body from his. The hat, the mittens, the blue coat zipped high with her exposed fingers. She stood before him fully armored as the lady in the blue coat. But she wasn't, and she left without saying goodbye.

Donovan didn't move. He remained at the table and watched her stand on the southbound platform above—waiting to go somewhere that wasn't her home, and then pulled the note from his pocket.

Someday, he would remember the skin of her thighs differently, and she hoped they would read like braille under his fingertips. "Open Me" is all they would say . . .

His eyes were drawn up by the ding-donging of the doors just in time to see her blue coat stepping through. "Doors, closing."

The book was hidden by newspapers containing a story that also jumped and skipped and rewound its way through time in a way that made everything feel predetermined. Donovan found himself slouched over in the chair, resting his face in the palms of his hands, trying to keep what he had, what he lost, and what he could still keep separated and untangled.

"You're still here."

The detective's head turned to check the time, and Donovan needed to speak before he said anything else. "Did you ever see her work? Emily's work?" The question was asked genuinely; a memory stuttered. They were on a beach, her head tucked against his neck, stars shooting across the night sky. "She told me there were three kinds of people in the world: those she painted for love; those she painted for money; and those she couldn't paint."

A tanned hand rose to rub more sleep from eyes not ready to be awake. "Why couldn't she paint them?"

Donovan knew Emily's paintings could be found and used however the police decided. "Because she loved them too much to let them go."

You were not for sale.

"It wasn't profitable."

The detective picked up the book and Donovan wanted to touch it. His hand reached for it while his body stood, moved forward, and then stopped.

He would not be driven by reflex, not in this moment.

The book tumbled out of the detective's hand and onto the floor. A slip of paper falling from between its pages. A slight miscalculation. A fumble. Donovan's instinct to catch something midair, avoid the collision with the ground, was just that. An instinct. But the smashed pages felt intentional when his fingers touched the paper and flooded his memories with the list of rules and how they'd broken them.

He was up, bent over, and closer to all he had remaining when he lifted them from the floor.

"Oh . . ." The detective's hand reached out, and Donovan saw how he avoided his eye. "Thank you." He touched the table in front of him, "You can just set it here."

But it wasn't that easy. How it looked. Who was playing what game? Donovan flipped through the book's pages knowing his eye would catch on any new detail just as quickly as the pages turned. The rules he held, penciled in Emily's hand, acknowledged their sins before they had been committed and then crossed out in a confession. ~~No hurting one another. No disappearing. No lurking. No sex. No kissing in public. No meeting in private locations. No seeing one another on Sunday. No discussion around why these rules are necessary~~ . . . and one more, written in his own hand.

To set it down, to return it to its previous location, to not mention it, screamed danger. Donovan could feel the heat rising, his fear and confusion growing. "Who gave you the book?"

The detective's glassless eyes squinted toward the paper. "What do you have?"

"Who gave this to you and why do you have it?" He hadn't sat down or distanced himself. He was tired of running from truth and into lies.

Fumbling for his glasses, the detective reached for the paper. "Let me see it, Donovan." His fingers wiggled and waved, unthreatening.

"People will see what they want to see in this." He handed back the book and held up the piece of paper the man struggled to read. "But it doesn't mean I did it."

"I don't know what it says. I don't know why it's here." A pause. "It wasn't like the other books on her shelf. I asked Obuchowski to make note of it when she wrote her report. That's all, a minor detail."

"There are no minor details," or moments, or words, or actions. "Is she the one who gave it to you then?"

"I don't know." The detective removed his glasses, rubbed his face and head and eyes and sighed. "I sleep a lot these days." He returned the glasses to their needed position, their lenses a magnifying glass. "Sometimes I wake up and find things. Things people have left. Gifts and what not." His hand whirled about. "I don't know who brought what half the time."

"And this time?" It felt too unsafe, too planted, too ready to collapse. "I can't say."

The book's pages had been bent in their landing, but the story would still read the same. Donovan wanted to tear them out, cut them up, put the words back together and receive a different ending. His eyes read through the list one more time before he held the paper up to his nose to check for her scent. "It's not the original." Everything felt fixed. "The original would have smelled like her."

Interference

When the search of the artist's collection *Between Drake & St. Louis* proved unfruitful in Lesley's investigation, he turned to Masterson's desk and observed its tidiness. Obuchowski had informed him that the photos given to him by the lady on St. Louis hadn't been logged in as evidence. "Maybe she didn't actually give them to him."

Obuchowski's expression was unmoved. "Or maybe she did."

The unease of it all left Lesley searching for a reason why. He let his elbows rest on the piles across his desk while he navigated himself back through the *In Transit* collection, taking note of faces, postures, backgrounds, and windows.

After several minutes, a certain character started to emerge. Lesley absentmindedly began making tally marks on a manila envelope to keep track of the image. *Between Drake & St. Louis* had already proved she repeated locations in her collections, and though some pieces were similar in content, no definitive faces had been repeated. This collection was different. There were thirty-two paintings in total and the tally marks told him six of the paintings contained the same man.

He went through photos taken at the gallery showing to see if he could find the recurring figure among the faces, shapes, and backs of heads that had been randomly captured during the event. But the only face he was able to connect was that of "concerned friend" Nate Aram and the wife standing next to him.

Lesley checked her other collections. *4:00-4:03* contained only abstract forms caught in sharp triangular images that felt not only threatening but inescapable. *His Dick to My Jane* did have repeated faces, but the faces repeated were of her husband and herself.

Phone in his hand, Lesley checked the time before dialing the artist's number and looked to see if Obuchowski was anywhere nearby. "Mrs. Monroe," he started talking before she'd said hello. "This is Detective Lesley Powell. Do you have a minute?" He could hear noise in the background and knew she wasn't at home.

"Yes, of course."

"There's a man who recurs in your last collection," Lesley paused, and she filled the gap with acknowledgment.

"He had a good nose and a curious expression."

A pre-recorded voice spoke behind her, and Lesley tried to make out what it was saying before he continued. "Is he a friend? Someone you spoke with?"

The noise behind her swallowed whatever she said next and only the last part came through, "Just some guy on the train."

"Do you know where he got on? Where he exited?" Lesley pressed the phone into his ear and plugged the other one.

"I know you're trying to be helpful, but he *really* was just some guy on the train."

"Uh-huh." The manila envelope seemed to say otherwise. "Did he know you were painting him?"

"I paint what I see."

"That doesn't answer the question." He pulled the chair away from Masterson's desk, just in case the pictures she had given him had fallen and Masterson had forgotten about them. "I can't seem to locate the information you passed on about the paintings that were taken . . ." The low rumbling in the line told Lesley she was on a train and headed underground. Her voice garbled before disappearing all together.

Placing the phone back on the receiver, Lesley checked the time again and grabbed his jacket. He needed to swap cars before picking up the boy's mother. He didn't want her riding in his filthy oven of a vehicle. It lacked care and would give an impression that she didn't need any help in having.

Obuchowski entered the room as he attempted to leave. "Any progress on those photos?"

Lesley checked his watch and shook his head. "I'll be back in a couple hours. We can talk about it then." Aiming for the parking lot, he tried to call Deb, but her phone went right to voicemail. "Hey, Deb, it's me, I just wanted . . ." But he didn't know what he wanted, other than a distraction. "Just calling to check in."

Tucking the phone back into his pocket, he set out on the half-hour trek of trading vehicles, trying not to see the manila envelope on the seat next to him as any kind of proof Masterson had failed. But by the time he found himself in the parking garage and seated inside Deb's car, he regretted not leaving that information with Obuchowski and couldn't start the engine without pulling up the paintings on his phone and sending them to her. *Maybe pull Brown-Line footage, see if you can ID this man? You'd only need to look at Kimball to Armitage between November and March.*

He waited for a response while gathering his collected items and chucking them into the backseat. There, in a normally empty space, Deb had left a pink scarf and a department store lingerie bag.

His phone vibrated against his leg, calling him back to the moment and the task that lay ahead, a one-word response, *Okay*. Lesley drove feeling buried in secrets. He was unable to shake his thoughts until he was parked in front of the boy's home and the mother exited the house holding blue and white birthday balloons that reflected light and bobbed in the wind.

He wasn't there just because it was the boy's birthday. He was there because every time a public meeting or call to action took place—she called Lesley. If it was a holiday—she called Lesley. If there was a rainbow in the sky, or a sale on Cheetos—she called Lesley—and not because she wanted to talk to him, but because she wanted him to know.

"He's not here because of you," she said, closing the car door and keeping her head obstinately forward.

"I know." He didn't need her to say it. Lines could be drawn between his morning watches and Jamal being seen as a narc. Everyone saw them, including Lesley.

Two hours later, with no word from Deb, and feeling plenty of responsibility on all fronts, Lesley sat with the Dupont files splayed out before him once again. He was trying to tell himself Masterson's notes had always been a little sparse. He was a "facts, and nothing but the facts" kind of guy, and frequently left out what he saw as minor details.

But the photos weren't insignificant, and Masterson was gone, had stuff to do, wasn't going to be around, and the combination of events left Lesley with questions he was leery to get the answers to.

"Want a sandwich, Old Man? I'm headed to Subway." Blakely appeared wired and ready for the long haul.

"I'll take a club on that cheesy bread, no pickles." Lesley picked up his phone as an alert came through. "You should grab something for Obuchowski. I haven't seen her eat all day." A thumbs up was given but no questions were asked, and Lesley checked his phone. Damien Quiles had just been picked up at Roosevelt High School, and Lesley had a friend, who had a friend.

Blakely had already left the building, and Lesley was more out of breath than he wanted to admit when he caught up. "Blakely!"

He was sauntering toward the vehicle, lit cigarette in hand, and he turned at the call of his name.

"I need a favor."

A slow wide smile emerged as he draped his arm across Lesley's shoulders. "No, Old Man, what *you* need is a light."

What You Have Said in the Dark

The songs of the Roman school's Friday Mass had been Nico's favorite part of all services since he was four. Now that he was eight, he had simply learned to hide his enthusiasm for it. All his friends enjoyed recess and gym. They liked to run and yell and play kickball or soccer. For them, Friday Mass meant remembering to wear their button-down shirts and ties. It meant sitting, standing, kneeling, and keeping their eyes forward even when their best friend sat across the way or in the pew behind them and the priest said something funny. They had to hold it in, suck it up, and keep their laughter to a minimum, something eight-year-old boys weren't very good at.

Those constraints of Friday Mass rarely bothered Nico. He liked the way their voices, the kids' voices, filled the church with sounds so close to God that even his arm hairs stood in praise. His body's response to their echoes bouncing back had once convinced him there could be nothing better, or more sacred, than children singing. But something he'd recently seen on his father's computer was an absence of that. A child singing, a man encouraging him to hum once his mouth had been filled. The image turned the sound of their singing voices away from Heaven and toward a sadness Nico couldn't quite detail. A sadness that sat deep within him, rolling around like a thistly doughball, showing him that life was not at all like the feelings he had during a Friday Mass, but something much more foreign and frightening.

This was made worse by "expression."

As a second grader, each week after Mass he and his friends were marched back across the parking lot and delivered directly to Mrs. Monroe's art room where "expression" began every class. He'd enjoyed it when he was littler, the way she would ring a tiny bell to let everyone know it was time to stop talking and sit still. The way she would light a candle, turn off the lights, and after a few moments of silence go around the room asking everyone to name what they were feeling in one word. He listened, watched his classmates, wondered if they knew, had seen, had experienced such gross nakedness as he had, and felt caught between knowing it wasn't meant to be discussed and really needing someone to help him understand.

"Happy," is what he'd said on his turn. It felt stupid and weird to sit in the dark and *express* anything—especially when vocabulary no longer accounted for what needed to be expressed.

Once everyone had their turn, Mrs. Monroe made them sit in silence with their eyes closed for a solid minute. Nico sat trying to ignore the fact that his expression had been a lie.

When the minute was up, she blew out the candle, rang her bell again, and turned the lights back on. "We're going to take a break from our auction items today and use up some leftovers." Mrs. Monroe began pulling out boxes of scraps. "I could use a break, you could use a break, and I think we should just go crazy. Have a little fun." Scraps of paper, scraps of material, left-over buttons, dried flowers, ceramic tiles, glitter, plastic jewels, string, you name it, she pulled it all out. "Now," she looked more serious than normal, "the only rule for today is this: what you make has to mean something *to you*. I don't have to understand it, your friend doesn't have to understand it—it just has to mean something to you." She looked around the class, checking to make sure her instructions were clear. "Does everyone understand?"

There was a silent response of nodding heads and then, without warning, she began dumping the boxes out into the middle of the room. The class erupted with the messy piles she created and added to, her voice needing to raise above their enthusiasm. "I've got the glue gun warming if you need it, let me know and I'll help you. Otherwise, this is all about *you*. Don't forget—the only rule is that it has to mean something *to you*." She gave her hands one firm clap, "Now get started."

His classmates rushed forward. Paper, twigs, broken crayons, laughter and shouting filled the room with a chaos Nico would have previously enjoyed being a part of but now needed to escape. After collecting his scraps and a few colored pencils, he sat at a lone desk in the corner and stared at his blank sheet of paper.

God hadn't answered any of Nico's questions about what he'd seen on his father's computer. He hadn't spoken to him directly like Adam or

Moses. He hadn't offered him any signs or tried to ease his uncertainty by providing peace. And Nico tried to understand His silence patiently, not wanting to feel alone or forgotten or unworthy, but it was hard.

The closing song at Mass that day had said, *I the Lord of sea and sky, I have heard my people cry, all who dwell in dark and sin, my hand will save*. Nico found himself wondering if he'd recognize the hand, and what it meant to be saved. No amount of thought kept certain things from hurting.

The boy from the computer had been young, on his knees, on top a toilet. Singing. Nico drew him, and then covered his nakedness with black scraps of paper.

There had been a man, a hairy man, his face hidden, body close to song. Wiggling. Nico scribbled wild black hair and the pink of his private part.

Sitting in a room full of chaos, he uncovered the boy's mouth and tried to understand why it had opened. The yucky feeling in his body, telling him the mystery was a sin, also told him to cover it up again. To cover the man and the things he couldn't un-see, to crumple the paper, throw it away, wait for God to clear his mind, send him an angel, save him.

"Nico." Mrs. Monroe said his name softly while kneeling beside him. Her unexpected voice and closeness made him jump. "I'd be interested to hear what you're working on here."

He didn't want her on her knees. He didn't want anyone on their knees outside of Mass. "Nothing." He placed a hand over his paper and felt the sticky glue cover his palms. He couldn't let her look and risk the chance she'd pull back the cover and find what was hidden.

"Nothing?" She smiled. "It's never 'nothing' with art."

"Can I use the bathroom?"

Mrs. Monroe trapped his hand under hers. She looked up at the clock and then turned toward the rest of the room. "Five minutes, everyone. Start putting on those finishing touches and get ready to go."

When she turned her attention back to him, Nico snatched up the paper, crushed it into a ball, and quickly asked again. "Can I use the bathroom?"

Her face stopped smiling as she looked from the paper in his hand back to his face. "What's going on with you, kid?" Making herself more comfortable on her knees, she rubbed her hand across his shoulders like she was trying to shake something out of him. "Did something happen? Are you having a bad day?"

He didn't have words to say.

"Whatever it is, it's better to talk about it than to not."

And he felt ashamed by what he'd seen, but also shame for having looked.

"I'm always here to listen. No matter what, okay?" Her hand once again rested on his and he quickly stood up. "Nico." She rose like she might grab him, an action that caused Nico to run from the room without permission.

Three seconds of silence later, leaning against the bathroom door, Nico threw his picture in the trash and waited for the bell to ring.

Confession wasn't an option yet, but he wished he could talk to a priest, or even the friend of a priest. All Nico knew was that he needed someone closer to God. Someone God might speak to in return.

A push against the bathroom door startled him out of his thoughts and out of the way. Thomas Aram, who had been Nico's Faith Buddy four years prior, occasionally visited the school when serving as altar boy for funeral masses or christenings during the week.

"Hey, Nico. Long time no see."

Nico watched him wash his hands and wondered if God had heard him.

Irregularities

Emily entered the Armitage station weighed down by bags and thought and Donovan stood opposite the turnstiles. "Here," he offered his hand across the gate, "let me help you."

His words had startled her, and she stepped back, stopping the flow of traffic behind her. "What are you doing?"

"I wanted to see you before I left." He'd meant what he said, that he would see her again. "I've got my friend's wedding this weekend, the big speech. Remember?"

A man tapped her shoulder in a huff. The line was growing, and she stepped aside to let the people pass instead of walking through herself. "You shouldn't be here."

"I haven't seen you . . ." The people dispersed, but she remained on the other side. "I thought maybe you'd ride south with me to Clark and Lake—"

"Don't."

"Don't what?"

"Show up. Be sweet. Act like this is a thing—because it's not." She motioned between the two of them. "This isn't going to happen. Okay? You're just some guy on the train. Leave it at that." At the first turn of the stair he heard her call him back, but the thundering of an approaching train felt safer and easier to catch. "Donovan! Wait!"

He stepped onto the train and left her safely on the outside.

The lights were blinding, and the faces that inhabited the thirty to forty tables spread across the ballroom couldn't be seen. He'd practiced the speech a hundred times, pacing around his apartment and in front of a few students, but he had no idea how it would land in the real world.

Luckily, it seemed to be landing well. People laughed, took up space, allowed his tongue time to rest before moving on.

"At any rate, as we stood there drunk and peeing on a dumpster . . ." In his mind, he was running, lightly tapping his toes in a rhythm to keep himself focused and remain on track, "Jimmy told me he'd be asking Tilly to marry him when he got back home."

It felt like a school day with engaged students.

"It wasn't exactly the proposal I was hoping for, given our love for one another . . ."

Until it didn't.

"But I knew from experience, he'd make a great husband."

Things would be different after this.

He pushed forward through the clapping, forcing the crowd into silence, his words coming faster and faster, waiting to collide, trying to pile up, and he stopped mid-sentence, raising his hand to block the light and look out into the crowd.

They see you.

"Before we raise our glasses to the happy couple . . ."

They see you, and they know.

"I'd like to share a quote by Mignon McLaughlin . . ."

You will never have a Tilly.

"'A successful marriage requires falling in love many times, always with the same person.'" Picking up his glass, he raised it into the air and turned to his friend. "May you continually be falling."

People were drunk. The band was loud. He had to stick to the perimeter to avoid his mother's questions about his date and why she couldn't make it. But no matter where he went, bridesmaids wanted to dance and forget they were bridesmaids.

"I don't dance," he had to shout above the music. "I'm not a dancer."

"Come on, one dance, you deserve it." The bridesmaid wore a salmon -colored dress and tugged on his hand.

"No . . . thank you though." She wore lipstick. He hated lipstick.

"You know, you're not very fun . . . I thought you'd be more fun."

I'm not here to amuse you.

He watched her take her shoes off and knew he could fuck her without dancing.

Jay appeared, out of breath and weary. "Jesus, man, save me from Mom."

Everyone needs saving at some point.

"Jay, this is Alice." His brother was indifferent to lipstick. "She wants to dance."

Chut-chut, chut-chut. Chut-chut, chut-chut. She'd held his hand while apologizing. *Chut-chut, chut-chut.* And bowed her forehead against his chin before letting go. *Chut-chut, chut-chut.* What was one bad encounter when she continued to appear? *Chut-chut.* Each day a little warmer. *Chut-chut.* Each day a little less layered. *Chut-chut.* Each day a little more his.

Doors Closing.

 Possibility hung between them like positive ions.

"Rest your head on my shoulder. It's more comfortable than the window." The train rocked forward, bumping her head against the glass. "Here," tapping the spot where his mind had already placed her, "completely harmless—people do it to strangers all the time."

A quiet smile cracked her sleepy façade before she submitted. "Sometimes I think you're trying to ruin my life, Donovan James."

He was willing to push that button.

"You've already ruined mine."

She laughed even though they both knew it wasn't funny, and he closed his eyes trying to capture every sensation of her closeness. The weight of her head as she pressed it to his shoulder, the delicate holding of his arm after she'd fallen asleep; how her blood pulsated through her fingertips, through his jacket, lighting his skin underneath. Eventually, the combination of her rhythmic breathing and the warm sun radiating a scent from her head acted like an opiate, making his eyelids hard to reopen and his head impossible to hold up.

Their sleeping pinkies fondled creases. His hand moved. Her head turned. Through his sleepy haze and confusion, he saw Lily sitting at the opposite end of the train, watching them over the pages of a book. The deaf man, standing at the door, waiting to exit.

"Donovan." Her red hair straightened. Her coat tightened. "You shouldn't be here." More wakeful eyes. "You missed your stop."

Lily wasn't there, but the deaf man tapped anxiously on the door.

He exited the train in a brisk walk, but as he crossed Eastwood and headed toward Montrose, he broke into a jog. His legs were pulling him forward, faster, faster, his dress shoes smacking the sidewalk, his tie blown back over his shoulder, his messenger bag held out to his side to prevent it from bouncing against his hip. He didn't care if he looked insane running away in his suit, he *did* care that he *felt* insane and didn't know why.

On Montrose, an ice-cream vendor rang his bell, notifying all around that he was there. Donovan ran onto the street to avoid him. A car horn honked before he leapt back onto the sidewalk and away from the bell, *da-da—da-bing, da-da—da-bing, da-da—da-bing.* The sound chased him for blocks like a warning, or laughter, or a calling—he couldn't decide, but it was something else he needed to escape. Like the people, their smiling faces, and the red hair glowing in a spotlight of sun he couldn't outrun.

Then a bus stopped at California, and people, too many people, poured out onto the sidewalk, stopping his forward momentum. Blocking him. Preventing him. Forcing him to remain—*da-da—da-bing, da-da—da-bing, da-da—da-bing.* It was still there. A stuttered whisper only he could hear in his still river of movement.

Focus.

Focus.

And breathe.

The stroller containing two small brown-skinned children.

Focus.

The walker of a gray-haired man.

Focus.

Kids out of school.

Breathe.

Da-da—da-bing, da-da—da-bing, da-da—da-bing.

A vibration in his pocket started him running again. He didn't want to answer. He knew who it was, given the time of day, and he needed to outpace that conversation more than most others. He ran the entire way to his house in a fog of sounds and sights and tastes. He could feel the air trying to choke him, see the laughing eyes of those around him, and hear . . . he could hear it all pressing against him like the nightmare of standing naked in his third-grade cubby.

There was nothing to help him feel safe or inoffensive until he'd shut and locked the front door behind him. Then, dropping his bag to the floor, he loosened his tie, took off his jacket, and let it fall atop his bag. He kicked off his shoes and headed to the fridge. There were two beers there, not nearly enough to numb him, but he opened one and leaned back against the counter, placing the cold bottle against his forehead.

Unconscious awareness and rote movement pulled the phone from his pocket and began the voicemail. "Hey, Sweetie . . ." His mother's voice sounded sympathetic, like she was sorry to be bothering him, like her constant hounding about meeting his girlfriend made *her* feel bad when in all actuality, had she not hounded him to begin with, none of this would have happened.

It still would have happened.

"It's Mom, just wanted to confirm Memorial Day Weekend. I'm making reservations at the brewery and wanted a head count." It was always going to happen. "Your dad and I want . . . I mean, if *you* want to, we thought it would be nice to meet your friend Emily . . . just a casual thing, no pressure, it would just be nice to meet her. Anyway, call and let me know. Love you, Sweetie, look forward to seeing you." He hadn't told her Emily's name.

She'd kept the list of rules in her pocket and withdrew them at her convenience. A reminder to them both of what they'd promised. But the words lacked meaning when the smell of her skin was missing. Rubbing his head, Donovan massaged the memory of her weight, her laugh, her smell. Occasionally, he could close his eyes and capture her closeness without it feeling tainted. He'd remained in the hospital room, waited for the detective to wake up, so that those memories could be determined as true to everyone else.

Donovan set the list of rules on the table and waited.

Blue coats, yellow hats, and mittens.

Gone.

The detective picked it up, glanced it over, his expression and body motionless until he placed the paper back between the two of them. Face up. Exposed. "Did you kill her?" The detective gripped his legs and Donovan watched his eyes travel over the details of his face.

"See what I'm seeing here, detective, and tell me whether you would answer that question right now." He waited, and waited, but the man wouldn't fill in the gaps in his words. "Have you ever loved someone who gives you everything you need?" For Donovan, there were things that mattered more. "Have you ever loved someone and then been told it will all be made a lie?" He watched the detective's leathered thumb mindlessly twirl his wedding band and determined that it was more than a nervous habit. "It's just like the paintings, the sad man from the train, my utility . . . what we saw wasn't the truth." Donovan was more hopeful than he'd ever been while standing on those platforms waiting for her to arrive. "When I saw them, I thought she'd used me, avoided me." But the third-to-last train car wasn't her only source of inspiration. "The pictures can't tell the whole story, detective . . . that *list* can't tell the whole story—they're all interpreted with fear or want, and we only wind up seeing what we want to see. What we thought was already there." The clock ticked, and Donovan knew his time was limited, that he needed to speak first, steer the conversation to where it was important. "How did you know about the flash drive?" The detective rubbed his eyes before squeezing his legs again, like he was trying to wake some part of himself up. "You came to my house." He waited. "You said it was mine, remember? How could you have known that unless you'd seen it?" What the detective would say next would determine whether or not Donovan could stand up and walk away, but when the detective spoke, Donovan felt his hope slipping.

"Did Emily ever mention Nicodemus Papachristi?" Donovan had been asked this question too many times by too many people, and his response had always been no. "How about her relationship with Nate Aram?"

The question filled the room and didn't leave space for the air between them.

"I felt completely seen by her. Completely loved, just as I was." It wasn't a lie. It had never been a lie. "She told me she loved me, and I didn't even need her to—she said it and I already knew, it was like hearing my name, or that I'm a teacher, or that I run, it was just a part of me that already existed. Her words just dusted it off."

"There are plenty of other people for you to talk to about this. A therapist, for instance. I don't understand why you're here, talking to me." The detective began reshuffling papers. Once again exposing the book. "No charges have been filed, not enough evidence to charge you with anything—"

"That's because I didn't *do* it." Donovan sat up straight. "I didn't do it." *You'll spend the rest of your life in jail.*

Donovan tapped his toes on the floor and the voice out of his head.

The numbness of everything was beginning to wear thin. Her touch, her smell, the earthlike quality of her eyes. *Gone.* The way she laughed, from her belly. *Gone.* The dried paint left on her forearm, streaking her hair. *Gone.* Everything she was existed somewhere he couldn't reach; no imagined girlfriend-ness, no once-upon-a-time actuality, nothing left could allude to a future possibility. She was gone. All the doors were closed, and he was just beginning to feel it.

Interference

Eight days of summer heat and accelerating criminal activity passed before Lesley turned on the television to find it hadn't been turned on since the World Cup Final. Telemundo whispered quietly in the background while he paced the length of their apartment and Deb's phone rang its way to voicemail. "Deb, I've made us a seven o'clock reservation at Fork." He hadn't done so yet, but he intended to do so immediately. "We'll have dinner, we can see a movie if you want . . ." He paused and wondered if the timing was right. "I love you." He'd contemplated how to approach the subject of her having an affair and settled on doing what he should have done all along. Make time for her.

Lesley flipped to the traffic report while he waited for the restaurant's page to load. A picture of the lady on St. Louis appeared in the upper right-hand corner of the television screen and he quickly turned the volume up.

"The body of artist Emily Monroe was found Sunday morning by park maintenance crews cleaning up after Saturday night's festivities in Grant Park."

The anchor's words had been laid over footage from the music festival and then cut to a city maintenance worker. "It's just not what you expect, you know. I've been working down here every summer for fifteen years and never found a body."

Lesley's fingers began dialing Masterson before he could register his own actions.

"Authorities are asking for anyone who may have seen anything suspicious to call the Central Police."

"Yeah?" Masterson had answered, but Lesley wasn't sure what to say.

"Did you hear about the lady on St. Louis?" he found himself whispering.

There was a yawn across the line before Masterson spoke. "I had to close the case on Friday due to lack of evidence."

Missing photos had Lesley muting the television and massaging his scalp as he began to pace the room. "I'm sorry to hear that." Something was wrong. It felt more than wrong.

"I gotta get ready."

"Yeah." Lesley's eyes watched the movement on the screen in front of him. "I'll meet you at the station."

The possibility of letting it go and moving on was there. He thought about it as he began to gather his things, and then flipped through the local stations one last time before deciding to phone Central. He would make sure they checked the CTA footage for the man in the paintings. Then he'd let it go. There were other cases to solve, and this one wasn't his. Masterson wasn't his.

After relaying his credentials, Lesley was transferred, and then transferred again, and then put on hold before he was able to leave a message in the lead investigator's voicemail box. The inefficiency ate at him, but there were other things he was struggling with, things he felt both entitled to and ashamed of.

The coverage the artist's death was getting was two days after the fact, which seemed odd in and of itself, but Jamal Dupont's death had merely been a statistic in the morning newspaper. There weren't multiple bulletins being broadcast asking for help. If there had been, if people cared enough about a ten-year-old black kid living in Albany Park, then maybe, but Jamal had been a faceless number and that was it. Another kid apparently killed in gang violence. No one cared, and the reality of it burned up Lesley's remaining patience.

He drove his truck to work, windows rolled up tight in the heat so he could swear at the world and release some of his anger. By the time he arrived, the station felt expectant. Lesley walked directly to his lieutenant's office and knocked on her door. "Do you have a minute?"

She invited him in, asked him to close the door and have a seat. She started talking before he had a chance to ask any questions or file any complaints. "I'm glad you're here. We need to talk."

"Yeah, we do."

"I just got off the phone with the chief." She paused like she was waiting for him to respond. Lesley stayed quiet, confused by a pounding in his chest that had more to do with the lieutenant's expression and less to do with Jamal. "There's been a lot of discussion among the team regarding burnout." His confusion continued to grow. "I realize my own failure in not asking people to take time off when they need it. We're short-staffed as it is—"

"Is this about Masterson?" he asked, thinking Obuchowski must have said something—*had* to have said something. *He* too felt obligated to say something.

"This isn't about Masterson, Lesley. This is about *you*."

"What? I don't need time off." The look on Hollingsworth's face told him she believed otherwise. "I'm fine. I'm good, as a matter of fact. I may even have something on the Quiles brothers." He lied.

"You need to take some time off."

Lesley couldn't believe what he was hearing. His thoughts moved through the department, resting on each face, wondering who had said what and why *he* was the one requiring a break. "Is this Obuchowski's doing?"

She shook her head, "The Quiles brothers are feeling harassed. There've been complaints filed."

"Complaints? What kind of complaints?"

"Harassment," she said. "Both the family and the schools—"

"The *schools*?"

"Yes, Lesley, they're tired of you showing up every time you *think* one of the boys is involved with something. That's not the way policing works."

"I'm trying to build a case—"

"Your *case* lacks evidence." Her words forced him to perform a quick self-analysis of his behavior, and it complicated his ability to remain ambivalent. "We need to move you out of the neighborhood for a bit, Lesley. Give everyone a little breathing room." She used his first name to focus his attention on her personability, but she failed to take into account that they'd both received the same de-escalation training. "We're going to be pulling you from the case." The room rotated in a flash of red anger that left him unable to speak. "Take a few days off, get out of town, take Deb on a long weekend—"

"I don't need a long weekend, Rebecka. What I need is—"

"It's come down from the chief, Lesley. We'll be reassigning you come Monday." It was too surreal for him to believe. "Take a few days and figure yourself out. We'll regroup on Monday. No one has to know anything until then."

The words shifted in meaning before they settled on Lesley. "Like no one has to know about shoddy evidence or why Obuchowski has been going over all our cases—"

Hollingsworth tapped a pen on the desktop and examined his face. "When you come back on Monday, we can sit down and talk about the Quiles brothers. You can brief Detectives Blakely and Ranken. They'll be taking over the case." She plopped the pen into a ceramic container, signaling the end of their discussion. "You're just too close."

Lesley was struck by the ease in which it all took place. Never in his seventeen years of being a detective had he been taken off a case or accused of being too close. As a matter of fact, his closeness had previously been praised, regarded as a strength when he sat in cars on frozen street corners trying to find the rhythm of it all. "Why was the Monroe case closed?"

"Lesley—"

"She *died* within forty-eight hours—"

"People die." Her words were clipped. "We can't prevent that. We can only do what we do afterwards." But Lesley knew that wasn't true. "I have to get back to work. Take the weekend. We'll see you back here on Monday."

Lesley passed through the quieted station without making eye contact with anyone. His concern wasn't what they thought of him but a growing sense that he'd become an outsider in a world where being inside meant everything. As he walked through the parking lot, Blakely sauntered toward him holding up an unlit cigarette, and Lesley, now understanding the subtlety involved with needing a light or offering one, hesitated.

A book of matches was produced, and he watched the flame in Blakely's hand start and stall before completing its task. "So what's the play, Old Man?" Checking the lot for Masterson's car, Lesley didn't know how to answer. "He won't be in today." Blakely looked out across the

127

parking lot with an inhale that made the cherry glow bright and then let out a string of smoke rings like he hadn't a care in the world.

"Did you know you were taking over the Dupont case?"

He watched the flicked ashes fall to the concrete while Lesley watched him. "Just heard about it this morning—along with your little vacay." An inhale, a cloud of smoke. Ranken pulled into the lot. Blakely added a cigarette to a bush. And there was a buzzing in Lesley's pocket.

"We should grab a drink later." Blakely was walking backwards, toward his ride. "Yes? No? Maybe?"

"Sure, yeah." Lesley was thinking about the boy's mother and how she would view his being taken off the case. Moved out of the neighborhood.

"World of Beer. Eight o'clock."

He watched Blakely enter the vehicle, knowing his own removal from the case would be proof he'd not only failed—but was also *responsible* for Jamal Dupont's death. "Eight o'clock."

He had time before he needed to tell the boy's mother. But that conversation, and how it would go, held all his thoughts on the drive home.

His phone rang after the truck was parked in his building's garage. "Powell here."

"Detective Lesley Powell? This is Eric Sullivan, Emily Monroe's dad. We found your card at the apartment."

He'd only answered because he didn't recognize the number and thought it might be Central. "I'm sorry, Mr. Sullivan. I'm not involved in your daughter's case. You'll need to call Central." Lesley wished Obuchowski had given him her card, or that he could be better about letting calls go to voicemail.

"We *have* called Central. No one's telling us anything . . . I just want a chance to talk to someone who saw her before she died."

Another dead child. Another grieving parent. "I'm sorry." There wasn't room on Lesley's plate, or in his heart, or in his mind, to handle more. Especially one that wasn't even his. "I can give you the numbers for Detectives Masterson and Obuchowski, they would have been the last ones to see her." The man on the other end was quiet while Lesley read the digits. He listened to him repeat the numbers, thankful it wasn't his case, thankful it wasn't his fuck-up, and then disengaged the call.

The quiet ride up in the elevator, the cool darkness of the apartment. Lesley hung up his jacket and tossed his phone and keys aside before heading to the bathroom—the habit of the routine went unnoticed until his sleeves were pulled up and his face was wet.

When the a/c kicked off, he could hear the plastic of his phone vibrating against his keys in the bowl down the hall. Grabbing a towel, he followed the sound in case it was Deb calling to confirm dinner and then remembered he had yet to make the reservation.

The sound stopped and started again before he saw it was Blakely. "This is Powell."

"I've got something for you." He was already taking a drag. "Meet me at the Barnes and Noble off West Webster in twenty."

Jacket grabbed, keys picked up, the towel tossed atop the bowl.

Twenty minutes later, Lesley wandered the aisles of the bookstore until Blakely's voice caught him by a toy display. "Can you believe this?" Blakely held an insect catcher and a magnifying glass. "Not only do they give you the weapon, they also give you the cage." He placed the toys back on the shelf and began to stroll, his pelvis thrust forward in a gooselike swagger. "There wasn't much. Quiles's record was scrubbed after he turned eighteen," Blakely picked up a ball with a flashing light at its center, "and you already knew about his preference for opiates." He tossed the ball between his hands a few times before putting it down and moving on. "But you might not know he's been working for a cleaning company—some nonprofit out of Rodger's Park." Picking up a kaleidoscope, Blakely held it up to his eye, gave it a turn, and continued. "Normally the kids who exit Lawrence Hall go through Metropolitan Youth for employment, but he got hooked up with something else." Pausing, he picked up a small stuffed bear, examined it, gave it a shake to hear the rattle in its tummy, and then checked the price before looking at Lesley. "Metropolitan Youth has a drug program. I know that shit doesn't always work, but when you've got a kid with a known addiction—why not put him in the program?" Tucking the bear under his arm, he kept walking. "It doesn't make much sense, you know?"

"What's the name of the nonprofit?" Lesley followed him to the counter where he laid the bear down and handed over two twenties.

"Sticharia."

"Excuse me?"

"Sticharia." Opening the bag he'd just been handed, Blakely pulled out the bear and shoved it into his sweatshirt, leaving the bag behind. "Plural noun—some sort of vestment . . . I don't know, Old Man, but I think you need to start there, because, *personally* I think the reason you haven't been able to make a connection between the Latin Kings, the Quiles brothers, and Jamal Dupont is because there isn't one. Not a direct one, anyway."

Allegory

Kristin Cane sat in the one place where she could talk to other adults without being eavesdropped on by a dozen little sets of eyes and ears. For the most part, the teachers' lounge was a place of civil discontent where a gaggle of women congregated over lunch to bemoan the varying aspects of their love and work lives. Like the majority, Kristin's most frequent complaint was that she didn't have a love life at all. And in the absence of such, her days revolved around the singular happening of seeing "hot dad" walk his daughter down the hall to class. "I waited by my door all morning. Did anyone see him?"

Across the table, her friend covered her mouth with a napkin. "Her mom dropped her off today. Yoga pants and all."

The table's collective nod sent Kristin's eyes rolling. "What's her name again? I can never remember it— it's like my brain *refuses* to believe she exists."

The nods turned to laughter until Mrs. Camacho joined the group, setting down her oatmeal and Greek yogurt. "Isabel. Her name is Isabel." Mrs. Camacho liked to play it straight with her firm disposition and top-button-always-done appearance.

A recently hired pre-K teacher, who didn't quite understand the depths of Mrs. Camacho's judgment continued the conversation. "I was thinking the other day," a quick drink of her Diet Coke, "that Brad Pitt would play him in a movie."

"We've all thought it." Kristin couldn't help but respond and closed her eyes to picture it. "Brad Pitt from *A River Runs Through It*." The conversation paused in reverence.

"You realize you're coveting another woman's husband, right?"

Kirstin knew better and apologized for the transgression. Someone else, understanding that it was important to steer the conversation elsewhere at this point, voiced a complaint so frequently heard in the lunchroom that it didn't even matter who said it anymore. "Fifteen minutes is not enough time." The perfect springboard for a whole host of complaints.

"Max's mom actually sent a note asking me to heat his lunch today. I was like, yeah, that's not going to happen."

Kristin shook her head in disgust; she'd experienced the same thing the year before. "Buy a thermos, for God's sake."

"Miss Cane . . ." Mrs. Camacho had stopped spooning food into her mouth to provide a perfunctory look.

"Sorry." A bit of laughter floated through the room, but her shame for being called out twice in under a minute stuck like a thorn in the quiet that came after it. They'd reached that point in lunch when the rest of their time had to be spent in repentant silence, and Kristin desperately wished the fault had not been hers.

The unusual appearance of Mrs. Monroe gave everyone another chance at conversation. She entered with a polite smile and a few customary salutations before walking to the sink to rinse her lunch containers. "Miss Cane?" she asked, keeping her back to the group, "Do you have a minute to talk?"

Mrs. Monroe showing up to rescue her was like an act of God. In seven years, she'd never had a private conversation with the art teacher. "Right now?"

"If you can."

Kristin didn't need more than that. Mrs. Monroe began drying her dishes and Kristin tossed her sandwich back into the bag, "Enjoy the rest of your lunch, ladies." Swooping up her Diet Coke, she followed the art teacher out the door and away from judgment. "Thank you for saving me. I'm always saying the wrong thing in there."

"I have a hard time believing that." Mrs. Monroe smiled and opened the door to allow Kristin to enter the room first. "Sorry about the mess."

Mess was an understatement. Scraps of paper and cloth were strewn from a pile in the middle of the floor outward. Up and across tables. Resting on chairs. Glitter, glue, scissors. Popsicle sticks and pipe cleaners. It looked as if everything had been dumped out and then ransacked. "Did my class do this?" Kristin was mortified.

"No, not really." Mrs. Monroe stood beside her, hands in pockets, glancing around the room. "We were trying something new today, and it seemed to work out well." Looking at the place, *well* was not a word

Kristin would have used. "I'm wondering if you'd look over some art with me." Stepping over to her desk, Mrs. Monroe picked up a folder and carried it to one of the tall tables lining the walls. "I keep these portfolios for the kids until the end of the year, but occasionally something comes up that I want to talk with them about."

Kristin moved closer to the objects being put on display and wondered why she was there. Spread across the table were simple works of kid-quality art. A Christmas tree collage. An elementary sketch of a computer. A painting of water?

"I don't know." She was watching Kristin look at the work, her arms now folded over her chest, fingers tapping across the sleeve of her sweater.

Kristin leaned closer, trying to find what she was missing.

"Do you see anything?" Mrs. Monroe asked.

"I mean," the nervous expression on the teacher's face made Kristin pause, "not really. I'm sorry."

Mrs. Monroe drew her lower lip in with her teeth and nodded. "Okay." Arms unfolded, she brushed back her hair. "Okay. What about this piece?" She picked up the Christmas tree and handed it to her. "Tell me what you see."

Kristin held the collage and her feelings of confusion increased. "I see a Christmas tree without presents . . . a ceiling fan maybe? I don't know, what's this thing above the tree?" She pointed. "Maybe the tree is outside, and this is meant to be a cloud?"

Taking the picture, Mrs. Monroe turned it sideways and handed it back. "What about now?"

Kristin laughed as soon as she saw it. Like one of the pictures she'd been shown in an undergrad psych class, a different image emerged so strongly that even rotating the collage couldn't make her un-see it. "Someone's eating the tree?"

Mrs. Monroe nodded and swapped the picture for a different one. Kristin took each piece, eventually found some bizarre twist and handed it back. The process was repeated four more times, and though she found herself entertained, she still didn't understand its purpose.

"What about this?" Mrs. Monroe had returned to her desk and pulled a crumpled piece of construction paper from a drawer.

Kristin tried to flatten it out, and in the process of doing so, noticed some of the picture had been hidden under precariously glued scraps of black paper. "What is this?" She felt uncertain about what she saw, not because it was abstract, but because it was impossible for her to conceive it as unintentional. "Who drew this?" Turning the paper in her hand, she tried to find a name, and when it wasn't immediately visible, she flipped the collage on the table and panicked.

"Nico?" Looking at Mrs. Monroe for confirmation. "Nico did this?" She stared back down at the paper, wanting to peel back more of the black but too disgusted by what else could be hidden. "Have you talked to him about this? This is *not* okay."

Mrs. Monroe didn't respond. Instead she opened the folder and spread out a few more pieces. "There's nothing here before December, as far as I can tell." Again, Kristin felt her watching for a response. "And I'd found some of his choices curious since then, but nothing I could really put my finger on until that." She pointed to the crumpled paper. "After seeing that—"

"I feel like I'm going to throw up."

"I don't know what to do. When I look at that in conjunction with his last few projects, everything just looks—"

"Fucked up?"

Mrs. Monroe nodded and slid her hands back into her pockets. "I'm really concerned something's happened to him."

"You have to report it. *This* has to be reported."

"I know . . . I just needed someone else to see it first."

Confessions of an Unobserved Observer

It took Donovan exactly forty-five minutes to make it to the corner of Franklin and Superior. As soon as he rounded the corner, Adonis himself nearly bowled him over, seemingly as unaware of his size as he was his own perfection. He stopped abruptly and cupped Donovan's arm with his giant palm, smiling apologetically. "Sorry, man."

Standing so close to him dwarfed Donovan's sense of self. "No problem."

Adonis gave him a pat, right on his arm as if to thank him, and then continued in the direction Donovan had just come from and away from where he was headed. An older redheaded man had remained hidden by Adonis's bulk until then. He looked ready for a hike in his shorts and sandals, but his face beamed. "You don't have to take me," he said. "You should stay and enjoy the show."

Donovan quit listening and started walking. They were leaving, and at seven-thirty, heart thumping in his chest, he was arriving. He walked through the doors of the gallery and entered a part of her life that she hadn't invited him into. The music played loud enough to make it feel like a club. Violent strings and a pulsing bass line fit the title of the exhibit: *In Transit*. But it wasn't what he'd expected. He'd learned from his online search that the gallery had a well-lit and open floor plan. He'd believed their seeing one another would be guaranteed. But the room was crowded and when he looked around, Emily was nowhere to be seen.

Glass of wine in hand, Donovan weaved in and out of clustered groups of people who bore all the trimmings of having enough time and money to never understand "living." These feelings were compounded when a woman stopped a couple to take their picture for the society page of the *Tribune*. He'd never attended an event where the society page of any paper would feel the need to be present. This displacement left him wishing he hadn't come alone. A feeling he wasn't used to. A feeling he wanted to escape.

You should have invited the other lady.
Shhhh.
Sara. Because everyone needs a friend.

Toward the back of the exhibit, a group hovered in the corner around a small painting that could barely be seen from where he stood. It piqued his curiosity enough to push him forward, make him stay, pull its story into view.

You were never meant to be here.

The texture of the painted wool coat was palpable. The crook of the nose obvious. The green of the scarf Donovan had lost just days before he'd first noticed the lady in the blue coat and her smile that said, I've been there. The painting was of him, in a single seat, reading *The New Yorker*.

She's already seen you.

A small card to the right of the portrait read: *An Unforgettable (un) Known*. Not For Sale.

Here is your utility.

The room suddenly felt much too small.

This is what she needed you for.

The music too loud.

A painting.

The air too thick.

Your usefulness has expired.

The shine of the stainless-steel trimmings inside the train. The awful fake wood paneling. It was all just as detailed as he was.

You're just some guy on the train.

He moved to the opposite wall in an attempt to separate himself from his own image, afraid someone would recognize him standing so close. But when he lifted his eyes, he was again met with his own reflection. Standing on the platform, snow blowing all around and piling on his shoulders, covering his new scarf. The view of him waiting on the platform came from inside the train. *He* was looking in. Waiting for something more than warmth.

She knew you were waiting for her.

The card to the right read: *Being There*. Not For Sale.

Wouldn't it be nice to have a friend, Donovan?

A deep seed of resentment planted itself with the shame and embarrassment he felt remembering those mornings, knowing she could have eased his suffering and chose not to.

Emily let you stand there like an idiot.

He glanced around at the other paintings immediately within view, angry that he'd come, angry that she'd exploited him, angry to see his utility put so easily on display without care or permission.

This is all you ever were to her.

Shut up.

Others were there. Others were recognizable, but their haecceity was missing.

The girl with the giant headphones and freakishly white Keds who always stood in the doorway smacking her gum was there, but not really: *i-sol(n)ation.* $675.

The businessman who wore his baby in a forward-facing papoose was there, but not really: *Daddy's Got a Day Job.* $800.

The older Vietnamese women who would get on the train with their carts full of knitting supplies were there, but not really: *Read Pham Dawn.* $1500.

Everywhere he looked, he saw something known to him, but he was there, explicitly idealized.

The poor schmuck, waiting in vain. That's what the painting should have been titled.

"Shut up." A thought said out loud, but only meant for him.

Shhhhhhh.

He recognized himself in one last painting.

The woman with hair the color of pennies rested her head on his shoulder. He sat looking out the window, his chin resting upon her head. Her hand was cupped between his. Hidden from view on his lap. The man was not *really* him, but it was. The woman was not *really* her, but it was. They were in the background of the painting, something no one else would immediately notice unless they knew the experience of where they sat and the intimacy she occasionally granted him.

The painting was no less than 3'x5' in dimension; large, full of color and motion, and they were there—*Hidden, In Transit* and Not For Sale.

The confluence of feelings he experienced while looking at the painting was extreme on either end. As naked and used as he felt in the other paintings, he wished to hang this particular painting on his bedroom wall and fall asleep looking at her there. That yellow dress falling loosely over her knees as he held her hand. His heart, mind, and body ached with the perplexity and obscurity of it all, leaving only one thing that could steal his mind away. The familiar electric current that told him she was near.

It was panic that overtook him as he looked out the window of the gallery and saw her standing outside with a small group of people. She held a cigarette and was laughing. Her aqua-colored dress clung tighter than any fit he'd seen her wear before. It highlighted the skin of her milky and noticeably voluptuous breasts in an unexpected way. Maybe this was the real Emily, smoking and leaking cleavage.

Maybe you didn't know her at all.

Her smile gave way to a ghostlike expression when she saw him watching her through the window. The idea of her as a stranger distracted his thoughts of yellow dresses. It fueled the shame and anger the other paintings had left and made him look away.

"I didn't know you were coming." Her voice came from behind him. "I wish you would have told me." He felt her move and thought she might touch him, welcome him, say she was glad he came. But her arm raised and gave a wave instead. "Mr. Aram! It's great to see you. Thanks for coming!" And then she walked away. No "hello." No "goodbye." No "thanks for being my subject." Donovan didn't need to remain.

Instead of getting on a train and being reminded of his "just some guy on the train" usefulness to her, he walked to Montgomery Park, a space completely void of her memory, where he could lick his wounds in private.

The sun was just beginning to hide itself behind an elm tree, but some light remained on a grassy knoll where he could sit and watch its golden rays dance against the water. The colors made him consider stories of Heaven, a place or thing he had never been able to comprehend and thought of it now not simply because the world itself felt incomprehensible but also because a part of him wished to be done with it.

"Mind if we sit in the shade?"

Emily tried to pass him an open bottle of wine. She had taken off her shoes, and her freckled toes played with the grass underneath her feet.

When he didn't take the bottle or look at her face, she walked over and sat in the cool shade of the elm tree. He watched her from behind, the sway of her hips made more apparent by her dress, and he hated her for being there.

You should have called Sara.

Shut up.

Reflection-checker, mind-reader, eyeglasses that have their own sub-category.

Stop.

The golden flicker of the water—He tried to concentrate on that, but Emily had polluted the space and he rose to leave. "I don't think I want to see you again, Emily."

"Yes, you do." The assuredness in her voice caused him to turn and look at her. "You always want to see me."

It was strange how he could hate her, want to strangle that part of her he thought he knew. "You just left me standing there." But his accusation lacked venom and sounded pathetic even to himself.

"I didn't ask you to do that." And the truth of her response stung. "I've watched you for over a year now, Donovan, and suddenly your bag is caught in the door and you think we're lovers."

"Fuck you."

"No," she shook her head. "You don't get to say that to me. I don't owe you anything—"

It didn't occur to him what he was doing until after he'd charged back and tackled her fully to the ground, ready to humiliate her the way she'd humiliated him.

But instead of fear or concern, she looked at him with expectancy and didn't attempt to push him away.

She'll see you now.

The bottle of wine tipped in his wavering. It glugged its contents into the grass. She panted its aroma into his thirsty mouth.

Open her.

When the moment lingered without resistance or encouragement, he rolled off of her and onto the grass. "I think you owe me a bottle of wine, Mr. James." His erection had been pressed firmly against her body, and he knew she had felt it. "We should buy two."

Her fingers traced the outline of his ear while his eyes stared up between the leaves of their shade. "I need a minute," he said.

No, you don't.

Donovan would report that they drank both bottles of merlot purchased from a convenience store a few blocks away. And that they talked about "nothing" until a little after midnight. That "nothing" included cell phones, portable isolation culture, YouTube, Jesus Christ, and The Beastie Boys. It turned out Emily knew every word on *License to Ill* and *Paul's Boutique*, something she once believed meant she would marry Adam Yauch. How they wound up talking about Jesus, Donovan couldn't exactly say, but he knew it led to the Beastie Boys—the details were just a little hazy.

At ten minutes after two in the morning, they took the elevator down from the Montrose platform and sat at the bus stop waiting for a cab. "Why didn't you kiss me in the park?" She held his hand close to her chest and swung her legs across his lap.

"Because you're drunk."

"Not in the beginning."

He really wanted to walk her around the corner, to his apartment, and remove her dress.

She ran a thumb over his lips and caused an increased tightness in his pants. "I've tried to imagine where you live," she said. He never wanted to imagine where she lived, only how she could exist with him. "What it would be like to walk barefoot around your apartment . . ." He imagined that every day. "What books you have on your shelves." Leaning in, she brought her lips a whispered breath away from his. "I want you to know I think about you, Donovan."

He could feel his fingers tightening on her upper thigh as his ability to separate imagined girlfriend-ness from rational decision-making diminished. He said, "I love you," and felt his lips brush against hers in their movement.

Open her.

The cab horn honked and woke them both.

Drunk and aching from the evening's events, Donovan entered his home, walked directly to his bookshelf, and started pulling books out, flipping them upside down, and shaking them until at long last a card fell out.

Under thirty, thinks men will step on her.

"Sara?" he whispered into the phone, "it's Donovan."

Wears glasses that should, and do, have their own subcategory.

"Do you know what time it is?" she asked.

Noise could be heard in the background; he knew she wasn't sleeping.

"I'm drunk. Come sleep with me," he said.

Attention-demanding whether deliberate or not—but probably at least subconsciously deliberate.

There was a long pause from the other end, and he pulled the phone away to see if the call had dropped.

"Where are you?" she asked.

And forward, let's not forget forward.

"4417 North Wolcott, 2B."

That night, with Sara sprawled out naked next to him, he dreamed he was in his mother's kitchen. She told him everyone was already dead and scraped black char from a cast-iron skillet. In another room, a dove called. Its cage hung in front of a Christmas tree and contained a Nativity scene covered in shit. Mary's praying hands were on fire and the bird pecked ferociously at them as if it were trying to put out the blaze. Donovan wanted to save her—but the bird gave one last peck and Mary's hands fell to the straw below. He reached in to grab them, extinguish their flame, and, turning Mary over, saw that the left side of her face was covered in char. When he tried to reattach the hands, the entire figure burst into flames, leaving the bird to peck at his fingernails. It was then that Donovan realized Baby Jesus was missing. He put a small crucifix inside the manger to make up for the absence of God, but the crucifix was not meant for the manger and would only float above. It hovered where an angel should be. He watched the suspended crucifix, knowing Baby Jesus was dead, knowing we'd crucified an angel, knowing he could not make the Virgin whole without simultaneously destroying her.

Donovan woke in a cold sweat. Sara lingered. She wanted to make him breakfast or get coffee. She wandered around his apartment wearing his shirt, looking at his things, reminding him again and again of what they'd done and making it clear she was willing to do more. Avoidance and subtle silence didn't work.

The abysmal hope he'd felt in believing she'd be gone by the time he'd finished showering, cleaning up his facial hair, brushing his teeth, putting on more layers than necessary and tidying his hair—all of which he did slowly to extend a twenty-minute task into fifty, was ruined when he opened the bathroom door to find her sitting among the books he'd tossed on the floor the night before. Still not dressed, still wearing his shirt.

"You don't seem like the kind of guy who'd leave books on the floor." She said it without looking at him and holding the green clothbound copy of *Macbeth* his grandmother had given him.

He was insulted not only by the sight of her touching something his Nan had read and annotated but also by the supposition that she could assume anything about him. He took the book, brushed the cover free of her, and placed it back on the shelf. "I don't think you know me well enough to make that judgment."

He wasn't the kind of guy who left his books on the floor. Nor was he the kind of guy to take a married woman home, even though she'd asked, even though he'd really wanted to. He also wasn't the kind of guy who made drunken late-night solicitations for gratuitous sex with a woman he cared absolutely nothing about—and yet there he was, stuck being two out of three things he wasn't.

Carefully avoiding any kind of contact, he began picking up the only mess he had control over.

Emily hadn't called. He'd checked his phone six times throughout the night and she hadn't called.

You fucked Sara. She fucked Adonis.

The layers were making him sweat.

Sara stood, handing him the few remaining books before lifting his shirt over her head and tossing it onto the bed. Exposed. Unapologetic. "I figured this was just a booty call."

Her body was tanned and fit, like she spent time climbing mountains naked. He wanted to look at her and feel something stir inside him, some kind of sexual desire that wouldn't make him feel like such a dick for having fucked her without reservation. But the only thing he felt was shame.

"Maybe you'll call again?" Glancing over her shoulder, she smiled at him. "I mean, it *was* fun, right? Girlfriend business aside?"

The skirt he'd hungrily pulled up and then eventually removed was slid back over her hips and her underwear were tossed into her purse before she slipped her feet into her sandals. "I don't mind being a pinch hitter."

He will remove Emily's dress eventually.

"I can be discreet, you know."

She will stand there, breasts exposed.

Sara approached him, "However, you should know that once you start drunk-dialing other women while fighting with your girlfriend, it's pretty much game over."

Heavy. Milky.

Sara returned to the bed and pulled her t-shirt down over her body.

You could fuck her one more time before she goes.

"I . . ." his hands wanted to fidget but there wasn't anything within reach. "This . . ." he looked toward the bed and tried to phrase his words carefully, "isn't something I'll be doing again."

Yes, you will.

Checking herself in the mirror by the door, she removed her sweater from a hook and slid it on. "I believe you believe that," and threw her purse over her shoulder. "But I don't."

Fuck her.

"I'll see you, Donovan."

After every trace of his experience with Sara had been placed in the washing machine, he lay down on his bed and struggled to recapture how Emily had felt pressed under him on the grass. Her hair a mess of red. Her hands moving across his body. Her breasts full and heavy, thighs parted just enough for her heat to radiate toward him. The smell of her skin was lightly bloomed with Ivory soap, red wine, and a trace of something warm and floral. He would replace her soap in the shower during his next trip to the store and search for the smell of her warmth at the florist, but all these images kept being swallowed by Sara's tiny firm body, undoing his pants in the dark, trying to complete the fantasy he'd started with Emily. The more he tried to forget the feeling of Sara's ribs and spine, or how his fingers had searched her skin for flesh with give, the harder it was to remember the moments that led him there.

Every morning the following week he stood on the platform by 5 a.m. and waited until 7:15. Emily never appeared.

Donovan shook his head and stared at the floor. "That shawl was a gift, a birthday present from him. Nate Aram." He couldn't help but wonder what other parts could have been undone or made different. "What if he hadn't given it to her?"

"Then I'm sure there would have been something else." It was a cold and matter-of-fact statement.

Looking at the detective, Donovan wanted him to understand how "something else" couldn't be imagined. "They showed me pictures of it wrapped around her neck, her eyes open. Afraid. Her hands up like she tried to pull it away and failed."

But the detective didn't care. "Tell them the flash drive was *yours*, the pictures were *yours* . . . Emily *gave* you the coat—"

"And then what? Everyone would think *I* did it—that *I* killed her."

"Did you hurt her?"

It wasn't as simple as that. It was as if the man had never been in love, never lost his senses, never failed to consider the consequence of a few words. "We hurt each other, Detective Powell."

"Well," he nudged the paper closer to Donovan, "I'd say Emily's a little worse off."

"The dead don't feel."

But you do.

The detective left a pause, waiting for Donovan to look at him. "Sometimes the living don't either."

Run or jump, it doesn't matter.

"Have you had any contact with Lily Ziyad since all of this?"

The words made Donovan feel sick. In need of escape, he got up to move to the window. "No."

"Have you wanted to?"

It won't open. You'll have to run.

They were twelve stories up and facing the setting sun. "The only person I ever wanted to see was Emily."

145

Interference

There was plenty of time for Lesley to admit failure before Monday, but he knocked on the mother's door wanting to prove he wouldn't need to. "Sheila." He only said her name in private and always said it with a clipped "la".

"Detective."

Standing on the other side of the screen it was hard not to notice how she didn't invite him in. "Do you have a minute for a few questions?" She rolled her eyes and widened the opening of the front door as she walked away, leaving Lesley to open the screen himself as she always did. "Does the name Sticharia mean anything to you?"

The house had fallen into disarray since the boy's death. Cans of half-drunk soda could be seen sitting lopsided on top of surfaces where toys had been buried by over-due notices and medical bills. "No."

"I've been looking through the files, going over statements. The day Jamal was killed, you said something at the station, something about him being involved in programs."

Sheila turned down the music she'd been listening to, "I already told you—"

"No, you didn't."

"Well, I told the fat one then." She flipped open a pack of Marlboro Light 100s that sat on the kitchen table and chucked it aside when she found it empty. "This is the problem with all of you." Snatching a bag from a chair, she dug through it and pulled out a fresh pack. "You don't hear a goddamn word we say."

"What was the name of the program and how'd he become involved?" He didn't want to think about Masterson's notes or why they failed to contain that bit of information.

"Some do-good white lady in the neighborhood," she opened a window, stood by it and tried to fan the smoke out. "I never trusted that . . . giving him paint, paying for his registration."

"Giving him paint?" That she said the woman was white narrowed the results enough to keep the potential do-gooders limited, but mentioning paint made them more so.

She pointed the cigarette at Lesley. "This is exactly what I'm talking about. I told you all this when he was caught tagging—"

"Do you know the name of the woman?"

"No, but I can show you her building. It's right on St. Louis, just next to the mosque." A pit developed in Lesley's stomach. "We can march our asses over there right now—"

"That won't be necessary." Lesley needed to sit. He needed to think. He needed a drink.

Sheila rubbed the cigarette out in a plastic ashtray held in her hand, "Maybe it's not necessary to *you*," set it on the table and headed for the door, "but it's necessary to me."

"She's not home." He needed to prevent her from going over there. "I already know she's not home." But when the mother's eyes turned with suspicion, he knew he had to say more. "I think the woman you're referring to is Emily Monroe." The problem was, he didn't have answers. "She was an artist, and she lived in that building."

"And what's she have to do with my son being beaten to death in an alley not more than four blocks from her home?"

Lesley was tired of feeling defeated. "I don't know."

She started full-steam toward the door, and Lesley knew all she'd have to do is turn on the news and those pieces would fall together.

"They found her body Sunday morning in Grant Park. I don't know any of the details—why she was there, who she was with, how she died—"

"Was she murdered?"

"Yes."

Shelia covered her mouth and began walking circles in the entryway.

"Can you tell me the name of the program your son was involved with?"

Crying, motioning this way and that way but nowhere specific, she began to speak. "He'd go to the community center—on Saturdays . . . he'd go and do that . . ." She nodded to no one other than herself and

147

went back to her cigarettes. "I told Detective Masterson all this . . . He's the one who called when Jamal got picked up—said he was at the school, trying to talk them out of pressing charges and that someone else would be bringing him to the police station."

The pieces floated around in Lesley's mind like the scattered wreckage of a sunken ship, and his eyes rested on the table. "Do me a favor, don't talk to anyone about this for the next few days."

She hesitated. "What's going on?"

"Just don't talk to anyone, okay, Sheila?" He waited for her to agree. "I'll be back after a while."

He left Deb's car parked in front of the Dupont home and walked to St. Louis, keeping his eye on the cross streets behind him. Things felt different from the street. He could see the varying colors of the faces that passed him, smell the foreign foods being sold on corners out of insulated containers, hear the music pouring from speakers outside of stores selling cheap clothing and off-brand electronics. The difference between patrolling the neighborhood and walking its streets forced him to recognize and experience his distance from those who lived their lives there. People like the boy who had lived just four blocks away.

St. Louis was lined with lush green trees and humidity. Apartment buildings and houses, no more than three feet apart, blocked the breeze floating west from the lake but also prevented the trash of the ever-busy intersection from blowing in and littering its sidewalks. A lone ice-cream vendor had stopped to please some small children, but other than that, the street was free of potential bodies and golden snapbacks.

The woman who came down to let him in had black hair piled on top of her head in a way that left patches of her scalp exposed. Her undone-ness brought him into the present. This death. This life. These people.

"I'm Detective Lesley Powell."

She shook his hand. "Yvette."

"Do you have a minute? Unofficially?"

"Officially or unofficially, you're the first cop we've seen since they told us she was dead." She held the door open and waved him in. "I don't know how you-all handle things back here in Chicago, but this shit would never fly where I'm from."

He wanted to say that things didn't normally work this way, but he no longer knew if that was true. "How long have you been in town?"

She let him lead the way up the stairs, "Since Sunday. Alex has been staying with us while he finds a house—he got the call at a little after eight and we were on a flight by noon."

The apartment had been left open and Lesley entered without ceremony. The windows of the sunroom were open, whipping in the waves of hot air able to float above the shorter homes across the street. The apartment felt emptier, a feeling he recognized and hated all at once.

"I'm sorry for your loss." She looked back at him with skepticism. "This is a terrible process to have to go through, and I'm sorry for your loss."

Yvette raised her hands to her head, tears filling her eyes. "It just doesn't make sense. None of this makes any sense."

Lesley gave her a moment before moving forward. "If you don't mind, I'd like to ask you all a few questions while I'm here."

Looking down the hall, "It's just Alex and I. Eric's staying downtown—wants to stay close." By "close" Lesley understood she meant close to where his daughter had died. He imagined the father in the park, looking in bushes, walking the path of her last steps, trying to find any remaining trace of her. "I could call him if you want."

"I don't want to drag him all the way out here. I'll go see him when we're done." Following Yvette down the hall, he questioned the legitimacy of his own presence in the home.

"Alex, this is the detective Eric called—Detective Powell." Alex sat in the dining room, shoulders hunched, head bowed, eyes staring blankly at the table in front of him. "He has a few questions for us."

His face was pleasant and boyish in a way Lesley hadn't expected. It exuded a kind of innocent perfection that was striking even while the rest of the man appeared a disheveled mess. He looked like a child waiting to be held, but when he stood he proved himself a beast of a man, six-foot-four and broad as an ox. Lesley knew, had the couple been seen together, Alex would have been the memorable one.

His soft palm swallowed Lesley's hand into his. "I'm not sure what I'm supposed to do here. I think M would offer you something to drink."

149

Striking blue eyes accented his face and were made bluer by the redness surrounding them.

"I'm fine, thank you . . . I'll just take a few minutes of your time." He waited for the pair to sit before pulling out a chair and taking out his notebook. "I'm wondering if Emily had any affiliations with youth or after-school programs that you know of."

Alex tucked his messy blonde hair behind his ears and tried to free his face of tears and snot before wiping it all on his pants. "She sometimes ran an after-school art program where she worked."

"Anything else?"

Alex's Adam's apple moved as he swallowed, and the tears that returned to his eyes slid obstinately down his cheeks despite his best attempts to stop them. "She did other things. She did lots of other things." He held a string with his fingers, twisting, knotting, pulling. Lesley knew he was waiting for his lip to stop trembling before he spoke, but the string became too much and his eyes overflowed. "Do you know if she was pregnant?" The stiff jerk of a silent sob before he hastily covered his face, and Yvette moved to comfort him.

"I'm sure they would have informed you of that by now." Alex wiped his nose with the back of his hand and Lesley pushed forward. "Do you remember a kid named Jamal? Jamal Dupont? He was killed in the alley off Drake—"

Yvette and Alex both nodded, but it was Yvette who spoke. "She was devastated—wound up finding out at the grocery store."

"Which store?"

"The one up the alley."

"Did she report being close to Jamal?"

Alex pushed his hair back again, rubbing his hands across his face. Lesley wanted to give him a moment, but in his pause, Alex got up and took the small hall to the right of the kitchen, leaving Yvette to answer the question.

"I don't know about close. I know she was fond of him and wanted to help, but she never said they were close."

"And were there others? Other kids she talked about? Projects she was involved in?"

Yvette appeared irritated by the question. "She worked at a Catholic school. She loved kids, and art, and community—she was taking ASL classes so she could talk to a guy on the train, for Christ sake—so, *yes*, there were other kids—*yes*, there were other projects and programs and people."

Lesley wanted to give her a minute, but there were too many things he needed to know. "Did she paint him? The deaf man?"

She wiped her face and pulled a tissue from her pocket. "I don't know."

"What about the paintings that were stolen? Do you happen to know which ones were taken?" Rising from her chair, she beckoned Lesley to follow and headed toward the kitchen. "She kept a ledger. She's listed all her work in it for about twenty years . . . How much they sold for, whom they were sold to, where donations went—you might find something in there."

He believed Alex had gone to clean his face, wash the snot from his hands, and collect himself, but when Lesley followed Yvette down the small hall off the kitchen, they found Alex sitting on the floor of the studio, sorting through his wife's paintings. "Where have all the people gone?"

Yvette rubbed his shoulder and took a seascape from his hands before heading back into a storage space attached to the studio. "They're being shipped back to California, remember?"

Alex's eyes continued to search the paintings surrounding him. "I thought she hated landscapes." And then he rose at the room's center. "Landscapes and seascapes . . . I wish the people were still here." There was a madness about him that Lesley couldn't pin to grief. "She thought there were entire worlds inside of people." Alex's words seemed to make him pause and then, saying nothing else, he left the room.

"Is he okay?" Lesley turned his attentions to Yvette coming out of the storage room with a book in her hands.

"No." She pushed it toward him, and there was only a slight sting to his conscience when he took it. "His wife just died."

Lesley looked at the book in his hands. "Would you mind if I took it? Dropped it off tomorrow?" The ledger contained names, dates, and places. He'd look them up, track them down, find out if there was a connection.

"Give it to Eric when you're done," she said, guiding him out the door. "He'll want to keep track of it for her."

They entered the dining room where Alex stood close to the white-board, dry-erase marker in hand. "Mr. Monroe?" Lesley wanted to say goodbye, offer his condolences, but Yvette tapped his elbow and shook her head before leading him down the hall to the front door.

"It wouldn't matter if you stripped naked and danced a jig beside him right now. He wouldn't notice you. Not while he's at the board."

The voice of Emily Monroe worked its way into his head.

He can do that . . . But he can't do this.

Lesley left the car and walked up Lawrence to the Brown Line station. A ride through the Loop and back would provide two hours of uninterrupted thought and research.

The ledger had divided Emily Monroe's works up into purchases, donations, gifts, those kept Not For Sale, and the artist's newest category, Stolen. Lesley started there and found himself unsurprised by what he learned. When over half of female homicide victims were killed by ro-mantic partners, the first thing one needed to do was identify who those romantic partners could potentially be—married or not. Six of the eight paintings stolen contained the unidentified man and increased the likeli-hood that she *did* in fact know him, at least a little.

Concerned friend Nate Aram's name appeared as one of three locals to purchase her work. He had chosen the most intimate piece from the artist's collection, *His Dick to My Jane*, a fact that only moved Lesley closer to believing there was more to their relationship than Emily had mentioned. The piece had been purchased directly from her two days before any paintings had been listed as stolen, and his name was the last to appear in the artist's hand within the ledger. It wasn't completely in-conceivable that Aram entered the studio, saw the collection containing the unidentified man, and came back to remove the threat. Then, when that didn't work . . .

A quick search showed Aram and his wife, Isabel Escamilla, on numer-ous society pages at parties, attending fundraisers and benefits, dripping money with their white toothy smiles and perfectly executed styles. Lesley briefly wondered how people had enough time to spend so much of it putting on airs when an article from 2009 showed Isabel Escamilla shaking hands with a man wearing a construction hat outside The Windy City Project. The brick building was a small nonprofit focused on the performing arts. It had added four chapters around the city in just as many years, and the power duo were the primary stakeholders, but there was no tie between that program and the ones offered in the boy's neighborhood.

The other local purchases had been made by Kadi Burk and a man named Nicodemus Papachristi. Kadi Burk had been tagged on both Nate Aram's and Isabel Escamilla's social media pages. Her own Facebook account indicated a close relationship with her art teacher and explained her small, inexpensive purchase from *Between Drake & St. Louis*. Unfortunately, despite the plethora of activities the two of them shared, there was no mention of Burk being involved in city programs like Sticharia, Metropolitan Youth, or the Windy City Project.

Lesley recognized Nicodemus Papachristi's face from the accounts he had just been examining. Papachristi acquired the most expensive and expansive piece from any of Emily's collections—*What You Have Said in the Dark*, $13,000. Paid for in cash on January 6, a handful of days before the boy had died. Papachristi appeared to be a suave, older gentleman, and the most high-profile person on the list. He'd received the Hope Award for his display of Christian ideals and values through his acts of service within the community. The award had been given by the school where Emily Monroe worked, and his children attended alongside the daughter of Aram and Escamilla.

The list of projects and programs funded or supported by Nicodemus Papachristi varied in size and stretched from L.A. to Thailand. Public records proved he owned little chunks of real-estate throughout the city; a few housing projects on the South Side, and a spattering of warehouses used by his shipping company Christi Limited.

A little digging into the company circled everything back to Nate Aram. Christi Limited was represented by Ockham, Handler, and De-Witt, a law firm specializing in environmental law where Aram was a paid specialist. He handled the environmental-impact assessments of the firm's clientele, the largest of which was owned by Papachristi.

Looking up and around as the train pulled into a station, Lesley checked his location. They were at Sedgwick and still approaching the Merchandise Mart. He had time. What bothered Lesley, given his experience with how crime spread and which neighborhoods were "safe," was that none of Papachristi's money, despite its extensive reach, seemed to land in or around Albany Park. As a matter of fact, a very clear border existed around the neighborhoods stretching from Mayfair to Uptown and as far north as Rose Hill. It created a bubble. A nexus.

Keeping track of the details, Lesley moved on to those paintings listed as donations. Out of the six pieces she'd donated in the last year, two had gone to auction fundraisers supporting cancer research and three could be traced to children's charities, all of which involved STEAM projects, but none located in Albany Park. The sixth piece was donated to the Chicago Hearing Society where she'd taken her ASL classes, and nothing there could lead him back to the boy.

Lesley passed the last stop in the Loop, and the train's signs changed to read Kimball again. Time was limited to more than a few train stops. Repositioning himself and changing his focus, Lesley moved onto those paintings Emily had chosen to *gift* people. Peter O'Shea, Brian Daniels, Georgia Russell, and someone named Mica McDowell. The men were easy. Peter O'Shea owned the market at the end of Emily's alley, one that had been tagged a number of times in the months leading up to the boy's death. Peter had no association with any charities or city programs other than Little League. He coached a team on the South Side where he lived, but neither Jamal nor Damien were involved in sports.

Brian Daniels, someone Emily mentioned routinely speaking with, was a philosophy professor out at Loyola. He did fund-raising once a year during Autism Awareness month, but outside of that, his community and city involvements centered around talks given and books published on the philosophy of perception. The other two names had to be narrowed down via their likelihood to have encountered Emily based on social-media evidence. There were seven Georgia Russells in the Chicago area, one a CTA worker at Emily's most frequent stop, and a Mica McDowell could be found working at a pub directly next door to that station. Neither woman showed connections to anything outside of being, or having, transit-related acquaintanceships with Emily—a fact that increased their likelihood of being able to identify the man in the stolen paintings.

Lesley stopped at a Mexican restaurant a block over from the Kimball station and ordered food so he'd have another place to sit and think. Everyone's attention had been focused on potential gang activity where Jamal's death was concerned. The likelihood had been probable, but Lesley had never been able to connect Jamal's Monday through Friday, 7:15 to 7:37 a.m., 3:35 to 4:05 p.m. life to anything of the sort. While Lesley sat on street corners not minding his own business, there were things happening elsewhere, at other times, potentially involving other people. And none of it had been documented.

Matriculations

Each Saturday, Brian Daniels rode the train alone, stopped by Dunkin' Donuts for a coffee, and drank it on his walk from the Loyola station to Madonna Della Strada Chapel. Sometimes, when the weather was nice, he drank it slowly, so he could stand just outside the chapel doors and look across the ocean-like lake. But it was inside the chapel where he felt the most peace.

Surrounded by its white walls, he would light a candle for his mother, a candle for his father, and then make his way halfway down the left side of the church, where he would pull down a kneeler and pray, "Jesus, I trust in you."

Even when it's hard. And it's really, really hard sometimes.

If there were lights in the chapel, he'd never seen them on. He didn't show up for scheduled Masses or holidays. He preferred to sit alone, in the quiet, with the windows around the top projecting enough light during the day to make the gold wall behind the altar sparkle and glow as he said, "Jesus, I trust in you."

Please help me protect Abigail. Help me to save my wife.

He and his wife, Olivia, had been sold on the version of parenting that consisted of hugs, kisses, sleepy-snuggles, and bedtime stories—the pleasure of watching their child grow, and learn, and discover—not autism and the hell of what it can mean: the communication barriers, the severe anxiety and depression that only appeared to be growing with size and age.

No one ever told them all these things could combine into a force so mighty that they'd have to hire caregivers, multiple caregivers, just to make sure things were less likely to end in death or disaster.

Just the day before, he and Olivia found themselves sitting in the library of their daughter's school. The school's attorney, counselor, nurse, and superintendent sat on one side of the table, while the family's attorney, Abigail's psychologist, her at-home ABA therapist, a social worker, and someone from Disability Services appeared on their side. IEP meetings used to feel quaint. They involved Brian, Olivia, Abigail's teachers, an ABA therapist, and the school's principal. They would sit around tiny desks, pushed together, and his wife would bring snacks, understanding that the meeting would run long and people would be tired. But the space they required grew with Abigail's behaviors, and Olivia had stopped bringing snacks.

"We mentioned at the beginning of the year that this was tenuous. We promised to do what we could, and we did, but we no longer feel able to support Abigail here at the school." The principal slid a printout across the table, a familiar logo of a blue puzzle piece top-and-center of the page. *Long Term Solutions: What If We Just Can't Do This Anymore?*"

"What is this?" Olivia had grabbed up the paper so quickly he'd barely read the title. "What are you implying?" There were tears before he understood the cause.

"We've also noticed—forgive me, Olivia—an increase in marks."

"What?" Placing his hand on her arm, he kept his wife in her seat.

"On you."

Brian had stopped seeing the little scratches and bruises so long ago that he'd forgotten she could exist without them. The cast his hand rested on was one of the things they'd blown off as "lucky"—lucky the chair didn't hit her head as intended.

"We've had Abigail with us now since preschool, and your injuries keep increasing." It was like hearing that cigarettes were going to kill you. "She's only going to get bigger."

Olivia returned the paper to the table and he read the first few words, "Residential placement is a personal decision," before she was on her feet using words he'd never heard her use before.

"Olivia, honey," he tried to coax her back into her chair, but she ripped herself free from him.

"Fuck you, Brian—fuck all of you." Her purse, an extension of her hand, swung violently toward wherever her finger landed before moving again. "I have given up my *life* for Abigail and you're saying I'm not enough? That I can't handle her, or love her enough—"

"Mrs. Daniels, no one is saying—"

"Everyone is saying!" She picked up the stack of papers and threw them toward the opposing side. "You brought papers saying!"

"Mrs. Daniels, if you could just sit down and—"

"No, I am not sitting down, I am not listening to this." Snatching up her jacket, she headed to the door. "I'm taking Abigail with me. She won't be coming back."

Brian sat in the littered silence of the room following the slammed door and the distressed moans of Abigail being taken out of an activity and led away by her mother.

"I'm sorry." In every direction, toward every person involved, for every event. "I'm sorry."

He stood on the train far removed from where he'd be standing with Abigail and let the chaos of the afternoon travelers unfold around him without interest or concern while his mind rehashed the "luck" of his wife's broken arm, the broken nose five months prior, the pencil in her thigh, the locked-up knives, scissors, razors, their plastic dishes and tin coffee cups, nothing breakable that could be used as a weapon.

Back in the chapel, Brian found it difficult to know what to pray for and tried to let his faith carry him through. "Jesus, I trust in you." He repeated the words slowly, meditatively. *Whatever that means, whatever that entails.* "Jesus, I trust in you." That day, he spent an hour on his knees, murmuring over and over, "Jesus, I trust in you," until finally he felt heard. A peace fell over his heart, and he knew it was time to stop.

Making his way along the lakeside path, past the library and toward the Crown Center, he saw a familiar face that allowed him a detour. "Good morning, M."

Her smile was always kind and warm, but her candor continuously caught him off guard.

"Morning, Brian. How's God today?" Shifting over on the rock where she sat bundled against the weather, she tapped the space beside her to invite his diversion.

"Mostly quiet." The rock wasn't quite wide enough for them to sit side-by-side, so they sat with their lower halves pointing away from one another while his left shoulder leaned against her right. "But He's still here."

She smiled and offered him some coffee from her thermos before growing more serious. "A boy in my neighborhood was killed last week . . . beaten to death in an alley."

"Oh, God. I'm sorry."

"It makes me wonder," she squinted past the snowflakes that fell between them, "if He's ever really been here at all."

"He has. And He will continue to be." Brian didn't know how to justify his response as he looked across the frozen lake, but he believed it to be true.

"There's so much," there was a sigh, "so much shit in the world, you know? Kids suffer so much, Brian. They suffer so much, and no one hears them." They hadn't been in the habit of baring souls, and her heaviness was new and unexpected. "I'm sorry," she said, "I'm sorry . . . How's Abigail doing?"

"Good . . . fine . . . yeah . . . she's good." He knew it sounded like a lie but hoped it would suffice.

"I painted a picture of her a while ago." Taking a drag of her cigarette, she avoided his eye. "I'm not going to use it in my show, but I wanted you to know."

He felt uncomfortable by the confession and what it could mean; what she'd seen, how it had been captured. "Why aren't you going to use it?"

There was a half-smile. "I felt like it violated this," she said, motioning between them. "I couldn't show the painting without asking your permission, and it felt too weird to ask."

It had been at least four years since he'd first seen her there by the lake and said hello, and yet every morning they rode the train together for one stop and never said a word to one another.

"Do you still have it? I'd like to see it." The images he had in mind were chaotic and made him feel embarrassed.

Nodding, she rubbed her cigarette out on the ground. "I do. She's got those pink headphones on, and the sneakers she used to wear that had green flowers."

He knew the pair. Abigail had refused to give them up, dug them out of the trash, rejected wearing anything else. He hated those shoes.

"I've just been waiting for the right time to give it to you. I didn't

159

want you thinking I'm some crazy lady painting your kid." She stared out at the lake. "I loved those shoes. I felt they said so much about her."

A few moments of silence passed before she reached into her bag and pulled out her phone. Brian watched her nimble fingers swipe over the screen while he continued to imagine the images she could have contrived from Abigail on the train. The hitting, the face scrunched up in an angry moan, her hands forever immortalized mid-flap.

"I just love the way you love one another." Looking down at the screen, he saw his daughter. "I wish all children had that kind of love."

Abigail held his hand next to her face and dangled a sucker out of her mouth. Her tiny little chin pointed upward, her eyes crinkled with the slightest hint of a smile as she looked up at him, calm, happy, her feet captured in a moment of dance. It was like seeing her with fresh eyes. Eyes that didn't know she'd broken her mother's nose at least twice and exhausted his marriage. Eyes that couldn't see her smashing television screens because a movie wouldn't be restarted or a DVD had a glitch. Eyes that were free of having to see her and decide how much more medication would be required in order to keep her home and safe. The image invoked the memory of her laugh, her joy in little things, and the softness of her hand in his.

Seeing her there, she appeared full of hope and promise.

Jesus, I trust in you.

It was embarrassing to be caught so off-guard by ten years of emotion left to spill out, onto, and all over the shoulder of a familiar stranger. But she stayed put and didn't say a word while he told her everything—all the details of love, parenting, medication, residential homes, feeling like a failure, his concern over his wife—everything came out in a tsunami of grief and long overdue confession. Everything he couldn't say to God, he said to her, and in the end, she looked at him with a complete absence of judgment.

"I'm sorry." Brian wiped his face and tried to compose himself, but the tears kept coming.

She shook her head and wrapped her arm around him. "Please don't apologize. Out of all the people in the world, you have nothing to apologize for."

Mosca

Self-doubt and flagellation came and went. But there were times it didn't matter that none of it was real. The fictionalized part of Donovan's life made the mundane happenings of grocery shopping, television watching, and weekend plans sound more enchanting than when he reported them as an almost-thirty-year-old man with no love life or prospects. His parents asked questions, wanted to know more about *him* and the things he enjoyed doing—things he could say he did with *her*. People suddenly listened. And he was entrenched enough that the words no longer felt like a falsehood when he opened his mouth.

Helping to fuel the illusion was *Hidden in Transit*, a painting Donovan determined to be evidence that Emily avoided him, not because she didn't like him but because of how much she did. It was therefore okay that he hadn't seen her again for days. He had proof she'd return to him eventually, and that much wasn't a fantasy at all.

You are not okay.

Shhhh.

This is a pillow.

I can smell her soap, light the candles and—

You don't even like Corona.

She's here.

No one's here but you.

The phone rang and, given the time of day, Donovan knew it could only be one person. "Hello?"

You'd rather talk to your mother?

"Are you ready for graduation?" Her voice rang on in his ear and didn't allow him to answer. "We're so excited to see you—Jimmy and Tilly are coming for the barbeque. Alice will be here—"

"Alice?"

Yeah, Alice. The girl from the wedding.

"She and Jay have really hit it off."

It could have been you, Donovan.

"I can't believe how well he's doing."

All you had to do was dance.

"He's working and talking about moving out."

Your pot-head brother is fucking the bridesmaid and moving forward while you're fucking a pillow.

"Of course, I don't want to jinx it but . . ."

Do you like it?

"I think she just might be the one to help get your brother's life on track."

Or would you rather something else?

"And she's a sweet girl, a really sweet, sweet girl."

A sweet girl you could have fucked if you'd just danced.

"*Jesus*," Donovan snapped. "Shut the fuck up already."

There was silence, and then an "Excuse me?"

Shhhh. Donovan could feel himself slipping and closed his eyes. *You are not okay.* "I'm sorry, that wasn't meant for you."

"Well, I don't think you should talk like that to anyone, Donovan."

You're going to lie again

"Of course not. I'm sorry."

and again

"Do you talk to Emily like that?"

and again.

"Of course not, Ma. Jesus, it was just the television."

More silence.

Eventually, no one will believe you.

"Are you doing okay?"

"Yes, please continue."

Not even her.

Eyes closed, Donovan listened for the sound of a train in the distance. His mother's words starting slowly, tentatively, until they once again reached full-speed. "Everyone's looking forward to meeting her. Do you think she'll be too overwhelmed with all the people?"

"Who? Alice? Everyone already knows Alice, don't they?"

"*No*, Emily. Do you think *Emily* will feel overwhelmed?"

What are you going to do? Bring your pillow? Introduce it to the family? "No, Ma, I think she'll love it."

"Your dad wants to put the blow-up mattress in the den, said you could sleep in there."

Are you going to lay it in your childhood bed and whisper sweet nothings into its cover?

"Is that okay? Will that work?"

You're such a fucking loser.

He didn't know if he could hear the ding-donging of the doors, or if it was all in his mind. *Doors Closing.* And he lay there, quite still, trying to determine what he thought and what was real.

"Are you okay?"

Sometimes after he'd gone to the gym, he could still hear the dribble of balls and squeaking of shoes, even though he'd only heard the sounds from a distance.

"Donovan? What's going on with you?"

What's going on, Donno?

Sometimes when he heard the sound, he could actually feel the grip of the ball's texture in his palm. The stuttering of his feet across the gym floor.

"Donovan?"

He tried to feel the train.

Do not attempt to board or alight this train while doors are closing.

And couldn't get in.

You are not okay.

A handful of gifts were placed in a canvas bag, gifts he'd purchased for the students who had been with him since their freshman year. Students who knew him. Students who saw him. Students he didn't understand how much he would miss until he entered his classroom and saw their smiling faces all together for the last time.

"Whoa, Mr. J, look at *you*." Kamal took out his cellphone and snapped a picture while snickering.

It was a three-piece windowpane suit.

"Whoever said straight white boys don't know how to dress never met you."

He wore it with a pale gray shirt and a navy tie that carried specks of red and charcoal, allowing the flare of his pocket square to boast brighter shades of red and blue in an otherwise gaudy display of paisley floral.

"How do you know he's straight?"

"He's got a *girlfriend*." Kamal looked at him. "You've got a girlfriend, right?"

"Does it really *matter* if I have a girlfriend?" He'd shined his black shoes and pulled out his warmer-weather dress coat. "I mean, look at me. Who cares when I can dress like this, right?" He turned around, hands out to his sides, soaking up the fact that knowing how to dress had never been his downfall. They laughed, and took pictures, and agreed with him. But there was a pain in his chest that none of them knew was there.

Knock knock.

Donovan had begun buying gifts in early February. He handed Kamal a package, "This is for you. I'd wish you luck, but . . ." And the group carried on.

Which door do you choose?

"Wait, did you actually get me . . ." A voice rang from the corner and a box was held up, "Wooden Battleship, baby. Bring it!"

Door number one?

Dreadlocks and travel.

"Oh, how did you know?" A journal brought to a nose, the smell of leather.

Door number blue?

A constellation of freckles . . .

"You're the best, Mr. James." Purple cats and shooting stars.

Door number she?

"I have something for you." A tiny box that sent a chill through his spine and down into his gut.

She wants to fuck you.

"A playlist." She lifted its top, exposing a thumb drive.

If you agree to meet her.

"Something to remember me by." Lily removed the object from its box and slid it into Donovan's breast pocket.

164

It would be that easy.

"'Transgression Through Literature: How Depictions of Immorality Shape Society's Acceptance of Misconduct'," Donovan said.

"Excuse me?"

"Great minds think alike." He handed her a flash drive of his own. "My thesis."

Her expression lacked the appreciation her peers had shown, but her brown eyes stared more intently. Her hand slipped the gift under her gown, into a pocket closer to her skin, and then came up to his collar. "The acceptance of misconduct," pretending to straighten it, pretending that the pressure of a single finger traced down his neck wouldn't affect him. "Nice suit." Marking him with her scent.

"Hey, Mr. J—" His awareness jerked away from her and back into the room. "We need a picture of all of us together." Voices sprang from every direction, adding distance between himself, and her, and the part of her that clung to his neck. Choking his thoughts.

"Are you a chaperone tonight?"

A laugh forced itself up and out, "Hell, no. You think I want to be responsible for this?"

You are responsible for this.

"Donovan." A knock on his door. Ann looking irritated by the commotion. "The kids need to get to the auditorium."

"Take a picture first?" He could show her it was fun; it was harmless, everything was fine. "Just a quick one?"

Ann entered the classroom and did as he'd asked with eyes that searched faces. A mother, sniffing out the bad seed, and blinding everyone with the flash. "Now," she said, handing the camera back, "to the auditorium."

Lily's hand reached for his like it belonged to her. "You'll find me afterward?"

"Of course."

"Lily." Turning her away from him and toward the door, Ann glanced back at Donovan with a non-smile that said, No, you won't.

He stayed just long enough to see the diploma touch Lily's hand.

On his back, phone cupped into his palm, Donovan worried its next vibration would tremble more than his hand.

I know everything about you. Every thought in your head.

But he answered the call anyway. "Hello?"

You won't be able to take this back.

"Hi." She too was on her back, in another bed, another room. Waiting. "What do you need?"

You know what she needs.

"Can we see each other?"

She wants you to take her clothes off.

"I'm not sure it's a good idea."

Like Sara. You just closed your eyes and pretended. Remember?

"You said we could."

She has more flesh; longer legs—and that ass. She wanted you to see it.

"Yeah, I . . ." Feet on the floor, eyes on the shelves. *Lolita. Just for you.* "I'm not sure it's a good idea right now."

"But I'm here."

"I know."

You just close your eyes.

"And, Mr. James?"

"Yeah?"

"I won't say no."

Pretend.

What did you think would happen?

Donovan stood on the southbound platform and yelled, eyes closed, fists clenched, throat burning, not caring that the train he was meant to board wasn't covering his sound.

Did you think she'd magically appear with luggage and play your girlfriend for the weekend?

Heads turned, and people stared, but it didn't matter.

You haven't even seen her.

None of it mattered.

You're just some guy on the train, remember?

He was supposed to be heading to Midway, catching a plane, showing up with his girlfriend and proving everyone wrong.

You should just jump.

"Shut! Up!"

"Doors closing."

He watched the train pull away, grabbed his weekend bag, and fought his way down the stairs, into the busy station, looking for Georgia.

"Georgia?" He shouted, louder than he needed to. "Georgia?"

"Georgia's not here—she went home at two—"

"Have you seen Emily? Red hair, blue coat all winter?"

The woman's face scrunched in irritated concern. "Sir, I have no idea who Emily is—"

"Emily. Red hair, pale skin. She wore a blue coat all winter—"

"You can repeat yourself all you want," she said, shaking her head, "but that ain't gonna help." Donovan watched the deaf man enter the station and cut his way to the front of the fare-machine line, pushing buttons, causing additional noise and chaos in the already busy space.

The woman quickly turned toward the sound. "Sir! Sir! You can't do that, stop pushing buttons."

Donovan saw Lily step in front of the man, her face appearing angry in a way he hadn't seen before. "He's deaf and he will not understand you yelling at him."

Take her instead, introduce her to your family.

Donovan couldn't tell if she was real.

You could tuck her into your childhood bed.

The thundering overhead told him he could catch the train if he tried.

She's real. And she wants you.

Donovan didn't take his shoes off or remove his coat. "We missed our flight."

His father was not pleased. "What do you mean you missed your flight? Your brother's already on his way to the airport. Your mom's making dinner."

The six-pack he purchased at the corner market remained on the coffee table within easy reach. "We had an argument, and we missed our flight—"

"Well, you should have called sooner."

The remote rested untouched at his side.

"Jesus, Donovan, what's going on with you?"

"I'm sorry. I'll catch a flight tomorrow."

He sat on the couch through silently ringing phones and countless unheard voice messages. He then found himself in the bathroom, looking in the mirror, left eyelid drooping due to lack of sleep and alcohol consumption.

He'd stared so long that he could no longer see the reflection as his. It felt more real that way; foreign actions and strange behaviors were easier to digest.

"Good night, asshole."

It was noon before he bothered to check the time or rebook his flight. He read the number of his credit card to the woman on the other end of the line, then texted the flight information to his brother. The next two and a half hours he remained flat on his bed, watching the light shift across his room as the minutes passed. When the time came for him to leave, he didn't pick up his empty bottles, or change his clothes; he didn't even bother to check in with the asshole in the mirror. He just took hold of his suitcase and dragged it out the door.

Emily sat at the front of the train car, fitted in a sleek green dress and tucked next to the window. She looked like a trapped animal gazing back at him, her limbs jerked to escape, but the suitcase and body next to her prevented the action.

Chut-chut, chut-chut. Chut-chut, chut-chut.

Standing awkwardly in the aisle, gripping his suitcase in one hand and a steel pole with the other, Donovan wished time could stop, or rewind, or fast-forward him away from the situation.

Chut-chut, chut-chut. Chut-chut, chut-chut.

Emily sat unnervingly straight and still, eyes cast out the window, body turned away from him until the train entered Irving Park and she pushed past the person next to her, not waiting for them to move their baggage or adjust their position. "Excuse me."

Donovan attempted to stop her exit by grabbing her arm, but she jerked away and stepped onto the platform without looking back.

"Doors closing."

There was an ocean inside him, deep, dark, full of life that swelled in a panic as the train pulled away.

Chut-chut, chut-chut. Chut-chut, chut-chut.

He could feel its waters stirring, bringing its depths up to the surface.

Chut-chut, chut-chut.

Before any conscious effort could be put into the decision, Donovan turned and punched the Plexiglas window, ripping open his knuckle and silencing the train car.

The last paragraph of the article read: *No words are entirely untranslatable; none are entirely transparent. A pragmatic view of how words work is the only view of them that accounts for our persistent tiny triumphs and sudden comic errors. Sometimes they obscure; sometimes they're plain; often they fail us.*

Trapped in his airplane seat, dried blood across his hand and shirt and pants, Donovan let his eyes roll over the sentences several times, recounting his last words to her until they spilled from his mouth. "I love you."

If it weren't for those words, if he had acted, kissed her, not called a cab, taken her home.

It's over.

"You realize you have blood all over yourself, right?" Donovan found himself riding down the 96 in less time than he'd hoped, and Jay was casting nervous sideways glances in his direction. "Everything okay with you, Donno?"

Surveying the side of the road, and the speed in which it passed under them, Donovan rolled down the window and stuck his head out. He considered opening the door, falling, feeling the concrete smack and shave his skin.

Maybe you'll get hit by a car.

He checked the side mirror.

Better to wait for a semi.

Head hanging out the window, he closed his eyes and he imagined it.

"What the fuck are you doing? Keep your head in the car and buckle up. Are you stoned or something?"

"Jesus, shut up." Clasping his face, Donovan lowered his head to his lap and took several deep breaths.

There are going to be questions.

"You're gonna need to clean yourself up before you see Mom. You'd freak her right the fuck out looking like that. She already thinks there's something wrong with you."

You better come up with a good lie.

Or you could just tell them the truth.

Donovan saw his parents' car as they pulled into the parking lot of the brewery.

Did you bring your fuck pillow?

"I'll grab you a change of clothes." Engine off, Jay opened his door. "You get to the bathroom and clean yourself up. I'll order us some beer and keep Mom busy."

"I'm not okay."

"Yeah, I can see that." Jay handed him the keys and turned to the back seat, rummaged through Donovan's bag. "Make sure you don't bring your bloody clothes to the table."

"I think I need help."

"Here." Jay handed Donovan fresh clothes and returned to his seat. "What the hell is going on with you? Dad said there was a fight, but I wasn't expecting blood."

"I'm not okay."

"Did you hurt her?"

Quiet, quiet, the smack of the concrete, the ripping of his skin. "No."

"I've never seen you like this before, Donno. It's not good."

Silence. Breathing. He wanted them both to stop.

Jay cupped his hand over Donovan's shoulder. "Dad's gonna try and push your buttons. Don't let him."

The button has already been pushed.

"Oh, honey." Hugging his mom made him feel defenseless. "It's good to see you." The tightness of her squeeze, the rub, the scratch, the pat on the back that signified she knew more about his heart than he wanted her to. She held him close, rubbed his back, spoke soothingly, just as she had when he was ten and he thought Jimmy had to move away. "I'm so glad you're here." Pulling out a chair, she motioned for him to sit while his father ignored his arrival by staring at the menu. "Are you doing okay? Your father said there was a fight."

He saw her eyes, struggling to see him.

"It's the end of the year, things are stressful." Donovan looked across the table at Jay, who watched him closely, nudging him with glances and brows and subtle movements, coaxing out the right words. "I think the combination of work and the anxiety over meeting everyone just got to her . . . and I didn't handle it well."

"That's a surprise." His father spoke without looking, and Jay shook his head, warning Donovan not to engage.

"Oh, come on, Don—"

"You know, Laurie, I'm still pissed off. You went through all the trouble of making dinner, had the room set up, dessert made, and he didn't even call until Jay was at the airport."

"I'm right here, Dad. Yell at me, not Mom."

But this was the way it had always been. "It's okay, Donovan, don't worry." Reaching out, his mother patted his hand while her smile said, Please, don't make things worse.

The smell of their freshly placed beers brought forth the memory of his father's breath, planting seeds, blaming him, crushing his existence with words pitched violently in his direction: *Why are you crying? You're like a little girl, for Christ sake. Stop that stuttering business and use your words. Jesus, Donovan, why can't you just be a normal kid with normal interests? You know, you keep acting like a little fairy, and no one's gonna want to be your friend. Maybe if you stopped living in fantasyland and spent some time in the real world every now and again, you'd be able to form a proper sentence.*

"It's always been the same with you."

You're still that stuttering kid to him.

"Oh, Don, leave him alone."

"Laurie!" His father's hand struck the table in a gesture familiar to Donovan, "I'm sick of this, his entire life—"

"Hey, maybe we can talk about this later, at home, where it's private." Jay said, trying to be good, trying to keep things safe.

"No, I want everything out in the open. Right now."

Who are you?

"Are you *gay*, Donovan?"

A stuttering kid. Some guy on the train.

"Is this *girlfriend* of yours actually a man?"

Seen and unseen, all at once.

"I mean, Jesus, I would prefer you just admitted it so we could move on and stop being lied to all the time."

Donovan thought of the car ride home, the maximum speed the car would travel. The smack. The scrape.

All their images of you removed.

"Just say it, for Christ sake." *Who are you?*

Donovan's fingers curled around the knife placed conveniently to his right. "You want everything out?" He could stab his own throat, die a regret in his father's eyes.

"I do, yes."

"You're an asshole—"

"Donovan." His mother took the hand that held the knife.

"You've done nothing but ridicule and humiliate me my entire life."

No words are entirely untranslatable; none are entirely transparent.

"When was the last time you heard me stutter? When was the last time you saw me cry?"

"Donno." Jay rubbed his forehead and closed his eyes.

"I'm not that same kid anymore, Dad."

Sometimes they obscure.

"I grew up. Learned to run. Learned to speak—"

Sometimes they're plain.

"And I'm tired of your voice living in my head telling me that nothing's changed."

"And yet you still won't answer the question."

"Don, *please.*"

"You're an asshole."

Often, they fail us.

Jay repositioned himself across the table.

"That's the only thing that hasn't changed."

At 5 a.m. Donovan woke to a text from Lily. He laced up his running shoes on the edge of his childhood bed and plugged in his headphones. Quietly closing the front door behind him, he looked across the street at the house where Jimmy used to live. The driveway was still cracked, but the new owners had put maroon shutters up against the pale-blue barnlike house and installed a white metal fence around the front patio.

You are marooned.

I know.

The trick, he had learned, was to concentrate on the smacking of his feet against the pavement and the cool air coming in through his nostrils before it exited hot through his mouth. Two miles up, he connected with the trail where he had once learned to escape his thoughts, but neither the trail's recently added length nor the speed at which he pushed himself could stop them. He had to go back, he had to see Emily, he had to find her and make her understand.

The detective kept talking, kept asking questions, kept forcing Donovan to live and relive moments that couldn't be changed or undone, and the pressure inside him was mounting. "She said you gave her the key on July 5th."

"Lily took the key. I didn't give it to her. Why would I give her the key?"

"Because it was easy."

He's not wrong.

"And you liked her."

You did like her.

"And she wanted to be with you."

Again, and again, and again.

"Did you ask her to pose with the coat? Did you take those pictures?"

Did you ask for that?

"Emily gave me the coat, like a memento. I had the coat; she had the book—"

"Did you ask Lily to pose with it on?" Pictures conflating memories. "If you didn't want her to have the key, why didn't you ask for it back?"

Angry thoughts. Bad thoughts.

Just thoughts.

"I was trying to help her."

He'll never understand.

"Is that how she wound up in your bed?"

He'll never understand. They'll never understand. You'll never understand.

"It was after . . ." There was a before, and there was an after. Before Emily, before Lily, before flash drives ruined everything and the truth spiraled out of control. There was a before this moment, a before when he knew the difference between fact and fiction. But it was the after of this moment, this conversation, that would define who Donovan was. "It was after I took her home with me on the Fourth of July—she was drunk and in danger and nothing happened. I put her to bed, that's it. I put her to bed and slept on the couch."

No words are entirely untranslatable; none are entirely transparent. Sometimes they obscure, sometimes they're plain; often they fail us.

"Then what?"

"I went for a run the next morning, and she was gone when I got back."

He could see the skepticism. He'd seen that same look on the face of every detective he'd spoken with over the last few weeks.

"But you knew she had it. Didn't you, Donovan?"

Whether he did or didn't was irrelevant. Neither would change the story's end.

Donovan sat looking at the detective while his father's words ran circles in his mind: Y*ou have to do what they say, son.*

All the acceptance he'd ever needed, summed up tight with one little word.

Son . . .

Realized. Represented. Portrayed.

Actualized.

Interference

It wasn't until Lesley received his chips and salsa that he realized his first mistake may have occurred years prior to the death of Jamal Dupont. The hours of the boy's life Lesley hadn't been privileged to witnessing were the hours where the real problems had occurred. Lesley had known this for a long while, and had focused all his attention on those hours in relation to the Quiles brothers and their activities. He'd been certain they were involved—so certain that he never acknowledged the potential for the Quiles's own problematic hours or what led one to juvenile hall and the other to golden snapbacks. He needed to rewind everything. Move back in time and see old complications under a different context.

Damien Quiles was sent to Lawrence Hall at the age of fifteen after brutally stabbing his mother's boyfriend, Tyson Cuthbert. Lesley hadn't been involved with *that* case, but a year prior to it he and Masterson had investigated a spate of burglaries involving a methadone clinic two doors down from Globe Cargo where Cuthbert worked.

The chain connecting the barred security doors of the clinic had left a narrow gap they'd initially overlooked. But as more burglaries took place, he and Masterson had to consider someone small enough to squeeze through the space—a woman. A small woman who was desperate and needing a fix. Looking at the information now, Lesley reminded himself of what he'd already known: boys, young boys who could once fit through windows, lost their value after puberty broadened their shoulders.

Damien, who had admitted to the stabbing for reasons that didn't go beyond "being sick" of Cuthbert, may have outgrown his usefulness and finally been big enough to fight back. But maybe there was more.

Lesley knew Globe Cargo was the kind of hole-in-the-wall place where one could purchase phone cards, Turkish coffee pots, powdered coffee creamer, and generic brands of foreign snacks that could only be identified if there was an accompanying picture or you read the right languages. It was also the kind of place where one could send and receive packages, luggage, and letters from home. The shipping aspect of things felt as close to a connection as he could find, and so he wrote down all the pieces he could think of: *Jamal Dupont, Emily Monroe, Albany Park Community Center, Damien Quiles, Lawrence Hall, Globe Cargo, Tyson Cuthbert, Metropolitan Youth, Sticharia, Nate Aram, Isabel Escamilla, Nicodemus Papachristi, Christi Limited.*

He began his next internet search with the most unlikely combinations: *Jamal Dupont, Emily Monroe, Sticharia.* Nothing. *Damien Quiles, Nate Aram, Emily Monroe.* Nothing. *Nicodemus Papachristi, Tyson Cuthbert, Jamal Dupont.* Nothing. *Isabel Escamilla, Metropolitan Youth, Globe Cargo.* Something.

Lesley paused before clicking on a pdf file from a Cook County Board of Commissioners meeting. The names weren't all together, they were spread across one hundred and seventy pages of "net warrant by fund summaries" and "vendor reports."

Papachristi's name and signature appeared under an agenda item toward the end, a letter documenting why the safety corridors needed for the students whose closing schools would have them traveling greater distances should be handled via the tax allotments provided to each district.

Closing schools and tax allotments kept Jamal and footbridges close in Lesley's mind. He spent the next two hours finding names and pinpointing locations on maps. A Spanish entertainment and tabloid newspaper owned Globe Cargo and shipped its papers there. Those papers were then delivered to an office space in Rodgers Park rented by Isabel Escamilla. Whatever legitimate business Escamilla could be running out of there, Lesley couldn't find. But vendor reports showed something was happening—$4,800 had been paid for computer systems and design.

The man who performed the work was Yasser Najjar—the primary stakeholder of Sticharia, a nonprofit group contracted to empty trash bins and scrub toilets for Christi Limited, *and* Damien Quiles's employer.

No amount of digging provided Lesley a physical address for where Najjar could be found, and the addresses given for both his business and that of Sticharia varied across public documents.

After all the lines had been drawn, a larger story was evident. One he hadn't been told. One he still couldn't see the whole of. But one that power and money had actively worked to keep hidden. He'd been placed on leave and pulled from the neighborhood because someone, some-where, didn't want him to know *this*. Whatever "this" might be.

Rodgers Park, and the rented space of Isabella Escamilla, became his next point of interest.

Lesley added news alerts for crimes and suspicious activities surround-ing the neighborhood in question. He rode the Brown Line to Belmont, waited for the Purple Line, and tried to keep track of the time he had left before needing to meet Blakely at eight.

His thoughts were rushed, and stubborn, and hot with the speed at which they traveled, each one spinning him in a new direction he didn't have space in his head to contain. There were too many details. Too many things to consider and hold up and try to keep straight. Too many people crammed onto the platform at Howard. Too much noise. Not enough space until Lesley stepped from the station to the street and the world seemed to pause.

Expansive use of neutral-colored concrete, smoggy air, and the time of day made it easy. The stillness of the area gave him time to let his thoughts settle without taking anything else in. But the dust collecting on his black shoes bore a sharp contrast to the occasional passing of white sneakers and reminded him, in quiet ways, that he was never meant to be standing there.

The address he was looking for sat across the street from a commu-nity center and was located in a rundown strip mall between a shawarma shop and a nail salon. Its windows were covered with newspaper the way some businesses are when they're going through a remodel or shut-ting down completely. But no signage was displayed, and the door was locked.

Lesley stepped inside the shawarma shop where a large man behind the counter pretended not to speak English once the first question had been asked. He then tried the same question in Arabic, but the man held up his bear-like paws saying, "I don't know. I don't know," and shooed Lesley out the door. He hadn't known what he would find, but he hadn't expected such a clear sign of keeping one's mouth shut.

At the nail salon next door, Eastern European women wore white smocks that made them look like doctors. They worked against a backdrop of white walls and white furniture with bright pink accents. More like something you'd see on the edge of Wicker Park and Bucktown. "Can I help you?" a voice called out to Lesley. "No openings until tomorrow, but you can leave your name." It suggested that he might be there for a service and this caused him pause as he glanced at the sign-in book lying open on the counter.

Years of habit reached for his badge and he said his name, not realizing his mistake until after a different woman began to speak. "Is this about Emily Monroe?"

The space was disorientating. It required a quick scan before Lesley was able to pinpoint the face attached to the voice.

Isabel Escamilla sat in an overly large white chair. "Don't worry. It wasn't me." Her foot held by the woman sitting in front of her, she smiled. "I wouldn't kill someone for sleeping with my husband—I'm not the desperate kind." Lesley knew that just by looking at her. "Besides, she'd moved on." She raised her manicured nails to give them a once-over. "Nate and I saw her. She was wearing the shawl he gave her for her birthday when she stepped right off the path and into the bushes with her crooked-nosed little friend. It reminded me how much money I'd unwittingly spent on my husband's whore and how much of a whore she was." Sighing, she rested her hands on the arms of the massage chair. "Do you have any questions I haven't already answered? I've got a plane to catch."

This was not the way Lesley had envisioned the trip going.

The bell above the door rang and the woman at her feet got up to sign for a package.

"I'm not here about Emily Monroe. But I am here to talk to you." He watched her expression shift from smug to confusion.

"I don't understand."

"I wanted to ask you about Yasser Najjar."

Isabel Escamilla gave a quick tilt of her head. "I don't know a Yasser Najjar."

"The man you paid to do computer work next door." He pulled out his notebook. "Do you have any idea how I can reach him?"

Her pause gave Lesley time to make note of the crooked-nosed comment. "I wouldn't know anything about that."

"It's your office though, right? The lease is in your name?" He gave her time to respond, but she remained quiet. "Public records show Yasser Najjar listed 7653 North Paulina Street for a cleaning company he owns."

She eyed him up and down before saying anything. "I have no control over what people write on papers—"

"Did you have computer work done?"

"My husband took care of it—"

"Would you mind if I had a look next door?"

"I would actually, yes." Coming down from her throne, Isabel Escamilla slipped her feet into a pair of sandals and approached Lesley, bag in hand. "As I said, I have a plane to catch, but if you give me your card, I'll have my husband call you."

Lesley hesitated in handing her the information. "Where are you headed?" Her outstretched hand wiggled dancing fingers and he faked a pat-down of his pockets, "Sorry, I'm out at the moment, but if you give me your number—"

She slipped one of the salon's business cards across the counter. "Write it here then."

A lot of information can be gathered from a cell phone number, and Lesley paid attention to his gut.

Her nails were too long for her to take the card without looking alien, but he watched her slip the number into her phone case. "And—not that it's any business of yours, detective—but I have a commercial to film in Spain."

It was not a coincidence. None of it was a coincidence. Lesley checked his watch and calculated train times. "Great. If you could just have your husband give me a call."

She tapped her phone's case.

"Right. Okay. Travel safe, Ms. Escamilla."

Lesley made a note to see Nate Aram the next morning. He might dial the wrong number before then, but Lesley couldn't risk anymore afterhours visits with people who were potentially involved. He was still considering the consequences of his trip to Rodgers Park when he exited the Purple Line at Davis and remembered the one thing in his life he shouldn't have forgotten. He checked his watch just as his phone began to buzz in his pocket.

"I've been waiting for an hour. There *was* no reservation—"

"Deb, I'm so sorry." Lesley stopped at the bottom of the stairs, knowing it was too late to make things right.

She hung up, and he remained motionless. Other passengers made their way past and around him like fish swimming upstream.

"Bum a light?" Blakely's voice came from behind. "Gotta keep moving, Old Man."

"I have to get home. I'm sorry, I had plans with Deb and . . ."

Blakely nodded slowly, studying the faces around them. "I'll wait with you then." He looked at Lesley. "I mean, I don't have a wife, so I don't know how it works, but I imagine she's pissed." He headed back up the stairs and Lesley followed him, hoping the next southbound train would arrive quickly. "*I'm* pissed. I was looking forward to that beer."

The reader board read "Loop 28 Minutes," and Lesley pulled out his phone to send Deb a message. *I'll be home in an hour and three minutes.* Then he remembered he still had to pick up her car. Blakely eyed the empty platform and pulled out a cigarette.

"You can't smoke up here."

"You gonna give me a ticket?" He smiled at Lesley and tossed the lit match onto the tracks while exhaling a plume of smoke. "They gonna give me a ticket?"

"Just do me a favor and toss it if any women or children come up."

Blakely laughed, "This is your problem, Old Man, your problem and your gift." Lesley didn't ask for clarification, and Blakely peered down onto the street where people waited for buses in light unfitting for the time of day and then stepped back from the railing. His eyes remained on the parking garage across the street. "Masterson knew about the lady's involvement with the boy." He didn't look at Lesley. "I have a friend who says he began working with the Bureau of Organized Crime last October—something called Project Lake Effect."

"That's bullshit." Lesley couldn't look at him.

"There was a flash drive found on Emily Monroe's person. It wound up getting separated from the other evidence, misfiled at the wrong station. Taken care of, perhaps?"

"Masterson had nothing to do with that. He wasn't there—he said he closed the case on Friday."

Blakely took a drag and gave himself time to exhale before continuing. "Do you know that for sure?"

Lesley checked his watch, and then his phone. There were too many things floating, too much for him to consider.

"People say a lot of things, Old Man. It's what they *do* that's important." Blakely's body moved like he was stretching his shoulders and cracking his neck, readying for a fight. "I'm ready for that beer. Got a five spot I can borrow until Monday?"

"I don't carry cash."

"Check." Blakely rubbed his nose before his eyes fell to Lesley's jacket pocket. "You seem like a guy who would carry at least a *little* cash."

Wanting to know what, but not wanting to know how, Lesley slid his hand over his pocket to find a small bulge where there hadn't been one before.

"It contains compromising pictures of a young *lady*—she's questionable in age." Blakely looked back out onto the street and flicked his remaining cigarette over the ledge, no care to the people below. "They were taken at two locations and added between April and July of this year—"

Inside the pocket, Lesley's fingers recognized the item as a flash drive, and he knew he shouldn't be holding it. "How did you get this?"

Blakely turned around and relaxed his back along the rail. "Don't worry, I didn't steal anything. I'm *borrowing* it for you."

"Well, I don't want it." Lesley tried to hand it back, but Blakely held up a hand.

"Because I need to bum a *light*, Old Man." There was a tired plea in his voice. "I need to bum a light, and you're the only one I know who isn't balls-deep in this shit right now." Blakely's arms and hands conducted the movement of his words. "You never gave up on that kid. Your instincts were spot on, and you got *close*, so close that they took you off the case, gave you a long weekend, and will be booting you out of the neighborhood come Monday." There was a long pause, and Lesley could tell Blakely was choosing his words carefully. "The bureau wants you out because you're getting in the way."

"But in the way of what?"

"Bigger fish." People could be heard entering the station, and Blakely spoke quickly. "There's a connection . . ." Voices could be heard coming up the stairs of the northbound platform, and Blakely flipped his hood up over his hat. "I'm gonna go grab that beer." He was headed down the stairs before anyone reached the top.

The Probability of Collisions

Outside the Armitage station where she worked and the few blocks surrounding her family home in West Lawn, Georgia Russell was accustomed to the anonymity of a city that held nearly three million other people. She didn't have to worry about running into the lady from church if she shopped in Hyde Park. Nor was there ever a concern that the store clerk would stumble upon her getting her nails done in the Ukrainian Village after work.

The density of the population made keeping up a very fine-tuned set of appearances possible and easy to maintain. As a young adult, she'd learned that crying in public spaces, where she lacked a sense of belonging or community, felt safer. There was no privacy for her to lose or reason to care. No one would stop and ask if she was okay, offer to get help, or bring it up the next time she saw them. Unfamiliar people, in unfamiliar places acting against the social norm went ignored.

This had been a source of comfort for Georgia almost her entire life. Worlds didn't collide or overlap. She could stand on the Polk platform just a few blocks removed from the worst news of her life and cry undisturbed. Everyone there assumed why she was crying. She was sick, someone she loved was sick. Everyone was dying, so no one needed to act.

But Georgia also knew something else: even in a city containing eleven thousand people per square mile, God had a plan—whether she liked it or not. And on this day, his plan seemed to consist of inviting the familiar into a space where familiarity meant something else.

The blue coat of her friend caused the smile she wore Monday through Friday to instinctively reveal itself. A face could not match feelings when the script was broken. She straightened her wig, quickly wiped her eyes, and transferred the black of her makeup from her hands to her pants before raising her hand to signal her presence, "M! Mrs. Monroe!" She thought it better to expose herself because "Georgia" would never miss a friend. "Good Lord, what are you doing all the way out here?" They came together for a hug, and she felt the faintest slipping of her wig's cap across her scalp. "It's too cold for exploring."

M laughed and adjusted her cap with one hand while the other lifted a large flat black bag. "I had a preview meeting today." She cast a childish grin. "I'm totally not their girl, but I thought I'd try anyway."

"What are they after? Of course you're their girl." There was a relief Georgia initially ascribed to being forced to pretend things were normal and fine. But as she watched M's eyes, hands, and mouth, all alive with expression and vulnerability, she knew God was at work.

"I actually have no experience painting murals," she laughed and rocked back onto her heels. "I also have no relationship with cancer but . . . I'm pretty good without that." She shrugged. "It would just be nice to do something meaningful *and* make money—which is horrible and makes me a terrible person—"

"You're not a terrible person." Georgia gave her arm a motherly squeeze. "Money pays the bills, unfortunately." She knew too well. "Damned as it may be."

"I don't want to be wasting my time, Georgia." There was a tone in her voice, a tone that said what she really feared was wasting her life, not her time, and Georgia could relate.

"You just gotta hold on." A westbound train pulled in and a sea of people rushed into their own lives, moments where they knew every second counted. "You just gotta hold on and know the good Lord is always working."

The train left an empty platform, and M seemed to put their unfamiliar location into context. "What about you? What are you doing here? Are you okay?"

Georgia knew her face. They'd been learning one another for almost seven years. They'd exchanged Christmas gifts and cookies. They'd stood under the heat lamps of the station and lamented the polar vortex. They'd shared drink recipes and barbecue techniques, bemoaned the humidity of the summer months, discussed weekend plans, shared their opinions of the public school system, God, and the city's staggering crime rates.

185

Georgia knew M, and knew she needed to try out the words on some-one other than her husband or children, but the words just weren't ripe enough yet. "Oh, I'm just fine, love. Don't you worry about me."

M's eyes wandered the edges of her face, examined her hairline. "I feel like that might not be the truth." There was a slight slant in her brow. "But I'll believe you if you tell me again."

It was either a dare for her to lie, or a chance to offer the truth. "I just like to ride these newfangled Pink Line trains every now and again." All the things she'd come to use as a disguise—wigs, false eyelashes, heavy layers of makeup, and fake nails—suddenly felt like beacons calling at-tention to, and away from, the one thing she didn't want to say. "I used to come here with my momma when she was sick." Looking at M, "The trains weren't so good then."

Their platform was filling with young interns, seasoned profession-als, and those she recognized from waiting rooms and acts of urban in-attention. Her train would be arriving soon, and she wasn't ready to step back into the pulsing city. M reached out and took her hand, knowing without being told, and opened the door to the confessional Georgia had been trying to avoid.

What she'd wanted had so rarely mattered that she'd come to want very little in life. "I don't want my children to know and change their lives." It was that simple. "I don't want my husband watching me with sad eyes." Maybe her wants were selfish. "I don't want people standing by, just waiting for me to die." Georgia didn't want to hurt anyone with the truth. "All I've ever wanted is for things to just keep moving." And this truth would change everything. "I don't understand why we can't just keep happening until the good Lord calls us home." The obligation of death was one of the hardest things to reconcile. "When you're dying, living becomes very different. For everyone." Her words, as quiet as her tears, needed to come out. "I'm gonna die, M. I'm gonna die, and I'm not ready for everything to change yet."

M blinked and freed her tears; they landed with a knock on the plat-form. "How long do you have?"

Georgia didn't need to consider the question. "Six months?"

M's tears continued to fall even as she rolled back her shoulders and nodded in acknowledgement. "Okay."

"I'll get the summer." Turning her face up toward the heat lamp, Georgia smiled. "I'll get to feel the sun on my face."

Squeezing Georgia's hand, M adjusted her body toward the pretend sun. "Sounds like a plan. I'll bring the beer." The irreverence and frankness made Georgia laugh. "But in this moment, I think we should eat." She looked at Georgia. "I'm starving. Are you starving?"

The question called attention to her body, and it was strange to hear its response. "I am, actually."

M's smile widened as the train quietly slipped into the station. Its doors slid open without catching, or jerking, or sputtering. "Well, then, let's go get some lunch."

Elementary Particles

Self-sabotage. That's what this has always been about. Ruining every-thing before anyone or anything else can.

Donovan boarded the Brown Line at Montrose and rode it to Kimball.

You know how it looks. How you *look.*

A sandwich shop in a small strip mall directly across from the station allowed him the perfect place to sit and watch people come and go.

How long are you going to sit here?

Red hair in the sea of browns and blacks would be easy to spot.

What will you do when you see her?

He waited, eyes trained out the window, imagined seeing her up close where he could touch her, grab her, stop her from walking away, stop her from pretending that *Being There* meant nothing.

"I'm sorry, you must leave now, you cannot sit here anymore. Manager said."

A young man dressed in the yellow and green of the restaurant's branding lifted Donovan's cold cup of coffee from the table and began to wipe the table down.

"I'll take a cup of soup then. Can I get a cup of soup?" Fumbling for his wallet, he found cash and held it out in his shaking hand. "I'm waiting for a friend."

"Your friend is not coming. You need to go." The server's words were emphasized by the fact that he threw the coffee into the trash.

"I'll leave after the soup, just . . . let me get some soup first."

In order to show his innocence, Donovan held out some cash and looked in the direction of the manager, waiting for a nod of concession. "What kind?" he asked.

"It doesn't matter."

Donovan's eyes scrambled back toward the Kimball station.

Two hours staring out the window, and you think you missed her in the last thirty seconds?

He felt the money being snatched from his hand.

She's not here.

"You leave with the soup."

A car pulled into the space just outside the window and the instant glare of its windshield was blinding. "Fuck you." It didn't matter that the obscenity had been muttered under Donovan's breath and directed at the car. That obscenity seemed to be the last straw for the man in yellow and green because he tossed a to-go container down onto the table and ordered him to leave.

All Donovan could see were black and green spots when he reopened his eyes. "I just want to eat my soup. Let me eat my soup."

"Two hours too long. Manager said." He pointed at the door.

Donovan pushed back his chair and slowly stood up. The scraping of the metal legs across the concrete floor screeched through the four walls of the restaurant with a bone-cracking density that made his jaw clench.

"Don't forget your soup." Donovan didn't want the soup. It was never about the soup, and they both understood that. But the manager stepped out from behind the counter and the raised container was pressed into Donovan's chest."You take the soup."

"I don't want the soup, okay?" As he pushed it away, the lid popped off and spilled its thick contents onto the server's shirt and down onto the floor.

"You get out!" The manager approached in a fury of beady eyes and swinging fists. "You get out and don't come back!"

The door snapped open, and Donovan stepped out apologetically, but when the door began to swing slowly shut Donovan thought he saw blue reflected in its glass.

Eyes darting back and forth across the street, trying to find the color, trying to spot red, forgetting all that had transpired in a frenzied need to get across and stop her.

The slight ripping sound of his wallet getting caught on his pocket, the ding-donging of the doors, the beep of his card being registered at the CTA turnstile. They all seemed to happen at once.

"Doors closing."

Donovan spun away, flinging his wallet and card across the pavement. Eyes and bodies stopped. Took note. Brought him to his senses.

He held up both hands, palms facing outward at his waist to show he was harmless before he moved to pick them up.

It wasn't until he found himself aboard a train that he realized the blue he'd seen wasn't Emily. All the elbows and knees expressed the warmth of the world around him. Summer was almost there. Summer meant no more blue coats. Summer meant no more possibilities of morning train rides.

You were never meant to see her. Remember?

Donovan felt a woeful disconnectedness from those around him. The exposed skin of people laughing, headed to buy beer and steaks and hotdogs. His family would be barbecuing that day. Friends would be over. Jimmy would be there. People would ask questions. Phone calls and texts would be sent seeking more information, wanting to know what happened, wondering why he left.

His mother had tried not to cry when he said goodbye to her. She stood in the kitchen, same pink bathrobe she'd always worn, pouring her first cup of coffee. "Maybe I should come with you."

"Mom—"

"Or Jay, maybe Jay could come—"

"Mom—"

"Just for a few days. Just until you're feeling better." He hugged her because he needed to be held, but he also knew it would shut her up. "I love you so much, Donovan."

"I love you too, Ma."

He changed into his running clothes and tried to do the right thing. He couldn't stand to be anywhere. No location was safe for long. Stillness brought thoughts that made him act irrationally. *Pa-tat, pa-tat, pa-tat, pa-tat, pa-tat, pa-tat, pa-tat, pa-tat, pa-tat, pa-tat, pa-tat, pa-tat, pa-tat, pa-tat, pa-tat.* His usual route was blocked off for a Memorial Day event, pushing him south down unfamiliar streets with uneven sidewalks. *Pa-tat, pa-tat, pa-tat, pa-tat, pa-tat, pa-tat, pa-tat, pa-tat, pa-tat, pa-tat, pa-tat, pa-tat, pa-tat, pa-tat, pa-tat.* Every few blocks he found himself turning up the music playing in his ears, drowning out everything else. *Pa-tat, pa-tat, pa-tat, pa-tat, pa-tat, pa-tat, pa-tat, pa-tat, pa-tat, pa-tat, pa-tat, pa-tat, pa-tat, pa-tat, pa-tat.* His heel came down on a slanted edge, rolling his ankle, bending his toes up and back before his shin made excruciating contact with a cement curb. The smack of the concrete. The ripping of skin. His hands grabbed at sticky bits of flesh, feeling for the protruding bone that would account for the pain.

It felt like a misshapen dream when Lily's face materialized over his. Her lips moved as she looked down at him, lying on his back. He couldn't believe or begin to comprehend the amount of work the universe had to have put in to make him this miserable.

She pulled his earbud out, exposing him to the sounds of the world and her repeated question. "Are you okay?"

What will you do now?

Her long black hair dangled between them, drew attention to the romper hanging away from her body and exposing her bralessness.

Now that you can't run.

The pain radiated up to his knee, his heartbeat pounding in everything below his ankle.

"Let me grab my mom's car." She stood up and looked around. Tried to keep her hair from blowing into her mouth. "Do you think you need to go to the hospital?"

All Donovan could think was, "What are you doing here?"

Pulling the remaining earbud out, he closed his eyes and concentrated on the sounds around him. Cars passing, the hydraulic brakes of a bus, and music. There was music passing by, coming and going, sending mixed messages. He wanted to push past it all, hear the birds, the tapping of a squirrel's feet, the screaming of the cicadas.

They haven't been born yet.

"I live right around the corner." Lily pointed when he opened an eye, and he couldn't understand the lack of cicadas. He felt like they should be there. Screaming. But all he could hear in the distance was the ringing bell of an ice-cream vendor.

This has already happened.

Lily, tucking her hair behind her ears, said, "Just wait here. I'm going to run home and grab the car."

What will you do now?

She stood, turning away, glancing back, shading her eyes from the sun, "I'll be right back."

You can't run.

The garage door began sliding open the instant the tires hit the driveway. The tidiness of the garage caught him off guard: clean concrete, white ceilings and walls, nothing stored. Its purity was so foreign that he felt immediately diseased and drawn to the car's interior. Tan leather, not a mark or smudge present on the dash. The spotless floor mat now tainted by a few drops of his blood.

"I'm sorry I—"

"Don't worry about it." She eyed the mat before quickly getting out. "I'll take care of it." When his door opened, she bent over and her fingers touched places never felt before. "I thought it was just your shin." Keeping her eyes on his injury, she rose, the romper returning to its rightful place over her chest. "Maybe we should take you to the hospital? It could be broken."

"It's not."

Her eyes met his with uncertainty.

She's afraid of all the wrong things.

"Do you think you need stitches?"

His "no" was directed at many things. "I have some butterfly bandages at home."

"We have some here—"

"And I'm going to need my ankle wrap."

"I can do that too."

He wished he had run anywhere else.

"I should go." Taking hold of his legs, Lily began to lift them up and out the door, forcing Donovan to either move his body or bear the pain. "Really, I should just get home. I can take care of it there."

"Don't be silly." She knelt before him and he had to look away. "We do need to get your shoes off before we go inside though." He could feel her struggling to undo his shoelace. "What are you, some sort of professional knot-maker?" His eyes were drawn in the direction of her laugh, and he wished he'd paid more attention, wished he would have known he was running toward her and not away. "How did you manage this?" Only a single door separated him from the space where she lived and showered and did homework. He felt trapped by events outside of his control and believed the universe meant to prove he was nothing. That what he wanted meant nothing.

One shoe off.

"Is anyone home?"

She shook her head. "My dad had a conference and my mom went with him."

He needed to look away, to think of anything other than her kneeling in front of him. "What do they do again?"

"My dad's a psychiatrist and my mom cleans house. Not other peoples' houses, just our house. She has OCD, remember?" Cupping his ankle in the palm of her hand, she delicately slid off his second shoe. "She's deaf and she has OCD."

He tried to sound sympathetic and hoped she wouldn't look at him. "Yeah, yeah, of course. It's just easy to forget when you're so . . . "

"Normal?"

The word "normal" made him need to look at her. It wasn't a word he would have ever used to describe Lily and he was surprised that she'd chosen it for herself. "On top of things. Ahead of the game even."

His words left her lips curled into a tight smile that said, You have no idea.

You can't run.

"We'll need to use my bathroom. My mom's not allowed in there, so it won't matter if there's blood." The door opened and exposed the house's hotel-like structure. Wide, open, decorated out of necessity and function rather than aesthetic comfort or pleasure. There were no signs of life present within the home as they passed through. No pictures on the walls, no paper of any kind lying around, no plants, no smudges on the wood floor, no throw pillows to clutter the furniture. Nothing that expressed warmth or hospitality, just bright, natural light pouring in from giant windows that could easily expose any flaw.

The space had him reconsidering Lily, all the times she'd waited for him, all the prep periods she'd intruded upon. All the things she'd said that he'd only pretended to hear. The silence of her life. He'd had no idea. Maybe everyone was meant to hate their childhood.

No.

"And here we are."

She stopped outside a threshold. Looking at him, flustering him, making his words feel clumsy before they could leave his mouth. "I should have had coffee with you. When you asked," he apologized.

No.

Seeing her beginning, he felt he understood. "Everyone needs a friend, right?" His thoughts turned to Sara and how she'd said the same to him. "So let's do that before you leave for college."

Her smile said, Thank you, while her lips said, "I don't need you to feel sorry for me, Mr. James."

"I don't. It's not—" But then the bedroom door fell open and another dimension of Lily came into view.

Her walls were painted pink, not a soft or bright pink, but a hard-plastic, Barbie-car pink with flowing curtains around her windows and carelessly hung prints by famous painters tacked to her walls.

Her bed was a mess of white linen, with a rainbow of Christmas lights hanging from the ceiling above. Books and stacks of paper were mixed with toys she'd probably outgrown a decade earlier, a strange museum of her past. A parade of ghosts. Every age of her existence watching them enter her bathroom.

"Sorry." She flipped on the light. "I wasn't expecting company."

Donovan couldn't imagine a time or circumstance where company would have been allowed or felt welcome in this home. But he stood and looked at the makeup littering the counter where black cords attached to items that rested upon the debris like ships in a sea of colored plastic.

"Here," there was a faux fur cover on the toilet's lid, "have a seat." The fur tickled the backs of his thighs as he began to sit, and Lily turned to wrap her hair up into a bun, turn on the faucet, wash her hands, wet a wash rag.

The heartbeat in his ankle became a deep throbbing pain. She stepped closer, leaned in, and reached up toward a shelf behind him.

The fabric of her romper grazed his face, and he could smell the warmth of her skin wafting through the thin material separating her flesh from his. It didn't matter that he tried not to, would have *preferred* not to.

"Here we go." She used a basket of medical supplies to push back the sea of plastic on her counter, then kneeled before him for the third time in under twenty minutes. "Let me know if it hurts."

Does it hurt, Donovan? Being here with her?

The warm wet of the wash rag made contact with his shin, and he could feel it pulling at the dried blood trapped in his leg hairs.

"Did you like your gift?" She didn't look at him.

He felt conflicted about lying but assumed that sparing her feelings was best. "I did. Thank you." He had yet to open the flash drive and explore its contents. He didn't care for the music of teenaged girls. Not even when he was a teenager.

"Good." The cloth on his leg stopped moving as she looked up at him. "I could give you more." He smiled a smile of reassurance and she flushed. "If you want." She rose, rinsed the rag.

"That would be great."

She returned to her kneeling position, this time placing her thighs on either side of his left foot, with his toes dangerously close to their intersection. She held a tube of salve and worked it with her fingers, pressing and rubbing before removing the cap, sliding her thumb up toward its tip, collecting the cloudy thick gel that shot out across her fingertips. "Do you want to rub it, or should I?" Her smile was more seductive than he'd expected.

He'd gotten it wrong. "I think I should call a cab," heart now pounding in his ears, making his words sound quiet in his head. "I need to get home."

"Does it hurt?" Her pursed lips blew across his wound, one hand holding the back of his calf while the other lightly anointed the gash in his shin. "I'll be gentle."

His height accentuated his ability to see the space left open by her falling neckline and he tried to look away, but her kneading and blowing and rubbing kept drawing his attention back to her.

Do you like it? Being alone here with her?

She wiped her fingers on the rag and pulled a package of bandages from the basket, her eyes watching him as she freed tiny butterflies from their wrapping. "I'll grab you my phone in just a second." Her thumbs slid up the sole of his foot with pressure enough to keep it from tickling before she released him and stood up. "It's okay," she said.

Donovan closed his eyes, thankful that she was standing, thankful she was no longer touching him.

You can't run.

He needed space, and clarity, and a cab.

What will you do now that you can't run?

A light sound opened his eyes. Romper at the floor by her feet, bare breasts staring at him with dark brown-tinted points. She stepped closer, took his hand and brought it to her chest. "Maybe this will help."

She's afraid of all the wrong things.

The tip of her nipple, naked and rubbing, caused thoughts he needed escape from. "Lily. . ." She brought her mouth to his and the animal within pushed her away. Brutally. Vehemently. Dangerously.

There was the thud of her head hitting the wall, and the yelp she emitted —like a dog who'd been stepped on.

Donovan closed his eyes and saw Emily standing on the path, stepping into the brush, falling to the ground. "She would have never forgiven me for that flash drive. She would have thought I was someone I wasn't." It was true in the way all words could be true.

"And who was that?" the detective asked.

"A creep."

Say it.

"A potential pedophile." Donovan looked the detective in the eye. "Lily was eighteen—"

"Miss Ziyad was fairly graphic in her details." Hands reaching for papers, fingers flipping to pages. "It's all right here—"

Donovan spread his legs and motioned to the space she had inhabited. "She stood here. I scooted her out of the way," again he motioned, "and then I left."

"She was naked, you became violent—"

Donovan knew not to speak. He knew what she had said. But as he looked at the satisfaction dripping from the detective's smile, he smiled back and spoke anyway. "And thanks to Sara, no one believes her."

A newspaper was raised. "Your relationships teetered on the edge of something predatory, made you look sick whether they're printed here or not—"

"I wasn't sick; I was never sick."

You are sick.

"What happened after Emily found the flash drive?" Donovan had grown tired of having the same button pushed over and over again, and when he failed to answer the detective pushed on. "You said Lily took your key and that's how the pictures happened. So why not admit it was yours? Tell the truth. Clear Emily's name."

The answer wasn't that easy. "Sometimes you need people to see the you that isn't inflated or contaminated by something else."

"That's not seeing, Donovan. You can't isolate moments and say they're who you are. It just doesn't work that way."

"You have pictures on a flash drive, you're a sexual predator," Donovan replied. "You have a coat in your bed, you're a creep. Some paintings go missing, you're a thief. You save someone, you're a hero. You kill someone, you're a murderer." He pointed to the stack of newspapers, "You make a living out of isolating moments and saying that's who someone is."

The detective's smile said, And I know who *you* are, Donovan James, while his mouth said, "Touché."

Interference

By the time Lesley got home, Deb was asleep in bed. He paced the dark apartment in sock feet, phone in one hand, notebook in the other, carefully sidestepping the creaks in the floor he knew existed until he worked up enough desperation to view the images on the flash drive. Once that desperation was found, the computer refused to cooperate, it needed updating, and a restart, and Lesley once again found himself pacing, watching the progress bars, chewing on his thumb nails, wondering if this was a sign not to take his indiscretions any further than they'd already gone.

He removed himself from the room, entered the kitchen in search of food he'd yet to eat and found the cheese and cold-cuts he'd had for dinner two nights ago still sitting on the counter. Normally, Deb would have cleaned it up; it would have been something he never had to remember that he failed to take care of. Now, it sat on their counter dried out and waxy. Ruined. Unsalvageable.

Pulling the bin out from under the sink, he scooped the food into the trash and, appetite lost, returned to his computer and waited.

There were only two kinds of files on the flash drive, mp3 and JPG. The music files appeared to be just that, but he started there in case they were meant to be significant and sat through ninety minutes of music, incongruous to his mood, before turning his attention to the photographs. His nervousness over what would be found in the JPG files quickly veered toward sickness once he began to go through them. A girl with long black hair in varying poses of undress. Blakely was right, her age was questionable; some of photos were taken with a childishly pink background with stuffed animals behind her; others in a different location, one with white sheets, a navy comforter, and a blue coat. None of the details meant anything to him. What he saw was potentially child pornography, and someone didn't want it to be found.

At 5 a.m. he heard Deb's alarm go off and waited for her to finish her shower before he attempted a conversation. Lesley needed to get downtown in order to keep the promise he'd made to Emily Monroe's friend. "I thought we could ride in this morning."

Deb was busy, gathering her things, not revealing her expression. "I have a meeting I have to set up for."

"We could still ride together." He hadn't slept and still wore his clothes from the day before, but he needed her to know it wasn't too late. He'd make a change. Things were going to be different.

"Have you seen yourself, Lesley? Look, I don't have time for this. We can talk later."

But she did have time. Lesley watched Deb enter the train four cars up from where he stood once he'd gathered his things and allowed his feet to carry him through the morning heat, up the stairs and onto the platform of the closest transit stop. She had time. She just didn't want to waste it with him.

It was a feeling that sat with him while his mind remained lost in thoughts over truth, and words, and actions, and Deb. The boy, he'd been told, never left Albany Park. Never took the train downtown, never saw Sears Tower or the river dyed green. Never ate a Chicago-style hotdog or tasted a Pequod's pizza. His life had consisted of the blocks between Lawrence and Argyle, Bernard to Avers. That's what he'd been told. That's what he'd believed.

"Did you ever take him to the lake for a swim?" he'd asked.

"I never had the time."

But time was a resource people used in the wrong way and didn't understand until it was too late.

At Adams and Wabash, Lesley descended the stairs to the sound of street musicians drumming on overturned buckets. Traffic halted, horns honked, a stream of passengers crossed the street, and the train rattled the rails above them. Downtown was an assault to the senses, a discord of sights, sounds, and smells that made it hard to be present with death when so much life continued happening.

Eric Sullivan stood under the round lit bulbs of the hotel's overhang where shoppers passed by with bags and smiles and conversations untouched by the tragedy he was experiencing. It was easy to recognize him; his full head of red hair and burly beard were almost as out of place as the Patagonia-brand clothes he wore.

"Detective Powell." Lesley shook the man's hand and handed him the ledger. "Do you have time for a coffee?" Nodding, the man followed him to an outdoor café where they waited in silence until they were seated at a table. "I'm incredibly sorry for your loss, Mr. Sullivan."

Removing his glasses, the father tried to clean the tear smudges his thick lashes had left behind. "No one is telling us anything." He smelled clean, fresh from a shower, just how his daughter had smelled when Lesley met her. "I don't understand what happened. She's all I had left—I can't imagine my life without her." His words passed away, and his glasses remained off. "What did she look like the last time you saw her?" The hope in the question chilled Lesley's insides as he pictured Emily on her back porch. "Do you remember what she was wearing? What did she say? Was she afraid?"

Lesley shook his head. "Not afraid, no. Sad, but not afraid."

"And what was she wearing?"

It seemed a macabre endeavor to describe her, but grief doesn't care, it only wants what it wants. Right then, it wanted every detail of her alive and painted for Eric Sullivan to see. "She was wearing a linen dress," Lesley's hands moved with his words, "grayish purple." He watched the father's head nod as if he knew the dress he spoke of. "Some canvas shoes—"

"Toms, she loved her Toms."

"And her hair was pulled back in a low ponytail, or maybe it was a braid?" That detail, he remembered the wisps, the bits of hair that fell out of place, "I think it was braided."

Her father pulled a photo from his pocket and set it on the table between them. "This is my favorite picture of her."

Lesley moved the photo closer and felt the acid rise in his stomach. She'd been caught mid-laugh, her smile was wide, her mouth partially open, and her pale skin, freckled and clear of any makeup, radiated a joy Lesley hadn't seen her express.

All of that was well and good. "It's beautiful." But her red hair came down from beneath a yellow stocking cap, catching flakes of snow in its long strands, and rested across a blue coat Lesley knew he'd seen just hours before. "Is this her coat?"

The father leaned in, peered at the photo, and Lesley knew Eric didn't need to check the coat to answer, he simply wanted to see his daughter.

"We bought it last year, after Christmas." A soft smile with sad eyes. "She was just so beautiful, you know?" He slowly sat up, hands wiping his face. "Such a beautiful soul."

Lesley tried to hand the photo back, but Eric shook his head. "I would like you to keep it," he said. "I want you to see her like that." His head nodded in agreement with his words while his hands began searching the pockets of his pants. Lesley was hesitant to tuck another dead child away with the frayed edges of someone else's. "Do you know where the blue coat is now?"

Eric looked confused. "We thought it was at the cleaners."

"Do you know if she would have loaned it to someone? A friend maybe? A young girl?" Lesley had only been to the artist's house twice, but he knew that the photos of the young girl couldn't have been taken there. The architecture didn't match. The photos of the girl showed modern design features and paint colors incongruent with the Monroes' home.

"She would have given it to anyone if she thought it would make someone happy." Eric Sullivan's confusion shifted. "I had no idea anything was happening outside of Jack." His hands sat firmly on the table. "If there's something more you can tell me . . ." Lesley shook his head. "If you think he had anything to do with this . . ." Eric placed his glasses back on his face and really looked at Lesley for the first time. "She wanted to help in any way she could."

"The cat?"

Lesley looked at the man and tried to understand what he was saying. But Eric Sullivan shook his head and his eyes couldn't contain his tears. "The cat was named after him."

"After who?"

"The deaf man, *Jack*." He wiped his eyes. "It worried me, how upset M told me he got sometimes—I didn't care what the girl told her, it still worried me."

"What girl?" Lesley withdrew his phone, wishing he had a picture of the girl's face as he pulled up photos of Emily's paintings.

"The girl who helped teach the ASL classes. Lily. I think her name was Lily." Some pieces came together. Others drifted away.

"Is this Jack?" Lesley pointed to the recurring male who appeared in the paintings. "Is this Jack?"

"I wouldn't know." Eric shook his head. "I never met him. I don't know what he looks like."

Running

"There's actually a building opening up on Willow." Vicenta, St. Jose-maria's librarian, talked with her mouth full because she knew her time with M was limited. "I just talked to my sister about it this morning. She's going to call and see if they're interested in walking through this afternoon."

"That's great, thank you—I really appreciate your help."

Vicenta hadn't done anything except tell her sister what was needed, "It's really generous of you to do what you're doing."

"Yeah, well, the money has to go somewhere, and their current build-ing sucks."

"It's still generous." Conversations about the money Papachristi had given her for the painting made M uneasy from the start, so Vicenta steered the conversation back to where things were comfortable. "How are the ASL classes coming along?"

"Meh," she laughed and pushed her salad around with a fork. "I thought Jack tried to ask me for my coat today, so they could be going better."

"Maybe he did. It's a good coat."

They both laughed, and M checked the time before leaning back in her chair. "It will be interesting to see what happens when Lily leaves for college next fall. Hopefully I'll know what I'm doing by then—her mother never speaks."

"You'll get there." What motivated the art teacher to become involved in the Chicago Hearing Society had never come up, but Vicenta believed in the virtue behind the undertaking, despite the bad name that "charity" had acquired of late. "Can I ask you something?" M looked at her, nei-ther granting permission nor blocking it, but clearly understanding what would come next. "I know we haven't talked about it, and I respect that. But maybe if you stuck up for yourself—"

"It's not about me, Vicenta. People want to make it about me, so they don't have to look at the real problem—"

"But if you just . . ."

M shook her head and began collecting her lunch items. "I don't need to defend myself. I'm not going to let them chase me out of here as long as that man is still walking around receiving awards."

The library door opened, and Vicenta's heart sank. The principal walked in and rested her eyes on M. "Just who I was hoping to find—I need to speak to you before this afternoon's assembly."

M smiled at Vicenta. "Thank you for the company." She turned to the principal. "Let me drop my stuff off downstairs and I'll meet you in your office."

"Of course." She waited for M to leave the room before turning to Vicenta. "It would probably be wise of you to avoid your little luncheons with Mrs. Monroe. You don't want to give people the wrong idea." Vicenta stood in penitent silence. "I shouldn't think I'd need to remind you of the scholarships and student activities Nicodemus makes possible to those who couldn't normally afford such things. Your children have received a generous education because of people like him." Vicenta wanted to look away, toward the church, find her strength. "It's important to our school, as well as our spiritual community, that Nicodemus's good name and reputation remain intact. Father Michael will look graciously on your support, regardless of how things work out."

"I'm afraid I don't understand."

"There is a time to keep quiet, and a time to defend. Right now, the church and the school need your defense." It was short, it was sweet, and it was to the point. "Do we understand one another, Mrs. Alzira?"

"Yes, ma'am."

"I'll be sure and let Father Michael know the church has your support." As quickly as she entered, she left again.

Vicenta stood in the silence of the library and prayed.

The Uninvited Absurd

It was seventy-nine degrees by 6 a.m. on the last day for C-track schools. Donovan stood with his eyes closed on the bubbled blue portion of the platform, the bubbles there to remind him that if he should collapse, he could land on the dreaded third rail and perish like an insect in a bug zapper. He felt that calling. The breeze could simply topple him. An accident.

The screaming horn of the approaching train warned him to step back. Eyes closed, both hands holding the strap of his messenger bag like a parachute, he waited to feel the vacuum of air as the train pulled in. A vacuum to suck him out, toward the metal.

It will be quick.

Horn piercing. Platform rumbling. Blue bubbles bursting. The whirl came and sucked him forward as a grab at his elbow jerked him back.

"Hey, man, step the fuck back." A kid, at least double Donovan's size, dressed in his Marine fatigues, ready to go to war and not understanding that a war was right there, happening now. "You're gonna get your ass killed if you keep doing shit like that." He pushed Donovan onto the train.

You're going to have to tell them you broke up.

Anna Karenina's head landed between two train cars.

Jimmy will be here for the Fourth.

How fast was the train going?

Jay's coming for the World Cup final.

What was her sense of time?

And your parents—

Shut up.

The sun was already illuminating the world around them, spotlighting some familiars who looked at him as if he'd already passed.

They'll disappear. By the end of summer, at least one of them won't exist.

You'll assume they've fallen into a different routine, found a different transit option.

Different familiars will mark timeliness.

"Donovan."

You'd never know if death and a decomposing body forced their absence.

"Hey, Donovan."

The train doors opened at Paulina and a woman who was not Emily boarded.

Oh, she's familiar.

Her hair was blonde by bottle, and the bottle had been an expensive one.

Do you remember that woman, Donovan?

She wore a wrap dress of black and white with heels that looked fairly lethal.

Your dad introduced you to her at the Christmas party. Remember?

Her painted red lips smiled at him as she effortlessly pulled a wheeled tote behind her.

"Donovan?"

He didn't want to turn toward voices.

She had red lips then too.

Women like that made his dick limp.

And those black heels. Do you remember her heels?

The symbol of his impotence forced him to exit the train at Southport to wait.

And you wonder why your dad thinks you're gay.

"Donovan!"

It was a test, and you failed.

The air was muddy.

"Stop!" Another grab at his elbow. A bit of hair had flown into her mouth and she struggled to set it free with full hands. He was surprised to feel the reality of her cheek against his hand as it moved to brush her hair away. "I've been calling for you." Out of breath, another blue-green dress, weighed down by bags and holding a large brimmed hat in her hand.

Emily, standing in front of him. Real.

Four weeks of imagining the grab it would take to prevent her from leaving allowed his hand to slip around the back of her neck and squeeze just a little tighter than appropriate.

You're not going to fail this time.

I know.

"Donovan."

Kiss her.

"Please don't." He was close, she wasn't afraid, he squeezed a little tighter and her head turned away. "Don't make me regret this."

Their feet remained on the bubbled blue portion of the platform.

Resting the hat she had given him for ransom on his lap, he opened the computer and loaded the St. Josemaría School website. Images of the school's interior cycled through, and he pictured her there, in those rooms, in that dress, working with those kids.

Dear Emily,

I need to see you again.

Donovan

The bell rang, and the first of his final classes of the year began to enter.

"Morning, Mr. J."

Her response would not be instant.

Five hours later, he sat with his fellow teachers and wondered what time Emily would be free to meet. Brief messages between classes had fed his morning, but by the end of fourth period all correspondence had ceased.

"Are you with us, Mr. James?" Everyone in the room was staring at him. "You're ready to be moved to 305 by Tuesday?"

A vague acknowledgment allowed him to retrace the conversations that had been taking place around him for months. The closing of schools, the shuffling of five thousand uprooted students. How efficiency experts concluded that extra staff wasn't necessary, and that the remaining teachers simply needed different classroom designs and more effectual use of wall space.

Wall space.

"My mom's bringing church kids down this weekend to help get stuff moved. She told them it's an act of service."

"Room 305 isn't going to accommodate your roundtable approach, but I'm sure you'll make the best of it."

What will you do with your wall space?

An email notification came through on his phone, and his thoughts were thrown back to Emily, what she would say next, when he could see her, how much of her she'd let him hold, or see, or touch without kissing. A tightness that had been coming and going all day grew.

He pulled out his phone and read the message.

Dear Donovan,
    No one else uses my name.
    I like that you do.
    Something came up and I won't be able to see you today.
    But I will see you soon.
Your friend,
    E m i l y

He read the message several times. The first lines begged things of him while the last felt like the vacuum of a passing train pulling him in, zapping him into nonexistence.

Your friend

Like black stilettos and red lipstick to his groin.

You are not friends. You have never been friends.

The afternoon sun was hot. He removed his jacket, rolled up his sleeves, and moved into the shade near the stairs. It didn't matter if he looked ridiculous holding the large brimmed hat. Trapped inside it was her scent, a scent he would take home and lie with in his bed.

"I'm surprised you didn't wear a hat—you always have a hat." The blonde man-bun caught his attention before he spotted the blue-green of her dress.

"I told you, I was late." She was flushed from heat and weighed down by flowers and gift bags while her Adonis carried her normal accoutrements.

"I'll rub some aloe on you when we get home." They reached the top of the stairs.

A discernible unease enveloped her face when she saw Donovan standing there in the shade. She didn't allow the expression to last and quickly smiled a smile that wasn't secret, though it was unknown.

To Donovan's surprise and discomfort, she stopped in front of him, pulling Adonis in his direction. "Alex, this is Donovan, we ride the train together sometimes." Her eyes begged for many things, but filling her void wasn't one of them. "Donovan, this is my husband, Alex."

"Nice to meet you, Donovan." His smile was wide and cheerful, as if it were actually nice to be standing there, in the heat, meeting the man who rode the train with his wife.

Sometimes.

Donovan gave a nod but refused to give anything more.

"We were just talking about hats." Her husband pointed to the one Donovan held. "That looks like a good one." Emily looked out around the people scattered across the platform, and he turned his words toward her. "Nice big brim," a joking poke of an elbow. "Something to keep you from becoming a lobster."

Her smile was weak, and Donovan wanted to punish her for bringing her husband into their equation. "You should probably take him up on that aloe," he said.

The third rail isn't close enough.

As he watched them head around the corner to where he and Emily used to wait, Donovan could hear blood pumping in his ears. She'd polluted the space, its memory, their morning, and a white-hot rage grew inside of him when she stepped onto the first car without looking back.

"Doors Closing."

Tan legs took the seat next to him. He looked and saw things he knew he shouldn't. She smiled, and her smile said, I know how this works. Lily pulled a book from her bag and pretended that he was no one.

"What are you doing? Why are you here?" They hadn't spoken or communicated since she stripped naked in her bathroom.

"I'm just riding the train."

And her innocence could no longer be assumed. "I don't have time for—"

"Nice hat." It was a joke, a tease, a familiar cruelty. "Holding it for a friend?"

He wanted to choke the jest out of her voice. Make her see that it wasn't a game. "I think you should move."

"Don't worry." She patted his thigh. "I am." The train arrived at Fullerton and her sudden absence left the smell of cosmetics and antiseptic behind.

Over the next couple of weeks, and still unable to run, Donovan began taking longer walks, wandering the Albany Park neighborhood, glancing in windows, tuning into voices, waiting to hear the screeching of cicadas like electricity screaming through the lines overhead. He walked alleys not yet baked in the summer sun and smelled the mixture of trash, laundromats, bakeries, and tamales being sold on street corners. He watched the kids playing cricket on the corner of Ainslie and Pulaski and saw a woman throw her husband's clothes out the window on Central Park. But he did not see Emily until the evening of June 30. A barbeque, a sudden blackening of the sky, lightning, rain, their table umbrella snapped in half by the wind. People ran squealing up the back stairs to what he assumed, and later verified, was her apartment. Adonis attempted to get the meat off the grill, and there she stood, holding a plate over her head. Laughing.

Jimmy called before nine-thirty. "I'm not going to be able to make it for the Fourth."

211

Donovan threw the ball he'd been tossing in the air toward the wall and hoped it would bounce back and break something big and important.

"Tilly's mom and dad are coming."

He wondered where he would go and what he would do with his suddenly free holiday.

"Jay and I are still coming for the World Cup."

"Yeah." A toss.

"Tell Emily I'll make it up to her then."

A miss.

"We look forward to it."

A shattering.

Donovan sat up to find the glass face of the clock behind him scattered across the floor.

Another gathering of people. This time a couple with a handful of kids Emily would pick up, whirl about, ruffle their hairs, tickle, and make faces at. They blew giant bubbles early in the day while the children squealed. They drank and listened to music that mashed against other songs playing from other yards, and Donovan had to watch her dance in order to discern which beat was theirs. He liked the way her body moved; she didn't take herself seriously, everything was play. The play of her hips, play of her bare feet, play of her arms swaying back and forth. It all filled him with a sort of ecstasy.

You need to move. Go get a drink before someone sees you, calls the cops, has you arrested.

He'd visited the market at the end of her alley a handful of times when he knew she wouldn't be there, but he didn't want to leave this moment.

Fine. Stay in the open. Be seen.

Outside the mosque parking lot, next to her building, he could stand and see the shaded kiddie pool between the brownstone building where she lived and its garage.

He watched her round the side of the building, turn on the hose, add fresh water to the pool where children splashed. In the shade she removed her hat, stepped in with the kids and held the stream of water over her arms, splashed her face, eyes closed, mouth open.

She wants you there, watching her up close.

Her every movement begged him to join.

Move closer. Let her see you.

Pressed against the fence, waiting, soaking it in, memorizing the nuances of her Being-in-the-world.

Call out to her.

She pushed the hair out of her face and her eyes opened in his direction.

Say her name.

Frozen by the sight of him.

Do it now.

Stepping out of the pool, she retrieved her hat and turned back into the yard where he could no longer see her, and he could no longer be seen.

The blue first caught his attention as he rounded the corner toward his house after too many drinks and in need of a distraction. The blue was long and flowing like Emily's arms had been while she danced in the sun. But this blue had tan shoulders curved from its top and a leg of equal color peeking out from a slit like someone eyeing the audience before the curtain was pulled. Anxious and expectant.

Pausing, he watched the three men standing around her, sizing her up, smiling, one hand holding a drink while the other remained close to their cocks—a subconscious maneuver Donovan had tried to avoid in the presence of attractive women but knew he sometimes failed at.

The blue was *her* blue. The lady in the blue coat before she was Emily and said the word *friend*. Twice. Both Emily and the color left him feeling less than innocent. He wanted to meet someone and take her home. He wanted to watch that blue fabric cling to her from behind and wondered if the thick gold belt around her waist was difficult to remove. He'd want to take it off and run his hands uninhibited over and under but not removed from the color. Emily's color.

Friend was a shitty word. If you're really friends, it doesn't need to be made explicit. If it needs to be made explicit, maybe you should just fuck and get it over with.

One of the men leaned in, saying something while he cupped the woman's tan arm. The thought of skin on skin fed Donovan's mind with images of what the men would do with her, given the chance.

Images removed from blue. And Emily. And everything decent.

He looked away and then back, wishing to be closer, removing the belt himself. Red hair. Pale skin. Emily would never wear that belt.

A tanned hand rose and tucked a bit of dark hair behind her ear with a familiarity that discomforted him. Brown nipples, pink walls, and white linen bedspread.

See the blue, flowing, peeking, touching. You could touch her. Taste her too. Smell where there aren't any powdered cosmetics or antiseptics. She might be clean, but she's not pure, Donovan. You know that.

He no longer felt lost in a sea of drink and potential distraction. He felt smothered in responsibility. She raised a plastic cup and drank its poison. They all had a good laugh when she attempted to look up at a bright purple explosion of light and toppled backward.

You know what they'll do if you leave her there.

Her leg falling all the way out of its curtain.

They'll probably fuck her right there, in front of everyone.

Two point seven million people in Chicago proper. At least half could be distractions.

Or you could take her home.

Her profile turned his discomfort into obligation.

Where no one can see anything.

"Oh, Mr. James," she whispered when he laid her in his bed. "I was hoping you'd show up." She passed out as soon as the gold belt had been removed.

He knew how it looked, but there were things Donovan had learned between her death and this trip to the hospital. Things that shifted under
the appropriate light. Emily's phone had been shut off for the five days
Donovan couldn't reach her. That fact had been highlighted by a different
detective whose fingers pointed out mobile data confirming he'd spent a
handful of days and evenings following her throughout the city. Parks,
beaches, the downtown library, three visits to Kincade's, a half-dozen
coffee houses, one trip to the art museum, her last moments at Millenni-
um Park.

"The evidence is damning." The detective picked up the list of rules
and let it dance between his fingers. "You should have been charged by
now." Donovan had come to save himself, but from his first sighting of
the book's cover he understood that the detective didn't believe in his
innocence.

"Why did you do it?" Donovan asked.

"Do what?"

"Let me go that day, if you thought I was guilty."

"Guilty of what?" The detective's smile said, *I never thought you
were innocent,* while his mouth said, "I never thought of you as anything
other than a lie."

A creep. A weirdo. Hidden.

"Her biggest lie, as a matter of fact—everyone else had been mentioned to at least one other person, but *you* . . . no one knew about you
outside of Georgia Russell and Mica McDowell." The detective picked
up the list of rules, folded it, told him to take it. "I think she did love
you, Donovan. I do." He waited until the list had been hidden from view
before saying anything more. "But I think there came a time when she
might not have loved you anymore."

It happened.

"I want to know what happened after that."

215

There was a crushing stillness in the room, like time had stopped at the moment of impact and would remain there forever. Blue shawl. Bleeding head. Eyes wide with fear. Donovan found his hands on his thighs, elbows pointed outward.

Run.

Interference

Exiting the bus at Kingsbury Street, Lesley found himself in a small industrial area by the river. He'd driven by the spot more than once but never felt the pulse of the place because he hadn't stood there. The glow of melting steel as it pours, the heavy banging of metal, shooting sparks, the rattles of a drill, a truck so heavy it shakes the ground under your feet.

He had planned to visit Nate Aram, but Eric Sullivan had pointed him in a different direction. Lesley paused and watched a woman heading into the Hearing Society, a building stuffed between all the banging and rattling. He had expected something more official, something that looked like a Lincoln Park business with exposed brick and reclaimed wood. Instead, once through the door, he felt he'd entered the Department of Welfare. Cracked cushions, some decades-old signage, linoleum flooring, and that institutional green paint he'd assumed was popular at some point in the 1940s, chipped, scraped, and peeling in places people could easily pick at.

Behind a pane of glass, a large woman holding a piece of cake opened a window to speak to him. "Can I help you?"

Lesley stepped closer and noticed streamers and other party decorations strung up behind the partition. He also noticed a sign stating that the office would be closed the following week while they prepared to move to a new location on Willow. Hopefully, that location would be better.

"Birthday?" he asked while checking the bulletin board behind her.

"Going-away party. What can I help you with?" Her eyes were stern and calculating.

"I'm Detective Lesley Powell," showing his badge briefly this time and fully aware of his transgression. "I'm trying to locate a man named Jack, and a woman who works here. Her name I believe is Lily?"

"We're not allowed to provide information regarding any aspect of our client care, including who we do and do not provide services to, but I *can* tell you that Lily left for college today." She held up the cake before sitting down, and Lesley repeated her words in his head.

"Young woman? Black hair?" His eyes tried to focus on the board behind her where drooping staff photos were held up by single pushpins. "Maybe you could tell me how Lily got along with this woman." He felt for the picture of Emily in his pocket before holding it up. "Her name is Emily Monroe. You may have seen her in the news—"

"Sir, we are not allowed to provide information regarding any aspect of our client care."

His eyes landed on Lily's portrait. "I'm not asking about your services, or your client care—"

The woman rose quickly and set down her cake. "Sir, I'm afraid I'm not going to be able to help you, and I'm going to ask you to leave."

He shook the photo of Emily, trying to get her to look, but she turned her head and he placed it back in his pocket. She didn't need to look. The intensity of her reaction told Lesley all he needed to know. "I thank you for your time, Miss?"

"Evelyn Janson."

"Thank you, Ms. Janson."

Blakely had given him the flash drive for a reason, but Lesley couldn't make the pieces fit. There were no visible lines to draw between the girl in the photos and things like shipping companies or Sticharia. She clearly had a connection with Emily but, blue coats and photos aside, that connection seemed to exist in deafness. A deaf man named Jack. A dead cat.

The more information Lesley gathered, the more he lost track of the boy and the events that led to his death.

Damien Quiles was there in his mind, but he could no longer see him without Sticharia, or Yasser Najjar, or Papachristi, or Globe Cargo and Spanish Tabloids.

He needed to talk to Nate Aram, and he needed to be careful.

When Masterson's digits appeared for the first time in over twenty-four hours, Lesley disregarded the call. A short bus ride and fifteen minutes later, a round man with an oddly familiar face and schoolboy laugh stood talking with the receptionist when Lesley arrived at Ockham, Handler, & DeWitt.

Instead of making Lesley wait, the man led him back to Aram's office while making idle chit-chat about the weather and licking doughnut sprinkles from his fingers. "A lot of people don't know how the Lake affects the weather, but this humidity is something else, isn't it?" They'd reached the door, and the man gave a quick knock before turning the handle. "Detective Lesley Powell is here for you." Pushing the door all the way open, he motioned Lesley into the room.

The Lake's effect on the weather . . . Operation Lake Effect, Masterson, the BOC. Lesley tried to catch sight of the man one last time before he left, but he'd already made his exit.

"Detective." Nate Aram came from behind his desk, his white smile missing, and shook Lesley's hand. "How can I help you?" His hands came to rest on his hips, his feet spread shoulder-length apart, a sort of power pose that made him a barrier.

"I'm trying to locate Yasser Najjar. Your wife told me you had his contact information."

Aram's arms folded across his chest. "Yasser Najjar?" Lesley nodded. "I don't understand. What does he have to do with M?" He shut his office door and returned to his seat behind the desk, motioning for Lesley to join him.

"I don't know that he has anything to do with Mrs. Monroe's case. I'm just clearing up a few details on another case."

Aram laced his fingers and leaned in, resting his arms on the hard surface in front of him. "This is about her phone call, then."

Lesley didn't know what call he was referring to and remained silent, allowing Aram room to continue if he chose.

But he didn't. He leaned back in his chair and ran his fingers through his hair. "I think maybe I need to talk to someone before I start answering any of your questions."

"I'm only here for contact information, Mr. Aram." Lesley needed to calm him. "The address Najjar gave for Sticharia matches your wife's office in Rodgers Park, so, really, it's just a clarification. A minor detail." Aram wasn't so easily convinced. "I don't think it's anything more than confusion on his part."

Aram sat up, hands between his knees. "I still need to call someone." Lesley wanted to rise from his seat when Aram moved to pick up the phone.

He gave a light turn of his hand, tried to look calm, focused his attention on the children pictured and framed on Aram's desk. Hoping. "All I need is a phone number."

It wasn't until he'd followed Lesley's gaze to the faces of his children that he placed the phone back on the receiver. "Well, I've never spoken with Yasser personally." Aram began moving papers, opening drawers, shuffling things about and then handed Lesley a business card. "But you can talk to Nicodemus. He has Yasser's information." Lesley glanced at the card. A high-gloss black that said "Christi Limited" on one side and listed his contact information on the other. "Sorry I couldn't be of more help." Nate Aram stood and headed to the door, opening it, making his desire for Lesley to leave known.

"No, this is great. Thank you." Tucking the card into his pocket, Lesley stood. He felt the needling of unanswered questions. "Both you and your wife thought I came to see you about Emily Monroe."

The statement changed Aram's expression. "You're a detective, and M's been killed. Of course we'd think you were there about her."

Even though Lesley could see the logic in the man's words, his gut told him there was more. "Did Mrs. Monroe know Yasser Najjar?"

"Not that I know of."

"But she knew Nicodemus, right?" Nate Aram slowly resumed his posture of power. "What was their relationship like? Do you know?"

"I'd say that's a question best left for Nicodemus."

Given the man's stance and his propensity to pick up phones and start dialing numbers, Lesley knew to stop there. "Thank you for your help, Mr. Aram."

He headed to the bus stop thinking of matryoshka dolls and how many pieces one set could contain. He had to consider the likelihood that Papachristi was receiving a phone call at that exact moment to notify him of Lesley's impending arrival. Both the dolls and the phone call troubled him.

He'd hoped to talk to Georgia Russell before catching a train, but there was more traffic than he'd expected when he arrived at the Armitage station. Checking the time, plotting his moves, he grabbed a cup of coffee from the 7-Eleven across the street and waited under the trains' trestles where he could watch, and maybe catch, a glimpse of a familiar face.

Irritation buzzed, like the phone in his pocket, a ticking timebomb, jerking to a rhythm he didn't recognize and couldn't ignore. An alert informed him that a raid had just been done at Globe Cargo, but before he could read the report, he received a call that couldn't go unanswered.

"Where are you?" Deb's voice was full of frustration, and in the background, a faint *swoosh-swoosh* rhythm of her driving past parked cars.

"I took the afternoon off." He wondered where she was going, when she'd gone home to pick up the car.

"Don't give me that bullshit, Lesley. I'm so tired of the bullshit." An approaching train drowned out her next words, and Lesley welcomed the noise. When it passed, he asked her to grab dinner with him later. "Are you kidding me right now?"

He rubbed his forehead and tried to push her words away while his phone continued to buzz, buzz, buzz, against his head. "I'll make things different, Deb, I will. It's just this *case*—the boy, I just can't—"

"I thought things would get better, Lesley, I really did, and I've tried—"

"Don't say whatever you're going to say." Preparing for the crash he could feel coming, he leaned over and put his head between his knees. "Just don't say it."

"I'm done, Lesley."

"Deb, please."

"I've rented an apartment and I'll be moving my things out this evening." The weight of her voice stuck to his limbs like anchors he would have to drag around and carry with him once she was gone. He didn't know how he'd be able to move. "I want you to know because I don't want you to be there when it happens. It would be too hard for me."

He tried to grab his handkerchief, clear his sweat, but his keys tangled and rattled and slipped from his hand in slow motion. He found himself amazed by the number of thoughts he could have while they fell. People had reported a similar phenomenon in potentially deadly moments.

"Are you hearing me, Lesley?"

"I'm hearing you. I'm hearing you."

"I don't want you to be there when I come home."

"I love you, Debra."

There was a pause, and he hoped she was contemplating what to say, whether "I love you too" was appropriate under the circumstances or if she needed not to say it to prove a point. "We'll talk soon," she said.

Lesley needed to feel what was happening. He needed to picture Deb packing her things and not coming back. He needed to imagine going to bed, not just that night but every night of the foreseeable future, without her. Instead, he stood up and walked across the street and into the station where the doors had been left open and the air was cool and breezy.

"Mrs. Russell?"

Her smile disappeared with his voice. "It's never a good sign when someone calls you by your last name."

"Detective Lesley Powell."

"It's definitely not a good sign when they're a cop." A man entered the station and she forced a smile, gave a "Good morning," and waited for him to pass. "I was wondering if anyone would come by." She blotted her heavily lined eyes with a knuckle. "I'm assuming you're here about M."

Georgia Russell's shoulder-length wig shook with her scalp and Lesley tried not to notice. "I am actually, yes." He waited, irritated by the steady stream of stop-and-go traffic within the station as another passenger came through. "Did you ever see Mrs. Monroe here with a young lady named Lily? Black hair, just graduated high school—"

"Oh, I know who you're talking about." She smiled, waved her neon-green nails, and waited. "I never saw her with M, but she waited for Mr. James out there every morning." A train pulled in above them. "She also has a friend, a deaf man. She passes through with him occasionally." People could be heard coming down the stairs. "Excuse me a minute."

Mr. James. Another name to remember, to hold onto, to try and make fit or throw away. Seven minutes passed before the station was clear again. "And who's Mr. James?"

"He's a teacher up at Lincoln Park, a friend of M's."

The woman was interrupted by more people entering the station, and Lesley took out his phone, pulled up the paintings, moved the device in her direction feeling an overwhelming impatience with the world.

"Next Thursday's my last day," she said. "M and I were going to drink beers on the beach." She took his phone into her hand and he wanted to be kind because her eyes were filling with tears.

But time was running out. "Retiring?"

"You could say that." She smiled at the photos. "I always thought she kind of fancied him." She looked a moment more before handing back the phone. "I imagine he's pretty shaken up over this."

"So this *is* Mr. James?" Lesley needed to be sure.

"Yeah." The expression on her face slipped from melancholy to indignation. "You don't think it was *him*, do you?"

"I'm just putting the pieces together."

"Well, you can chuck that piece right out the window because that's just crazy, you hear me? Crazy."

Another passenger, another smile turned on, and Lesley waited. "Did you ever see Mrs. Monroe with anyone else? Friends? Acquaintances?"

Georgia looked away. "M talked to everyone." It was clear she didn't want to be seen crying, but a giant tear fell to the concrete floor below. "She was kind that way . . ."

Lesley took a moment to pull up a few more photos. Nate Aram and Isabel Escamilla, Nicodemus Papachristi, Damien Quiles. But before he showed them to Georgia Russell, he took Jamal's photo from his pocket. "Do you happen to recognize this boy?"

Where there is hope, there is possibility.

A shake of her head.

"How about this one?" When there is possibility there are choices.

"No."

"What about this couple, do you recognize either of them?" In the choices there is action.

"I'm afraid not."

"And him? Do you recognize this man at all?" And actions make the man.

"I only recognize Mr. James."

Scattering

Friday afternoons had been slow for months, and Mica McDowell had grown nauseatingly accustomed to the harassments of her day-to-day life. The polar vortex, which had stretched itself through March, helped coffee and cocoa sales across the street at Starbucks, but it had been death for the pub business, driving everyone but the diehards away. Mica craved the return of warm weather, a catalyst for workforce lunches and happy-hour associates. All those customers drank quickly and tipped well. Instead, she was stuck with Jared.

"Change the music. I hate this shit." He was the kind of middle-aged white guy Mica saw most regularly. "Steve Miller. Put some Steve Miller on. I know you've got it." He drank cheap beer, and he drank too much of it.

In an attempt to give him as little attention as possible, Mica reached one hand to the music player's dial while the other sent a message to her mother.

"Why'd you turn it down? Turn it back up."

The front door opened behind her, and Mica tossed her phone under the bar, increased the volume of the music to just a little too loud, and turned to see how many menus she needed to grab. "Hey!" She was surprised by the appearance of M, a warmer-weather, Monday through Friday kind of gal, who usually came in alone, stayed for a single beer, and chatted up the servers while she was there. "Two of you today?" Seeing her *with* someone meant she'd sit further from the bar and focus all energy on her guest like it was serious work to have actual company.

While Mica filled their water glasses, she thought about their first *real* meeting. M had been drunk, messy drunk, crying on the floor in a bathroom stall, and Mica held her hair while she puked and sobbed and divulged details about herself that she believed would send her to hell.

If the toilet bowl had been a confessional, her sins would have been forgiven.

Jared tapped the counter. "Hey, what time do you get off? We should have a drink. You never have a drink with me."

"And that's not going to change today, or any other day, Jared." Water glasses filled, she rounded the bar and headed toward the table.

M ordered, glancing at the man across from her. He smiled when she said, "I was thinking about doing a flight, trying something new."

"Trying new things is good," he said. "I'll do the same."

It was hard for Mica not to watch her and hope this was the start of something new and good in her life. The way the two smiled at one another, like everything was a secret between them, made Mica wish her boyfriend Kristof were there.

They both worked in the service industry and had picked up an armchair psychologist's understanding of nonverbal behaviors in public settings. She wanted to watch M's table with him. They could discuss whether it was a first date, a last date, if the couple was happily married, on their way to divorce, or having an affair. Kristof would take issue with the gold band on the woman's left hand because it was clear the two of them weren't married. "No one has that kind of chemistry after a few years," he'd say. "Definitely an affair."

But Mica didn't want to believe that. She understood the necessity of fake wedding rings and rarely let them interfere with her interpretations of the body cues she was trying to decipher.

"Wedding rings are just as easy to put on as they are to take off," she'd say. A ring, or the absence of one, could both be a lie.

Coming down the stairs from the bathroom, Jared whistled to get her attention, like she was a dog, like she was his bitch, and she wished she was a poorly trained one, capable of attack.

"How about you grab me another." Empty glass on the bar, he sat down and waited for her to follow his command. But she didn't.

She finished preparing the drinks for M's table and on her way to deliver them, said, "I'm going to check on your food first—sober you up a bit."

"I don't need sobering—I need another goddamn beer."

She knew better.

Taking the doorway that separated the two halves of the pub, Mica found herself in the shuttered dark of the other side where the kitchen lay hidden in the back corner. Unlike the enduring shine of the bar where Mica spent most of her time, the kitchen side had upstairs, downstairs, and outdoor seating. Lighter, more dispensable furniture. And it only opened its doors and turned on its lights at night or on game days when the crowd could get loud and rowdy.

The kitchen was always open, but when the rest of the room was closed, the vacant space made the florescent lights of the kitchen glow offensively. "I don't see how you work back here."

The cook smiled and placed her food on the pass-through. "I don't see how you work out there."

Mica believed she preferred the other side for its sturdiness. But she knew his words were directed at the pawing, and the catcalls, and the unsolicited invitations to "get together sometime." Those things she could do without.

"How's it going out there anyway?"

"Slow." She grabbed the food from the pass. "Got a drunk guy at the bar and a couple at the window."

"See, it's better back here." He turned up the volume on his radio and gave her a wink. "Not a drunk in sight."

To her relief, Jared stopped talking and began eating once his food was placed in front of him. His eyes set on the TV, Mica slipped him an RC and tried to remain invisible.

Three tables came and went. Someone picked up a to-go order. M's table remained quiet, and then Jared started talking again. "Are you still seeing that one guy?"

She'd begun drying glasses, a task that forced her into his immediate line of sight. "His name is Kristof, and yes. We've been together for seven years."

"Does he still wear earrings?"

Gauges, they were gauges, but she didn't feel the need to correct him. "Yep."

"When are you gonna find yourself a real man?"

Jared's definition of "real man" included things like: does manual labor, drinks a lot of beer, is the boss in every relationship. "Not everyone can be as manly as you, Jared."

Mica's definition included: stands up for the underdog, isn't afraid to express emotion, understands the meaning of "partner".

There was movement by the window, and Mica looked to see the man take M's arm as she tried to leave. It looked inauspicious until M smiled and he let her pass.

Moments later, her date stood at the bar, tidy little beard across his chin, dressed like a hipster version of Mr. Rodgers. "Could we grab a pitcher?"

She liked his smile. It was a kind smile. "Sure. Do you want fresh glasses?"

"I think we're good. Thanks though."

Mica pulled the tap to find only foam dispensing and swore under her breath. "Sorry, it might be a minute."

"Don't you think she deserves a real man?"

Mr. Rodgers looked confused but held his pose when he looked toward Jared. "Excuse me?"

"A real man," Jared pressed on. "You know, someone who knows how to take charge."

Mica was sick of the conversation. "Jared, leave the guy alone." The awkwardness of the moment flushed her face, and she bent over to check the CO_2. "He's drunk, just ignore him."

But he was looking at Jared while his soft, well-manicured hands tapped fingers on the bar, and Jared gave a drunken laugh. "What would you know?" His hand gesticulated too close to the man beside him. "You probably don't got balls enough to fuck with—"

"Shut up or leave, Jared." Mica set two filled pint glasses atop the bar in front of M's date. "These are on the house," she said. "I'll bring you the pitcher as soon as I've swapped out the keg." Jared tried to stand and fell back into his seat. "And I'm going to call *you* a cab."

Mica moved to take his plate and glass from the bar, but Jared smacked her hand away. "Back off, bitch—" And before anything else could happen, the man with his polite smile and well-manicured hands grabbed Jared's shirt and pushed his chair off kilter, leaving it on the verge of falling backward.

Jared looked panicked, but his movement caused the chair to angle back just enough to where he might fall, and the man looked like he'd let it happen. "Apologize."

"I'm not going to apologize—" This time, the chair's tipping was intentional. "Okay—Jesus, I'm sorry." Jared submitted.

"Say it to her."

Mica met Jared's eye and saw her own fear reflected back. "I'm sorry, Mica."

Returning the chair to a position of safety, the man leaned in, whispering something into Jared's ear. "Thank you," he said, raising the glasses, and then walked back to the table like nothing had ever happened.

Jared put on his coat and threw some cash down on the bar.

"Let me call you a cab."

He left without comment or look.

Rules

Donovan went for his first run in six weeks and returned home to find a note Lily had left lying on his desk. "I woke naked in your bed. Hope you'll help me remember." She'd placed the flash drive she'd given him on top, circled it with the green pen he used for grading, and then scrawled: Open Me.

Crumpling the paper, he buried it in the kitchen trash under some Chinese takeout before digging it up and burning it in the kitchen sink.

The flash drive itself was something less innocuous. At least that's what he told himself when he plugged it in and began opening its folders. There were six in total. Donovan opened all of them.

You could keep it, for when you're alone.

He didn't allow his eyes to fall on the details, but he still felt the gluttonous devouring of one who has been starved too long.

That's what you do. What you've always done.

He ejected it. Held it in his hand. Contemplated its demise. But a text message pinged, and the flash drive was buried under sticky pads and staples in the back of his desk drawer.

The message read, "Meet me at Kincade's. Noon today." And he tossed the phone aside. Didn't recognize the number. Didn't think it was meant for him.

People hide what they don't want others to find in the first place most people look.

Is this where they look?

No one's looking.

He slammed the drawer shut and paced the space full of scattered sensations.

While the whole affair was being washed from his sheets and skin, images of her limbs lingered; the flash drive left a ghost to haunt the less-controlled portion of his being.

His brother called three times while Donovan was in the shower.

"We're coming in Friday evening and leaving Tuesday morning—Jimmy got an extra day." The washer was on Spin, and he laid his upper body across it trying to shake free his mind. "I hope your lady friend can handle us—and she better fucking like soccer, Donno, or I'm going to be pissed."

Lily would willingly play his girlfriend, but the thought made him hate himself more than he already did. She might be able to pass for twenty-something physically, but mentally she was a mess of teenage everything, and no one would ever buy it, not even Jay.

Then there was Sara.

She wouldn't pretend to be anything ever, not with her clothes on anyway. So she was out, even if everyone *could* believe they were dating.

Tinder was an option . . . and much cheaper than a prostitute. Both of which he'd considered in order to appease his mother and quiet his father.

She'll have to have red hair. They know she has red hair.

Not just anyone can pretend to be Emily.

Not with the lights on.

Shut up.

They'll see your disappointment.

The room smelled like burnt paper and evoked blue images. He sat at his computer, still in his towel, not opening the drawer but trying to determine what to do with his physical need for release.

He considered recording himself.

Who for? Who will you show it to?

He reached for his phone, and it vibrated in his hand, an unknown number calling to remind him of an unknown message sender. He silenced it, sent it to voicemail, restarted his phone, and found that the caller hadn't left a message.

The unease he felt over the mystery number was the catalyst for the next email he sent.

Dear Lily,

Nothing happened. You put yourself in a dangerous position last night that could have ended tragically. Please have more care in the future.

Sincerely,

Mr. James

He stared at the Message Sent across the top of his screen and waited for his despondency to either abate or push him over the edge.

On the southbound platform at Armitage, he stood where he could look down at the street and watch whomever came and went from Kincade's. Recent events led him to believe the message could have been from any number of people he never wanted to meet face to face, Lily's parents perhaps, Adonis even.

Maybe it's someone from work who saw you last night, drunk—with an even drunker Lily.

He didn't recognize a single person entering the pub before noon.

Or maybe it's a cop, dressed in plain clothes, holding another flash drive.

Fifteen minutes later, still no one familiar had appeared.

It's her.

She entered Kincade's twenty minutes after the message had told Donovan to be there, and he could feel the trap of her peach dress filling his body with a mixture of hair-on-end terror and galvanic excitement that he needed to suppress before he'd be able to head down and into the pub.

She wanted to make you wait.

"How are you doing, Mr. James? Good to see you taking the stairs again." Georgia had new hair. It was shorter, with highlights, and noticeably a wig.

"Yeah, I'm feeling much better."

Two steps from the door, she continued talking. "M just passed through here looking for you." She laughed and shook her head, "You two do more asking about each other . . ." Her words kept rolling out, igniting new fires.

"Sorry, Georgia, I've got to run."

"Okay, love. I'll let her know I saw you."

Instead of telling Georgia not to bother, letting her know they were meeting or asking what he really wanted to know—how many times and how recently Emily had asked about him—he walked the thirty feet from the station entrance and into the dark interior of Kincade's.

Once his eyes had time to adjust, he found Emily looking at him from across the room. She'd taken off her hat and her bag hung on a hook, implying that she intended to stay even while her lack of smile said, I won't be staying here with you.

He approached cautiously and tried to slow his heart rate with controlled breathing, but his hands dove for the cover of his pockets and his guilt made looking at her difficult.

Her expression didn't change when he reached the table. "You're late," she said.

"I didn't know it was you."

"I just assumed after spending so much time watching me from a distance, you'd forgotten how to watch me up close." There was no response for that, but at least she'd gotten that part of the conversation over with quickly. "What were you thinking?" She was angry; he recognized it in the way her eyes became smaller and her brow collapsed.

"I'm sorry—"

"Don't be sorry. Be careful, and dammit, Donovan, don't be a creep. You can't just go around stalking people—"

"I wasn't stalking you—"

"You weren't stalking me?" He shook his head, knowing very well that though he believed he was technically correct, she'd push the subject further. "What would you call it then?"

"Watching—"

"Watching?" The anger lit up her face. "How long have you been 'watching' me, and how do you think it makes me feel to look up and see you lurking around my house?"

The lump in his throat and ringing in his ears prevented an immediate response.

"Donovan—"

"You watch people all the time."

"What?"

"All those paintings from your show—you watch people all the time."

"That's different."

"Tell me how."

"I don't follow people."

"I didn't follow you. I found you—"

"You're disturbed."

She stood up, like she'd be leaving, and he blocked her. Stepped close enough for his body to touch hers and grabbed her like he'd imagined doing so many times before. "Don't leave."

It wasn't clear if it was fear he saw or something else floating behind her eyes, but she didn't attempt to escape. "I need to ask you something in all seriousness, Donovan, and if I find out you lied, I *will* file a restraining order and never see you again." Her words threatened, but her body remained brushing his. "How long have you been watching me?" He opened his mouth to answer, but she stopped him, "Tell me the truth—because I'll know if you're lying."

"Almost a month—"

She stepped back. "You're lying—"

"I also waited for you at Kimball on Memorial Day."

Her expression bore all the signs of discontent. "Why? Why would you do that?"

Honest. Be honest or she'll leave.

"You stopped showing up—"

"I'm married."

"I don't care."

Their last morning together, on the platform at Paulina, her head had fallen against him while he held her hand and traced the skin of her forearm with his fingertips. He'd touched her, and she'd let him.

She'd turned her head up and breathed him in, let her lips rub across his neck. "I don't know how to stay away from you," she'd said.

"Then don't," he'd replied.

He chose to remind her of this moment. Step closer. Let his fingers read the bumps of her skin. She didn't pull away. "You've always wanted me to find you, remember?" She withdrew enough to look at him. "Then it won't be your fault."

He pressed his nose into her hair, and she whispered, "That doesn't mean I wanted you to stalk me." His touch, or words, returned her to her seat. And though it may have been the only place for her to go, she left her exposed legs vulnerable to his touch. "I should be terrified of you. You realize that, right?"

"Are you?" She turned her face away from his and didn't answer. "Why'd you ask me to come here, Emily?"

"You still have my hat."

"Your hat?"

"Yes."

"I don't think that's why at all." He slid onto a seat next to her and she tucked her legs under the table, hid the most precious parts from him.

"We need to *understand* one another, Donovan. You can't go lurking around corners watching me. It's not okay."

You're going to kiss her.

I know.

She knows you're going to kiss her.

In a test of her commitment, he slipped his hand under the table and onto her leg.

She squeezed his fingers, stopped their motion but did not push them away. "We need to establish some rules, Donovan. That's all." Watching him as closely as he watched her, her lower lip disappeared into her mouth as a pitcher of beer arrived and glasses were set down.

It's only a matter of time now, isn't it? You can take her home to fresh sheets. She's not afraid. She likes it. Likes what you are, sees who you are, wants who you are.

"I think if we just establish some rules about what *can* happen and what can't . . ." She pressed her hand into his, let her fingers caress the space between his. "And I could really use a friend."

He nodded, unbelieving. "I'm not your friend, Emily." Her mouth moved, and he waited.

"I can't have sex with you," she said.

"And I can't be your friend."

She moved in her seat, trapped his knee between hers. "What if that's the only way we can see each other again?"

Kiss her.

"Because I want to see you again, Donovan."

Leaning closer, his knee now pressed between her thighs, he could feel all he imagined coming true. "I'm going to kiss you."

She laughed, a belly laugh, and held up her hands in protest, "No, that's where you're wrong—"

"I'm not wrong."

The rest of the pub exploded in cheers shouting 'GOOOOOOOOAL!' and Emily adjusted her position on the chair, reached for her beer, drank more than was necessary. "This was never supposed to happen—you were just a guy—"

Unable to hear the rest of the sentence, Donovan stood and kissed her. One hand on her neck while the other held her head in place. Daring her to resist, daring others to see, daring himself out of fiction and into reality.

"I'm not waiting on platforms anymore." He didn't move, her face was flushed and her eyes wide. "I won't lurk, but I *will* see you."

Her head bowed against his chin, and he knew the right shampoo had been purchased. "There need to be *rules*, Donovan. I'll see you, but there have to be *rules.*"

Fuck her rules.

He refilled their pint glasses and determined they'd need another pitcher. "I want to see you every day, Emily—"

"I can't see you every day."

Returning to his seat, Donovan felt in control of her and their fate. Believed that his will and actions would propel them forward to where he wanted them to be. *Knew* they would be. "I want to see you every day, and I don't mean on a train. I want to see you in the world, take you places, do things with you, take you home with me, show you my books—let you walk barefoot around my apartment, introduce you to my family, wake up with you in my bed—"

Her eyes closed and cut off his words.

"Tell me you don't want it—that you don't want to see me—"

"It's a lot more complicated than that." Her eyes tried to warn him, but the threat wasn't real.

"I don't want to hurt you."

"Then don't."

Kiss her again. Quiet her, she didn't want you to stop.

"I love you, Emily."

235

He watched her take the stairs up to the ladies' room, and then he grabbed her bag. Her phone had messages, messages in the order of: Donovan, Dad, Yvette, Kadi, Alex. Calls in the order of: Donovan, Nate, Unknown, Kadi, Dad, Alex, Yvette.

He didn't have time to check anything else, but he did have time to send and accept a request for Find My Friends before hanging her purse back on the hook.

"Donovan?" He'd been lying in bed waiting for the call she'd promised when he exited the train at Montrose. "I can't see you on Sundays."

"I love you." She didn't say anything in return, but he didn't say it for reciprocation. "Tell me what you do first thing in the morning." His imagination traced the skin of her thighs, hands following hands, up under dresses, the breath of her sighs adding to the reality of their now.

"I do my asanas."

He could hear their actuality in her inhale. "Tell me more."

"Yoga. Ninety minutes every day."

He rolled over onto his stomach and imagined her there. "Will you show me? How you do it?"

A light laugh traveled to his ear and tickled down the length of his spine. "Will you do them with me?"

"Yes."

Yes.

"We have to do it early. My day doesn't work otherwise."

"You can spend the night with me. We can do it when we wake up."

"Donovan." Her tone held a smile underneath. "Remember the rules."

They met at the coffee shop by his house. She walked through the door shaking her yellow umbrella behind her, and he wondered how to greet her. Should he stand? Should he hug her? What he wanted to do was forbidden by rules he'd agreed to while half drunk and willing to say anything to make her stay.

Noticing the hesitation of his stance, she smiled. "I'd kiss you if I could." She pulled out a chair and set her umbrella on the floor. "I just want you to know that."

He ran in the morning, took a shower, met her at an agreed-upon location that had been determined the night before while they each lay in their respective beds.

She slept naked. Between the long silences that would spread between their phone lines, Donovan found himself masturbating, hoping she was doing the same. But each time she'd simply fallen asleep listening to him breathe.

She glanced occasionally out at the lake between wild scribbles on the notepad in her lap. Donovan could feel the spin of the earth pushing against his will. Time passing, whether he wanted it to or not. "When do you have to be home tonight?"

She didn't look up or toward him. She just smiled. "When do *you* have to be home?"

The smile was a game. It said, It's just a game. "I'm not the one beholden to time."

"Neither am I," she said, her smile suddenly absent.

The skin of her arm was cool to the touch when he sat up to stop their trajectory. "My brother and best friend will be here tomorrow evening, and I'd like you to meet them." The *whoosh* of her pencil stopped, and he could feel her watching his profile after he'd looked away. "There's nothing in the rules that says you can't meet my people. And they'll be here through Tuesday morning, so there's plenty of time"

"I can't meet them. It's insane."

Flipping through the pages of her sketchbook, she stopped on an image of the sea, or lake, or some large body of water, and began to add marks to the page. The ease in which she fell into this activity, picking it up where she had left off, made him feel they too were something she could easily pack up, put away, and expect to remain unchanged by whatever length of time she chose.

You won't let that happen.

Patting the surface above his heart, he asked her to hear it. "Lay with me a minute."

Tha-thump, tha-thum. Tha-thump, tha-thum.

A hesitation. A turning. A setting aside before she placed her head to the center of his chest.

Tha-thump, tha-thum. Tha-thump, tha-thum.

Closing his eyes, he touched her, felt her back loosen under his fingers, smelled the warmth rising up from her head.

"I wish I could stay like this forever." Whispered words of assurance and the curl of her pinky around his.

A hawk circled in the clearing, children could be heard laughing, and the steady sound of a basketball pounded in the distance.

Donovan had been passive. He had allowed the detective to steer his thoughts away from his remaining possibilities and back to memories that were being rewritten no matter how hard he tried to stop them.

He'd lost sight of the man's utility. What could be seen and actualized there in his lifeless body. "This was never about me, or Lily, or Jack, or even Emily, was it?" He waited, and nothing came. "No one cared who killed her or that kid. None of those things mattered to whoever talked to Sara." He didn't know if they mattered to him either. Not in the moment. Not when his story had spiraled out of control and all his previous actions pointed to a freak, a weirdo, a murderer.

"I imagine they've promised to destroy the evidence against you?" The book was buried under a stack of papers containing stories Donovan never wanted to know the details of and still spent hours reading.

They triggered questions. Drew on his worst fears even while their truths lacked his reality.

You just gotta do what they say, son . . .

Words, his father's words.

"Was it your partner who talked to Sara?" Donovan took up the newspapers that had been sitting between them and began going through articles in search of what he needed. "It says here—"

"I know what it says."

"So maybe it was him." He watched the detective's face, could feel his stillness. "Some sort of strange trade—your wife for a video—"

"It wasn't Masterson."

Donovan felt the room tilting in his favor. "Then who?"

But the detective shook his head. "You know, maybe you should be asking yourself what they actually have on you, Donovan." The man's chest moved when he drew breath, a strange incongruence to the rest of him. "What haven't they shown you?" Hair down, blue coat barely parted. "Do you know exactly what you're doing?" A freedom from consequence. A lack of complete judgment. "Or are they using you?"

What is your utility?

239

Interference

Lesley needed a container. He needed one person or place in which all the names and faces fit. He stood alone on the northbound platform waiting for a train to Montrose, phone in hand, seven more minutes to wait. Georgia Russell had identified Lesley's first known unknown in the Monroe case: the man from Emily's paintings. No relationship to the boy, Sticharia, or Christi Limited. Just a teacher at Lincoln Park High School. Outside of his class webpage, James lacked any kind of online presence at all.

The rush had passed, and the street below held an unfamiliar level of quiet that was only interrupted by the occasional soft coo of a pigeon hiding in the shade of some rafters. Scrolling through classroom photos, James could be seen standing with students in graduation gowns, everyone smiling and happy. Pleased to share a moment with him.

Nothing looked particularly off. Nothing on class discussion boards felt or looked out of the ordinary. Donovan James presented as an attractive man who was an active and engaged teacher, well-liked by his students. But what if that wasn't the whole picture? What if Emily Monroe lied about knowing him for reasons outside of infidelity?

Lesley scrolled through more photos and stopped on a familiar face. Black hair, a different smile, a cap and gown instead of bare skin and a blue coat. The moment was met by the thundering of an approaching train and Lesley held the phone close to verify the student's name: Lily Ziyad.

He tossed everything aside upon entering the train and tried not to think of the voicemails from Masterson he'd yet to listen to. He could only hold so much.

Donovan James. Lily Ziyad. Emily Monroe. A flash drive. And a deaf man named Jack.

He rested his head on the window and let the vented air blow up his neck, around the back of his ear and jostle the hair on his scalp.

News alerts on his phone were few and far between. The raid at Globe Cargo was a blip that left Lesley considering the possibility it

240

wasn't a coincidence, but a signal to something or someone still out of his purview.

The set containing Emily Monroe, Lily Ziyad, Donovan James, and a deaf man named Jack all belonged to public transit. The set containing Emily Monroe, Jamal Dupont, and Damien Quiles all belonged to Albany Park. The set containing Emily Monroe, Nicodemus Papachristi, Nate Aram, and Isabel Escamilla all belonged to St. Josemaría School. Lesley could *make* sets. He could make sets upon sets, but Emily Monroe, Damien Quiles, Metropolitan Youth, Nicodemus Papachristi, and Jamal Dupont lacked a container. Arrows could be drawn, but there was no single *thing* gluing them together.

The fact that no one had been taken into custody for the murder of Emily Monroe needled him when coupled with the unviewed CTA footage and the discovery of Donovan James. It also made having "bigger fish" to fry feel more likely when, whatever that fish might be, could be the set of sets containing all others.

Donovan James had to be seen. Papachristi had to be seen. Yasser Najjar needed to be questioned. And no one, as far as Lesley could tell, was doing that.

Exiting the train at Montrose, he headed down the stairs and into the heat. James lived just a few short blocks away from the station, and Lesley needed him to be home. He knocked on the door and waited. Nothing could be heard moving beyond the door and he knocked again, louder this time. "Donovan?" Lesley called with another, more urgent banging on the door. "Donovan James?" He tried the knob, found it locked, and banged again. A crashing came from inside, followed by a stumble, followed by a "Hold on."

James opened the door with squinting eyes and mussed-up hair. He was not as Lesley had expected. Not the man he'd seen pictured and painted, smiling or waiting. There was no snow piling on shoulders or hopeful expressions. He wore a cream-colored short-sleeve button-up and blue shorts that, judging by the number of creases, he'd been wearing and sleeping in for days.

"I'm Detective Lesley Powell." He waited, but James just stood there waking up and not offering any reaction. "Would you mind if I came in? Asked you a few questions?"

James paused, glanced over his shoulder, and then looked back at Lesley. "I've been sick. I just woke up. My house is a mess—"

"It'll only take a minute," Lesley placed his hand to the door like he would come in anyway and James stepped back, moved in, began tidying up along the way.

The lights were off in the apartment and the curtains were all closed. It took Lesley's eyes a moment to adjust. James tidied sheets and blankets on a bed near an alcove and then attempted to tidy himself. "I haven't been feeling very well," moving his hands over hair, then shirt, then arms, like he was trying to get warm. "I haven't moved for a few days."

Opening curtains, James shed light and familiarity. The white sheets, navy comforter, and shelves lined with books had been visible in the flash drive photos. The girl, Lily, wearing Emily's coat there on that bed.

The scene had Lesley altering his first question. "Would you happen to know where Emily Monroe's blue coat is?"

"Yes." His hands stayed put in his pockets, but his toes gripped the carpet underneath them. "It's here. She left it here."

"Intentionally or unintentionally?"

"Intentionally. I'm sorry, who are you again?"

"Detective Lesley Powell." Emily lied about something larger than infidelity. Or she didn't.

"Did she leave the coat here for you or for Lily Ziyad?"

The question visibly knocked James off balance. A slight sway of his upper body was followed by the shuffling of feet. "She left it here for me. Why are you asking me this? What's going on?"

"So the flash drive was yours then." The words intentionally left Lesley's mouth a statement and not a question. "She found it, took it so you wouldn't have it."

There was a pause, not an "excuse me" or an "I don't know what you're talking about," but a pause, and the pause was enough for Lesley to force further assumptions. Push Donovan James with logical leaps that would fill him with fear and make him speak—sell her out or shed some light on how she wound up dead with the flash drive in her pocket.

"Then she was strangled in a park before she could do anything with it."

"What?" James lunged forward, toward Lesley, reaching for him but not touching. "No. No." He was bent over, scrambling, finding a shoe, wrestling it on. "What d-did you say?" Another shoe, another scramble, a dialing of a phone. "Say it!" The phone was tossed, and James stepped toward Lesley, grabbing him like he'd shake the words out of him, but his own words felt stunted and his grip was released. "Tell me. Again."

Lesley repeated the words with more emphasis. "Strangled, to death."

Donovan James pushed away. "I don't believe you." Picking up his phone he headed for the door. "I don't believe you."

If this were a case, a normal case, and Lesley were on it, he would have followed him out the door and shown him proof. James's reaction had not been to the flash drive—he could give two shits about the flash drive—it was the fact that Emily Monroe had been murdered that James didn't want to believe.

Lesley's options on who to call and what he could say were limited. Standing alone in James's apartment, Lesley glanced around for the coat as he made his way to the door. Wondering if he should lock it, wondering whom he could call, then noticed a lump in the bed. An irregularity. Everything else was neat. Undisrupted. Pleasantly placed. And so he took the three steps back and flipped down the blankets.

A sweatshirt and the blue coat. Donovan James had been sleeping with them both.

"I need to speak to you. In private." Masterson's voice wasn't the one he'd expected when he dialed Deb's number. "As soon as possible, Lesley."

The sun had peaked and begun its downward motion. The light shone directly into the stairwell leading up to the platform. People in motion, the heat of the day, Lesley needed it all to stop. "Okay." A clipped response. "Hartigan Beach. Half an hour."

The cubby seat was open when he boarded the last train car, and Lesley stepped into the privacy its walls provided. Masterson's messages had started mildly. "It's Masterson. Call me." Then progressed. "Powell, stop fucking around. Call me." And progressed. "Whatever you're doing, I need you to stop." Until Lesley felt sick by what he had to say. "Look, I'm asking you, as a friend, to stop. Just back off this one. Let it go. For Deb's sake, and for yours."

Was that a threat?

All the calls had been made in the last two hours.

Lesley redialed Deb's number, and no one answered. He tried Masterson's phone, and no one answered. He stared out the back window toward the city, not knowing if Deb was okay.

Taking the train up to Hartigan Beach meant a backtrack and a transfer, but the park was fairly unused, and the neighborhood was familiar. Masterson sat on a bench between beach and playground. He sat up, moved to stand, and then remained seated. "Lesley."

"Tell me nothing's happened to Deb."

"Nothing's happened to Deb."

"And nothing's going to happen to Deb, right?"

"I don't know." Masterson looked close to tears. "None of this has gone like it was supposed to."

Lesley could hear his blood pumping in his ears.

"This isn't who I am, Powell." Masterson wiped his palms across his pant legs. "They showed me what they had and—"

"Who?"

"I wish you'd never gone to see Escamilla. I don't know how you got information on Yasser Najjar, but asking about him . . ." Lesley waited. "They're going to call you in and strip you of your badge." Masterson shook his head. "Everything I've done is for nothing."

Lesley wanted to sit down, rest the legs that were barely holding him up, but any time he thought of moving he saw himself hitting Masterson.

"What was it about the kid anyway? Why did you care so much about *that* fucking kid?"

The world spun violently around him. "Because no one else did." He watched Masterson and no longer recognized him. "Not you, not the force, not the community or news channels—when did you all decide that a child's life wasn't important? That *Jamal* wasn't important—"

"It's bigger than the kid!" Masterson stood up and stepped further into the sand. "There are things happening that need to be stopped, Lesley. It's . . . it's bigger than the kid—"

"Tell me how. Tell me how something else is bigger than a child's life."

"When it's multiple lives." Masterson turned to face him. They were separated by ten easy steps. "Najjar's name came up eighteen months ago in connection to a trafficking ring out of Baltimore. A truck full of refugees was dumped in a panic. Twelve people died." Lesley remembered the story. "The truck could be traced back to deliveries made to Globe Cargo, but a federal investigation didn't find anything—including Najjar or how to locate him."

"What does this have to do with Jamal Dupont?"

Masterson shook his head and kept talking. "In January, a call was placed to Child Protective Services regarding Papachristi's son, potential sexual abuse of a minor—"

"What does this have to do with the boy, Masterson?"

"Christi Limited could be traced to Najjar through transportation services and a handful of youth programs which, up until the phone call, gave them nothing—"

"Jamal Dupont, Masterson! I'm through fucking around—"

"Jesus, Powell, are you hearing me?"

He was hearing him. Nate Aram's comment about a phone call had been illuminated. There were people being exploited, children in danger, and the entire thing was fucked. But Lesley *didn't* know why he'd been given the flash drive or how Jamal was involved in any of it.

"The FBI had a kid on the inside, someone they touched base with, asked questions of." Masterson paused, and Lesley feared where the lines would connect. "They'd been tracking groups of kids coming out of lockup. The kind of kids who would be vulnerable—unstable homes, addicted to this and that, willing to do what they had to."

"Damien Quiles."

Neither one of them spoke for several moments. The warm evening air blew off the lake and around them. Whipping loose material. Causing dust devils in the sand.

"They asked me to keep you away from the Quiles brothers—"

"Who did?" Lesley felt himself teetering toward violence.

"He was their best chance."

"Who?"

Masterson no longer looked at Lesley. "The BOC brought me in last October. Showed me everything they had."

"You should have fucking told me."

"I couldn't tell you. You know that—you know how it works."

Lesley was enraged over how things "worked." "So it was one of them—"

"Papachristi's homes and businesses are being raided as we speak."

"Good."

"No, not good. Your actions forced everyone to move before they were ready."

"Don't you dare make this about me." He watched Masterson's hands go into his pockets. "What do the Quiles brothers have to do with the Monroe case?"

Masterson's eyes shifted away and out toward the lake. "Emily Monroe had relationships with both Nate Aram and Nicodemus Papachristi."

"So what?"

"The BOC saw her death as an opportunity. A Plan B if things fell through with Damien." All the physical signs coming from Masterson told Lesley he was struggling, but Lesley couldn't trust what he could see. Not anymore. "They wanted Papachristi. There couldn't be any question over who killed Monroe."

"What does that even mean?"

"They didn't want her relationship with James to complicate a murder charge." Lesley couldn't stop staring at Masterson.

"And if Donovan James is guilty?" Masterson was there, but he wasn't. There, but not the man Lesley had always believed him to be. "Why are you here, *Bill*? Why are you doing this now?"

Masterson acknowledged the unfamiliar calling of his name with a look of disgrace. "Because everything is fucked. And I want to make right what I can." He pulled a phone from his pocket and held it in a clenched fist. "I couldn't destroy it. I thought I was doing the right thing but . . . I couldn't destroy it." He stepped forward and handed Lesley the phone. "It's a complicated business, Powell, who goes free and who gets caught."

That had never been true. Not for Lesley. "No, it isn't."

Phone in hand and video loaded. Lesley saw Jamal standing in the half-lit dead-end alley of Drake. Piles of snow all around him. An apartment building no more than ten feet from where he stood, and Joey

Quiles no more than three feet in front of him. Joey held a baseball bat and his taunting was drowned out by the snickering of others and the boy holding the phone. A child whose voice had yet to drop.

Lesley's heart beat in his throat. Masterson distanced himself from the cracking sound he knew was coming. Knew the sound would draw Lesley's eyes back to the phone to see Jamal not moving and Damien running on the screen.

"What are you doing?" Damien yelled and grabbed the bat from his brother, holding it up before giving him a stiff enough push to knock him down. "What are you doing?"

Jamal started to stir, tried to stand. He spit blood into the snow, and Lesley knew teeth had come out with it.

"He's a narc, D," Joey shouted. "He's gonna get us all sent to juvie if he doesn't shut the fuck up."

"Who are you talking to?" Damien turned on Jamal, poked him with the bat. "You want my brother to go away? Get locked up?"

"He does, D." Joey was up and talking, but the kid holding the phone had stopped laughing and started moving.

The image shook and shifted away from the boy, the bat, and the brothers. The sound of snow under the kid's feet interfered with whatever else was being said until he stopped and whispered to someone else, "Go watch the street—quick, go watch the street."

A crack, a cry, an "Oh, shit," tinted with surprise and fear before the phone swung back around.

"Turn that fucking thing off." Another voice, another child speaking. The phone fell to the snow and the video stopped.

Lesley's eyes jumped quickly to Masterson then back at the screen. He wanted to speak, he wanted to advance, to do the right thing, watch the video again—see who could be IDed, keep this thing moving, bring justice to Jamal, peace to Sheila, but he had to accept his largest fear.

Jamal's death was his fault.

Lesley threw up on his shoes. Masterson spoke with a broken voice. "I was sent to make sure Damien Quiles wasn't involved. They needed him on the streets, he was the only one on the inside."

Taking the kerchief from his pocket Lesley wiped his face and tried to see Masterson but couldn't. "Who else knows about this?" Masterson shook his head. "Who?" Lesley moved closer, ready to use force if necessary. "Blakely? Obuchowski? Hollingsworth? The chief? Who?"

"No one." He raised his hand and stopped Lesley's forward motion. "I collected the phone and never gave it to anyone." His words were matter-of-fact. "I knew what they were after and what would get in the way." Masterson made familiar motions Lesley didn't want to see. "They believed James would get in the way. I believed James to be a real and actual threat. I asked you to go with Obuchowski because I knew you'd see everything I hadn't done. I knew you'd see James."

"But who cares if I saw Damien Quiles, right? Who cares about the death of a black kid—"

"Fuck off, Powell. You know it wasn't like that."

"I don't know anything." Lesley stepped forward, ready. "What is it that you expect from me right now, Masterson? Absolution? Permission? What?"

"I want you to understand!" Masterson gripped his head and closed his eyes. "I thought I was doing the right thing."

"So forgiveness." Lesley didn't have space in his heart for that. "You showed me this," phone held up, "tell me you've known all along. Let me ruin my career *and* my marriage, and now I'm supposed to forgive you. Tell you it's okay, that I understand all your lies and sneaking around and your shared fucking cigarettes."

"This isn't about Deb."

"It *is* about Deb! It's about all of it." Lesley tucked the phone into his pocket.

"If you take that video in, Papachristi and Najjar—all their shit goes unaccounted for—"

"And if I don't?"

Lesley walked toward Sheridan with bits of vomit still on his shoes. He placed the phone in one of the station lockers, and forty-eight minutes later, back at his truck, he called the station to say he was headed in.

The normal buzz of the station was missing. The eyes of his compatriots avoided him like dogs who knew they'd been bad, and it occurred to him he could just leave, walk out the door, buy his new truck, and never come back. He didn't have to have the conversation. He didn't *need* to admit fault where truth was involved, and all of these people would probably rather he disappeared.

But that wasn't who he was.

"My office, Powell."

His sergeant entered behind Lieutenant Hollingsworth, and the door closed before Lesley realized it wouldn't just be the three of them.

The lieutenant from Central and the chief of police were waiting behind the superintendent, and two plain clothes were there to make things official.

He wanted to look them in the eye, see what muscles twitched and know how deep the well ran.

After he'd been asked to place his gun, badge, and phone on the desk, it was the plain-clothed woman who began to speak.

"You're being relieved of your duties as a detective within the Seventeenth District until Internal Affairs has finished reviewing your activities and the potential interferences surrounding the murder investigations of Emily Monroe and Jamal Dupont."

She was like a robot in a brown pencil skirt and no-nonsense flats.

"You will not be allowed to enter this precinct, clear out your desk, or have communications with anyone involved from either district until a ruling has been made.

"It's imperative that any and all information you have gathered is released to District One, and that you cease any and all communications with members of the victims' families, as well as those they knew and associated with in the community.

"Any further collusion or badgering of witnesses will lead to your immediate termination from the force and the increased possibility of criminal charges.

"Because you will be unable to access your files after leaving this room, we ask for your compliance in helping us locate the information you have gathered.

"Our investigating officers have already done a sweep of your home to prevent your accidentally withholding any relevant information.

"Your willingness to cooperate will be noted and taken into account during our investigation and subsequent determination."

His phone vibrated an emergent pulse on the desk as the room fell silent, and Lesley thought of the flash drive still sitting in his computer.

"This is where you do the responsible thing, Lesley," Hollingsworth urged.

"I don't have anything to give you, ma'am."

Her look of concern quickly transitioned to one of parental condemnation. "Well, if you do, we'll find it."

Lesley bore the remaining conversation and gained more insight than he gave before being escorted from the station.

He climbed into his sun-baked truck and dug through his glove box for his emergency phone. He needed to call Deb, make sure she wasn't home.

"I've been calling you." Her congestion when she answered told him she'd been crying. "The cops were here, Lesley. Why were the cops here?"

"I'm on my way." The sun coming through the windshield was hot on his thighs and he rolled down the windows for air he could breathe without feeling sweat on the inside of his mouth. "I'll be there in twenty."

But the twenty minutes didn't prepare him for the wreck he walked into. "What is this?" Deb stood in front of him, eyes swollen from tears. "What is this and why do you have it?" In her hand she held the flash drive.

"It's evidence . . ." Lesley tried to approach her, but she threw the drive at him and walked into the living room where her last bag sat overstuffed with items, ready to leave.

"Bill called to tell me they were coming." She was crying, struggling with the zipper, trying to force too much into too little until her fists came down at her sides. "What have you done? What's going on, Lesley?"

Reaching for her, he took the hand he'd promised to love, honor, and cherish and led her to their dining room table. "I can't tell you everything, but I'll tell you what I can."

He spoke. She watched him with eyes more sad than bitter and then rested her head in her hands while she continued to cry. "I love you, Lesley." Her positioning allowed him to see the naked indention of a tan line where her wedding band once lay. "Bill called, told me I needed to leave—and all I could think was, how do I save you?" Uncovering her face, she folded her arms in front of her and looked at him. "But I can't save you, can I?"

He reached for her hand and she let him take it. She *had* saved him. She'd seen the flash drive, recognized it as being out of place, and put it in her underwear not knowing what it was or why it would matter. "I'm sorry, Deb. I really am."

Rising from the table, she released him. "Me too."

He called her a cab because she was too upset to drive and then carried her bags down to the car. As much as he wanted her to stay, he wanted to know she arrived at her new life free of further damage.

Sitting on the edge of their bed after she'd gone, he stared into the empty closet across the room and thought about what to do next. The boy's closet was still full, had shoes that looked freshly kicked off lying by its door. Emily Monroe's closet would soon be cleared of her clothes but would remain full of her scent. The others would all be the same. By the end of the month, over forty homicides would be committed, each one leaving a trace of the victim behind. Lesley could see the emptiness of his own closet; but couldn't imagine Deb really being gone. Not like them. Never to return.

M-Theory

Bring everything together.

Alex sat with his back to the door staring at the whiteboard in front of him.

Monster. Mystery. Membrane.

The three people sitting with him and the one pacing behind them hadn't spoken a word in over ninety minutes.

Mother. Master. Magic.

Occasionally an excited inhale was heard. The pacing would stop.

Matrix.

Someone would approach the board, zero in on a possibility.

Bring everything together.

Inevitably a sigh followed, and positions were resumed. The footsteps behind them eventually aligned with the ticking of the clock.

Eleven strings. Nothing left open.

Six months earlier, they all believed they'd made a breakthrough in the use of loop quantum gravity to help support string theory's concepts of higher dimensions and supersymmetry—something they'd been working on for three years straight. In their excited rush to publish their findings, one of the variations of the Wheeler-DeWitt equation made their findings impossible, forcing them into a kind of stalemate that required them to either find the problem in their own theory or the flaw in the Wheeler-DeWitt variation.

Alex was consumed with discovering the failings in the variation, while the others assumed the problem was their own.

There was the sound of a door shutting, and Rakesh, a short Pakistani with the face of a twelve-year-old, leaned in, saying, "Alex, your wife is here." But the words didn't translate properly in Alex's brain.

"Psst, Alex." It was his nearness more than the words that drew Alex's attentions from the board, and the little man motioned toward the door with wide expectant eyes. "Your wife."

The phrase, unfamiliar and too far from where his mind was, muddled his perception, but he turned in the direction of his compatriot's eyes and saw her standing there.

Blue coat unzipped, hat lopsided on her head, mittens held in her hands, her unexpected appearance signifying that he'd forgotten something very important.

"I'm sorry." He didn't know what he was apologizing for, but he figured it was big. "I'm sorry I forgot."

Her smile confused the situation, and she threw a thumb toward the door. "Can I talk to you for a minute?" The whiteboard didn't allow for interruptions.

Eleven strings. Only one of them is time.

"Can I have a minute?"

The others sat watching, waiting to see what he'd do, and Rakesh leaned in again, whispering but not whispering, "We'll save our discoveries until you come back."

Alex turned to see she'd already stepped outside. Forcing his decision and not taking into account that he'd apologized. "I'll be right back."

Bring everything together.

Before the door had closed behind him, his wife had ensnared him with her arms and lips. A trace of alcohol rising with her breath. The absurdity of her interruption made him laugh, not because he thought it was funny but because he couldn't understand.

Mystery.

"You're drunk."

"I'm not drunk," she said, pushing away from him. "I haven't seen you awake in four days, and I'm horny."

"M, you can't interrupt me for that."

Her hands immediately plunged into her coat pockets, recreating a sign of protest that his little sister used to use. "What *can* I interrupt you for, Alex? Death? A housefire?"

Looking back at the door, Alex tried to understand the unpredictability of it all.

Matrix.

"I hate it here," she continued. "I want to go home—back to California."

Her sexual appetite dissolved into unexpected tears. "I'm so fucking lonely here."

Anomalies.

"I want to be around someone who loves me—who *sees* me."

Seeing her tears, he wiped her face.

Quarks.

"I want a friend, Alex. I *need* a friend."

A paper at home talked about black holes and quarks.

Irregularities.

"Are you listening to me? I want to go home."

"Okay."

Her emotion stopped. "What?"

It was as if her presence there was universally necessary for him to move forward.

Magic.

"Let's go home. I can come back later."

She wiped her eyes with her mittens. "Okay?"

"Let me just grab my coat."

She waited for him in the hall and held his hand on the way to the train. She talked about needing time, more time for connecting, less time for drinking wine by herself. He could picture the paper's location, east-side wall, second shelf—it should be in a green magazine holder, forest green was the color of 1998, all 1998 papers were in forest-green holders.

"Maybe we could take a trip—a weekend trip out of the city. Rent a car, find a cheap hotel somewhere, eat room service in bed . . ."

"Now's not a good time for traveling."

A baby cried. A mother swooped. Smiling, holding, soothing. Never alone.

Mother.

A baby. M's puzzles were linear.

Eleven strings. Nothing left undone.

With the front door barely shut, he removed her blue coat and kicked off his boots. There was enough time to accomplish two things before he headed back. Both had purpose, and both were potentially necessary for things to work normally again.

Unzipping the back of her dress, he slipped it off her shoulders and let it drop down to the floor. With her undergarments, boots, and leggings still in place, her cold hands slid up under his shirt, and over his chest while he unfastened his belt and loosened his pants.

Mother.

It wasn't easy. Her leggings and underwear were pulled down enough for penetration, but the wood floor was hard against his knees, and her boots caught the hair of his legs.

She tried to remove his shirt and got it stuck on his head.

She laughed, and he could smell her breath through the fabric.

Uncomfortable.

Bring everything together.

Shirt removed and testicles smashed in the process. A pause for re-adjustments. Accidental hair pulling, sighs of pleasure, gasps for more, tender bites, and the moment of completion.

Still inside her, he grabbed his shirt to slide between them as they separated.

He looked down the hall toward his shelves and the whiteboard, and her words began again. Looking at her there, one hand cupping his shirt between her thighs while the other stroked his back, he almost wished he had more.

Time.

"Will you come to bed with me?"

His fingers began to unlace one of her boots.

Take it all apart. Unwrap everything. Put it back together. Connect it all.

"I need to find a paper." He slid the boot off and inserted his fingers into her sock to slide it down, rubbing her foot along the way, stroking each toe individually. Each one a dimension, taking up space. "We have the web conference with Caltech tomorrow."

Her hand stopped moving across his back. "It's *Saturday*."

Again. "I'm sorry." The second boot was loosened and removed. He felt the muscles of her foot flex, and her toes point as he rubbed his fingers across the arch of her foot while removing her sock.

"If you keep rubbing me like that, I'll definitely forgive you."

M.

Time.

Her cheeks were flushed and her breath shallow. She held herself with one hand flung over her head. "Please don't stop."

Five more toes, ten dimensions of space. She took up all of them.

There's only one for time.

With her underwear hidden inside them, he gripped her leggings and guided them down until she was finally naked. He started at her ankle and did what she requested, watching her flesh give to the pressure of his fingers as she fell silent to his caresses.

Nothing left undone.

When he reached the top of her second leg, he stopped and patted her milky thigh. "I have to get to work."

She cracked him a half smile and reached for his hand. "Do you love me, Alex?"

Her drunkenness had made her absurd.

Irregularity.

"Of course I do." He shook his head and stood up. "That's why we're going to have a baby."

He didn't bother with clothes before walking out to the dining room, and M's voice rang up the hall. "Excuse me?"

Propositions known and unfamiliar.

Matrix.

He took a joint from a tiny box atop the hutch.

Membrane.

Lit it with an inhale.

Magic.

And stood staring at the board.

Master.

"Alex?"

Mystery.

"What did you say?"

Mother.

When he finally looked back to see her, only their clothes remained.

Extenuating Circumstances

"What will you do with your boys' weekend?" Emily's head jostled against his shoulder with every bump of the bus. His hand tightly held on her lap like something she didn't want to lose. Pressing. "It will be weird not to see you." She raised her head to look at him, "I've grown accustomed to your face."

And hands.

And lips.

And tongue.

"You could join us." He wanted her to know everything, every dirty detail of his corduroy-induced impotence and newly inspired mastur-bation schedule; the anxiety he felt every time they said goodbye; the self-restraint he required each time they were together and he witnessed her bare skin. Things that couldn't be mentioned. Things you don't say to someone you want to keep. Rules that were bent in her favor.

"You know I can't." Her hand came to rest dangerously close to the place Donovan had little control over. "But I . . ." Phone, buzzing in his pocket, vibrating her hand.

"You what?" Her movements suspended. His leg moving, just a touch, just enough to bring her hand closer to where they both wanted it to be.

"You should get that." Pulling away, she pointed to his pocket. "It could be them."

He did what she said, hoping they'd find their way back to this mo-ment.

"Hey, Donno, we're about an hour out—Jimmy wants to take Emily for drinks some place nice, so you pick the place and I'll change into something decent before we go." It was Jay, calling to solidify plans that *could have* happened had he not called right then and ruined the moment.

Sitting between the window and Emily, he didn't have much room to navigate the conversation discreetly.

"You there, Donno?"

"I'm here." Donovan turned down the volume and tried to switch ears, but Emily had heard her name and prevented the shift with the grab of his hand and a mischievous smile. She leaned in and he could feel the warmth their bodies created together.

"So find a place and tell her to meet us there at seven—or she could meet us at your house. Whatever you guys want to do."

The bus stopped and opened its doors. A group from the methadone clinic entered and they shuffled into the back, filling the seats all around them.

"Sound good?"

"I don't think Emily's going to make it out tonight."

"Give me a break, man."

She squeezed his thigh, and he turned to look out the window. "I can't help it. She's really busy."

"It's a good thing I've seen pictures of this chick, otherwise she'd be the worst made-up girlfriend in existence."

Emily's face expected answers. "Alright, Jay, I've gotta go." But her hand remained close to his arousal. "I'll see you in a bit."

"You told them I'm your girlfriend?"

Donovan saw the distant eyes and quiet antsy demeanor of their newest companions. He was thankful they'd remain oblivious to his humiliation.

"What pictures do you have of me, Donovan?" The slightest move brushed her hand against his dying erection; they were three miles and seventeen minutes from her stop, and dirty little secrets were trying to escape.

"I need you to see things from my perspective."

"And what perspective is that?"

Focus was necessary. He repositioned himself, placed her hands back onto her own lap to avoid the distraction, and tucked the phone away before explaining what made perfect sense to him. "The very definition of a girlfriend is a female companion in a romantic or sexual relationship." He'd thought about it and determined his use of the word was legitimate. "A relationship based on mutual interest or involvement." She closed her eyes and bowed her head like she was praying, praying him away, and he quickly took back her hands. "I don't know what you think we've been doing all these months, but I would say it's been mutual, a mutual romance that *is* involved and teeters on the verge of being sexual."

She covered his mouth and rested her forehead against his. "Don't say anything else," releasing his lips, "please." Taking his hands, she pulled them back toward her, closer to her hips and then held either side of his face. "I want you to kiss me." He could taste her breath. "Kiss me like it's true."

He stood on the edge of her facts and his fictions and needed her words to let one of them slip away. "I need you to say it." He could feel her. "Say you're my girlfriend."

She moved his hands, let her legs fall just wide enough that his fingers could slip easily between them. Her whisper, her sigh, the rushed relocation of her bag to block an accidental show for those who might care to look. "I want to feel you, Donovan."

He could sense the danger of not being able to stop. "Say you're my girlfriend."

Parting of thighs, hips raised, her hand pushing his. "*Shhhh.*"

"Say it, and I'll do anything." Fingers, passing, tipping, tracing around. "Say it."

"I'm your girlfriend."

He went deep and curled his fingers back. Her breath was a fire in his ear.

"I'm your girlfriend."

He felt her lack of fear or hesitation. Her arms pulling him closer.

"Please don't stop."

He felt the suction of her lips bruising his earlobe. Her steady stream, soaking dress, hand, and seat.

There was no escaping the image of her like that. It was the most brave and taboo act he'd ever committed. The arousal it caused came in unexpected waves that required immediate release each time they fell upon him, a lapping of distraction, release, distraction, that caused not only a desire for more physical contact but also more adventure in doing so.

Friday night, after he'd gotten drunk with Jay and Jimmy, he phoned her multiple times begging to see her. Saturday, after he'd sobered up over brunch, he called and attempted to apologize. Sunday, despite the rules, he sent her messages, asking if she was okay, sharing details of the World Cup final he was no longer interested in.

By Monday night, his apartment looked and smelled like the frat house none of them had ever lived in but all secretly wanted to. Jay's bed on the couch hadn't been made since his arrival, and days of clothes were bound within its blankets. Jimmy's space was a little more cared for, a blow-up mattress by the desk, almost made, bag on top unzipped and spilling. Beer bottles and cans littered the few horizontal spaces that didn't contain books and take-away packages. Scraps of quickly eaten meals were scattered everywhere but the bathroom.

They were celebrating their last night together by playing coffee-table poker. There were cigars and whiskey. Between games, Jimmy left to call Tilly, and Donovan lay back on the floor, checking to see if he'd heard from Emily. Reading an email from Lily.

"Maybe she's not good for you, Donno," Jay poured him a generous three fingers of Jameson and set it on his chest. "I mean, you're depressed all the time, she doesn't care enough to meet your friends or family." Checking his watch, "Dad thinks you made her up to avoid blind dates—"

"I didn't make her up."

"Well—"

Jimmy came back in and sat on the pile of couch blankets. "Who didn't you make up?"

Donovan said, "Emily" while Jay said, "Lily."

Donovan sat up, "Her name is Emily—"

"Lily's the student, Emily's the girlfriend." Jimmy had come in late but could at least keep track of the players.

"Lily, Emily, Emily, Lily, it doesn't matter. They're like the same person—"

"Fuck off, Jay." Donovan tossed his phone aside, done with the conversation.

"They're both invisible."

The doorbell rang and shot an unexpected wave of nervousness through Donovan. It didn't sound normal. It wasn't the quick half-ding of food being delivered, but a long-tailed note that still sounded incomplete.

Jimmy rose to answer. "You two play nice. I'll get the pizza."

"I left the cash up there." Donovan pointed his cigar toward the counter, but Jimmy had already rounded the corner. "Jay, could you take him the cash so I don't have to look at you?"

"Don't be shitty with me because your girlfriends are ghosts."

Donovan chucked a pillow at him, "Seriously, fuck off."

"It wasn't the pizza." Jimmy's voice sounded like a warning, and Donovan turned to see Emily standing next to his friend through thick layers of smoke.

It made him question his reality.

"I'm Emily," she extended her hand to his brother. "You must be Jay?"

The room was quieter than it had been for days, and Donovan jumped to his feet feeling sick and unprepared. "Yes," he said. "That's Jay," and motioned to his friend, "Jimmy."

Her smile said, Don't be nervous, and her mouth said, "We met at the door."

Donovan didn't know what to do. He couldn't take his eyes off the reality of her being there and wasn't sure how to control the situation without certain bombs being dropped.

"Could we interest you in some whiskey? A cigar? A game of poker?" Jimmy had always been better at this stuff, not good, but better. "Pizza should be here any minute."

Emily accepted all three.

She had her hair pulled back in a pigtail near the crown of her head and was wearing a navy-blue linen jump suit with sandals that wrapped her ankles and left the pinks of her toenails exposed.

Jimmy retrieved his traveling humidor, Jay rounded the counter to grab a glass, and before either task was complete, the bell rang again. She gave the go-ahead and the entire universe submitted to her command.

In the bathroom, there is body wash, shampoo, an extra razor and a toothbrush.

He motioned toward the couch where he'd imagined her sitting so many times before. "I'm glad you're here."

But she chose a seat on the floor, next to where Donovan had been sitting, and patted the space next to her.

What if she looks?

Pizza, whiskey, and cigars doled out, the four of them gathered around the coffee table. It felt slippery, like the right question could blow the whole thing apart.

"So how long have you guys been dating?" Jimmy asked.

She looked to Donovan for help and he tried to smile but it stuttered somewhere around the corners of his mouth. "Six months, maybe?" It was a good answer until she laughed and filled him with a naked dread of potential truth. "But I've had my eye on him for a lot longer than that."

Reaching out, she touched the scruff of his beard and her smile said too many things for him to determine.

What if she sees more of you than she's supposed to?

"I'm writing a book about love—"

"Oh, Jesus, Jay, let's not get started," Donovan interrupted.

All she has to do is look.

"Jay's been writing this book since middle school," Jimmy explained, leaned in to offer the details, and Emily tilted her head to catch his words in her ear.

How many men lean in?

How many does she tilt her head for?

You could be nothing to her.

Jimmy had finished, and Jay was suspicious. "So what can you tell us about love, Emily?"

This was a characteristic not often seen by those without years of personal experience with Jay, but Donovan knew his fishing techniques, and his heart pounded in his chest.

She slid her hand onto Donovan's leg and rubbed it with her thumb. Her smile said, I'll play your game, while her mouth said, "It's complicated."

There was a nod of agreement from Jay. "Why do you think the book's not done yet?"

Everyone's looking.

Donovan excused himself to the bathroom and quickly compiled the evidence of his lie, tucking it all neatly behind the trash bin under the sink.

Emily sat next to him, unafraid to touch, or laugh, or provide the occasional kiss as a sign of affection. She made herself comfortable, used the bathroom without asking, got herself water, more whiskey, offered to refill plates of pizza, and it was almost better than the imagined scenarios he'd concocted in his mind. The problem was, he couldn't determine if it was real or for show, or how long it would last. He couldn't decide if he should be alarmed, or angry, or happy about her imagined girlfriend-ness coming to life, or, more importantly, how far he could push it.

"Do you want to stay the night?" It was late. It was a not-so-innocent question meant to test her commitment to the part.

Her smile said, I *will not* play this game with *you*. "I've got time before I'm stranded. The trains don't stop running until four."

"If she stays," Jay interjected, "will you stop pouting?"

Time kept slipping. Donovan could no longer keep track of where she fit or how long she'd been there. The cards he'd been dealt didn't amount to anything; they felt like noise in his hands, a static interference in the actual game they were playing.

"Donovan never said you were a cigar-smoking card shark." Seven hands in, the majority of the chips had been slid across the table in her direction. She collected them quietly as if she wasn't keeping track.

Jay tossed his cards onto the table. "I'm out."

Then Jimmy joined him.

Donovan kept his cards hidden but added them to the pile.

Emily laughed and exposed her hand, "I've got nothing, you guys. Come on, I thought the point *was* to bluff." It felt like the most real play of the evening.

"I wish Tilly were here. You'll have to come up for a weekend so she can meet you."

Jay choked on a bong-hit and pulled out his phone, "Speaking of which."

"Jay . . ." Donovan knew his parents had asked for evidence.

"Mom would kill me if I came back without a picture." He held up his phone and Emily smiled at Donovan.

He couldn't determine what her smile said, but he recognized it from maroon corduroys and Whole Foods bags where mittens kept hidden what blue coats didn't want him to know.

"You should probably move your bong," Jimmy laughed.

Donovan kissed her to stop the loop of Adonis kissing the side of her head.

"Shit, okay, one more time."

He kissed her and stopped when his thumb felt the little gold band he tried to ignore was missing.

Whether she noticed his noticing was a mystery; but he took the missing ring as a sign and *not* a calculated play. A sign that he was winning. A sign that her absence had been due to late-night talks with a husband she no longer wanted, and that her arrival that evening, her comfort in his home, were in fact true displays of a future life where his mother and father would find her joining them around their Christmas tree and filling their home with the grandbabies his mother so desperately wanted.

He kissed her again. "I love you," he whispered into her ear and her hand found the back of his head, fingers flitting over memories dug into the back of his neck and then rubbed in, and around, until her sighs and yeses were inescapable in his mind. "I think you should stay."

She glanced behind them toward the bed before returning his gaze with a smile that didn't feel like pretending.

When it was time for her to leave, she slipped her feet back into her sandals. "It's been really great to meet you. I can't wait to come up so we can all hang out again." She looked at Jimmy and smiled. "And meet Tilly."

"Well, everyone's heard loads about you, so . . ." Donovan gave him a pat, as if to thank him, but it was really just to shut him up.

Their imagined future had grown after cards had been put away. They'd moved onto the couch where she laughed at childhood stories that never mentioned stuttering, or therapy, or his parents thinking he was gay.

Emily turned to Jay, "I look forward to reading your book someday."

"I *don't* look forward to you kicking my ass at cards." She laughed, and Jay held out his hand. "Be good to my brother."

Donovan watched the interaction with discomfort and then grabbed her hand for a quick escape.

Their steps fell in line once they'd reached the sidewalk. He thought of Sara, walking to George's for ice cream, the possibility of being seen in the early morning hours holding hands with his future. "I'm glad you came."

"I needed to see you." Her steps slowed and threw them off and then stopped all together. "You can't *really* know someone without seeing what they're like in their home with their belongings and friends."

She knows.

"Well, now you know." Panic struck, but he forced a smile even as he felt the doors outside his mind closing.

"Maybe." Her eyes turned before her head followed them. A train could be heard one stop down. "I have to go," she said. "I need to catch this."

He leaned in to kiss her but she moved too quickly away from him to notice. "You know me, Emily." He watched her walk the twenty remaining feet to the station. Knew she could hear him. "Maybe I'm the one who doesn't know you."

He avoided conversation and returned all her objects to their natural places in the bathroom. He watched her dot travel across his phone screen until she was home. He imagined her stripping her cigar-fumed clothes off and sliding into bed with a naked Adonis, begging his forgiveness, quieting his questions by spreading her legs.

He woke at eleven soaked in sweat, the air once heavy with smoke had turned soupy with humidity and made breathing gross and difficult to perform. Jay was snoring on the sofa, Jimmy's bed had been deflated, the shower was running, his bag already packed and sitting by the front door.

Reaching over his head, he felt around the wooden blinds and attempted to shut the windows. The upside-down backwards action required more brain function than he had at the time. He gave up and grabbed his phone.

Nothing except another email from Lily.

Emily's blue dot was at Loyola by the lake. He watched it and waited for her to call.

On Sunday, he watched her dot land at a hotel off Damen in Wicker Park and counted the hours it stayed there.

You are marooned.

Sara made herself at home. Donovan couldn't determine if he liked this or hated it. He hated that he couldn't like her even out of spite, and he hated her for not being someone else. But she said yes to anything he wanted to do, and he didn't hate that, not when so many fantasies had built up without release. He knew his life could be settled and different, like Jimmy and Tilly, if he at least *wanted* to like her. But he didn't, and he couldn't, so he hated her for that as well.

After spending five nights and four mornings hoping Emily would reappear and find Sara in his bed, Donovan tried to avoid the motions that told him Sara was preparing to go. She threw underwear in a bag and stretched a tank top over her torso, not bothering with a bra. "I'm leaving for Vietnam on Wednesday." The news came as a surprise. "There's a story there I'm hoping to make work." He didn't ask any questions, but he did feel panicked by what he would do with his time. "I'll be back in a few weeks." She kissed him like it was normal. "I'll get ahold of you then."

As soon as she was gone, Donovan began ridding himself of her. He stripped and showered and swept and washed everything from sheets to throw pillows. Four hours later, smelling of bleach and the sweat of his work, he said he'd meet Lily at Oz Park.

He assured himself that their recent exchanges had proved innocent; book recommendations, questions about his thesis, updates on a few classmates, a couple of inquiries reflecting her anxieties about moving away for college. He reassured himself that because there had been no more pictures or *open me* suggestions, a meeting, in neutral territory where no fear of possibility existed, would be fine. The presence of her, or Sara, prevented him from lurking beyond blue dots. And there were rules about such things.

It had only been three weeks since he'd rescued Lily from trouble and laid her drunken body in his bed. They walked for two hours before she stopped at a bench, not sitting, but ready to if necessary. "I'd like to see you again before I leave, if that's okay."

"Yeah, yeah, absolutely. Let's do dinner or something."

Her smile sent flash drive images of face and skin and hair all her own. They mixed with Sara's willingness and Emily's breathy yeses.

"I'd like that," she said.

He would have liked her more if her future with stilettos and red lipstick wasn't so obvious, but when she leaned in and pressed her body to his in a hug goodbye, the thought of taking her home and pretending that future didn't exist tickled his mind.

It's really that easy.

"Until next time, Mr. James."

He turned to avoid unintended contact with parts of himself full of their own intention.

"Maybe you should start calling me Donovan." He created the space necessary to mind himself. "The whole 'Mr. James' thing could get weird."

Her smile was as wicked as the images he struggled to squelch. "I think I like Mr. James more."

He spoke what they both knew to be true, "You're all trouble, Lily Ziyad."

And she one-upped him, "You haven't seen trouble yet."

Donovan shouted between beeps, circling the couch with his phone pressed to his ear. Yelling into the receiver, listening to what he'd just said, deleting his own unconvincing noise. Pacing a circle where only he understood the secret. "Emily, it's been two weeks and I've heard nothing from you . . ." Delete. "Emily, this is Donovan . . ." Delete. "Emily, you're a very bad girlfriend . . ." Delete. "I don't know what I'm doing . . ." Delete. "I didn't understand . . ." Delete. "What about the rules, Emily? There were rules about disappearing, and you've fucked them up—fucked everything up, do you hear me? Do you understand?"

Delete.

□   □   □
═══════════════

The detective looked Donovan in the eye, "I'm going to be honest with
you now, and I need you to listen to me."

The wire tickled Donovan's chest, and he felt it loosen under his fingers when they pulled across his skin.

A reminder.

"You're being used in ways that you can't possibly comprehend, and
I need you to stop and think for a moment." The clock ticked. "I can't
tell you how she got the flash drive or the video—but I can tell you all
the information gathered pointed to places people weren't meant to see."
Donovan felt uneasy about the detective's sudden hurriedness. "There
was no way to predict how that story would unfold. I didn't have all the
pieces, and I sure as hell didn't have all the answers, but guilty people were
going free and the innocent ones . . ." A tick . . . tick . . . ticking.

You gotta do what they say, son.

"You were a block from the *Tribune* when you were shot."

"I was." The detective nodded.

He has to say he talked to Sara.

"It had to have been you."

"There was enough information on both cases for everything not to
be lost if it was all made visible to the public. But it wasn't. Your relationship with her twisted."

The police had said he stalked her—they showed him evidence to
back it up. They said he'd left all those creepy gifts, and that the flash
drive was the last one.

But Sara had told a different story.

"If the police had the flash drive, Donovan, they could solidify their
case against you beyond a reasonable doubt." These words somersaulted
through Donovan's mind.

"They told me everything that was on it."

"Did they?"

It didn't make sense. They'd seen it, he knew they'd seen it. Seen *him*.

"Or did they name names and mention a blue coat?"

Donovan couldn't afford to falter, but his tongue felt too large for his mouth and allowed the detective to continue.

"Sara has the flash drive, Donovan. And she did more than allude to the images. She connected those images to Emily through the blue coat and then used Emily's association with Papachristi to prove her involvement in a child pornography ring. Are you going to allow that to happen? Are you going to allow people to believe that's who Emily Monroe was?"

He could have left. He could have left right then, and everything *might* have been fine, but he sat firm and listened.

A tan hand wriggled down between mattress and rail and pulled out a small manila envelope. Photos were unfolded, one he'd been shown, one he'd seen, one he couldn't escape. "What can you tell me about this?" The detective showed him one, and then the other. "Here, use these," fingers reaching for glasses, passing them over. "Look." Pointing. "Do you see that there?" It took a moment to make it work. The glasses needed to be at the right angle and Donovan's head a proper distance, but even then, the little blue cross was very difficult to discern among the shrubbery. "It's missing." His finger highlighted the complete absence of the cross in the second photo.

Donovan felt trapped by his own confusion.

"What can you tell me about tiny blue crosses, Donovan?"

"Nothing."

A memory. A twist, a turn, a rubbing.

The detective flipped through a few more photos. Showed him the numbered evidence markers that remained after Emily's body had been removed. The hair strands left from where she'd initially hit her head. The smallest bit of thread left by the catching of her skirt. The pencil that fell from her bag.

Years-old candy wrappers and cigarette butts had been collected and marked, but any trace of the cross was gone. Erased. Deleted.

"I don't see why this matters. I don't understand what you want me to see."

The photos were tucked away, placed back between mattress and rail.

"It's a discrepancy, Donovan. Something intentionally or unintentionally left from view."

The words still didn't hold meaning.

"Like your relationship with Emily. The real one. Not the one where she used you to get close to Lily—but the one where she loved you."

It felt like a trap.

"How guilty do you look if they don't actually have the flash drive? If it was never logged as evidence?"

Interference

Lesley rose before daylight and drove Deb's car up to Loyola. He wanted to sit on Emily Monroe's rock, where she spent her Saturday mornings, and think. He'd lain awake in bed most of the night listening to the air conditioner turning off and on like the ringing of a bell alerting him to the fact that someone else would die. Could die at any moment. It didn't matter what he did, or what he said, or what side he was on. People were going to die. Had already died. And innocent people were going to continue to be harmed in the process.

Parking the car, he took to the path. The sun was just beginning to rise, creating a horizon that couldn't be separated from reflection. The lake was familiar, but the quiet made it new. There were no sirens or traffic, birds flew overhead while light waves lapped against the rock barrier separating path from water. Everything had changed, and everything had remained the same.

The vastness of nature stretched out before him. Beautiful, peaceful, and wildly removed from all his thoughts. The universe didn't care what happened or what anyone had failed to do. The warmth of its sun still felt good when it came after months of ice and snow, and a low-humidity morning with a cool breeze was still refreshing after so much heaviness.

Lesley followed the trail to the white, flat rock and gazed down at the cigarette butts littering its base. He could tell by the varying brands that Emily Monroe hadn't been the only person who sat there, but she was precisely the person he'd come to see. Her death. Her killer. Her friends and family left to wonder. Lesley watched the gold of the sun bounce its reflection off the water. Staring long enough, there was no beginning and there was no end, a feeling more congruent with all he felt. He was sitting on the edge of infinity.

"Would you mind if I joined you for a minute?" Lesley looked up to see a clean-cut man with a leather messenger bag and a cup of Dunkin' Donuts coffee. "I had a friend who used to sit here. She recently passed away."

Lesley rose and extended his hand, "Detective . . ." But he wasn't a detective anymore, and he realized he'd have to learn how to introduce himself, have conversations. "Lesley Powell. We might be here for the same person." Lesley could put these pieces together. "You must be Brian Daniels?" He nodded and shook his hand. "Mrs. Monroe spoke highly of you."

"I came to watch the sunrise for her." Smiling out toward the lake, he brought the coffee to his lips and then paused. "It's a shame what they're saying about her, you know."

"What who's saying?"

The gentleman looked surprised, "That article in the *Tribune* this morning. It said she might have been involved with a sex-trafficking ring." Lesley looked away, back out at the water. He didn't believe it to be true but knew a connection could be faked through a flash drive found on her dead body. "I mean, I wouldn't have claimed to know everything about her, but . . ." Daniels sighed with the slightest of shrugs. "I know she had a good heart, touched a lot of people." He pulled some keys from his pocket. "A man from the train was passing these out Wednesday morning after the news broke." Attached to the chain was a small cross made of twisted blue ribbon. "You don't just do that for anyone."

Lesley took the object into his hand. The cross matched the color of her coat, the color of the shawl used to kill her, the color of the ribbon wrapped too tightly around the neck of a cat. "Do you know the man who passed them out?" At the cross's center, the letter M had been written in childlike scrawl.

"I know him as a guy I sometimes see on the train . . ." Lesley handed the keys back, and Daniels slipped them into his pocket. "I think he's deaf, and maybe a little unwell, but I'm only on the Brown Line for one stop."

"How many of those did he have?"

Brian Daniels chuckled. "A freezer bag full. If you were on the second-to-last car of the Brown Line that day, you were getting one. He made sure of it."

No one would have had time to make that many crosses between the breaking news and the morning rush. "Were they all the same?"

"They were," he nodded and pulled the keys back out to look at the cross again. "I thought it was a kind touch."

The sun had risen, and Lesley's phone began to pulse. "Excuse me a minute." The number wasn't immediately recognized but the voice was.

"Where you at, Old Man?" Lesley heard the urgency in Blakely's voice and turned from Daniels. "They've taken Deb and Masterson into custody."

"What?" Lesley gave a slight wave of his hand and moved away from the rock, toward the path, toward the street, toward Deb's car. "Why Deb?"

"They were brought in under tampering charges—"

"Deb has nothing to do with any of this." Lesley stopped at the street. A crosswalk away from the phone, and the video, and any potential justice for the boy. "What do I need to do? What can I do?" He would grab the phone from the nearby transit station. Hand it over, set Deb free.

"James was taken into custody yesterday after your little visit to his house."

"I don't care about James—"

"But you *do* because he identified you as the person who told him Monroe was dead, *and* he mentioned the flash drive."

"Shit."

"They didn't know they'd lost it."

"Blakely . . ." Lesley pressed and rubbed his forehead, "why—"

"Look, it was found on her person, sent to the wrong station, misfiled under a different case—there's good reason they can't find it."

"Jesus, Blakely."

"Don't do anything, okay? All the wrong people go to jail if you turn it over now."

"I can't leave Deb in there."

There was an unexpected pause on the other end of the line, "So what are we gonna do, Old Man?"

Lesley aimed for downtown, watching his rearview mirror, phoning ahead, and giving credentials that were no longer his. For most people, the boy's death was never more than a newspaper statistic, but Blakely was right. As unfair as it was, a white woman murdered in a park downtown demanded more answers and could be used to their advantage. There was a story there. A story that would take over news stations, and in turn set Deb free and bring justice to the boy.

But Lesley knew it was risky.

It took fifteen minutes to be transferred to the lady covering the story. "This is Sara Barrett." His rearview mirror said he might not be alone. "Where's good for you?"

He knew better than to go someplace visible. "Billy Goat Tavern." It was 7 a.m. and the location should have been hidden enough if he could get there without a tail. "But just in case, I need you to write a few things down." A car pulled out from Illinois Avenue, cutting off movement and gaining the attention of a traffic cop. Lesley turned left, then made a right, then found himself under the orange lights of Lower Michigan Avenue.

She said, "I'm ready," and Lesley began to talk.

"Donovan James, Lily Ziyad—there's a deaf man named Jack who rode the train with them—"

"Wait, wait, wait."

In the underbelly of Michigan Avenue, Lesley found a place where he could pull between dumpsters and delivery trucks. "You need to write it all down—Damien Quiles, Jamal Dupont, Sticharia, Metropolitan Youth." The red and green lights of the tavern glowed across the street. "Globe Cargo, Christi Limited, Cook County Board of Commissioners, Yasser Najjar." He waited to make sure he wasn't seen or followed. "Nicodemus Papachristi, Isabella Escamilla, Nate Aram." He dropped the moving images of Jamal Dupont's murder into a lingerie bag with the flash drive and covered them both with a pink scarf.

"Everything else will be there in five."

He waited to see the woman as she'd reported herself: dreadlocks, black glasses, carrying a green bag.

Once she entered the tavern, Lesley did as he and Blakely had agreed. He took the stairwell up three flights and found the little-used elevator Blakely had used for drops in the past.

Lesley wondered if he'd look. If Blakely would feel the weight of the bag and check to see what, other than the flash drive, was there.

The bag was dropped. The doors were closed. And moments later a text came through, "See you on the flipside, Old Man."

The transfer was complete. Now, it was up to Sara Barrett.

The air on the sidewalk clung to him once his shoes hit the pavement of Lower Michigan Avenue. For the third time in under twenty-four hours there was stillness in the air. This time nothing paused or settled. This time the silence suspended Lesley between terror and relief.

Voices of people coming down from the upper avenue could be heard on the stairwell behind him. In front of him, a cyclist rode by close enough to cause a breeze when they passed.

He stood, waiting to cross the street, while another disregarded stop-light caused horns to honk and tires to squeal. He felt his own awareness of sound. His shoes, tapping once he began to move through the chaos of drivers shouting at one another in unconcealed anger.

He thought about what he would do and where he would go after Deb was free and okay.

A loud pop like a backfire settled his plans. He would buy a truck, take a road trip, ride donkeys through the Grand Canyon, but Lesley was suddenly very confused by his position on the sidewalk and his close view of the ground.

"Sir?" The face was dark and close and terrified. He heard the shout-ing of motorists become screams. "Sir, try not to move. We're going to get you some help."

Gum smeared on the cement. A roach wandering through shadows. An empty Dunkin' Donuts bag trapped under a tire, its stapled receipt blowing in the breeze.

"Can I get your name? What's your name?"

The bell above the tavern door kept ringing.

Disaffiliation

An explosion of thoughts and feelings affected Nate Aram's sympathetic nervous system when she said they could meet at The Robey. Fight or flight had never been a preferred sensation, and so he attempted to ignore the pit in his stomach by not asking any questions and pretending that a hotel bar was a perfectly reasonable place to meet.

He also stopped to buy her a gift. Just in case.

He'd seen her in the pale blue fifties-schoolgirl dress before. Sometimes with a sweater over the top, or a shirt underneath; sometimes with winter boots, leg warmers and leggings. But it was summer, and hot, and there weren't any added layers, just a sleeveless linen dress with a boat-neck collar and a pair of canvas shoes.

"Thanks for taking time to meet with me." He placed his hand on her back and they exchanged an awkward set of cheek pecks like neither of them fully understood how to interact with one another anymore.

Patting the chair next to her, she closed the book she'd been reading and pushed it aside. "What's up?"

He thought of the gift in his pocket, wondered if she had a room. "We shouldn't be meeting here. You know that, right?"

She shrugged, "It's where I was heading when you called."

"And why is that?"

He joined her at the bar and she leaned in to whisper, "Cockroaches." The bartender deposited a glass of wine in front of her and she stopped him from leaving. "Could we also get a seltzer water with lime?" This was Nate's preferred drink. "Unless you want something stronger?" She looked at him and smiled. "You *did* sound rather serious on the phone."

Nate knew that adding alcohol to the mix would only increase the likelihood of bad decisions and he waved the bartender off.

"You made it sound like you're breaking up with me." Her laugh told him she didn't understand the detriment of their relationship, or the consequences of being found there together.

"This isn't a joke, M."

"Oh, I didn't think it was." She thanked the bartender for the seltzer and slid it closer to Nate.

"Isa intercepted a call from Kadi about your party."

The wine glass hadn't reached her mouth before she returned it to the bar. "What party?"

"Your surprise party."

"Oh, *that* party." She gave a light laugh and took a sip of her wine. "Who's coming and when is it happening? I'd like to be prepared."

"Goodness, M, this isn't about the party—"

"I'd still like to know."

"Isa has completely lost her mind about you. I've never seen her so mad." He tried to see M as the familiar stranger he once knew. "She said if I didn't stop seeing you, she'd take matters into her own hands."

M choked a little on her wine, her hand rising to her chest while her face contorted with confusion. "What is *that* supposed to mean? It sounds rather threatening, doesn't it?"

"It's not a threat to you, it's a threat to me. She's going to divorce me." Resting his head in his hands, he stared down at the bar and struggled not to enjoy the fact that M had reached out and begun rubbing his back. Trying to soothe, trying to comfort.

"Come on," she rested her head against his, "she won't divorce you. Nothing's happened. Nothing is ever *going* to happen."

But they were there, in a hotel, and he remembered what it was like to comfort her and feel needed. "How long are you staying? Do you need money for the room?" He moved to pull out his wallet, but she touched his arm to stop him.

"Don't be ridiculous, Nate." Her smile rang through her voice, full of humor and missing the point. "You're not paying for my room." She gave him a playful elbowing. "That is, unless of course you *want* Isa to divorce you."

The casualness with which she acted frustrated him. Her touch confused him, led him, pulled him in even while he tried to remain firm. "This isn't funny. Okay, M?"

"I just don't understand why you're here," her exasperation bubbled to the surface, "why you had to see me now. Right this minute."

Her disappearing smile quickened his pulse. "This entire situation has gotten out of hand."

"What situation?"

Her confusion compounded the problem and made it hard for him to pinpoint a line of argument she could follow. "You never should have gotten involved with Papachristi."

Her eyes widened, and he watched her recoil. "*Involved* with him?"

"You know what I mean—"

"No, no, I don't. If you think for a single instant that 'not doing' was the appropriate call to make, then you can go fuck yourself."

"That's not nice—"

"Nice? We're talking about *children*, Nate, not a few bootlegged DVDs."

He took her hand, an act he'd done at least a dozen times before. "But maybe you have it wrong."

Her head shook. Her lips crooked up in a wry smile.

"This isn't how I wanted things to be. I wanted to be your friend, but I can't lose my marriage, and Papachristi is one of the firm's largest—"

"You wanted to be more than my friend, Nate Aram." Her eyes met his with a truth that felt cursed, and he withdrew his hand from hers.

"That's not fair, M."

She realigned herself on the stool, turning to him, resting her legs against his, "Why are you covering for him?"

"It's not about him."

"But it is—you just said it was."

Nate couldn't look at her the way she looked at him. "Isa is going to divorce me. That's what this is about."

She shook her head, "This isn't about Isa—"

"It is about *Isa*. It's about my marriage, to *her*—"

"Then why bring him up? Why mention Papachristi at all?"

"Because it complicates things—taking him on complicates things. It draws attention to you and everything you do."

"Everyone I talk to?"

"Yes."

"So it draws attention to you?"

They sat in a silence far more awkward than their hello kiss had been. Getting some cash from his wallet he set it next to his untouched seltzer, watching, wondering, wishing she'd chosen the location for him and not someone else. If only this once. "I'm afraid I'm not going to be able to see you again, M."

She swiveled on her seat and took up her glass of wine. "The feeling is mutual."

Taking up his jacket, he slipped the gift he'd purchased from its inner pocket and slid it toward her. "Happy birthday. I'm sorry I won't be able to make the party." He wanted to watch her open the gift, see the thin blue material draped across her shoulders. But she ignored it, slowly returning to the position he'd found her in: book opened, head bowed, seemingly oblivious to anyone else around.

"You know," she said, "if you're involved in any way, it's going to come out."

He didn't need to respond, he needed her to listen. "Everyone knows Alex is gone and you're alone for the summer." She didn't look up or toward him. "You should be careful, M. Try and keep a low profile until you can get back to California."

"Goodbye, Nate."

Dirty Little Secrets

His eyes rested on the naked Barbie with matted red hair and a blue ribbon tied around its neck that she'd dumped on the table in front of him.

"I need to know it's not you." Shaking hands spread the other objects out and closer to him. "I need to know it's not you." There was a torn-out pornographic picture of a redhead in bondage, a bottle cap that read, 'A Prost to Extenuating Circumstances,' a broken paintbrush, some false eyelashes, and a nail that looked like a smaller version of a railway spike.

"The first package was a flower—a black lily. I thought it was from you," she laughed nervously through tears as she searched the pub. "I thought you were being sweet."

"I've never left you any flowers."

She hadn't looked at him, not once since he'd arrived, and he made a quick glance around the pub so familiar to them. The table they first sat at, by the window, facing the street, with the Armitage stop hanging over it in full view. The table by the side door where they'd written their list of rules and then spent weeks breaking most of them. Another lunch, another beer, at the counter where they chatted with the one waitress who always seemed to be there, she was there now, busy behind the bar, taking orders from those more interested in the Cubs game than the disturbing mementos Emily had spread before him.

He was thankful to be in the corner, hidden by the lack of light, thankful the music and television sounds covered their conversation and her tears, but he knew she'd picked Kincade's because of its ease of access to a quick train escape and that the number of people meant she'd be safe if he was, in fact, a creep.

"Then there were things like," she picked up a brooch and a ring, "random pieces of jewelry, a plastic snake, some rotten fruit, hair clips—"

"I haven't left any of these things. I've never left you anything." Trying to comfort her, he placed his hand on hers, but she reacted as if it burned and pulled her hand into her sleeve. "Emily."

"I need a drink. Can we order a drink? I need . . ." She covered her face with her hands, and her crying increased to silent sobs.

Donovan excused himself and made his way to the bar. He didn't want to look back and draw attention to what was happening, but the waitress was already looking over his shoulder with suspicion. "Is she okay?"

He had to check for himself. "I think it will be fine. She's having a bad day."

She placed a stout on the bar. "I was just getting ready to take this to her. Tell her it's on me."

"Thank you." He smiled, thankful she hadn't come over, thankful she hadn't seen the chaos of items spread out, or the suspicion of his guilt. "If we could get a couple waters and two club sandwiches, that would be good." She put the order in and said she'd bring the water, but he didn't want her at the table. "Could I also grab a beer?" He needed time to clear it off. "I can come back for the water."

Beers in hand, he turned back toward the table. Emily looked a mess of sleeplessness and lacked whatever she did that made her skin bright under all her freckles.

"Here you go. Food's on the way."

Still, she hadn't looked at him. She drank half her pint while he returned to the bar and was crying all over again when he got back.

"Let's get these things off the table."

His hands moved to touch them, but fear and her words stopped him. "They stole my paintings."

"Who did?"

"I don't know." It was a defeated shrug. "They didn't take all of them." Her hands rubbed her face like they could calm her tears. "But they took the most important ones," then touched her chest, "to me, the ones that mattered *to me*."

"When did this happen?" Whatever instinct drew his hand toward her again also made her pull out of reach. "Emily, please—"

"It was that Friday," her hands slid between her and her seat, "after the bus." The tears had stopped, but she still avoided looking at him. "They broke in through my back door and took them from my studio. I'd been with you all day, so it couldn't have been you—"

"Why would it have been me, Emily?"

"They were paintings of you." The words, combined with her eyes finally landing on his face made the hair on his neck stand on end. "They were all the paintings of you."

Sitting with fists pressed to his lips, he stared across the table at her and tried to determine what he was feeling. "Can we get all this stuff off the table?"

Her face crumpled and was once again buried behind hands. "I need to know none of this was you."

"This wasn't me," he said, motioning to the items on the table. "The paintings weren't me." He leaned in closer. "I don't know what else you want me to say."

"They killed Jack."

"What?"

"Jack, they killed him—"

"Who's Jack? Jesus, Emily, what's going on?"

She looked frantically around the pub. "My cat," shaking hands wiped her face. "He's not actually my cat but . . ." Head, wagging, "It's not important. I mean, Jack *is* important but . . ." Her words and motions were all over the place.

"Emily—"

"I need to know it wasn't you."

"It wasn't me. Why would you ever think it was me?"

"You were watching me!"

"You watch people all the time. That doesn't mean you go around killing cats."

They let the comment rest between them.

"I'm afraid, Donovan."

He wanted to touch her. He wanted to continue unwrapping the presence of her. He wanted to hold her and keep her safe. His phone vibrated, and he knew it was an email from Lily. Then Emily's gold band caught light, and he knew there were things between them that neither wanted to know but should be asked, or told, or handed over. These things needed to be either forgotten or forgiven, but they couldn't be avoided, not forever, not anymore.

As much as he didn't want to ask the question, it had to be asked. "What did your husband say?"

Her eyes wiped by her sleeves, "He doesn't know."

"What do you mean, he doesn't know? How can he not know?"

"I haven't told him."

"But you're his wife, it's *his* house—" She collapsed onto the table and cried. "Emily."

Donovan moved his chair closer and rubbed her back without her flinching away or resisting. He felt her skin relax under the bulk of her sweater and brought his head down to hers. "Let me have them pack the food up. You need sleep."

There was a resurgence of tears. Her voice squeaked, said she couldn't go home, didn't want to go home, not right then, not for a while.

"*Shhh*, okay, it's okay. I'll be right back." He returned to the bar and changed their order to-go and then quickly moved to put all her horrifying little tchotchkes back into her bag before their food appeared.

The waitress, who didn't frequently step out from behind the bar when it was so busy, delivered the food herself and addressed Emily directly. "Are you doing okay? Can I do anything? Call anyone for you?"

It was a slight performed in sisterhood and meant to protect women from men who caused harm. Donovan noticed, and he felt betrayed. He had once protected the waitress from a man much worse than himself. "I've got her."

But she didn't budge, she waited instead for Emily's response, which came with a smile that said, Thank you, and words that told half-truths. "I'm sorry, my cat died, and I just feel a little emotional. I'll be okay."

He picked up her bag of secrets and tried to make sense of dead cats, stolen paintings, and a husband who wouldn't notice any of it. "Come on," he said once the waitress had left, "let's get you out of here."

Donovan led her out, and up, and on, and she didn't object when he guided her off the train at Montrose and down the stairs around the corner to his apartment.

Despite the heat of the day she was wearing a pale gray sweater with long sleeves and jeans. He'd never seen her wear jeans and felt betrayed by their unexpected appearance on her legs and hips. Her hair was down in its normal fashion but untamed and bulked by the humidity of the great lake that stretched its fingers over the city year-round, causing weather systems and circumstances all its own. Emily was not unlike the lake.

He watched her eyes and nose, both red and dripping against her will, continuously being wiped by a tissue in a hand where a gold ring had reclaimed its space upon her left ring finger. Even this broken facet of her appeared perfect and beautiful, something he needed to keep. But she wasn't something he needed to grab and not let go of; she was there, like a deer, ready to expose her neck to the mountain lion if the mountain lion should be him.

She kicked her Converse off in the entryway and pushed them toward the closet with her foot, mirroring what he normally did with his own shoes.

They were alone, and in his apartment, but not in the way he'd imagined it to be.

"Go ahead and make yourself comfortable." In the kitchen, he grabbed two plates and two cups and two sets of silverware and knew it wasn't for show. "I'm going to set you up with some food, and then you can nap, or watch some television, or read a book—I've got lots of books, whatever you want."

It wasn't how he had imagined, but it was real, and its realness encouraged him to continue speaking while she stood at the counter's edge looking at the space as if it were new to her.

"Do you see other people?"

Donovan had planted evidence around his apartment to prove her presence, and the thought of her discovering it ignited the tips of his ears. "What do you mean?"

"Other women—do you go on dates, have sex, see other women?"

"Emily." The conversation wasn't one he could afford.

"It's understandable if you do, I just . . ." She looked back out into the apartment.

"You just what?"

"I don't know. I guess I just want to know—maybe it's one of them, maybe you have a jealous lover, maybe there's someone I don't know about."

"You're the only woman I see," not necessarily a lie. "The only woman I *want* to see," but this was closer to the truth. "There's no one else." He wrapped himself around her while she stayed stiff-armed against him.

"Only you." He smelled her head and was thankful for clean sheets and empty trash bins. "I love you, Emily." It was a relief when her arms slowly rose to slide around him in return.

"Can you just hold me for a while?"

He steered her to the space where his fantasies of her were the most vivid and unencumbered. It wasn't what he'd imagined, but she was there, lying in his bed. That she cried herself to sleep against him, still fully dressed, didn't matter.

The food went untouched. Emily slept through the night and then woke him early the next morning to say she had to get home.

His arms and hands tried to coax her into remaining, "It's okay, just stay, everything will be fine." The scent of her told him he'd need to switch out the body wash in order to maintain her presence.

"I have to meet someone at nine," she whispered.

He thought of her disappearing. He thought of her wandering out his door and never coming back. He thought of flash drives and Sara and the flesh he'd yet to see. "Why don't I come with you." Her body gave into the hands that found their way under her sweater and slid across her back. "We could spend the day together. I could take care of you."

Her laugh said, I don't need that kind of caring. "You can come, but you'll have to stay out back." She wouldn't disappear. "There's a meteor shower tonight." Her jeaned leg cautiously found its way over his, and he knew she could feel his intention pressing into her. "I want to sleep under the stars and do asanas at sunrise."

She was there, and he didn't want to think about her husband, or the cat, or who she was meeting and why it couldn't be put off. He didn't want to think about the rules now that all but one had been broken, and so he pushed himself against her and rolled her onto her back, landing on top, pinning her under him.

"I want to make love to you."

Her hands ran down the sides of his face and her fingertips lingered in his beard, "I have to get home and shower. I have a meeting."

"You're not saying no."

"I'm saying I have to go."

It was almost time; the ticking clock sounded the way patiently forward, allowing their bodies space while advancing the inevitable. He wouldn't let her escape. He knew what he needed to do and how to get her there; he just needed time, and time meant following her, patiently, wantonly, through the next few hours, so that in the end she would be his, and naked, and her girlfriend-ness would be fully realized.

And so he followed. Donovan stood behind her as they entered her building, excited by the proximity of her life and the possibility that her husband would find him there and know where she'd been all night.

"I need to shower." She unlocked a door just inside the vestibule that opened to an unlit wooden staircase descending into darkness. "I know it's not ideal, but you can wait down here or head over to the park—"

"I'll wait here." He continued to follow her. Down the stairs and into a cobweb-infested shell of what could have been a garden apartment a hundred years prior, but now contained only remnants of furniture, a few yard tools, some bikes, and a coin-operated washer and dryer.

Her smile said she was sad. "When I'm done, I'll pack what I need and meet you back here." He leaned in to kiss her, but she looked back to where they'd come from and pointed. "Would you mind shutting and locking that door? I'm going to head up through the back."

He thought she would wait, but as his foot hit the first step, the door behind him closed and she was gone. She closed one door, he closed and locked the other.

Ivy had grown over what windows were available and left the space unusually cool for the time of year and the heat outside. He didn't like to imagine her there, in that space, with cobwebs and dead cockroaches on the cement floor.

A screech and turn brought the sound of water through the pipes, and he imagined her naked above him but was unable to hold it because her shower was brief and he'd yet to see her naked. Her fear, even if it had momentarily been a fear of him, had lessened her resolve and heightened her attachment.

Above him, he heard the vestibule door open and then a doorbell before a buzzer rang. He heard the visitor open the second door, the one that led up the stairs to the front of her apartment, and he wanted to know who it was and what they were doing there that was so important. After a few moments his curiosity won, and he opened the back door, stepped out into the concrete cubby hidden under the stairs and waited to hear something. He wasn't lurking. He was waiting for them to come down. He'd watched and learned that Emily liked to bring people down into her little garden patio and believed it only a matter of time before she brought this visitor down as well.

It took longer than he'd hoped, but eventually he heard a door open and a woman's voice come out. "And the man who made the initial report, are you romantically involved with him?"

Donovan's heart beat wildly in his chest and his ears filled with cotton, waiting, waiting, waiting.

"My life's not nearly that complicated. He's the father of one of my students, and we have a few mutual friends."

Donovan wanted to believe her, but he thought of her phone, the messages, the calls, the hotel, the little blue dot, the three weeks of no contact, and turned, tripping over a stack of empty planters stacked on a small table—crashing, clanging, scattering.

He froze.

"It's just my neighbor doing laundry."

Donovan was kept a secret, hidden in a basement full of webs and roaches.

At 7:23, after they'd spread out some blankets, opened the wine and put food between them, Donovan watched her watching some children digging in the sand and felt she could slip out of his life at any moment with little consequence to herself. What he wanted from her wasn't just the temporary physical manifestation of girlfriend-hood, a romantic meteor shower at the lake, or a home-cooked meal. None of these actions would mean a thing if they didn't mean everything, and his name had gone unmentioned.

All he wanted was for her to stay, never leave, never disappear and break his heart and make him call Sara, or look at flash drives, or take walks in parks with girls who would one day wear black stilettoes and make his dick limp. He wanted her to be warm. Full of yeses. And his.

"Why didn't you tell them about me?"

Emily's head fell against his shoulder. "It would complicate things." Her arm looped through his. "Things are already complicated enough."

He watched the children raising their heads to see the sand they'd tossed in the air. "You thought I'd done all these things—"

"I didn't think you'd done any of it." She looked at him, accentuating the sincerity of her words. "But I needed to be sure." A deep release of breath as she returned her head to his shoulder and pulled him closer. "You're the least complicated thing in my life right now, Donovan James. I didn't want to change that."

Dead cats, cryptic messages, naked Barbies, and stolen paintings. *Of you.*

He didn't want to pull away, but he needed to look at her. "What's going on in your life?" He needed to see what her eyes, hands, and lips said when she wasn't speaking. "What do you do when you disappear for days?" They darted, and brushed, and parted. "Why doesn't your husband know or care when you're gone, with me, or someone else—"

"There is no one else."

The children ran squealing past, their parents calling in the distance.

"But there's *him*, and there's *me*."

"He's in California," she said. "He got a job at Caltech and left last month."

Possibility smothered Donovan's fears. His apartment was too small, they'd need to move so she'd have room to work—there were Christmases and trips back to Lansing to plan for, a final "fuck you" to his father—

"I . . ." Her eyes said what her lips were too hesitant to speak.

"You're not going with him." The weight of seven months lifted by a single declarative. "I'm going to marry you, Emily Monroe."

In the distance, parents tried to calm children, offered them snacks, asked them to sit, steered their eyes to the sky where the show would soon begin. It all pointed to a future where he and Emily would sit and wipe sand from cheeks and brows and fingers. And her smile told him all of this was necessarily true.

"Should we lie down and get comfortable?" She moved pillows and blankets and thermoses full of cocoa. "I don't want to miss any of the action."

They wrapped together in a blanket, eyes turned up toward the heavens while their bodies flirted with intimacies yet to be explored. Donovan contemplated the unwrapping of her realness, a thing he now believed to be his, and fell asleep under shooting stars that lasted well into sunrise.

She woke him soon after his eyes had closed. Coaxing his body into the poses of her morning routine using words that were minimal and quiet and hands that didn't avoid those parts of him more carnally interested in her touch.

He felt sleep-drunk and underprepared for what the suggestive contours of her fluid body could achieve without effort. "You'll want to raise your chest." She was reclined, legs bent, feet tucked up next to her sides. "The best stretch happens when the top of your head is flush with the ground like this." He watched her neck bend back in a sort of ecstasy. Every vulnerable point of her body exposed.

Eventually the positions reached a point where her direction and guiding hands could no longer help. "Don't stop," he said. "I want to see you finish."

But she smiled and took his hand and led him to the edge of the lake where she slid out of her pants and tossed her shirt to the side. Standing before him, pale-skinned in peach-colored undergarments sheer enough to expose the complete form of her breasts and color of her nipples, she began walking backward into the lake. "Come on," she motioned. "I want to feel you out here with me."

Water crept up her legs and thighs, wetting her see-through underwear. Donovan felt hesitant to expose himself so thoroughly to her. Without walls or doors. Completely open to the world.

"I want you to feel me out here with you."

Clothes carefully discarded next to hers, he entered the water, unable to hide his body's desire for what she had yet to give, and he suffered the uncertainty of his lack of control.

"Come closer."

Each step he took forward seemed to encourage her backward movement until at last, water mid-breast, she stopped and waited. Two feet away, she reached for him, pulled him closer, and wrapped her arms and legs around him—causing fear that he would stutter, and panic that she'd laugh.

His body pressed rigidly against hers.

"It's okay," she whispered, and softly kissed his bottom lip. "I'm not going anywhere," she whispered, and slid her hand down between them. "I want this," she whispered, and pulled aside what material kept their intimacies apart.

She wasn't like Sara; her yeses were whispered into his ear like secrets as she guided him into her body and swam against him in a moment too brief for the memory to become anything more than a blinking of his eye.

Spent, and retreating, he felt her grip on him loosen. "I'm sorry." The shame and embarrassment were nearly too much. "I'm sorry."

She didn't laugh, nor did she smile. Her pale skin remained pressed to his, and her eyes, new and different, looked into him with an openness he'd never experienced while her lips moved air into his mouth and said, "I love you, Donovan."

"I don't care about the cross." Donovan wanted the detective to be telling the truth, but that truth was malleable and uncertain and didn't really matter as far as his future was concerned. "I need to know who talked to Sara."

They're using you.

"I wouldn't be here if I hadn't met with her." The detective stretched his fingers like he was trying to spread them wide enough to contain the situation, and Donovan's heart pumped in his chest. "I'm sure they probably wish they'd gotten to me first, but here we are." Hands gripped his thighs. Fingers digging into flesh. "I thought you were guilty; I really did, but . . ." He hesitated, gesturing toward the stack of papers and files. The book.

Donovan finally had what he needed. A confession that would erase all his sins.

He closed his eyes and breathed in a future that didn't involve prison time or accusations of pedophilia and murder. It was a future void of Emily's love, but now he could face that reality free from punishment.

Donovan felt free to speak the truth. "She saw what she feared when she looked at those photos," he said. "I never asked Lily for anything." Opening his eyes, he hoped to see a different ending. "But Emily would have never believed what I had to say about the flash drive." He breathed in through his nose and out through his mouth. "I'm not sure anyone would." Donovan felt his shoulders move in an unfamiliar shrug. "I had to do what they said."

The detective pushed the call button and Donovan prepared to leave. "It's not too late to do the right thing." He pushed the call button again. "Everyone will know the truth; the right people will be punished. All you have to do is say it was yours."

"The right people will never be punished for this, Detective Powell." A nurse entered the room, and it didn't matter what Donovan said in her company because all of it was over and he was free from blame. "Lily gave me the flash drive, but I never asked for it and I certainly didn't want it."

"So tell them that." There was a smile, a smile that said, I beg you, and for a moment Donovan wanted to believe it could all be made better with his words.

"What can I do for you, Lesley?" The nurse was far too cheerful for the occasion. "Are you needing some meds?"

The detective shook his head. "No meds, just some water and a light if you've got one."

She laughed and headed toward the door. "Sorry. No smoking in here today, sir."

He laughed and smiled and said, "It's all about the opportunity, young lady."

Interference

Lesley had been moved from the ICU and into a regular room where he'd remained stationed for two weeks. The surgery had gone well, they said, but that didn't mean he'd ever walk again. In a month, he'd be moved to a rehabilitation facility where he'd learn how to live in his new body more efficiently and safely. Then, with any of their so-called luck, he'd be home where others would need to provide services he could once perform himself. "Lucky," that's what they kept saying. He was lucky.

Sara Barrett's initial story led to an exposé that drew lines from Yasser Najjar, to Papachristi, to a handful of youth programs and facilities, to a string of missing persons, a child-pornography ring, and a trafficking operation that incriminated some of the city's most prominent business-men, politicians, and the police force itself. Nate Aram and Isabel Escamilla had been offered immunity for their cooperation in trials that would stretch for years, but Lesley knew they'd never make it that far.

The story of Damien Quiles, a casualty of all the aforementioned, had split the community surrounding his crime and the death of the boy in half. Damien had been a victim. His addiction issues were tied back to the trauma he had suffered at the hands of men who took from him, and demanded of him, things too insufferable to bear. He feared for his brother's safety should he too wind up in juvie. He feared Joey would be sucked into a life where choices were no longer his to make, and he killed Jamal Dupont to keep that from happening.

The press quoted Damien as having said, "The Latin Kings do less harm to the kids in my neighborhood than the systems you all made up to help them." And the extenuating circumstances surrounding Damien's actions lessened his moral blame in the eyes of the courts. He was charged with voluntary manslaughter and placed on house arrest until his trial.

Within forty hours of his release, no one could find him.

Because of the systems, because of their failures, because law enforcement had not taken action on smaller crimes and hidden evidence of larger ones, a full-blown federal investigation had been launched. The shit of it all rolled down to the men and women who, more often than not, were following orders of those well above them in power and rank.

Blakely had been questioned a few times by a few different agencies, but never in regard to his own actions. He'd made well-timed phone calls and met people in places that allowed him reasons for being where he was and doing what he was doing without raising red flags or calling attention to himself. If anyone was lucky, it was Blakely.

Alina Obuchowski, who had been hired to investigate the crimes being committed by police officers involved in Operation Lake Effect, had been put on leave and was under investigation for withholding evidence and the disclosure of classified information to the press.

Lesley had seen photos and interviews of Masterson and finally saw that the man *was* sad. He'd been indicted for crimes he hadn't been explicitly asked to commit. But Lesley's feelings toward him were complicated by a number of factors, including, but not limited to, images of him and Deb together.

Deb had been released without charge and that was as close to "lucky" that Lesley could feel. Despite the number of people being taken in and questioned, no leads surfaced in connection to his shooting. He was past the point of caring. Knowing who, he understood for the first time, wouldn't change anything.

So while Sara Barrett had shone a light on things that began to fall apart as soon as they were exposed, what everyone *really* wanted to know was who her source was. Whoever it was, their credibility held sway over the veracity of things being written. Speculations swirled, many names were suggested, and Lesley could feel a stillness surrounding his name like the calming of winds before a thunderstorm.

"I hope you're awake, Old Man." Blakely tossed the morning paper on the table left hanging over Lesley's legs. "What do you think happens now?" The headline read, *Isabel Escamilla Missing.* "Six people held and questioned, six people released, and look who disappears in under an hour." He threw himself into a chair, his ass barely catching on the edge, and reclined back comfortably. "A little birdie told me—"

"I don't want to know what your birdie said." Lesley pushed the paper aside. A conviction of Papachristi was growing less and less likely as the second hand moved forward.

"That lady, Sara what's her face—"

"Barrett."

"Apparently she's got a church full of people ready to paint Monroe as a bad seed."

"Look, Blakely, not right now." The Monroe case had yet to be solved, and the victim's relationship with Donovan James had been twisted one way while her relationships with Nate Aram, Papachristi, Lily Ziyad, and a deaf man named Jack Williams had been bent another. "I'm too tired for all of this."

Blakely's face held a stupid look that Lesley wished he could knock off. "What, you're not getting enough sleep lying there all day?" He adjusted his position, sat up, leaned forward, looked like a coach readying to swap players. "You know, I've been thinking. We should start something, you and I."

"Not right now, Blakely." He'd been at it for days. Showing up, trying to rile him, trying to invest his attentions on something like a future. But Lesley wasn't interested.

"Here, check this one." He flipped pages and handed him the paper again. "The paintings were found yesterday at the Chicago Hearing Society. Ziyad and Williams were *still* being questioned when Escamilla was reported MIA." He pointed to the information, but Lesley pushed it away. "Look, they're still trying to keep this investigation as close to Nicodemus Papachristi as possible, Old Man." Lesley remained silent, hoping he'd stop. "But it wasn't him . . ." He leaned back again, unable to get comfortable, too wired to sit still. "Don't get me wrong, he's a creepy motherfucker, but I don't think he'd strangle a woman in a park surrounded by thousands of people." A rub of the nose, a snort, a jumping up with a bounce that had him holding his clothes in place. "I'm thinking we should do a little independent investigative work on this guy once you're out of here."

"That's a terrible idea."

"Yeah, well, I'm giving my notice as soon as all this shit with Alina is worked out." What Lesley had believed to be a confabulation had turned out not to be. Obuchowski *had* been Blakely's date to the Christmas party.

"What do you think will happen with her?"

"Pssh—she's got this shit dialed. We don't have to worry about her." Obuchowski had never willfully or knowingly supplied information to Blakely or anyone else, and perhaps because he actually cared for her, Blakely never divulged information that would incriminate her in any of his actions. "Anyway . . ." He clapped his hands and returned to his reclined position in the seat. "A little birdie told me Donovan James is coming to see you *to*-day. It's all been arranged." It was Lesley's last chance to catch a killer, and he didn't feel up to the task. "He'll be wired, and so will you, so choose your words wisely, Old Man." Blakely checked his watch before reaching into his hoodie and pulling out a book with a bomb pictured on its cover. "I got this from a friend."

Lesley recognized the book's title but didn't fully understand its importance until he found a folded piece of paper tucked into its pages and pulled it out to read.

"If he believes *you* believe he's innocent, he should cop to the flash drive being his—"

"This isn't going to be enough."

Lesley set the book on the table in front of him, and Blakely handed him a manila envelope.

"We also have these." He waited for the envelope to open. "I have a friend who has a friend." Lesley shook his head and Blakely gave a few bounces. "Look, James is going to be antsy. He needs to be reassured." Blakely pointed to the discrepancies in the photos Lesley held in his hand. "It's another example of a police force fuck-up. You reel him in, get him comfortable, make him believe they don't actually *have* the flash drive . . . Then, when the time is right—"

Lesley looked at the photographs and the door began to open. "Blakely, wait." He turned with the sideways cock of his head and let the door close again. "I won't do this if there's any chance you'll get in trouble." Blakely's eyes rolled. "I mean it—You, you still have a chance to be happy, you know."

"Don't go soft on me, Old Man. It's all about those women and children, remember?"

"I'm just saying—"

"No, *I'm* just saying." His feet shuffled on the floor, convincing Lesley of the truth. "We'll be waiting downstairs. Push the call button and refuse your meds, that's the signal. James won't make it out of the building without cuffs."

Decoherence

Four days before she would be leaving for college, Lily stepped onto an air-conditioned bus and felt her heart beating with excitement. There were plans to arrange and details to work out, but she felt fairly confident that whatever they were doing would continue and be made more by her attending Michigan State.

Mr. James had told her the school wasn't far from his parents' house. He'd said that between him visiting his parents and Lily visiting hers, they'd almost certainly see one another. "It's possible to see one another six times a year just in our normal trips back and forth." He'd laughed, told her not to worry.

Yes, she wished anything about their relationship had been more concrete, but she certainly wasn't ready to give it up for some average No One who spent his time playing video games and smoking pot. She liked that Mr. James was a man. And she liked that he saw her as a woman.

She'd be leaving the city in a week and wanted to leave more pictures. Something fresh for him to think about when she sat across the table from him in a few days' time and suggested he take the next set of photos himself.

She'd replayed the fantasy again and again, but something always got in the way. He would say someone else's name, or not find her arousing, or hit her because he liked it like that, and all of these things made Lily feel bad. Like she lacked self-confidence and didn't believe herself worthy of him. Which she most certainly believed she was.

The photos started as a gift, a one-off, and then became a game of cat and mouse. After the key had been left on his desk for her, and she'd taken the first set in his bed, she returned to find the blue coat waiting for her there. After she'd taken those photos, he agreed to meet her in a park. They talked for hours, but never talked about that. He told her she looked grownup and confident, agreed to meet her again.

Every instance of Mr. James saying "yes" was followed by more pictures. But in all the times she'd visited his house he'd never actually been home. A silent agreement that felt excitedly violated by the smell of food coming from his apartment when she arrived this time.

He knew she would be coming. He'd confirmed their dinner plans and then chosen to stay. Four years of building excitement and tension aside, Lily was suddenly nervous about the fact that he was *there*, at home, waiting for her.

She slid the key slowly into the lock, wondering if she should have knocked first, allowed him the chance to let her in. But she decided to do things as she had been doing them, because maybe *that* was something he found exciting, and *maybe* even why he'd chosen to stay.

Entering quietly, she closed and locked the door behind her. She could hear the shower running and wasn't sure what she should do. Take off her clothes and join him, or just take off her clothes and let him find her.

"Lily?"

The sound of a woman saying her name startled Lily in all the ways "the other woman" could startle or be startled. All the questions that would follow. All the hate and resentment they both would feel.

"What are you doing here? How'd you get in?"

M. No more than eight feet from her. Stretching out one of his t-shirts, scrambling for some pants. It didn't seem fair that it was happening.

Yes, she'd seen them together. And yes, he'd left the blue coat in his bed for her to wear. But it was meant to be a fantasy. Something he could enjoy and not need to make real.

"What are you doing here?" M asked again.

There was humiliation in all she had done if it led to M standing half-dressed in his apartment. "Couldn't I ask you the same question?"

"No. You can't." M snapped.

Lily did not want to cry. Not in front of her. Not like that.

"I'm a grown adult, Lily—"

"A married one though, right?" M was haughty and Lily hated that side of her almost as much as she hated pretending the blue coat didn't matter. "Or does that not matter for some reason?"

"Look, I don't know *why* you're here, but I think you should leave. Donovan and I are in the middle of something."

Lily held up her key. Didn't want to walk away the loser. "I didn't know there was anyone else." Not really. *Not really.*

"I don't believe you—"

"There's a flash drive in his desk—"

"You need to leave."

"Ask him."

M put her hand on Lily's arm and moved her quickly to the door. "We'll talk tomorrow."

The door shut and Lily stood on the outside.

Her first instinct was to send Mr. James a message. A warning. An apology.

But a message on her phone from Jack read: *Must move paintings. They'll be moving in next week.*

And suddenly a different kind of threat became real.

The Unknown Known

For three days he slept next to her, unafraid, uninhibited, and unaware of the world happening outside the four walls of his apartment. He woke and let her guide his body into positions that eventually led them back to bed. Sara sent her last batch of pictures from Vietnam. Lush green landscapes and smiling faces. Lily sent an email reminding him of dinner plans he didn't view worth keeping. She would be off to college soon, and Emily was there for him to touch and taste and know more intimately than he'd ever known anything outside his own thoughts.

There was no competition.

"Would you marry me?" he asked while dancing his fingers across her back.

She had one eye free from the pillow under her head. "I would."

Sliding his face down next to hers, "Will you marry me?"

Her smile said, Yes. It didn't matter what her mouth said. Her body coaxed him beyond soreness and begged him for anything he had left.

"Don't ever leave me." It was breathless, and desperate, and earnest, and he held her full breasts as her motion came to a slow simmer above him and then stopped altogether.

"Did I say something wrong?"

She shook her head, and he could feel her breathing in his smell.

"What is it then?"

She lay down next to him and pulled him close, her fingers dancing through his hair.

There was hesitance, words that started untranslatable thoughts. And he gave her time to sort it, believed he had time to let her breathe.

"When Peter, my brother, died, I had to learn that sometimes people leave. It has nothing to do with what I want, or they want. Nothing to do with plans or futures or . . . sense-making."

Donovan raised his eyes to see her face.

"Sometimes people just have to leave—"

302

"I don't want you to leave," he said.

"I don't want to leave," she replied. "And if I ever *do* leave you, Donovan James, it won't be by choice."

God, he wanted to believe her.

"The list, give me your list." His body reached across hers toward the dress on the ground.

"It's *our* list, thank you very much." He rose to allow her movement, grabbed a pen, came back to bed. "Why, what are you doing?"

He took the paper from her hand, "Making an amendment."

There was laughter, and she held him.

Until death do us part.

Signed and dated.

The only rule fully acknowledged by them both.

Saturday came. Their days had hardly separated by dates and times, and Emily wanted to enjoy a concert in the park—be in the world with him, know what it was like to be a "real" couple while listening to the music of *Daphnis and Chloe*, the story of two young people who fall in love. Daphnis is taught to make love by another woman. Chloe has a list of suitors wanting to take her away. They eventually marry, and everything is fine. Except that it wasn't.

Emily insisted on making dinner while he showered. "I can take one right before we leave," she'd said, "so I don't smell like food." And then she kissed him. And he'd listened. He threw some towels in the dryer, started another load. Stood in the shower letting the water sooth his tired and sore muscles. Stood in the shower and smelled the chicken she was preparing, imagined her there, what she was wearing, her hair still a mess, cheeks still pink, smelling of sex. He believed this would be the rest of his life. His new normal.

If only he could contain it.

"Are you sure you want to go out?" Opening the bathroom door, he found her fully dressed, bag packed, front door open. "I thought you wanted to take a shower." His voice had startled her.

"I changed my mind." Putting the bag down, she retrieved her hat, the hat he'd had since the last day of school. "I should grab my coat too, get it to the cleaner before winter—"

"What's going on?"

"Nothing." She stood by the door, eyes and nose looking pink or tired, rubbing them both, pushing back her hair. "I just want to make sure I get it cleaned."

"Well, you won't need it tonight." He wanted to believe her. "We can get it to the cleaners tomorrow." But his heart beat high in his ears, "It looks like you're leaving." He looked at her there, shoulders up and back, head held high. "Are you sure you're okay?"

She gave a slow nod, but the tightened line of her lips told him it was a lie.

They sat like strangers on the train, her eyes skirting around for the quickest escape while he tried to think of ways to keep her.

She knows.

She doesn't know.

She's seen you, and she knows.

Emily hardly said a word, didn't eat a bite, held a small blue cross in her hand like she was praying the Rosary. Turning it, rubbing it, twisting a loose bit of its string. She looked everywhere but his direction until the concert was over and they were on the path between parks, heading back to the train. "I think I should go home tonight. It's Sunday tomorrow and I have things I should be doing—"

"You said you didn't want to leave."

She moved ahead of him on the trail and only stopped because he called out to her.

"What's going on?"

Her shrug, which he'd determined was never a shrug of indifference, was followed by six simple words, "I just need to go home."

But he could feel her slipping. It was in the words she spoke, the way her skin paled and flushed and her eyes darted between him and passing faces until she stepped off the trail to let people by, to not make a scene, and he pulled her into a covet of trees to prevent her escape, keep her from running, make her stay.

"Emily, what happened?"

She shook herself free of him, surrounded by shrubbery and darkness, stepping backward into the moonlight that peeked through tree limbs.

Her face, not her smile, her body, not her shrug, her Being, not her words, said, You're a stranger to me.

Out of fear, he reached for her and her skirt caught on a branch as she stepped further back. Fabric ripping, she tumbled over, stopped once by the sound of her head hitting fallen timber like she'd dropped a jelly jar on the wooden floors of his kitchen. She crumbled in a heap among the dead leaves and broken branches.

He dove forward in a panic and knelt beside her. "Jesus, are you alright?" His eyes adjusted and allowed him to see the slow trickle of blood exuding from her head down onto her shoulder.

"You're bleeding."

Scooting back, away from him, away from the possibility of all he'd imagined, she sat up, touched her hand to the back of her head and pulled a shawl from her bag to press against her wound.

"Emily, are you okay?"

He looked back toward the path, panicked, while her voice took on a kind of calm she'd never used before. "I think you should just go home, and we'll talk again on Monday." A calm, smooth whisper.

"I don't believe you."

"Well, I don't need you to believe me."

Again, he reached out. Again, she pulled away.

"I need time alone."

"Why?" he'd yelled. "So you can what?" His anger and fear were larger than him, and he could feel them roaring to escape. "Disappear? Leave me? Fuck someone else? Pretend I don't exist—"

"Lily told me about your flash drive, Donovan."

Her words were quick, the blood drained from his extremities, numbed his limbs.

She knows.

"She came to your apartment . . . while you were in the shower—and I didn't believe her!"

He stared at her there, crouched in the dark with dirt on her knees and brush in her hair. Heart racing, ears filling, doors closing.

"But I looked, Donovan, and there she was. In your bed, wearing my coat."

He tried to touch her, stop her, but this time she smacked his hand away and yelled, "Stop!" And he tried to tell her, he tried to make her see that nothing had happened, it was only her, it had always been her, there was never anyone else—could never be anyone else.

Then she hit him. This time with a closed fist right on his chest and then again, and again, and again until he caught her hand, and she released the shawl and smacked his face before he wrestled her to the ground. Holding her down. Pinning her tightly beneath him.

"Nothing happened."

She was afraid. Of him. He could see it, and feel it, and taste it, and smell it, like a sickness that had begun during his shower.

She'd packed blankets and candles that morning; they'd made love and plans and prepped dinner and made more love—then he took a shower and she fell ill. He couldn't make her well, not there on the ground holding her captive in the brush with dirt and trash under her back.

"I love you so much."

It's too late.

"If you love me at all, you'll get the fuck off me and leave."

She's seen you.

"Please, Emily."

"Donovan, this isn't love."

"Emily—"

"You need to go home."

"Please."

"Leave!"

Donovan looked at her.

You won't be able to take this back.

There was a knock at the door to remind him he'd been wearing the same clothes since Saturday. It also reminded him he hadn't washed his hands or brushed his teeth since conversations in a midnight wood, whispered sounds of ripping fabric, and the knocking of her skull—a sound much different from the knocking on the door that came again, and again, and again, this time a man shouting his name, too authoritative to be anyone he knew, too callous to be anyone helpful. The knocking came and reminded him that she would have rung the bell—she always rang the bell, she liked its sound, said it donged without the ding and had a long tail. He hadn't heard it until she said it, and then it couldn't be unheard or undone—like Lily, calling his name, or Sara sighing yeses into the dark of his room—there was a knock on the door to remind him. And then, the door burst open.

He ran the two and a half miles that separated him from the little blue dot on his phone. He ran up streets, through stoplights and honking horns. He passed people, and shops, and tried to recount the moments right before he'd run from her, blue shawl, bleeding head, on the ground, in the dark.

"Emily!"

He banged on the paned glass door with closed fist and saw the dried blood on his hand.

"Emily!"

He rang the buzzer and saw her, the moon making her blood look black.

"Emily!"

He grabbed the doorknob and shook it until he thought the glass would rattle itself free.

"Emily!"

Then came Adonis. Hair down, eyes red. Behind him a man with glasses and hair like hers. Then a woman whose black hair he'd seen dancing in the backyard with children and laughter and her.

The door didn't open. They stood silently on the other side, staring through pain, and he called her name one last time.

307

Donovan James had never been inside a police station. He'd had no need or desire to experience what took place between their walls, behind their doors. Pictures spread out, dates, times, phone records, the CTA footage they showed him again, and again, and again.

"We can make all this go away, Donovan—like it never happened."

She never happened. You never happened.

"All you have to do is tell the truth."

There were hours and days.

"You were clearly involved with other people—Lily Ziyad, for instance."

A visit here, a question there.

"Maybe you'd rather talk about her and the flash drive."

The unease of never being alone while being alone.

"You didn't love Emily Monroe any more than she loved you."

A scattering of days that became weeks. A photo slid forward.

"You'll spend the rest of your life behind bars for this."

Blue shawl. Bleeding head. Her eyes wide with fear as she lay on the ground.

"You stalked her."

An anxiety.

"She rejected you."

A constructing.

"You killed her."

A production.

"You either get Sara Barrett to name her source, or it all comes out."

His father sat next to him in the dark. Finally believed it all to be real. Slept on the couch Donovan could see from his bed. Answered his phone. Sheltered him from insults and questions and newspaper clippings too grotesque to be true. "I think you just gotta do what they say, son." He placed his hand on Donovan's knee and squeezed it. "Put this whole mess behind you." When Donovan couldn't stop himself from crying, his father tapped and shook his back. "It's time for you to come home so your mom and I can help you start over." His father pulled himself into an awkward hug between his own tears. "I love you, son . . . I really do." His body shaking against him. "I'm sorry I wasn't here for you sooner."

Son . . .

□　　□　　□

It was time for him to go. Run the course that had been plotted and leave the rest behind. He waited for the nurse to bring the water. He wanted to make sure the detective's needs were met before leaving. Once the nurse had left, he stood, took the book from beside the detective's bed, and held it up to his nose.

Frankincense and oranges, cigarette smoke, turpentine, and *her*. A melancholy. A drifting.

An End.

"It will be like it never really happened after this," he said, looking at the detective.

"Like what never happened?"

"Any of it. Emily. The hat, the mittens, the coat, the scarf." There was more, so much more. "I only ever wanted to know what she saw when she looked at me."

"What did you see when you looked at her?"

Donovan paced the room, opening the book, flipping through pages. "Fear."

"What did you want to see?"

He looked at the detective and was amazed that he still didn't understand. "Me. I wanted to see *me*—what she saw when she looked at me."

"Maybe you did."

You're the weirdo on the train. You can't even hold a polite conversation. Liar. It wasn't about you. It's never been about you. You are sick. Your usefulness has expired. You're nothing to her now. You're just some guy on the train. This is all you ever were. All you ever will be. The poor schmuck, waiting in vain. You are not okay. I knew you'd lie. You're gonna lie again. You are responsible for this. You're like a little girl. Little fairy. No one's gonna want to be your friend. Idiot. Freak. Stuttering kid.

"Did you kill Emily Monroe?"

Donovan handed the book back to the detective, watched his tanned hands take it while his eyes searched Donovan's face for something more.

"No." He pulled his headphones from his pocket, placed them in his ears, started the music.

Casting one last glance at the book, Donovan determined that Billy Pilgrim's passivity should be left with a man whose future would remain out of his control. A lesson.

"Donovan, wait."

But Donovan turned up the music, drowning the detective out, and stepped through the door.

Doors closing.

It almost felt like running.

Acknowledgments

The world is full of people who have helped in large and small ways, but I would like to give a special thanks to those who made the writing, and subsequent publication of M-theory, possible.

The McPlates, who bore my absence, both mental and physical, with a love and grace that was difficult to accept and hard to feel worthy of.

Caldera Arts Center in Sisters, Oregon, where I met my writing family. My heart still longs for your space and the people who filled it.

Nick Dybek, who bravely ran the first workshop of this manuscript's beginning. I hope to still be getting coffee with you when I'm eighty.

My fellow Wheel, Cheliss Thayer, who encouraged me from the beginning to give Lesley his own chapters. You were so right. Thank you.

My mentor, Chris Boucher, whose repeated refrain of "make it louder" allowed me to write Donovan as he now stands. You challenged me to take risks in my writing that I wouldn't have taken on my own.

My thesis advisor, T. Geronimo Johnson, who spent hours listening to me work through timelines, chapter orders, and when and where and for whom I could use italics. You were the first person to see the details of the moving parts and truly understand their synchronicity. Thank you.

Danilo Thomas, Christine Kelley, and Margaret Dalrymple at Baobab Press. How you showed your love and faith in me and this manuscript far exceeded any expectations I had when it came to being published. I would never want to do this without you.

Tiffany Cates spent five years navigating Chicago's transit and weather systems before moving to Oregon and earning her MFA in Creative Writing from Oregon State University. Strongly influenced by her degrees in philosophy and psychology, Cates writes around themes of personhood, the distance between self and other, and matters of free will. She is the founding editor of Townsend, a literary journal devoted to long-form fiction writers. Tiffany Cates lives in Corvallis, Oregon.